Brown's Hole

Please go to <u>www.ivanbosanko.com</u> for
more great articles, stories and books

Ivan Bosanko

D1736380

PublishAmerica
Baltimore

First printing

ISBN: 1-4137-2844-8
PUBLISHED BY PUBLISHAMERICA, LLLP
www.publishamerica.com
Baltimore

Printed in the United States of America

FOREWORD

No two pieces of paper signed by the same president have had a more profound impact on our country's history and the mass migration of its people than the Homestead Act of 1862 and the Emancipation Proclamation of 1863. Both did what they were intended to do: move and relocate people.

The secession from the Union crisis of 1860–1861 was not about the future of slavery in the entire Union, but about the slavery status in the Western Territories of the United States. The primary objective of the Civil War in its initial stages of conflict was to suppress the rebellion of the Southern states in an effort to keep the remaining border slave states still in the Union. Two overzealous Union generals forced President Lincoln's hand by issuing their own proclamations freeing the slaves in their military districts. President Abraham Lincoln immediately overruled Union Generals John C. Fremont and David Hunter on this matter. On January 1, 1863, Lincoln's own ultimatum announced that all slaves within all areas under rebellion would be declared free "thence forward and forever."

Thus the proclamation spawned a continual movement of people (slaves) to the North via the Underground Railroad, a system to help former slaves gain their freedom through a series of hidden shelters, travel arrangements and financial aid provided almost entirely by northern white sympathizers in their relentless quest to free the blacks from bondage.

The other document, the Homestead Act of 1862, spawned the greatest single migration of settlers the world has ever seen. Lincoln's successor, President Andrew Johnson, estimated it would take some six hundred years to settle the vast Western Territories—in less than forty short years, the impossible had been done: The American Frontier, and with it the free open-range cattle business, was almost a thing of the past. Under this act, a free quarter section (160 acres) in the West was offered to any citizen or intended citizen, 21 years of age or older, who would settle the land. Between 1863 and 1890, nearly a million people filed and homesteaded out in the West.

Year after year, waves of homesteaders claimed more land, stretched more barbed wire and put down stubborn roots, and moved deeper and deeper into the heretofore free public grasslands and range until open conflict, range wars, erupted as the inevitable outcome of this concerted westward expansion.

This continual crowding by the homesteaders forced the cattlemen to take to the trails once more. This time their huge cattle herds were driven to the intermountain wilderness of Idaho, Montana, Wyoming, and Colorado, including remote sections of the Dakotas and Utah where the hated homesteaders had not yet penetrated. Here in the last true wilderness, the cattlemen made their stand; come hell or high water or unfriendly bullets, they were not going to be forced to move again!

Again, following the relocation of these herds, small, isolated pockets of converted homesteaders became ranchers of sorts, stealing or rustling strays from the large herds to stock and restock their own small beginnings. Unbranded calves became "fair game" for anybody with the nerve or inclination to round them up and heat up their branding irons. Old cattle brands were replaced by new brands, many designed cleverly to cover or obliterate the first brand so that a "new bill of sale" eased everybody's conscience at the cattle yards, cowtowns and railheads of the West. At the turn of the nineteenth century, Steamboat Springs, Colorado, shipped more cattle to market than any other shipping point in the United States. True, many of the brands were of dubious origin to be sure, but those who pocketed the sale proceeds never claimed to be saints in the first place.

As with any expansion, large or small, all sorts of people followed the big cattle company herds; it was as natural and predictable as day follows night. And with it came the lawless element—many who came West were deserters from the Civil War, including those who plundered and pillaged the Kansas-Missouri borders before, during, and after the bloody war between the states.

The 1849 California Gold Rush provided yet another migrant push into the intermountain and high desert regions as many stragglers through hardship, circumstance or fate abandoned their dreams of striking it rich and settled for whatever means of survival were at hand—quite often at the expense of the large cattle companies.

Soon these vagrants became an intricate part of frontier life and coexisted with the ever-growing and profitable business of cattle rustling. Thus was born an accommodation of sorts between a new breed of outlaws and the small rancher: an unwritten but entirely enforceable code of conduct based on a mutual need for preservation and protection. From Landusky, Montana, south of the Canadian border, stretching southward on both sides of the Continental Divide, pockets of help and refuge sprang up for those who could and would take advantage of this unique understanding between the cattle rustlers and the struggling ranchers who sometimes dabbled in this profitable and oft-times very risky business or profession.

At first, this new breed of outlaws or cattle rustlers operated as loosely controlled gangs with little or no real planning, strategy or leadership, as evidenced by the flurry of hangings that took place wherever a lone tree, post or empty building with an exposed rafter could be found. Few bothered with the formality of a trial, especially when a quick rope could deal with the problem much sooner.

This changed dramatically during the span of years between 1870 and 1910, when the Outlaw Trail really came into its own. Just as with the Civil War's Underground Railroad, willing hands could be found to make the system work; but unlike the railroad, it all came at a price. Indeed, there were no signs pointing to such a trail or even its very existence, but those who used it and those who profited by it could've drawn a road map, either in their mind or on paper, it became that fixed in the intermountain regions of the Wild West.

This infamous trail spawned yet another enigma: three permanent hideouts for big-time cattle rustlers where stolen herds could be grazed and fattened without fear of interference or apprehension by the law. Hole-in-the-Wall in Wyoming, Brown's Hole in the very extreme northwestern corner of Colorado, and Robbers' Roost in southern Utah offered just such accommodations. Though each location was quite different in size, appearance and topography, each had three things in common: difficult but easily guarded and defended approaches or trails; plenty of good grassland to enable large herds to be pastured, even through winter if necessary; and friendly ranchers and their families. And of course it should also be mentioned that none of these hideouts had the obvious: a jail or a man behind a badge to keep it filled!

There was an old saying during those early days on the Outlaw Trail; it went something like this: It makes no difference who rides the trail, for any man with a past to hide or a price on his head is free to roam "nameless" on the trail provided he is good with a gun, fast on his mount, more clever than the lawman or posse chasing him, runs at least as fast as he can lie or cheat, trusts no one, has eyes in the back of his head and is a fool when it comes to adventure and doom. Indeed, in those early days on the trail, old age happened more by accident or providence than by careful design or plan.

However, that all changed with the appearance of George Leroy Parker, alias Butch Cassidy, and his gang, the Wild Bunch. No one person captured the free frontier spirit or epitomized its rebellion toward government control or encroachment than did Butch Cassidy. No one outlaw used the Outlaw Trail more to his advantage and treated those who hid, fed and sheltered him better than Cassidy. And no one was more careful to ensure that nothing strained or interfered with this unwritten code of conduct than Butch himself.

This relationship was not of the "Robin Hood variety" so romantically written about in jolly old England—no indeed! It was a cold, calculated understanding between outlaw and rancher alike; often it was the difference between survival and death for either, and more frequently than not, the money left behind by the Wild Bunch as a payment for services rendered pulled the rancher and his family through one tough spot after another. So unique and so strong was this bond that it would be hard to find any documented cases of abuse by either side during Cassidy's era.

Cassidy brought a level of professionalism unmatched in history to his career of outlawing. So thorough, so well planned and so well executed were his daring robberies of banks and payrolls that he left his pursuers—literally and figuratively—in the dust, using his infamous "Pony Express Relay System" of fresh mounts, fresh supplies and willing ranch hands as he and his carefully selected gang escaped time after time from hot pursuit.

It should be noted at this point that in many instances there was little if any distinction between the outlaw and the lawman or bounty hunter giving chase. Many a lawman had indeed traveled both sides of the law and often as not straddled a precarious "middle-of-the-road" moral existence when it came time to carry out his duly sworn duties and obligations. Some of the West's most celebrated and dime-noveled exploits by men attached to the lawman's badge fit this category perfectly.

The emergence of Cassidy's Wild Bunch caused people to take on an entirely new look or attitude about those who traveled the Outlaw Trail. Up 'til then, an outlaws was perceived to be some low-life character, a violent fool or an idiot who lived off Lady Luck and his gun. Too often he was seen in the public's eye as one of society's misfits who had to be hunted down like an animal—because that's what he was—by morally superior men wearing a badge empowered by the righteous law. This stereotyping of outlaw and lawman was anything but the truth. In fact, many of those outlaws who traveled the trail, contrary to belief, demonstrated uncanny wit and use of brains rarely matched by many on the legitimate side of society in those days.

It is important to also note that many honest ranchers and homesteaders lived along this trail trying to eke out a living on poor range or topsoil that barely supported an existence. These were a hardy, independent breed who wanted nothing better than to be left alone, who took instant dislike and distrust to strangers, new laws and any or all attempts by "self-ordained do-gooders" who circuited the trail, trying to exert their moral and religious beliefs upon the less educated, less experienced and more gullible. One could readily accept and understand their "cornbread or cornmeal philosophy" as earth given and earth grown. One old codger leaned back on the porch of his shanty and summed up his life or existence this way: "I'll be damned if Cassidy or some tin-horned lawman could ever make me leave my place…I love my place and these mountains…even if'n I'm near starved by them ever' two, three years. It'll take cold lead from a hot six-shooter by some behind-the-back sonofabitch to get me off'n it and then by cracky they'll have to plant me in it…now won't they? I'd swear to it on a stack'a Bibles three-feet high…'Course I ain't much bothered by cipherin' nor readin'…so guess you just half'ta take my say on the matter…right, stranger?"

Of the three permanent hideouts connected by the trail, no single location in the West, or on the trail for that matter, had such a colorful or varied history as Brown's Hole—much later renamed Brown's Park. This hole contained the greatest collection of characters—good, bad and somewhere in between—the wild and wooly West has ever seen.

The earliest known reference to this unique hidden hole was described in the writings of Father Oritz, a Spanish missionary in 1650. The Hole remained just as isolated and hidden from the white man until the General William H. Ashley expedition penetrated the Hole in bull-boats on the Green River. It was a harrowing experience as Ashley was a non-swimmer. The red-rock walls of the canyon kept rising almost perpendicularly straight up to great heights as the current grew swifter and swifter, being channeled into a deepening, threatening gorge. The Ashley party had to continue on—there was no getting out or turning back. Then they had to run the great rapids, going six days without food. Suddenly the walls drew back, the river widened and they shot out into the wide expanse of the Hole. A few more miles downstream, they came upon a great campground where thousands of Indians had wintered. Game was plentiful, the grass was lush and green, and they were awestruck by their discovery. This happened in 1825.

Kit Carson invaded the Hole in 1827 to trade with the Shoshone and Ute Indians. From that time on, until 1840, the Hole was home to the greatest of all "free mountain-man rendezvous" staged by the various competing fur companies. In that same year, Baptiste Brown, alias Baptiste Chalifoux, came with his Indian wife to trade furs. The ex-Hudson Bay fur trader and trapper decided to stay and make his home and living here, and thus this remote place was named Brown's Hole as he was its first White, permanent settler. It continued to be a home of sorts for many years to all the famous mountain men such as Jim Bridger, Kit Carson, Jim Baker and Jack Robinson.

In 1849, a band of Cherokee Indians drove a big herd of cattle through Brown's Hole on their way to California. From that time on, the Hole took on a vastly different character; it became a favorite wintering place for Texas cattle herds on their way to Montana. That was the start of the eventual conflicts between the small rancher or homesteader and the big cattle companies. Brown's Hole became a living hell to many from that time on.

In 1850, outlaws also moved into the Hole, using it as a base of operations and refuge, following repeated attacks on the wagon trains pushing ever westward using the Oregon-Mormon Trail just to the northwest. They stole horses and cattle and wintered them in the Hole until they could dispose of them. With such a large influx of outlaw gangs coming and going, the honest ranchers by way of circumstance were forced to appease and coexist with these desperados in order to survive. Thus was born the unwritten code of conduct between outlaw and rancher alike on the Outlaw Trail. This getting used to and learning to get along together gradually evolved over time. Disputes, arguments and just plain hot-leaded actions by both sides took their toll in those early formative years. Some 170 graves are scattered throughout the Hole, attesting to this "period of adjustment, accommodation and acceptance."

No lawman dared to enter Brown's Hole until the very late 1800s, and then under an alias to be sure. He was a so-called cattle detective hired by the large cattle companies to gather evidence and clean out the cattle rustlers. His name? James Hicks, alias Tom Horn. Hicks, or Horn, as the case may be, had been employed by the cattlemen's association in 1894 to clean out the cattle rustlers around Laramie, Wyoming. After gathering evidence and then following through with his "system that never failed" (used a 30-30 rifle), Horn did his work with a vengeance. Now Horn's services were again put to use—this time by the cattlemen's group of Northwestern Colorado.

And so the stage is almost set. You have the important background history and essential facts you will need in order to understand my story about Brown's Hole. But please indulge me a bit more. Let me properly introduce you to Brown's Hole, because if you know the lay of the land, it will help you to understand the story better.

Brown's Hole is quite literally a "hole," but on a gigantic scale—a miniature grand canyon of sorts, if you will. It is approximately forty-five miles square; half in Utah and half in Colorado with a sliver of area in Wyoming. On the south side, the Hole is sealed off by the imposing and nearly impassable heights surrounding Diamond Mountain. The Green River traverses its valleys as it disappears even more dramatically than it appears, plunging through Ladore Canyon. The north side of the Hole is guarded by Cold Spring Mountain—equally as formidable as the south side. On the west side, a series of terrible and treacherous badlands finally give rise until they form the shelf that becomes the Unitah Mountain Range. Only the east side offers fairly moderate but still bothersome terrain building up to Limestone Divide. The Hole's floor consists of good grassland spaced between sagebrush plateaus and low cedar ridges that are crisscrossed by numerous arroyos and gulches; some contain water, but most do not.

The Hole's perimeter consists of imperfectly defined red, yellow and white sandstone escarpments and walls, pitted with caves, maroon-colored rock ledges rising one above the other in stepladder fashion, knife-like ravines, and grotesquely eroded buttes and promontories jutting outward and upward. Old-timers talk about the Hole as being a "witches brew kind of country that could only have been created when the devil was at his drunkenest."

To reach the Hole takes a bit of doing too, as there were only three paths or trails in—two on the north side and one from the south. Each trail was surrounded by high ridges that provided easy spotting so that any outlaw could easily ambush with a minimum of risk to himself. In 1975, movie actor

Robert Redford, as part of an eight-person tour, visited the Hole and the other two permanent hideouts. They traveled on foot, horseback and by four-wheel drive vehicles to visit the three infamous hangouts.

From the visitor's talks and interviews with the ranchers and homesteaders along the trail, these old-timers and descendants of the trail left the Redford party with one inescapable conclusion: Little had indeed changed in these old, crusty, cantankerous people's minds. Oh, some of the glint and possibly an ounce or two of independence and orneriness may have escaped from their sunburned and weather-beaten hides, but it was still business as usual; they had no damn use for government interference or meddling, present-day politics, and new laws and regulations in approximately that order. To them, Butch Cassidy wasn't just an outlaw; Tom Horn wasn't just a cattlemen's association detective, bounty hunter or hired killer; and the Bassett sisters, who had lived in the Hole, weren't just cattle rustlers—no indeed! They were all larger than life itself. They were the embodiment of every boy or girl in America who ever went to a Saturday afternoon cowboy matinee, played cowboys and Indians, cops and robbers, or who had or dreamed of riding a pony down some dangerous trail with make-believe bad guys waiting in ambush to snatch the gold or carry off the fair maiden to God knows where.

Nowhere in the West did such hatred fester and spill over into violence between the big cattle companies and the small ranchers, on such a large scale, than what history tells us happened in Brown's Hole. So intense was this hatred, so determined were those in charge to exterminate these "nesters or homesteaders" at all costs, that the new term "Nestlers" was coined. To be called a Nestler, a small-time rancher or Nester who rustled cattle, was akin to being called something worse than an SOB in any language.

In conclusion, from the history of Brown's Hole, I believe both good and bad lived together, not because of their own circumstances but as a result of their own actions; that is, men by their own actions create their own circumstances for good or bad. Some of the best men did bad things in the Hole, and some of the worst of outlaws like Butch Cassidy (and I'll include Tom Horn here too!) did good things. And some of those who wouldn't soil their hands one way or another simply and quietly hired others to carry out their killing or dirty work in order to remain pure and self-righteous in the eyes of their fellow men.

The best way for you to really get into the story is to climb aboard a loaded freight wagon. Here, let me help you up! I'll grab your arm while you put your foot upon the grease hub of the wagon wheel. Easy does it, easy! There, you're safely up! Tell that big, smelly, mangy galoot holding the reins to move over, there's always room for one more! He's the bullwhacker, the ex-cowboy who hauls freight for a living. What's that, he says he's already got two passengers? Couple'a greenhorns from back East! Never mind his cuss words, they kinda go with the territory out here if you know what I mean!

Where are you goin' didja say? Best guess is you're headed south from the railroad station here in Rock Springs, Wyoming. Where to? Just listen to that sunburned, weather-tanned young man for a couple minutes more. Just listen to him! Golly, he's so excited about the new home he's taking his pregnant wife to that he plumb forgot to tell her they're going to settle down in a hole! Yes, you heard right, a hole! But as with all beginnings, you gotta get started first.

Hiya! Hiya! Giddyup there! Crack! Crack! Dammit now get a move on! Yahoo! Yahoo!

CHAPTER ONE

Old Henry Ettleman said, "It's a five-day ride to Rock Springs to fetch a doc. By the time you get there, you're either dead or cured of what ails ya."

"Are you sure that canvass is well tied down? We do have complete privacy from Tanner, don't we?"

Clay Barnett handled his wife's concerned questions with the same ease he used to unbutton his sheepskin coat. "Claire, I told Tanner he's to sleep and stay under the endgate section of his wagon 'til morning. Each night he'll be sleeping as far away from us as possible until we reach Uncle Beemis' ranch."

"Everything is so strange and different out here...How long did you say before we get to the ranch?"

"Figure on four more days at least, maybe five. I tried to tell you about distances out here in my letters. Remember?"

"Dear, there's a big difference between reading about all this wide-open space than being swallowed up in it! That's the way I've felt ever since you helped me up into that seat next to Tanner at the railroad station in Rock Springs."

"Hang in there, Claire, we're making good time. It's going to take a little getting used to, that's all."

There was complete confidence and a certain measure of safety in Clay's words; he'd given her the reassurance she needed and wanted. Suddenly she rushed into his arms. "Clay! Clay! Where are your lips? Eight long months I thought would never end! Today was worst of all! After seeing you again and not being able to touch you or say how much I love you and miss you...and want you."

They feasted on each other's lips with a hunger straight from their hearts. Claire moved into him, her body language sending an undeniable message that she wanted to forego any romantic build-up or preparation, so often the necessary ingredients to their past lovemaking. Tonight it would be more than just special between them. It was now she needed to feel and experience his passion being poured deep within her so that the longest day of her life could be closed out where it should be—locked safely away in her husband's arms.

Clay shed his sheepskin in record time, using it to sit down on while he undressed. Off came his cowboy boots. His cowboy hat sailed in one direction, his flannel shirt and jeans in another. He looked over at Claire peeling down. "Keep your boot socks on. Pretty nippy out tonight...Better leave your long johns on too, just make sure they're unbuttoned...We'll figure a way..."

She smiled at his inference. "Thanks for loaning me a pair of your long johns and bringing me that sheepskin coat. They kept me nice and warm. But tonight I want to be and feel like your wife once more, not just another rider. I will keep the socks on..."

Claire's modesty was never more apparent. She turned her back to him while she slipped the top of her long johns down, using the sleeves to keep it up fastened around her waist. Next, she lifted a flannel nightgown high over her head before letting it settle down comfortably over her body before stepping out of her long johns. Her last attention to detail came when she laid her sheepskin coat, fleece side up, on top of the two heavy buffalo robes Clay had intended to use for blankets. She turned around to see that he hadn't missed anything before giving him an approving smile. She commented, "I've sure taken to the nice, soft feeling of fleece. Should make us very comfortable before, during, and after."

Clay raised her just high enough to move her onto the sheepskins. He was on fire with a passion that had been quiet for far too many months.

Claire cradled him quickly between her thighs, her signal that she was smoldering, her needs only a shade behind his. "Let me help you, love...like

I always did. But first, I need to hear certain words, Clay—you still remember them, don't you? They're far too important to let slide…even now."

He didn't disappoint, he didn't dare. "I love you with all my heart and soul."

"You remembered, you remembered," she whispered. "Oh, I'm so glad…"

The bulge in Clay's long johns was never bigger. His need to be in her, never greater. Gradually, oh so gradually, Claire helped him ease into her. She felt him apply his own pressure, opening her up more and more.

"Don't stop, don't stop," she breathed. "Oh love, there's nothing like this…no feeling in all the world. Just take it easy…and give me more."

He cut their pleasure short suddenly by raising up on her. "Dang it!"

"What is it, Clay? I heard it too! Is it some wild animal?"

"Naw, it's the wind, changed direction, I guess. Does that a lot out here. It's flapping our canvass like crazy."

"But I heard a low howl…or maybe it was more like a moan or wail."

"That's the wind, Claire, really it is! Took me a month to really get to understand that the wind can play tricks on a person out here. That moaning sound will rise and fall with the wind. Not to worry, dear. I'd better move our lantern a bit closer…just in case."

"Good, that means I get to see you all the better…while we become one."

Clay reached out as far as his arms would let him. "I can't quite reach it. Mustn't let the wind tip it…could start a range fire."

He left a lot of unfinished pleasure under him—the lovemaking kind with Claire's reminder ringing in his ears.

"Don't take a minute longer than you have to. I'm not going anywhere…"

Clay grasped the handle of the lantern just in time to feel a gust of wind nearly knock him over while still on his knees. He could only watch in shock and disbelief while his privacy canvass went sailing out into the night.

"Clay. Clay!" She shouted, "I feel an awful lot of cold wind on me! What's going on?"

"Our privacy is gone! Better get up!"

The words he spoke had a double meaning as Claire pulled her nightgown down before sitting up. The lantern's light shed in two directions—on a man and his wife driven out of their lair of love and on a fully clothed freight hauler who had no business being where he was.

Clay tried to diffuse the situation. "I'd better catch up with that tarp before the wind picks it up to land it God knows where."

17

Claire, too, saw Tanner and saw red. She wasted no time confronting the barrel-chested man who'd obviously seen everything.

The only thing that saved Tanner from at least several slaps to his face, or possibly more damage, was the wind. It took both of Claire's hands to keep her nightgown pinned to her side. However, no wind in the West could've kept Claire from giving Tanner the tongue-lashing of his life.

"Just had to fill those beady little black eyeballs until they couldn't hold any more! Didn't you?"

Tanner shrugged his shoulders. "A free show's a free show!"

They stood eyeball to eyeball, boot sock to boot sock, neither about to back down.

"You could've done the right thing, Tanner, and turned away or stayed in your bedroll, WHERE YOU'RE SUPPOSED TO BE!" she reminded him.

"Since you put it that'a way, damned if'n I was gonna look over yonder or the t'other way. Like I said, a free show's a free show, and you done put on a purty good one!"

"What do you mean by that crack?"

"When I took you'n your man on at the depot, I see'd that watermelon ridin' on your belly, so I says to myself, 'Wonder if a knocked-up woman can handle some pokin' when the time comes?' Well, now I sure as shootin' got me my answer, right away tonight, when I see'd you and your mister agoin' at it sumpthun' fierce!"

"How dare you talk to me like that! I want an apology from you this very instant! Tanner! RIGHT THIS INSTANT!"

Clay arrived just in time to step between the two combatants. That didn't stop Claire from giving Tanner another verbal shot. "You must be twins, Tanner, because your dirty little mind sure matches the words out of your dirty little mouth!"

"Hey! Hey, you two, knock it off! Let's all try to get along for the rest of this trip. Four more days is all I'm asking out'a you two! From what I just heard, Tanner, you owe my wife an apology. Well, we're waiting!"

The short, stocky freight hauler stood his ground. "I called it the way I see'd it!" He turned to Clay. "Gimme that tarp! Follow me and I'll show you how to tie it down so it won't git blowed away no more!"

Claire walked away, still seething with rage over the obvious violation by Tanner of her most precious and private passionate moment. Clay, too, was very upset about the incident, but chose to let it pass for now. After all, he did need Tanner's services for a few more days; then there'd be time to let his feelings out.

Tanner went about tying and anchoring the tarp using the same side and front wagon wheel and tongue that Clay had previously used. Clay thanked the man for his help and then returned to Claire.

He found his wife sitting up, cross-legged, on their bed of two heavy buffalo robes. A thick robe hung loosely down around her, leaving two long-john-covered legs sticking out. He knew from the way she was dressed, all hope of rekindling anything except maybe a goodnight kiss was totally out of the question.

"The tarp is back where it belongs; we have our privacy again. Let's try to put this behind us…for now."

"I can't! I'm too angry to even think about trying to sleep…and I'm sure not in the mood…for anything else."

He sat up with his Claire, his mind alive with at least a dozen questions and most concerned Claire; however, several concerned Tanner. It was time to try one. "You don't trust Tanner one little bit, do you?"

"Only about as far as I can throw him."

They both chuckled over Claire's observation. Clay spoke. "That's about what I figured. It's starting to get chilly. How about sliding down even if you can't sleep?"

His invitation was hard to turn down, so Claire joined him.

"Snuggle up to me…like you used to," she said. "And put your arms around me. Always used to feel safe when you did that…back East."

Clay obliged like she knew he would. Claire turned her back to him while he gently pulled her back into the cavity between his hips. She raised her nightgown and robe slightly so he could feel her soft buttocks fill the space. It was a position, on other nights, that often lead to a wonderful, romantic encounter. Tonight, it served only one purpose: a good way to transfer his body heat to hers.

He raised up to kiss her earlobe. "I owe you an apology too. Got in too big a hurry, didn't take into account your condition. I wanted you so much…"

She turned over to face him, pleased with his concern. She pecked him on the cheek. "You know I'd never risk…unless it was alright, no matter how much I wanted you. I just wish you hadn't hired that horrible little man."

"So do I, but we're stuck with him for a few more days; then it'll be over so we can start a whole new life out here. As bad as it seems now, just remember it'll be just that much better when we get to your uncle's ranch. And speaking about Tanner, he may be about your height, but don't ever underestimate that man! He's strong as a bull! Remember the way he handled your trunks and boxes? Just wish you'da seen him a bit earlier when he loaded Beemis' flour and sugar barrels. He put me to shame, I'll tell you! 'Course those short, thick fence posts he lets pass for arms and legs don't exactly make him stand tall, like some six-footer. I'm a shade under six feet and he's like you, a good six inches shorter."

"Just 'cause he's about my height, that's the only thing I'll ever have in common with him! Thank the Lord!"

"Okay, you rode up front with Tanner today. Besides being short, what else?"

"Pockmarks all over his ugly face and I dare you to tell me he's got a neck! C'mon, Clay, where is it? Where, Clay? Where?"

"You're right, his head does seem to be resting right on top of his shoulders with no neck between. Only when he turns his head do I get the impression there's gotta be a neck in there somewhere."

Clay decided against pressing Claire any further. Tomorrow would be a much better time to get into their lives with personal questions he needed answers on. He sensed she'd relaxed enough now to take on one more. "I know you're not about to bring this up, but be honest with me, Claire. You think I did a sloppy job of tying down our privacy tarp, don't you? And that's the reason the wind blew it away so Tanner could see us put on our free show for him! Right?"

She tried to smooth it over as best she could. "Since you brought it up, dear…I made certain allowances for you being new out here…not knowing a whole lot about using rope and such. But Clay, that'll never excuse Tanner for spying on us! *Never!*"

"Alright, I'm not holding back what I think…no, better make that what I know happened tonight to wreck our reunion."

"I…I don't understand. What are you saying?"

He raised up on one elbow to peer down into her face. "Tanner told me he didn't think I knew beans about using rope because I'm a greenhorn from back East. I played dumb so I let him do all the tie-downs so I could watch. Oh, he cinched up a rope or two a bit tighter and he used a couple knots I'd never seen before…"

"Yes, go on."

"Beemis Markham showed me how to use a rope and tie knots the second week I was out here. Now, I don't claim to be handy with a rope or lariat like some cowboy, but when the job calls for a little rope work with a knot or two,

I know what needs to be done and I go do it. Claire, no strong gusts of wind ever tore our tarp way to give Tanner his free show. The only way the wind could've done that was with a lot of help from Tanner. He loosened that tarp, then lay back to enjoy the show."

They continued south toward the Hole on the second day of their trek with a stiff wind buffeting their backs, making them thankful their destination lay due south.

Clay had to volunteer to sit between Tanner and Claire to keep the uneasy peace from erupting into an old-fashioned free-for-all before they'd traveled the day's first mile. He need only glance sideways to see a far different Claire than he'd seen yesterday. Her pretty, round face now harbored hard lines and a deep scowl to go along with a determined, set jaw. Her blue eyes no longer danced with happiness and anticipation; instead they were dulled by distrust and fear.

Three hours passed in stone-cold silence, broken only by the creaking and groaning of the wagon and its wheels upon the hard, shale-like ground. The only words came from Tanner when he flicked his bullwhip over the team's rump to remind the four horses he was their master and he would set their pace, plodding ever southward.

"Stop your team for a minute!" yelled Clay. "Claire needs to get down to do some walking."

Tanner stood up to jerk hard on the reins. "Whoa up there! Whoa up!" The freight wagon lurched to a stop. "'Member it's your money," he grumbled. "You better had brung extra money, Barnett, 'cause it's gonna take that'n more if'n this keeps up, same as you done yesterday. 'Member, past five days'n I charge extra!"

Clay helped Claire down, then went to the endgate to untie his saddle horse. He motioned Tanner to go on ahead. He cupped one hand over his mouth. "This shouldn't hold you back but very little! Catch up to you soon with my saddle horse! You won't have to cut your pace any!"

They waited for Tanner to get a good lead on them before either took a step. Claire spoke up. "Haven't seen a living soul since yesterday when we pulled out of that cowtown. There isn't even a decent road out here, just some hit-or-miss trail. Mother said I'd end up in the middle of somewhere with nowhere to go. Beginning to think she was right. Is she?"

Clay let his horse trail behind. "This is sheep country we're passing through, that's why you haven't see hide nor hair of anybody. Once in a while you can spot a sheep herder's covered wagon or maybe hear a dog bark when he's being worked among the flock, but that's about it. Tomorrow, things will look a lot better, I promise! There'll be much better grass, which means we'll see a ranch or two, probably even get to wave to a couple of cowboys if they're close enough."

Claire continued walking. "If Mother could see you now, she'd never believe you're my husband, that's how much you've changed, Clay. Your cowboy hat makes you look even taller than you are. Last night, I discovered there isn't a pinch of fat on you anywhere. You're lean and suntanned beyond belief. The only things about you that I can still call my own are your deep blue eyes and your thin face. Even your hair has changed, no more darkening blonde shades, just bleached blonde through and through! Can't get over the way you've learned to ride and handle a horse. It's…it's almost more than I can picture, let alone try to understand or get used to. And the way you choose your words and the expressions you use, it's certainly not back-East talk. Not the back-East Clay Barnett I've known most of my life!"

He was pleased by what she'd said. He pulled on the reins to keep his horse in stride with them. "Thanks for all the compliments. Guess the only thing you left out is that I don't wheeze while I breathe and no more dry coughs or hacking at night when I lay down. Uncle Beemis said this dry climate is just what the doc ordered for my asthma."

"You're right, I haven't heard so much as one slight wheeze."

They continued on, each hesitant to press the other. "When I first got your letter saying you were expecting, I was upset…maybe a little angry at the time. Claire, it's not that I didn't want our baby, it's that we talked about this…and we agreed to wait having any more children until we got settled in out here. Remember?"

Claire stopped walking. She threw her arms around Clay. "I should've been more careful on our last night together when we made love twice. But dear, all I could think about was that you were leaving in the morning and taking Josie with you, and you two would be out of my life for weeks and months. Oh my Lord, been out here two days and this is the first time Josie has popped into my mind! Can you believe it? We have a four-year-old daughter whom I love and miss with all my heart, and my thoughts are just now getting around to her! How in the world am I ever going to make it up to her? How, Clay? How?"

He took her into his arms to kiss her concern away. "The same way you always do when you're around her: with lots of hugs and kisses. These past two days have upset you, that's all. Just wait'll you see her! She follows Aunt Maybelle around everywhere with her grownup talk and ways. Maybelle says she's really getting to be a good little helper!"

"Josie never was much of a baby. Hope she still misses me some or at least asks about me. Does she?"

"She misses you a lot! Every night, when I put her to bed, she always ends her prayer with 'and please, dear Lord, bring my mommy to me safe and sound, and tell Santa Claus to look extra hard for me when he brings my dolly, 'cause my new home is far, far away.' You did pack a doll, I hope? Josie's counting pretty hard on getting one."

"You bet I did! At least her mother remembered to do that! I can hardly wait 'til Christmas morning to see Josie mother her first dolly from head to toe!"

"We better start walking again; Tanner's losing us."

Claire didn't want to break up their embrace to deal with today. She looked up into her husband's eyes. "I was beginning to feel a lot better until you said Tanner. I'm afraid of him…of what he might do to us…"

He kissed her again and held her as close as her body would allow. "You're a lot stronger and tougher than Tanner realizes! He still thinks of you as some soft, back-East woman who will complain or cry at the drop of a hat! He doesn't know you like I do! Besides, if worse comes to worse, I can always count on Old Trusty here on my right leg to keep Tanner in his place!"

Claire broke from him. Her eyes narrowed then went straight to the gun holstered comfortably on his right hip. "What is it with you, Clay? And with every man I've seen since the minute I stepped from the train yesterday? Everybody's packing some kind of gun on either their right or left leg or both!"

She never waited around for Clay's answer. He got a firsthand look at what he'd known all along: a toughness called woman saddled with a determination that bolted up the trail under a heavy woolen skirt, going by the name of Claire Barnett.

"You don't understand, Claire! Hey, wait up!" He jerked the reins. "C'mon Dapper, we'd better catch her before she finds Tanner!"

Catching up with his wife took a bit of doing for Clay. It took a hard trot out of man and horse to finally cover the ground to corral one very distraught young lady. He pleaded with her. "Hey! Hey! I know what's on your mind, what you're going to say! Listen to me! That was a hunting accident ten years ago! This is different out here! Way different! Like comparing day to night!"

She stopped to catch her breath and to leave no doubt where she stood on the matter. "Dead is dead, Clay, no matter how or why! A gun took my father's life and robbed my mother of her husband and me of my dad! It changed our lives forever! We lost everything! My mother had to work for many of the same people who used to work for us until I was old enough to help out. Some fourteenth birthday for me, standing by my father's coffin, waiting for the funeral service to end so they could bury him! My mother and I vowed we'd never let a gun come into our lives again to cheat either of us out of the good life we once had. Mother can't do anything about her life! But I can and I will!"

They walked several hundred yards before Clay dared to plead his case upon deaf ears. "Today, you wondered why you never saw any other people. Out here, we say the same thing about the law. We say people and the law are mighty scarce because both are spread far too thin. There will be times when the law can't get to us in time to be of any help so we must give the law a hand when there's none around. So men like me strap on guns to make sure such things as our family, our property or own lives are protected. We call that taking matters into our own hands. Now do you see the big difference out here? Guns keep the honest man honest and serve notice to those who aren't that they won't be free to come or take as they damn well please."

Claire slowed her pace a bit, giving Clay hope that she could be giving his explanation serious thought. Some of the fire left her face and her jaw relaxed a trifle, allowing her usual soft, sweet voice to return. "I'm only going to say this once, so please give it all your attention, dear. I've always liked you since the first day I saw you in church over fifteen years ago. When you kissed me at our church social, I knew you were the one I would love and I have ever since! Clay, your gun must not be a part of our lives, ever! Take it off now! Hang it over your saddle horn until I can pack it away in my trunk tonight! When we reach Uncle Beemis, you must hand it over to him."

Clay swallowed hard, but refused to back down. "Uncle Beemis is the one who taught me how to handle it and shoot. If I did that, it'd be worse than saying I'm not man enough to own one. It's become a part of me, the same as drawing my next breath. I can't—no, I mean I won't take it off!"

"Either the gun goes or else I go!"

Day three did nothing to ease the growing tension between the threesome. Tempers flared over the most trivial things. What few words that were exchanged were far better off left on their tongues behind closed mouths. In short, the trying trip now promised nothing but a double dose of trouble from one end to the other. The only one who seemed to thrive on the entire mess was the one who had started it, the ex-cowboy turned freight hauler who called himself Tanner.

They camped that evening, still on the prairie as Claire so aptly put it, "out in the middle of somewhere." They glared at one another over cold beans, beef jerky and biscuits so hard and dry she was sure even a back-East billy goat's cast-iron stomach would've been tested to the limit.

Clay tried to say something positive. "Day after tomorrow, we'll be camping by some scrub pines. Should be able to gather enough twigs and branches for a pit fire. We can have a warm meal and chase it down with hot coffee. Now, doesn't that sound good?"

Neither Tanner nor Claire were moved enough to say anything.

Clay set up their privacy tarp while Claire scraped what few dishes they used and washed them in cold water.

Tanner cared for his team, using four buckets to grain, hay, and water each horse, drawing from supplies he kept in the back of his wagon. As each horse finished, he was tied to the opposite side of the wagon from the Barnetts until hitch-up time in the morning.

Clay tended to Dapper, his last chore for the day. He followed Tanner's lead by tying the gelding to the same side of the wagon. He removed the saddle and its blanket, intending to store both under the wagon to keep them from being stepped on during the night. Then an idea struck him. "What the heck?" he asked himself. "If it doesn't work, I'll be sleeping under the endgate next to Tanner, listening to his snores all night."

Claire was surprised to see Clay lugging both his saddle and blanket to their spot. Before she could utter any words, Clay got his in. "At night, cowboys use their saddles as range pillows. And under these range pillows they store their guns, just in case, same as I'm going to do 'til Tanner drives past the Markham ranch's main gate."

"And after that, then what, Clay?"

"That's up to you! I'm willing to compromise if you are! Look, Claire, neither of us trusts Tanner one little inch! Now doesn't it make sense to make sure we both do everything we can to see that the Barnetts arrive safely? Especially since you're carrying our child?"

The lantern's soft glow couldn't hide the change in Claire's face. Her hard jaw lines shifted a tad, and some of the worry etched above two eyebrows was erased completely. A faint smile appeared. "If I agree," she began, "it'll mean you must give up your gun for good once we reach the Markhams'. Do I have that promise?"

"You do, if that'll keep you from leaving me and going back to your mother!"

She threw her arms around her husband. Wet kisses followed nonstop. "Oh, I'm so glad we've worked our differences out! Now, I can tell you; I wasn't going back to mother, no matter what happened between us!"

"I don't understand. You and your mother have always been so close. What happened?"

Tears rolled down Claire's cheeks unchecked. "Oh Clay, mother's been on the warpath ever since you left! She's made these past eight months a living hell for me. I…I…should've been out here four months ago when our house sold. I know this is a terrible thing to say, but I believe mother was behind all those delays and excuses I kept getting while I waited around to collect the final money owed us. And when that didn't work, she and I really got into it. She said some awful things…about you…"

"I'll bet I can fill in some of it, but now that you're finally out here, let's get it said and be done with it. Then we can get on with our lives!"

Claire continued between sobs. "The last day packing my trunks was a nightmare! She came barging into my bedroom, shouting and screaming for me not to leave. She shook me and shouted in my face, 'You've already made two of the biggest mistakes in your life; don't make it three by going out West.'"

"I bet I know what the other two big mistakes were. Number one had to be when you married me…and number two came along when you let me take Josie with me. How'm I doing?"

"Two for two! Oh Clay, she called you a shiftless, worthless dreamer! Said dreamers live in their own world and never come into the real one. She said dreamers can't help being poor providers, husbands or fathers. She told me to stay back East with her so we could tell our neighbors and friends that you deserted us and took Josie by force. Then I'd be free to marry someone more stable—somebody she already had in mind!"

"Just for the record, how did you answer dear mother?"

"I pointed to our cute little house and told her in no uncertain words that my husband worked as a bookkeeper to save enough money to provide me and Josie with our very own home and that sure didn't sound like a dreamer to me and you must've joined our world long enough to do that!

"Good girl! Anything more?"

"Mother tore into me about you reading anything and everything you could get your hands on about the West. When Uncle Beemis' letter came inviting us out here, she said that proved you were a dreamer because you put Josie down and closed the door so she wouldn't interrupt your reading. 'Dreamers do that,' she said. 'They forget about being good fathers because they're too busy devouring every word in their dream world!'"

"And how did you handle that?"

"I went right on with my packing until I finished it. I told her, 'Let me know when the drayman comes to pick up my trunks because I'm going out West to be at my husband's side where I belong! Dreamer or no dreamer!'"

"Thanks, Claire, for putting your mother in her place. I know it wasn't easy."

"Clay?"

"Yes."

"Are you…a dreamer? After all, you gave up a very good job as a bookkeeper."

"Claire, I was nothing but a glorified note and figure-keeping clerk! Mister Henley never gave my suggestions or ideas any thought. My job was killing me, but I tried not to let on how miserable I really was. When Henley hired me, I took the job for only one reason: to impress you, not your mother! When your uncle's letter came, it gave me the way out to do what I've always wanted, to go west! Now here I am and so are you!"

A great dawn loomed on the fourth day over the limitless horizon, and for the first time Clay's letters came alive, really alive in the eyes, heart and mind of Claire Barnett. She saw the same rugged, raw beauty he'd been trying so hard to express in his letters to her. She also began to realize her husband was indeed a dreamer, though not the kind her mother had incessantly tried to drum into her head. The connection between the dreamer, the doer, and the visionary was never more alive than in the person of her husband. The wagon's creaks and jolts, dips and bounces, no longer became something to endure because with each turn of the wheel, a new sight, a different feeling, or a fresh scent took their turns greeting her. She had no choice but to gasp in awe at the mighty panorama unfolding before her because she, too, had changed from being only a spectator into a willing participant.

Tanner's wagon rode the crest of a high ridge giving Clay enough time to spur his horse hard to reach Claire's side of the seat. "Look! Look, Claire! He shouted, "There it is! The one with snow halfway down! That's Cold Spring

Mountain! From there it's only a half-day's ride to the ranch!"

Claire, too, was caught up in his excitement. "Everything's so clear out here!" She leaned forward, extending one arm towards the mountain. "It looks so close, like I can almost reach out to touch it!"

He laughed. "In about two more days you can! Distances really fool you out here! It seems like you'll never get there, then bang, you're right at its foot, looking up 'til your neck starts to ache!"

"Everything is so big out here. Mountains, ridges, valleys and the land between goes on forever! Is Brown's Hole like that?"

"Naw, you can squint real hard and you'll see the rim around the Hole in any direction. That's considered kinda small out here."

Clay rode alongside the wagon until the trail started down an incline. "Dapper's had a good blow; the trail's an easy downhill stretch for a spell! Time for your morning walk!"

Tanner's wagon lurched and pitched to a stop. Clay got off his mount to help Claire down. "Use the wheel hub, dear. It makes it that much easier."

"These stops are gonna keep takin' money outta yer pocket, Barnett. 'Member, you been told!"

"I know, I know, Tanner!"

Claire came up with a gem to counter Tanner. "The more you hound us about the money that's coming to you, the more I believe you don't think we belong! Even you, Tanner, had to come from somewhere, though I can't imagine where that could possibly be!"

Tanner mumbled something under his breath, then took his gut feelings out on his team. *Crack! Crack!* His bullwhip serpented over the lead two horses, leaving Claire with the distinct feeling he'd much prefer to have his long, leather-braided snake snapping and hissing over her and Clay's hides.

Clay held out his hand. Claire obliged by placing hers with his, a sure sign both were on the same page of life that glorious day. Dapper snorted his approval by nuzzling his master in the back, giving Clay a gentle push.

"Dapper's trying to tell us to get a move on," laughed Clay.

"You know, I've been too busy trying to find my way out here with you that I haven't even taken the time to admire your horse. I've never been around horses much, but I know a beautiful animal when I see one, and Dapper looks to be that and more. Am I right?"

"Yes, and then some. Beemis gave me this horse; it's an Arabian, the only kind he raises to ship back East to rich folks who can afford his prices."

"I'd like to learn to ride the way you do, after our baby is born."

"No problem. When you're ready, I'll do my best to give you what few pointers I've learned. Beemis showed me there's a lot more to riding a horse than trying to climb aboard and stay there."

Hand in hand, they continued on down the trail with Tanner's wagon getting smaller by the minute. The words stopped, but in no way did that end the communication between them; it had become that special once more. Clay decided to recheck Claire's feelings about Tanner. "Tanner's given us no problem since our first night out. How do you read the man now?"

Claire slipped her hand out. "No different than before. Each time you put up our privacy tarp, I feel his eyes upon me before I step behind the tarp to cut those stares off. He gives me the willies! I know he can't see through my sheepskin coat, but each day I ride with him, I'm not just getting his usual, dirty once-over. I can't shake the feeling he's trying to undress me, right up front with you riding between us!"

"He's rough as a cob and twice as crude, but there's a lot of men out here that way, Claire! It goes with the territory."

"C'mon, Clay, he's more than rough and crude, he's awful! I've seen you scrunch up your nose at least a dozen times sitting next to him. I'm sitting on the outside, and I can barely stand it when he passes all that gas!"

"Farts, Claire! They're called farts out here, same as back East!"

"I'm beginning to understand and like most of the changes about you, dear...but I see no reason to spoil it when you use language like that, no matter how big the territory out here gets to be."

Cold Spring Mountain loomed directly ahead, its snow-crested summit highlighted against the blue heavens, forcing them to look upward to catch its magnificence. Long tentacles of ice and snow stretched downward into numerous ravines, chasms and outcroppings, nature's way of warning the three weary travelers not to tarry too long, seeking the safety of the pass through its foothills.

Clay rode up to Tanner's side. He pointed in the direction of a stand of scrub pines. "Let's camp over there. Should be plenty of fuel to keep a pit fire going most of the night. I can already feel those cold drafts coming off the snowfields halfway down. That fire will cut the chill down quite a bit."

Tanner turned to look toward the northwest. A low, gray-looking bank of clouds caught his attention. "My bones ain't been wrong near forty years. Canada snow by morning, maybe sooner."

"Well then, we all need to get set-up as soon as possible. After you tend to your team, I want you to dig a hole about ten feet away from Claire's side. I'll string up our shelter behind it. There's enough daylight left to do a little bird hunting and still leave me time to gather fuel. Claire, how about you getting out your Dutch oven for hot biscuits and a big skillet in case I get lucky?"

Claire, too, had a suggestion. "Even if you don't bring back fresh game, there's a box of canned peaches next to my pot and pan trunk. Peaches should taste pretty good with biscuits and hot coffee."

"That's the ticket! Time to celebrate! Only a half day tomorrow!"

Claire shared Clay's enthusiasm, smiling and humming while she gladly went about opening her dish trunk and canned fruit box. Even Tanner must've caught some of the couple's excitement. Much of the scowl across his sour puss faded long enough for him to spade up the good earth.

Clay came back into camp wearing a grin a country-mile wide. Two sage hens dangled from his belt.

Claire rushed up to him as fast as her body would allow. "You never cease to amaze me, dear. You really do know how to handle a gun!"

He downplayed his prowess. "I can't draw'n shoot like some of the crack-shots out here, but Beemis showed me how to raise my left arm to lay my gun barrel across to steady my aim. Sure works for me!"

Even Tanner had to compliment. "You s'prised me, tenderhorn! Thought that gun hangin' off your hip was only to show your Mrs."

The first serving of Claire's baking powder biscuits, cushioned around a plate of fried sage hen covered lightly with gray, was fare fit for a king a la Western style. Clay did the honors with the coffee pot.

They sat around a steady pit fire, well stoked with sage-brush knots and jack-pine twigs and small branches to help hold the heat. While their conversation remained on the guarded and cautious side, nevertheless, it was their first meal together under much more pleasant circumstances. Claire finished her plate and did the polite thing. "Anybody for seconds?"

Tanner's eyes went into orbit just ahead of his mouth. "Best soppin' biscuits I ever ate!" He shoved his plate at Claire, nearly hitting her in the stomach. "Hit me with some more gravy, too!"

Claire was sorely tempted to do just that with the hot gravy. "You only need one hand to hold your plate; why are you holding out two?"

"One's fer them good vittles you cooked up, and the t'other is fer my money! All six day's worth, right now!"

Claire saw red again! She snatched Tanner's plate out of his fat, chubby fingers and pressed it hard against one cheek. "You'll get paid tomorrow when we get there, after our goods are unloaded, and not a minute sooner! And don't expect a full-day's charge for doing a half-day's job!"

Tanner gave himself away when he pumped both fists. "By God, it's a full-day's pay fer tomorrow or else I don't hitch my team up come morning!"

Clay jumped between. "Hey! Hey, you two! That'll be enough!" He turned to his wife. "Tanner gets a full-day's pay. I agreed to it before we picked you up! Should've told you before…had other things on my mind."

Claire was far from finished. "Alright, then how about us charging him for all that wasted time up in Rock Springs? And don't play dumb with me, Tanner! You know what I'm talking about."

Tanner relaxed his fists. "You're nuts! Ain't no time got wasted! None!"

Claire confronted him again; she was going to have her say. "I shouldn't wonder you don't remember 'cause your brain was pickled in whiskey! No sooner had you and my husband picked me up than you decided to stop in front of the first saloon we passed. Let's see, what was that Jim Dandy you tried on us? Oh, yes, here's the way it went!" She lowered her voice, doing her best Tanner imitation. "'Folks, need justa' minute, two at most! Gotta cut some dust clean outta my throat!' Some cuttin', Tanner! You took better than an hour to wet the dust down! Meanwhile, we set out front with your team stomping and snorting, and stomping some more! Darned good thing for you my husband knew how to handle those horses! Don't suppose you remember much about me sending Clay to find you in that place, do you? I can tell you this much, you stunk to high heaven from ten feet away! You left no doubt where you'd been or what you'd been doing! What a wonderful way to get started, Tanner! Yessiree! A Jim Dandy way!"

Tanner had been nailed to the proverbial cross but good by an outraged woman with enough talent to give the man a pretty good imitation of himself—drinking habit included. The best he could come up with was, "It makes me no never mind, but you done wasted my time too."

"Where? When, Tanner?" charged Claire.

"All them stops, so you could walk your belly!"

Clay jumped in. "No, Tanner, you're wrong! That's the reason you're getting the full day's pay for tomorrow. You're being paid very well for that!"

"I done some more waitin' on your Mrs. at the train station fer her to put them long-johns on under her dress, 'member?"

Claire couldn't wait to get her words out. "Five minutes, Tanner, that's all it took! How in the world can that be compared with your drinking? Tell me?

I'd like to know!"

Nothing would ever be settled between the two, of that Clay was dead sure. There was only one thing left to do, play the same role he'd played for the past five days: peacemaker. "Alright, you two, time to be doing other things. Tanner, I'm only going to say this one more time. You will get paid in full tomorrow after you deliver our goods at the Markham ranch. Anything else?"

"Thar's vittles left to eat! Gimme my plate back!"

Both men watched Claire go about fixing Tanner's plate. The last three pieces of sage hen were promptly scraped from the frying pan. She bent down to lift the lid from the Dutch oven to remove four biscuits, which she cushioned around the sage hen. Tanner's eyes grew big as marbles, watching Claire spoon the last of her gravy over the biscuits. She rose, looked at Tanner licking his chops, then let his plate fall from her fingers down into the fire. Eyes blazing to match the fire's flame, she calmly replied, "Didn't want your plate to get too cold. Looked like it could stand a little reheating. If you want seconds, you know where your vittles are."

Claire's display of defiance toward Tanner in no way dampened her show of passion toward her husband. The minute she stepped around the corner of her privacy tarp, she became a changed woman, bent on rekindling that unfinished business of four nights ago: making love. She unbuttoned Clay's sheepskin coat, along with hers, so she could move her body into his with an uncanny seduction action. Her eyes telegraphed her deep, abiding love, her lips covered his with smoldering desire, and her body all but invited him to lay her down, regardless of its shape. She broke the seal around their lips long enough to whisper, "Dear, how about getting that top tray out of my clothes trunk? Set it across our box of peaches, should do nicely for my vanity table. Now for my chair, another peach box will have to do for tonight. I need to freshen up a bit."

He never tired of watching his Claire do her magic act: transform herself into the most desirable woman he'd ever wanted or needed. Yet tonight, he felt it had to be extra special given the fact that four nights ago she had been stripped of the very thing she treasured most during their most intimate moments: absolute privacy.

She untied the silk sash under her chin, which held her lined sunbonnet on. She caught Clay's face in her mirror's reflection from the lantern lights. She smiled. "Thanks, love, for lacking my silk scarf through the sides of my bonnet! Great idea! No telling how many steps it saved by not having to chase it across the prairie when the wind caught it."

"Yea, kinda figured that meant Mr. Sweet Disposition had one less thing to bitch about."

"Cla-a-a-y! The word 'complain' does a much better job. Try it next time, you'll see."

He smiled to himself. Claire was not about to soften up on vulgar language, even if the West had more than enough room for such words.

Claire's deft fingers came into play, pulling the rosette-studded pin from her hair bun. Two quick shakes from her head and her hair tumbled nearly to her shoulders.

"You've let your hair grow," he commented. "I sure like it!"

His compliment pleased her so she rewarded him with two flirtatious winks coupled with her usual demure smile.

Clay watched Claire tilt her head while she put her hairbrush to good use to accent its natural sheen. Then she raised up slightly to allow room to slip the top part of her long johns down. For a second, she teased him with a quick peek of one breast in the mirror before blocking his view while she sponge bathed her face and upper body. That done, he guessed by the way she was crouching down, the lower part of her body was being attended to.

The part that always amazed him came next. Somehow her heavy woolen shirt along with her long johns were gone, replaced by a flimsy flannel nightgown that always settled down over her body without so much as a tug or pull. "How'd you do that?" he asked.

"Well now, Clay Barnett," she teased, "if I showed you how I did that, it'd sure take a lot of fun and pleasure away from both of us, wouldn't it?"

She tiptoed toward him with the pace of an Irish pixie, despite leaving her wool boot socks on. "Your turn, dear. I left plenty of hot water in the tea kettle."

"Better bank up the fire first," he offered, "then I'll see what I can do about taming five days' worth of stubble on my face."

Claire laughed. "See, you're using Western words again; they seem to come so natural with you. Anyway, thanks for reading my mind about needing to shave."

He banked the fire with sage knots and thick pieces of pine branches to hold the heat.

She tucked her legs under her nightgown and drew herself up. "Ooh, that heat feels so good. Don't worry, dear, I'll put my long johns on…later."

He bent down to plant a kiss. "Wow, I can sure smell your lotion and perfume! Bet you dabbed perfume in some special places, didn't you?"

She teased again. "Only one way to find out for sure…after you get rid of that prickly beard."

She became the spectator this time by watching him fill their washbasin. "Tanner hasn't asked to use our basin once since we left, Clay! No wonder he smells to high heaven!"

He found her face in the mirror, then went ahead applying lather to his face with his shaving brush. "You need to understand about soap n' water out here, Claire. Men like Tanner shy away from such things until a real bad case of hornies hits 'em; then they look for the nearest barbershop."

"Cla-a-a-y!"

"Okay, okay, change it to when Tanner needs a woman's services."

"That doesn't sound a whole lot better. What's a barbershop have to do with this?"

"Out here, it's called the fifty-cent bath special! Tanner gets a shave, then soaks the dirt off in a tub of hot water. Before he leaves, the barber slicks his hair down and douses him real heavy with lilac. One whiff of him in a saloon tells everybody he's ready to belly up to the bar to down some cheap, rotgut whiskey until he can gather up enough courage to proposition the first whore who can stand him and his lilac smell."

Claire shook her head with disgust. "If I live to be one hundred, I could never understand, let alone accept, such disgusting goings-on. The idea of some lady lowering herself to sell her body, it's…it's beyond comprehension!"

"First off, Claire, these aren't ladies we're talking about, they're whores, plain and simple! There are two things out here in mighty short supply: the law and good, decent, eligible women! Shucks, even the whores get marriage proposals real regular. A few even turn out to be halfway decent wives, if some hard-up man is willing to forget how many others she's serviced in the past!"

Clay's explanation of life's knocks out in the West did not set well with Claire. One word disturbed her to no end. "I don't care for the way you use the word 'service.' All my life, and I certainly hope since we've been married, both of us have been in the service of our dear Lord, serving Him by example, trying to live our lives by His laws. Have you forgotten them just because you're out West in this wilderness?"

He held the razor in midair, wondering just how to counter his wife. "No,

Claire, I haven't forgotten God's laws nor will I ever forget our marriage commitments. You have to understand the relationship between most men and women out here is a numbers game! Nothing more! Nothing less!"

She took the towel from his shoulder to wipe a spot of lather he'd missed. "Well, I can certainly see where I'm going to be doing missionary work out here in this Godless land! Our small organ you brought out will be put to good use as soon as I'm able after our baby is born. I hope you've told Uncle Beemis we will be holding regular church services in his home since I'm more than sure there isn't a church to be had in the Hole."

Claire had given Clay the opening he needed to change subjects. "Aunt Maybelle and Josie take turns dusting off your organ. She's hoping you'll show her how to play it. You will, won't you?"

"Of course, dear, and Josie, too, when she's a bit older. And speaking of Josie, I can hardly wait for tomorrow to come. I'm so excited about seeing her again. I've already promised myself I'll never let Josie out of my sight ever again!" She held up eight fingers to emphasize her point. "Eight long months, Clay! Far too long for our family to be apart! Never again!"

Clay knew he could've bet his last dollar on Claire keeping that promise. He took the towel back to finish shaving his chin. "After you put Josie down, you owe your uncle and aunt a great big hug and a proper thank-you for all the work they've done fixin' up our bedroom."

Claire put an arm around Clay's waist. "I don't want to look first and thank them second, so tell me what to expect."

He rinsed his razor in the basin and wiped it dry. "Don't expect to see hand-rubbed maple furniture. Beemis did a bang-up job of cutting and notching our bedframe, headboard and two dressers outta cedar logs he hauled and skinned. Your aunt, bless her heart, worked just as hard makin' our bedroom curtains outta fringed buckskin and for the curtain rings she used the leg bones from a deer I shot two months ago."

She squeezed him. "Just the way you talk about them, I can tell you think they're pretty special. What are they like?"

Clay stepped to one side to empty the basin. "Maybelle is deep South through and through. Have Beemis tell you how he met her, it's a corker of a story." He mused a minute. "Your uncle is some character, I'll tell you…come to think of it, he's a lot like the furniture he built for us."

"How in the world can my uncle be like furniture? How, Clay?"

He held her tight. "So help me, he is, I swear! Once you see our furniture, you'll more than see how that can be. Both are rustic as all get out and just as sturdy!"

Claire gasped, then laughed. "Boy, that's some description, I'll tell you. Any more characters like Beemis down in the Hole?"

"Just one, Henry Ettleman."

"Henry who?"

"Ettleman is his last name, Claire! He's something else; wait'll you meet him, too! He's our oldest and most respected rancher. He uses all his years of ranching in the Hole to come up with sayings to fit any situation that comes along. Boy, are they gems!"

Claire was highly amused by Clay's descriptions. "I've asked you before in my letters, dear, and twice since we started out, and you've never answered me. What are you going to do to make a living out here?"

"We, Claire, not just me! You'll have your answer in a minute, when I get back."

"Where are you going?"

"To check on Tanner."

Clay crouched in the shadows by the freighter's endgate, using the flickering light from the pit fire at the opposite end to penetrate enough darkness to find Tanner. A minute of eyestrain paid off; Tanner was where he was supposed to be: rolled up in his bedroll under the endgate.

He breathed a sigh of relief, then poked the large lump. "Hey, Tanner, you awake?"

"Damn sure, yes," he growled. "Soon as you and your missis shut up, then I'll git me some sleep."

"You can soon as I get back."

"Sumpthun' on your mind, Barnett?"

"Thought you ought to know. I had me some company along with a string of luck when I bagged those two hens. This kind of company rode bareback on paints and wore moccasins instead of boots."

"You see'd Injuns, so what? Nuthin' but friendlies, I'm sure...'Course you being' from back East, you like as not turned tail and run'd like hell."

"That's where my luck came in. At least a dozen of Chief Two-Moons' Utes whooped and hollered, doing their circle job on me. Good thing the old chief recognized me or else I wouldn't be here telling you about this."

Tanner raised up. Clay had caught more than his attention. "Don't understan,' Two-Moons has been friendly fer years...Wonder what's going on?" He scratched his beard. "I only see'd Two-Moons maybe once or twice in fifteen year or more. How's to come you know'd him so well?"

"It's because of that luck I've been tellin' you about. You see, my uncle Beemis and Two-Moons go back together quite a spell, been blood brothers for years! Ever since Two-Moons has seen me with my uncle, he figures I fit in as part of the deal! Get it?"

"Where's he camped? How close?"

"Let me put it this way, Tanner, the grease on your wheels' hubs won't ever get warm before we're at his camp. That close enough for you?"

Tanner scratched some more. "Yeah...yeah. See'd what you're drivin' at."

"I'd better saddle up Dapper while you hitch up tomorrow. I'll ride on ahead to make sure Two-Moons knows it's us. And for God's sake, don't even rest your hand or fingers anywhere near your holster. One shoot, Tanner, and it's all over for all of us! Are you clear about this?"

No man in the West could've walked back to his wife and given her a better guarantee of safe passage to their new home than Clay Barnett. For the first time in five days, he wouldn't have to lie awake to listen for strange sounds or rustlings in the middle of the night. There would be no need to doze with one hand under his range pillow, feeling the cold messenger of death at his fingertips, instead of being where it belonged, draped around Claire's body, pulling her into him, giving her an extra sense of security. Tonight, he was pleased by what he'd done, leaving him free as the wind to give Claire his undivided attention to be the husband and lover she expected him to be.

He sat on Claire's make-do vanity seat to pull off his boots. "Tanner's where I want him at last," he said. "There'll be no gunplay, no shots in the night, though in all honesty, I'm sure he knows we're too close to the ranch to be doing anything stupid."

Claire sat up with a robe covering her shoulders. "I felt a chill. Hurry up so we can snuggle under the warm blanket. I can tell by your voice, and your words, you're very pleased about something. What happened, love?"

He raised a finger to his lips. "Shh, we better keep our voices low. I'll tell you soon as I'm under the blanket."

Clay wasted no time getting undressed. He stacked his jeans and flannel shirt in a neat pile next to Claire's long johns, skirt and blouse. "Where's your sheepskin?"

"Under me," she whispered as he slid in beside her with only his long johns and boot socks on. "The only thing warmer than this lining is your body when we make love."

They laid together, their noses touching, their lips barely a kiss apart so that they had no trouble hearing each other. Clay kissed her tenderly. "I stretched the truth a bit, told Tanner I ran into Two-Moons' Indian tribe near here."

She returned his kiss, making sure he felt her moist softness full around his mouth. "Are they here?"

"Down the trail a mite...got Tanner believing one shot will bring 'em down on us quicker than he's got time to go after you. I made sure he knows Two-Moons would protect us no matter what he tried to pull. You can forget about Tanner tonight."

She hugged him again and again. "Oh, I feel so much better now, thank you, thank you, my love! One more thing, Clay...about your gun. Tomorrow's the day you hand over yours for good. Remember your promise to me?"

He nipped her earlobe. "No, I haven't forgotten...and after tomorrow...with my new job just around the corner...don't think I'll be needing one."

He saw the excitement building in her eyes; she could hardly keep to a whisper. "You've practically spelled it out for me these past days, but I was so upset and so worried, I didn't see it until tonight. All I had to do was figure out what Brown's Hole doesn't have and where you fit in, and there, plain as the nose on your face, it came to me. You're going to be standing behind the counter of your very own store, putting your own ideas to work, instead of being cooped up in that stuffy little office back East, with nobody paying any attention to you. How am I doing, love?"

"For that, you deserve an extra kiss. Here goes." Finally they parted long enough for Clay to continue. "Out here, it's called a mercantile store; back East, we called it a general dry goods store. Beemis and I have already picked the spot out, just across Vermillion Creek from his ranch. Two-Moons winters close by, so I should do plenty of fur trading, too. I'm also going to add a room in back so you and Josie will have enough room. We'll put in an extra crib for our baby and space for Josie to play. And when you're not nursing our baby, you could lend me a hand with the ranchers' wives—you know, give the woman's touch to needles, thread, yard goods, and women's unmentionables, things like that."

She squeezed him, her enthusiasm still building. "What a great idea! See, Clay, your plans are already coming forward! One thing, though. We must keep the Sabbath; our store will be closed on Sundays so I can hold church service at the ranch. Agreed?"

Clay bussed her cheek. "Of course, dear, I've already counted on that. I figure with Beemis, Old Henry and several other ranchers pitchin' in, we should be able to open our store by the time the spring thaws open the passes. I've done some pretty tight figuring and it's going to take most of our money to get started. Once we get going, things will loosen up for us and then we'll be able to move out of the ranch if we want to. Never hurts to have an option or two open, it's just good business."

Claire's smile broke into a laugh. "See, Mister Storekeeper, you're already a success and we haven't even unlocked the door. You know, for the first time since we started, I'm actually looking forward to riding on that hardwood seat up front with that disgusting, dirty man. We won't be ten minutes down the trail and he'll dig out a plug of toobacky, as he calls it, and say, 'Barnett, you ain't a man 'til you kin handle'a chaw of this.' Thank goodness that's not one of the habits you've picked up! After you turn him down, he goes ahead anyway, making sure I see that awful juice drizzling down his chin from the corner of his mouth. Then he flashes those ugly, yellow-stained, rotten teeth and lets go with a big wad, trying to aim it just so it misses over my knees."

He pulled her close so their bodies touched. "You've really got him pegged; boy, what a description! I'm glad you can see the good things happening out of this. One half day tomorrow with Tanner, and we'll be rid of him for good."

Their conversation stopped, each content with the feeling of closeness between them. Claire broke the spell. "Since there's so much we won't have in our new home…Don't suppose there's any sense in my asking, but when my time comes, is there a doctor in or near the Hole?"

He stroked her hair, then held her sweet face between his hands. "Well, my love, here's some good news for a change. No, we don't have a doctor, but we do have the next best thing: a midwife with plenty of experience birthing babies."

She smothered him with kisses. "Oh, my love, that's such good news! Day after tomorrow, I'm going to set out some good china and invite her over for a spot of tea! I'll have you go get her and then introduce us. You can leave the rest up to me; I've got a good feeling we'll get along just fine!"

"You're raising your voice, Claire; please keep it down."

"Alright, alright," she whispered, "but I need to know her name. What is it?"

He gulped, delaying the inevitable. "Seeabaka."

He waited for her reply; none came at first.

"Sounds awfully foreign, love...Can't seem to place her nationality. I do hope she speaks English. Does she?"

"I've never met or seen her, but both your aunt and uncle speak very highly about her. I'd have to say she's been around White women a lot, so undoubtedly she understands our language much better than most of her people."

"Around White women a lot? Her people? Clay, what are her people?"

Another gulp. "Indians. Ute Indians."

"No sirree, Clay Barnett! Not on your life! No sirree! No Indian savage is coming into my bedroom to touch me or my baby! GOT THAT, CLAY? NONE!"

"You're shouting, Claire, lower your voice. You don't understand; these aren't savages any more. Beemis has known them for years. They're friendly."

Claire's nose rubbed her husband's. "This is my final say, Mister Barnett. I don't care if Uncle Beemis hunts with them or whatever else they do out here, no Indian comes into my room!"

"Listen to me, you've as much as said you're gonna need help. If not Seeabaka, what then?"

He'd made a good point, one he was sure she couldn't get around this time. She turned her head to glance up into the night. Clay could almost hear the wheels turning.

"Besides those primers I'm going to use for Josie's schooling, you brought out every book we had, a lot of books on a lot of different subjects. Surely, there's bound to be one or two on medical matters such as childbirth. Starting tomorrow afternoon, I'm going through every one while I still have time...and with Aunt Maybelle's help, I'm going to do just fine, like other women have had to do out West."

Clay wasn't about to counter his wife after she'd made her position crystal clear. True, he reasoned, she was new and a bit green to the ways things were out here, but there was no denying she was cut from a special mold, the kind reserved for frontier women only. On that, she stood head and shoulders above any and all of his expectations.

A sweet voice interrupted his thoughts. "You...you haven't forgotten about us? About this being our special night, have you?"

He took her in his arms to kiss away those questions. "No, I haven't;

matter of fact, I was going to move the lantern a bit closer so I can see if those deep blue eyes are filled with the same kind of love I remember from eight long months ago on another special night for us."

Clay raised up to take hold of the lantern. When he slid back down between the blankets, he found his Claire ready and waiting. Her robe lay to one side, and her nightgown was above her knees, waiting for him to lift it as high as his passion demanded.

She knew he held the key to unlocking her love; it'd always been that way between them. He raised her nightgown, exposing her thatch of fine hair and her round belly. To her surprise and delight, he laid his head on her soft stomach, then turned to plant a wet, hot kiss on its highest part.

Claire stroked his hair. "Oh, my love, I'm so glad you did that, just like you always did when I carried Josie."

"Hey, did you feel that? What a kick! Wow!"

"Clay, you're talking too loud." Then she laughed. "If we aren't a pair. Keeping our voices down is never what either of us is used to." She continued stroking. "I'm carrying our baby the same way I carried Josie…Are you ready for another daughter?"

He raised up to catch the lantern's light on her face. "Well, if you're right, we can pretty well count on our baby girl having blonde hair and blue eyes, same as Josie and us. Correct?"

"I do have some cousins with red hair. All I ask and pray is that our baby is born healthy, no matter what precious life the Lord places in our care and trust."

"That goes double for me."

Claire waited for the passion to build in her husband. She didn't have long to wait. He raised his head for an instant as if seeking her permission to kiss further down. She opened wide to accommodate him, her way of saying yes.

She felt him kiss again and again, moving ever closer toward her thatch. Suddenly her passion broke free, matching his. She held his head gently between her thighs, moaning, "Oh my, my love, oh, my love," her way of protecting her modesty and yet allowing the pure pleasure he was giving her.

She waited for him to move back up. When he did, she whispered, "Oh, my darling, you must love me an awful lot."

He worked her lips from corner to corner, savoring her delicious softness, inch by inch. He stopped only long enough to reply, "I do, more than you'll ever know."

Claire moved slightly away so she could let him have her breasts. In the flickering light, she let him see, wanting him to touch, then taste to his passion's content.

She swooned, holding on, while he carefully measured with his hand, going over one breast. She felt his hand cup; then she felt his fingers lift gently, feeling its fullness and swollen roundness. He kissed her nipple, sending her into another world. "More, more," she urged. "Don't stop…please, my love…don't stop…"

Claire moved her nipple in and out between his hot lips, making sure he'd discover what she wanted him to.

He raised up. "Your milk's coming, lots of it. Tastes sweet and kinda sticky…"

"Yes, love, it started tonight while I was bathing them…I hope you remember to do something for me."

He didn't disappoint. He suckled hard for a minute, then raised up quickly to transfer some of her milk to her moist lips through kissing. He backed off slightly to watch the result.

She smacked her lips, using her tongue to gather in the last drop or two. "Oh, how I love its goodness and sweetness. God has given us this pleasure ahead of time, to take my milk the same way you did before Josie was born. Once I finish nursing our baby, there should be enough for you, too."

Clay went back to her breasts, eager to satisfy her wishes as well as his own desire. It would be hard to say who received the most pleasure, the one who gave the milk, or the one who took the milk.

Claire turned slightly to help him suckle. She kissed his forehead, her way of urging him to continue such pleasure. She ran her fingers through his hair, then quietly reminded him by saying, "Don't forget I have another, Clay, don't forget…"

He settled on her other nipple, making good sucking sounds, much to Claire's amusement and enjoyment. She closed her eyes, then offered up a prayer. "Thank you, dear Lord, for letting my milk come early. It brings us that much closer."

Clay stopped. He moved back up again, over Claire, his face flush with a readiness that needed no explanation or words. He sat up to position himself better.

Claire, too, read the signals and understood his need to be deep within her. She unbuttoned the lower part of his long johns. "Oh, my love, your seed pouch feels so full, so tight. Easy now, easy…Let me help you…"

He raised up over her. "Maybe I'd better make one last check on Tanner."

"Clay," she whispered, "you can't, not now."

"Whataya mean I can't? Tanner's seen me in long johns before."

"Not that, I mean the other."

He looked down. Claire's hand still held his hard shaft. "Oh, yeah…see what you mean."

She tried hard not to break out laughing. To counter, she cradled him and reached out with her free arm to bring him down to her lips for another passionate kiss.

He felt her take hold to make sure some of her wetness covered the head of his erection.

"Easy now, love…don't push. Let me help…easy…easy."

He had only to watch her face to see that he was in. He raised up slightly. "I'll try to keep my weight off as much as possible."

"No, love, I want to feel your body. Just let me…my way."

He marveled at the way she continued to position her body, using her legs to complete the cradle around him. He felt her arms come into play, wrapped around his buttocks, applying steady pressure, just enough to ease him into her.

Deeper and deeper he felt himself being pulled in, her wetness lubricating his penetration every inch of the way. "Please, love, try to make it last as long as possible; we've both waited so long for this."

Clay wanted to go wild now that he was in. Just stroke and shoot and stroke some more. He knew that would be cheating both of them out of such prolonged pleasure.

He started to use long strokes, and to his surprise, Claire moved up tighter than ever, forcing him to make love her way. She obviously knew him better than he knew himself. "I'm sorry, love," he blurted out, "it just feels so good. Don't want to hold back."

She smiled up at him. "It's alright, love. I understand."

Eight long months without intimacy suddenly became a beautiful ritual of give and take, thanks to Claire's careful planning and preparation. Their bodies moved in wondrous fashion, each now so considerate of the other's needs and desires.

Gradually, ever so gradually, Claire opened up, giving him more and more stroking pleasure. She paid attention to his breathing, waiting for the tell-tale sign. "Oh, my love," she whispered again, by way of encouragement, "when we do this, we are truly one. More love…just give me more. There's no feeling in all the world like this."

"Claire...Claire, I can't hold back...I can't...Claire..."

"Kiss me before your seed comes! Hurry!"

He pressed his lips firmly upon hers, trying in some way to compensate for the way he thought he was hurting her now by pushing so hard.

Claire gasped and held on. "I feel your seed, love! Don't stop. You must let it all come! Every drop!"

The more he pulsed and jerked, the tighter Claire clung to him, making sure their bodies absorbed as much pleasure as possible until she knew he'd spent his seed.

Then and only then did she release her cradle around him so they could stay locked together in sweet surrender.

Claire closed her eyes, savoring the pure pleasure each had given the other. She felt something light and slightly damp land on her forehead. She opened her eyes to look past Clay's head, up into the darkening shadows. "A tiny snowflake," she cried out. "It's going to snow, dear."

The romantic answer Clay had in mind stuck in his throat. Once, twice, three times, the serpent of braided leather coiled around his throat, strangling the very life and breath out of him. He struggled to gain his balance so he could face his attacker. Instead, he was doubled up backwards, like a jackknife, off of Claire's body up into two of the strongest arms he'd ever come across. The last thing he saw and heard was Claire screaming while she pulled her nightgown back down.

What happened next was a blur of life and death madness for Clay. Tanner's bullwhip was about to take his life. With one mighty effort, he freed his arms from Tanner's pin. He jabbed repeatedly with his elbows into Tanner's belly, trying to force the man to relax the death grip around his throat. For this effort, the man cussed and swore, then dragged him toward the fire. He felt hot flames lick at his boot socks; then everything went dark.

Tanner growled, trying to ward off Claire's blows to his head using Clay's saddle. Her screams infuriated the bullwhacker, but he refused to let up on his stranglehold around Clay's neck. He glanced around quickly to find her so that he might duck her next blow. He was aware of whirling white nightgowns everywhere that seemed to float without legs, but always sprouted arms and enough strength to deliver telling blows. He glanced up for some reason, only to see Claire hovered over him, mustering every last ounce of strength behind the downward swing of the saddle. This time the blow found its mark. His head felt like it had been split wide open. Blood gushed down his forehead, blinding him. He tried to turn to swat at the nightgown.

That was his last move.

"CLAY! CLAY! WAKE UP!" Claire screamed. "Tanner's down! What should I do next?"

She loosened the bullwhip around her husband's neck and tried to help him sit up. He coughed and gasped, pointing to his throat, then fell back to the ground, making strange, dry wheezing sounds.

"Clay! Clay! Can you speak? Clay! ANSWER ME!"

Somehow he steadied himself enough to sit up. Twice he tried to clear his throat; then he pointed a shaky finger in the direction of their bedroll. "Gun...gun," he wheezed, barely getting the words out. "Get...my...gun."

Claire's frantic face told it all. "What should I do if Tanner wakes up before I get back in time!"

He coughed, then cleared his throat. "You must pick up my gun to shoot him before he murders us!"

"I can't, I can't," she sobbed out. "I'm afraid of guns!"

"Then all this is for nothing; we're going to die!"

Clay realized Tanner was regaining his senses; he couldn't afford to wait for Claire to make up her mind. Still reeling from the effects of Tanner's bullwhip, he put every ounce of strength he had into rolling him over so he could get at his holster. To his dismay, Tanner's holster was empty; the man had bought his story, lock, stock, and barrel.

Claire, too, saw Tanner had no gun. Torn between her absolute fear of guns and the will to survive, she made a mad dash to pick up Clay's gun.

Both men sat up to take stock of their life-and-death situation—and both men realized Claire would determine who lived or died. They fought each other on the ground, kicking, clawing, hitting and wrestling one another, each determined to break free long enough to get to Claire, who was holding the gun, frozen with fear at what to do next.

Claire watched the free-for-all. Terror stricken that Tanner was gaining the upper hand, she did the impossible for her: She came at Tanner determined to kill him. It took both hands to steady her aim, but she pressed the barrel into Tanner's head, squeezed the trigger, and closed her eyes.

Click! Click, click! Click! Again and again, she squeezed the trigger; nothing happened.

Clay shouted, "COCK IT! COCK IT! PULL THE HAMMER BACK!"

Tanner rolled over on top of Clay. He pinned one of Clay's arms under his knee to free one hand long enough to snatch the gun out of Claire's hands.

"Go ahead, shoot me!" yelled Clay. "Two-Moons' braves will be here so fast, you won't have time to get to my wife!"

Tanner stepped away from Clay, still pointing the gun, first at Clay, then at Claire. "Stupid woman," he snarled, "don't know a damn thing 'bout guns! Well, I do! Both'a ya do as I say or else you're dead meat!"

Clay got up, determined to play out the hand of life he'd been dealt. "Claire, get behind me! Quick!"

Claire obeyed before Tanner could react. "Now what, dear?"

"When I move, you move! Rest one hand on my lower back so you can tell when I'm about to move. Tanner's only got one target this way."

Claire began sobbing. "I'm sorry about the gun."

"You did fine, you tried! If you hadn't nailed him with my saddle, I wouldn't be here, anyway."

To their surprise Tanner made a beeline for his bedroll, leaving the couple alone for a few seconds.

"What's he up to?"

"My guess is he's gonna come back with that big skinning knife he carries with him. I've got him convinced he doesn't dare shoot, so that knife will get the job done without the loud noise of gunfire."

"Be honest, Clay, how far is Two-Moons' camp?"

"Too far to do us any good for now, but you can get there if I keep Tanner busy before he tries to cut me up. Remember, just keep the rim we're on to your left and you'll run into his camp. Just mention the name Beemis Markham, and Two-Moons will take you safely to him."

She began to cry. "I won't leave you no matter what. I can't do that."

"You must, Claire; it's not about us anymore, it's about saving you and our baby, so Josie won't lose both of us. You must do this. There's no other way!"

Tanner returned with a vengeance, brandishing a ten-inch skinning knife. "I'm gonna carve you up, Barnett! Then I'll leave you fer those flesh-eaters and bone-pickers to fight over." He took an imaginary swipe. "Got plans fer your missis, too! Gonna mount her and poke her 'til there ain't no poke left in me anymore! Then ah'm gonna tell her to gimme some wiggle, like she done you. And when she ain't got no wiggle left, I'm gonna slit her from stem to stern!"

It had to be the biggest bluff ever tried above Brown's Hole. "Tell you what, Tanner, you can still walk away from this. You heard me right! I said walk away! Just leave camp! No questions or anything from us! We'll even throw in enough grub and water so you can make it back to Rock Springs!

Now how's that for a deal?"

"Deal! Fer what? Already got your house goods! Should fetch purty good money back in Rock Springs. Time fer talkin' done left with all your wind, Barnett!"

"Look out, Clay!"

Tanner jumped the fire pit bent on one thing: stabbing Clay Barnett to death. Two swipes produced nothing but cold air as Claire's warning allowed them to sidestep his bull-like rushes.

"Jump, Claire! Jump with me!"

They stood separated by the fire pit. Tanner now stood where Clay and Claire had been, and they in turn now occupied his spot. Tanner glared across. "Ain't gonna be so lucky next time. Only takes one time, Barnett, one time, that's all!"

Nobody paid any attention to the snow starting to fall or that the fire in the pit could stand banking. What a strange, macabre sight the three made. Tanner fully clothed with his buffalo skinning knife in hand, and Clay in his long johns and singed boot socks, backed up by one terrified woman clad only in a nightgown and boot socks using the trap door to Clay's long johns as her handle to dodge and duck, and stay alive.

"Claire. I'm going to turn my back for a second so he can't read my lips."

"I'm watching. Go ahead."

"The lantern is to your right. Grab it when I turn around. Next time we're on Tanner's side, make sure you get one of our blankets, you'll need it."

Tanner wasn't about to let their conversation continue.

"Look out, Clay! He's going to do something! I've got the lantern!"

Clay and Claire bobbed and sidestepped, matching Tanner's feints and fake charges. He felt his wife slip the lantern into his hand.

"Jump, Claire! Jump!"

This time the bullwhacker came in low, barely clearing the fire pit. He crouched down after landing, slashing out as Clay and Claire moved past him in the opposite direction.

Claire quickly rolled up one blanket. "I've got the blanket…What's the matter?"

The lantern fell to the ground out of Clay's limp arm. Gamely he tried to stop the bleeding, using his good hand to clamp around his forearm. "Must be cut clear to the bone. Can't stop the bleeding…My sleeve is soaked…didn't feel a thing 'til now…"

Tanner saw Clay holding his arm. "Winged ya purty good, didn't I?" he gloated. "Next time I'll stick it into your belly and watch you squeal n' kick like a stuck hog. You're done, Barnett! It's all over!"

Clay knew it was only a matter of time now. He risked turning his back once more. "I can't hold out much longer. I'm going to make a run for the nearest wheel. You run with me and keep on running. I'll break the lantern over the wheel, use the glass to fight off Tanner while you get away in the dark. Go to the woods first, then keep the rim to your left; it's your only chance. When I go, you must go, too!"

Tears nearly blinded her; her voice quivered, giving her agony away. "I'll do what you ask only because of our baby. Never forget how much I love you."

"Good girl." Then his voice faltered. "Tell Josie when she's older her daddy made one terrible mistake…Maybe she'll understand by then. You'll be there to help her grow up. Remember I love you with all my heart. NOW GO!"

They ran as though two lives depended on it, Claire's and the baby she carried. Tanner was caught off guard, but quickly gave chase, closing the ground between them.

Clay smashed the lantern, sending fragments of kerosene-soaked glass flaming out in all directions. He kept the handle and top metal cap, noting it still housed a large piece of jagged-edged glass, made to order for dealing out considerable damage. He wheeled on Tanner, slowly raising his wicked-looking tool. In the flickering light, Tanner saw a man rise out of the wagon's shadows with one purpose in mind: to make him pay for every inch of life he planned to take.

Somewhere behind Clay, out in the darkness, he heard these words fading fast. "Josie will know the truth about you because I'll tell her how her daddy gave up his life so that I could keep mine."

Clay motioned with his head. "C'mon, Tanner! Any time! Just remember, I'm gonna get lunch outta you before you even think about supper!"

A dirty taunt crossed Tanner's pockmarked face. He looked at the jagged glass, then at Clay's limp arm, dripping more and more blood on the ground. "Got lots more time than you got, Barnett. Believe ah'll wait 'til you bleed to death!"

Claire reached the stand of thick pines only to discover there was practically no light whatsoever once she stepped past its perimeter. Twice she stumbled over dead tree trunks, skinning both knees badly, trying to cushion the fall to protect her baby. On her second fall, her stomach churned violently, forcing her to vomit up her supper. She heard leaves and low branches being rustled by the wind. Dazed and sick, she decided to crawl in that direction. She took shelter in a thicket of bushes by spreading her blanket, then sitting in its center so she could pull its corners up under her chin to cut off the wind. Almost at once, the cold set in upon her, forcing her body to shake and her teeth to chatter. She moved within the blanket until she found support for her back against the trunk of a young sapling. Despite the coldness, she knew she needed rest if she stood any chance to make it to the Indian camp.

She awoke from her troubled sleep, her senses on guard, the tiny hairs on the back of her neck burning like never before. Something or someone was coming toward her. Was it an animal? Perhaps a deer or even an elk? Clay had pointed out a herd of elk just yesterday.

Crack! Crunch! Snap! Crack! Snap! The sounds were getting closer.

Common sense told her no animal thrashed around like that, no matter how dark. A new fear seized her—it had to be Tanner!

Something in the back of her mind told her to roll up in her blanket at once and lay still, perfectly still. Maybe in the darkness, she'd pass for a log—the same kind she'd stumbled over. It was too late to do anything else.

"Ah, there you are! Didn't git far, didja? Playin' possum ain't gonna do ya no good! Now git up! Ya hear me? I said git up!"

Claire was terror stricken. She was positive that Tanner had spotted her, darkness or no darkness. And his voice certainly sounded close enough to be standing only a few feet away. She cringed in fear about what would happen next.

"Alright, have it your way! I'm gonna kick hell outta ya! Then see how ya like it! Here goes!"

She gritted her teeth and braced herself for a punishing kick aimed at her stomach. Any second now, Tanner's boot would find its mark.

"Ouch! Ouch! OW! OW! Damn it!"

She couldn't believe her good luck; Tanner had to be hopping around on one good leg only a few feet from her. He'd obviously kicked hell out of a log instead of her.

He sat down on the log, waiting for his foot to stop throbbing. "Too damn dark out to see for sure," he growled out loud. "Damn the luck!

Mad as hell at himself, Tanner rose. Out came his skinning knife, ready to slash and cut anything that moved. "I know you're here," he snarled. "Gotta be! Damn weak-livered Easterner! Ain't got no gumption, no how! Big snowstorm's a'brewin' and ya got no clothes on or coat to tough it out! Got no boots neither! Ya kain't make it, you dumb, stupid woman! Afore you freeze that tight little ass ya got, I means to smell your perfume agin. Lord amighty, it sure did do me! Ya hear me? I said ya done me more'n any woman I ever met up with! Better'n even them whores up in Rock Springs! That's sayin' a lot by my figurin'."

The only answer Tanner's words received was a stiff gust of wind that chilled him to the bone. He rose, walking a few steps to keep his circulation going strong. He gingerly raised his good foot to feel the dim outline of another fallen tree trunk before planting his weight upon it. "Dead people kain't tell on nobody, ya know…But afore ya joins your mister, ah'd sure like another crack atcha! Ah see'd what'cha done with that perfume…where ya put it n'all. Sure do admire the way you gobbed it on your nipples an' between your tits. That was sumpthun', alright! Wished ita been me suckin' on them nice tits ya got, instead of your mister! Then ya let him chase that perfume down your belly, all the way to your varginny! Now that's where ah draw the line! That place is fer pokin' only, not kissin' like he done ya! Nothun' beats good pokin' ah always said, 'specially if there's lots a' wiggle coming from the woman when she's gettin' all that pokin'. That about the way you see it, too?"

Tanner started walking again, breaking twigs and small branches left and right. He stopped and turned around in Claire's direction, still convinced she was somewhere near, but where? "If'n that big storm warn't a'comin' ah'd sit here 'til daylight, then ah'd ketch y'an' get some fine pokin' in afore ah done ya in! Lemme tell ya how ah done in your mister. Shucks, all ah done was wait on him, that's all it took! Purty soon he hit the ground. Looked more like a wore-out old gunnysack than a man! So ah lifts him straight up by the hair n' gutted him g-o-o-o-d! REAL g-o-o-o-d! Twisted n' turned my knife in him 'til he bled like a stuck hog! I said stuck hog; nuthun' like the way a good man oughta die out here!"

Tears rolled down Claire's cheeks while she lay quiet, listening to Tanner's version of how Clay met his death. She was sorely tempted to throw off her blanket and tell Tanner to his face that one hundred men like him couldn't even begin to fill her husband's boots, much less the man. Two sharp kicks in her stomach caused her to wince, a not-so-gentle reminder that the odds were stacked against her, yet she must try, no matter the outcome. Clay's sacrifice demanded that much of her at the very least.

Tanner shouted his goodbye for all the woods to hear. "Ain't no Injuns 'round here, no how! Besides bein' a dead man, your mister was a liar, too! How's that suitcha?"

The snowstorm released its fury, piling up wind-whipped snowdrifts over the terrain, covering everything in its path. Again and again the wind rose in increasing waves of intensity until its own howl often matched that of the wolves that were known to roam the region.

Then in the midst of such fury, a lull interrupted its continued onslaught, giving the predators a chance to search for food to sustain themselves. A wolf broke from the protection of a thicket, embedded in the stand of scrub pines. His keen eyes traversed the landscape, looking for any movement at all that might offer a meal after giving heated chase. Nothing caught his attention, so he continued toward the abandoned campsite, hoping the human intruders had left a scrap or two to his liking.

Ten feet from Clay's half-covered body, he sniffed the air, trying to ferret out what it was that took priority over the hunger pains gnawing in his stomach. Once, twice, he circled the body, letting his own innate curiosity be his guide to moving in closer and closer.

Suddenly, he stopped and a low guttural growl erupted deep from within, exposing two rows of jagged, flesh-ripping teeth. He tilted his head toward the sky and let go with a mournful howl. The scent of death was everywhere, but this wolf wanted no part of it.

CHAPTER TWO

Old Henry said, "Brown's Hole's got to be the worst pest-hole in the West. You can bet anything missing will show up there sooner or later."

Claire's knees buckled again and again, but she refused to let the raging snowstorm claim her as its next victim. This same storm, which had been her ally in turning Tanner away, now became her mortal enemy. To make matters worse, she often glanced over her shoulder, fearful that Tanner had changed his mind and would somehow emerge out of the blinding snow to chase her down, ravage her, and then put his blade to work to keep her from telling as he'd done with Clay.

She trudged forward, following Clay's instructions to always keep the rim to her left, no matter what. In that manner, she felt she had to be making some progress, but the numbing question stayed with her, how much farther to find help? Every exhausting step she took, three relentless companions never left her: the bitter cold, the howling winds, and the blinding snow.

Gail-force winds seemed to be sucking the very breath out of her, so she stopped for a minute to turn her head away from the blasts, and to use her bare hands to peel the crust of frozen snow off of the boot sock that covered her head.

She managed to laugh out loud—Clay would've either applauded or laughed himself silly over the way she must look. The other boot sock doubled as a muffler covering her face to protect it from being frozen by the icy blasts. She'd ripped both sleeves loose from her nightgown and used them as leggings from her ankles up to her knees. For shoes, she had to bite through the outside lining of her blanket so that she could rip enough material to wrap her feet in. Two strips off the hem of her nightgown served as laces to keep her shoes tied to her ankles. Her poncho took a bit of ingenious doing. First, she centered what was left of her blanket over the broken end of an old snag, then pushed with all her strength to pierce it, allowing enough of an opening to poke her head through. Another strip of nightgown became the sash she needed to the tie the poncho securely around her waist.

Claire's feet began to feel like they'd been cast in stone. She realized that she was beginning to lose their circulation as the cold began creeping from her feet up as far as her ankles. She stomped hard with her next few steps, trying in vain to keep some sort of feeling in contact.

The storm heightened its fury, sending wind-driven sheets of snow directly at her. Visibility became nearly impossible, adding the new panic of becoming hopelessly lost. She floundered along as best she could, stopping only long enough to utter a prayer between chattering teeth. "Please, dear Lord…help me…show me the way for my baby's sake…and for Josie…Don't leave me to die here alone."

Suddenly the storm's fury decreased as quickly as it had risen. *Can it be an omen?* she asked herself. Had He heard her call for help after all? She forced herself to move even farther to the left, looking for her guide, the Hole's rim. A fresh set of tracks sent shock waves of fear up and down her spine.

"Tanner! Oh, my Lord, he's here! He's found me!"

She stared down in disbelief at the tracks. Then common sense took hold once again as she realized they had to be her tracks. However, her joy was short-lived; she knew now she'd been traveling in a circle to meet up with her own tracks. Which way to the rim? Forward? Backward? To her left? To her right?

She sank to her knees into the snow, a beaten woman without a direction in mind. "Clay, Clay," she cried out. "I can't make it. Please forgive me…I'm lost."

Claire lay down to die. She had given her all; there was nothing more to do. She'd lost all track of time, drifting off into her cold, body-shuddering, exhausted sleep.

Another force, another life wouldn't let Claire give up her ghost. It turned and kicked and turned some more until Claire was forced to sit up. She clutched at her stomach in pain and screamed aloud. "Ow! Ow! Ouch!" She plucked the ice from her frozen eyelids and looked about her. "Which way, my precious baby, which way?"

It took every ounce of strength to get up once more, let alone move one lead foot in front of the other, but that was exactly what Claire did. She picked a direction at random, more out of a sense of obligation to her unborn than anything else. She dragged herself and her frozen feet through the snow until she had spent herself into exhaustion. This time she knew there'd be no getting up. This time there'd be no resurrection from the dead, no matter how much the life she carried longed to see or cry or belong. Under her poncho, she folded both arms over her stomach, trying to pass the last bit of a mother's warmth and love to her baby.

The young Indian brave jabbed his pony in the flanks. He knew the storm had spent its fury, so he would be safe to look for a small herd of horses that had broken away from their corral during the height of the blizzard. One half mile north of camp, he came upon their tracks in the fresh snow, so he urged his pony on, hoping to overtake them soon.

One hundred yards later, he came upon a strange set of tracks that made no sense whatsoever, so he followed them down a short slope into a small ravine. He was puzzled. The tracks seemed more like blotches imprinted into the snow instead of the usual distinct animal or human footprint. Another thing that was hard to understand was the way they wandered, like an Indian who'd drunk too much firewater and couldn't find his wigwam. Though he'd never tasted the White man's whiskey, he was certain no Indian buck would've been crazy enough to have braved this storm.

Then he came upon her, the one who'd made such strange tracks. He knelt beside Claire and shook her while he tried to think of some white man's words. "Is your tongue still alive, White woman?" he asked. "Are there words left on it?"

The horse roundup was temporarily forgotten in favor of new excitement and commotion, the kind that a strange White lady had brought to Two-Moons' tribe. The old chief looked over the woman who lay before him. He walked around Claire, paying close attention to the roundness of her belly and the strange way she was clothed. "I've been around the White man for many seasons. I've never seen this before. Her time to bring new life is near…yet she has chosen to run away. I think a very bad man made her do this, took her clothes and drove her out into this storm. That is why she wears such strange clothes." He shook his head. "And the White man says we are the savages..."

He touched a finger to Claire's lips, feeling nothing but her coldness. Finally, he held it up for a closer look. He rolled his fingers over carefully, spotting a tiny droplet of moisture clinging precariously to his finger. "The Great Spirit will soon call her name... but maybe there is still time to save her unborn. I will send for Seeabaka; she has the gift and is wise in the ways of such things...woman things."

Seeabaka and two other squaws took charge of Claire. First, they removed her half-frozen clothes and wrapped her in a doeskin blanket. While the two women held her up, Seeabaka primed Claire with a very strong, hot herbal tea and waited for signs of life. Little by little, they watched some of the color finally come back to her face. "This is a good sign," said Seeabaka, "all of the White lady's water of life is not gone. There is still time to make her drop her baby."

Claire's eyelids fluttered; then she had great difficulty focusing her eyes. When she did, she saw an Indian woman staring into them. She tried to utter a sound and gave a feeble jerk.

Seeabaka's hand clamped Claire's mouth shut. "You must not waste your life water trying to scream or get away. Do not be afraid. You must help us. If you do, I will bring your unborn to this land before the Great Spirit comes to take you. Do you know my words, White one?"

Before Claire could ever even nod, one of the squaws forced a piece of rawhide into her mouth. "You bite down hard when too much pain comes."

One squaw held Claire up while the other forced her to crouch down in Indian fashion with her knees wide apart. "Good," replied Seeabaka. "There is no time for lazy White woman way to have baby; we must hurry!"

A half dozen squaws gathered outside of Seeabaka's wigwam, hoping to hear a baby's first cry. Instead they listened to one agonizing scream after another until several left, feeling sure Seeabaka's big medicine was too late.

Those who stayed covered their ears to keep Claire's cries from driving them away. Then the screams stopped. All was quiet—too quiet. Seeabaka opened the flap. "Tell Two-Moons to come." There was a collective sigh; that was the good sign they had waited to hear.

Claire slumped into a stupor. Her hair and her head were drenched in sweat. Two pieces of rawhide dropped from her mouth. Seeabaka started to dry the baby off while keeping her attention trained on Claire. "Hold her head up! I not wait to clean baby up!"

One squaw tilted Claire's head back while the other bathed her face with cool water from a skin pouch. Claire responded for a second, her eyes cleared up, and she made a slight gesture toward the baby Seeabaka held for her to see.

One thump, then two, and the baby gave out its first cry. "You have baby! Girl papoose! Take hurry-up look! See!"

The three Indian women watched an amazing thing. Claire's once contorted face, twisted by unbearable pain and agony, changed to one of quiet repose. They were witness to a miracle in transformation. Though no words would ever come, the three knew the white lady was at peace at last with herself and the world she left behind.

Two-Moons entered as Seeabaka finished cleaning the baby up. He was pleased. "You have done well, medicine woman. Who of our women has enough milk for this baby until we go down below to find green grass for the winter season?"

"Teekaka," the medicine woman answered. "Her breasts run with milk."

"Good, she shall be the new mother! As soon as we get our horses back, we will begin to move. This bad storm is an omen...We must move soon."

"Are we going to keep theWhite woman's baby?"

"This is white man's business. Wrap the White woman in a blanket and take her with us. I will powwow with brother Beemis; he will know what to do."

Two-Moons' tribe wasted no time getting relocated down into Brown's Hole as they camped across Vermillion Creek from the Beemis Markham Ranch. The chief sent for the robust, ruddy-complexioned, ex-Army scout. Seeabaka carefully unwrapped the Indian blanket for Beemis' inspection of Claire's body. Beemis took one long look, then turned away, a badly shaken man.

"Do you know this White woman?" the old chief asked.

The grizzled old veteran removed his spectacles, wiped his eyes first, then the lenses. The words came hard, but he said them anyway. "She is my grandniece." His voice faltered. "Would you mind covering her up again? I...I don't think I can handle it...right now. Put her in my buggy, too, if you don't mind. She's going home with me, where she was headed for in the first place! Where she belongs!"

Two-Moons placed his arm across Beemis' broad shoulder. "We have seen many strange things come and go, yet I know in my heart, as you do, there are things we cannot see far enough to understand. There is more here I think than comes to our eyes."

"You bet there is! My niece's husband must be up on top, murdered, no doubt! Soon as the pass opens, I'm gonna look into this...all the way to Rock Springs, if I have to! That's where he went to meet my niece!" Then he remembered. "Oh my Lord, my niece was expectin'! Where's her baby?"

Two-Moons was glad he had some good news for his blood brother. He motioned to Seeabaka. "Bring the White girl-child. The Great Spirit brought life to the baby through the hands of my medicine woman. Leave the baby with us, Beemis, until we go back on top when the chinook takes the snow away." He smiled. "We are both getting long in the tooth, my brother! Teekaka has much milk, enough for two! Leave it that way 'til the chinook!"

They shook hands. "Alright, but I'll be back tomorrow with my wife, Maybelle. She will want to see the baby and give her a Christian name. Wild horses won't keep my Maybelle away once she hears she has a grandniece who is alive and in good hands. Now, let me see the baby before I go!"

That afternoon Beemis buried Claire behind the main ranch house. True to his word, he returned early the next morning with his wife, Maybelle. He barely had time to help his silver-haired spouse step out of the buggy before she made a beeline to Teekaka's wigwam. The buxom-built lady made a big to-do over the baby, rocking and cooing the bundle of white-skinned wiggles she held in her arms. "Look, Beemis, her eyes are open! They're blue like yours and mine!" She kissed the baby's cheek. "Her name will be Ann Marie Barnett," she proudly announced. Then a wistful look clouded her face as she looked straight at Beemis. "I only wish her mother were here to do it herself."

"So do I! So do I, dear woman!"

The last thing Joe Cady wanted to do was disturb Beemis' breakfast, yet he knew this couldn't wait. The slim-built foreman stood by the kitchen door, removed his slouch of a hat, slicked down what was left of his greying hair to look presentable, then rapped soundly.

Maybelle, still in her robe, acknowledged his presence. "Come in, Joe, come in! Sure you won't join us for a cup of coffee?"

Joe stepped inside. "There's a bullwhacker out front by the main gate. Says he's the first freighter through since the chinook. Since we're closest to the trail, he decided to stop by here."

Beemis looked up from his plate, his round face the picture of prosperity.

"Well, what's he want, Joe?"

"Got some bad news or good news—It's all the way a feller sees it. This feller says he found Clay stickin' out'a snowbank. I lifted the tarp to make sure. It's Clay alright. The varmints left him pretty much alone...Guess the ice and snow helped some too. He's not in too bad'a shape...considerin'..."

Beemis turned to his wife. "Make sure Josie stays in this mornin'. Got me a coffin to make. Don't want her around me 'til I finish up! Keep her busy!"

Late that April afternoon, Beemis was ready to lay Clay to rest. Maybelle appeared, dressed in a traditional black dress, leading a frightened five-year-old girl by the hand. He waited until they stood in front of the coffin; then he read several passages from a small Bible and closed the short service by having them all join in by repeating the Lord's Prayer.

Maybelle turned to head back to the ranch house. Josie broke away and ran toward the coffin, sobbing her poor heart out. "My daddy! My daddy! I want to see my daddy! Please! My daddy!"

Beemis dropped to one knee to gather her into his arms. He stroked her soft brown hair and waited for her blue eyes to clear. "Josie, do you remember what your daddy called you the day he left to go meet your mommy at the train station?"

The sobs quieted down to mere sniffles. "Uh huh. Daddy called me his sugarplum."

"That's right! Now your daddy can't call you that anymore, but boy, would I ever like to. Do you suppose it would be alright if I called you that?"

Josie blinked back a stray tear or two, then looked Beemis straight in the eyes. "I...I guess so."

"Okay, Sugarplum, now what can I do for you?"

Josie's lips began to quiver. "You...you and Aunt Maybelle let me see my mommy before she went to heaven. If I don't get to see my daddy...well, maybe he won't get to heaven to be with my mommy!"

Beemis had been stumped by a child's pure innocence. He looked up to Maybelle for some help or at least an answer or two. She shrugged her shoulders, leaving him to deal with the delicate dilemma as best he could. "Sugarplum," he began, "you'll have to trust me on this, but I know for a fact your daddy and mommy are together in heaven, exactly where they should be! Now, now, you might ask, how do you know that for sure? And my answer would have to be because only good people who believe in God and say their prayers go to heaven. And Sugarplum, we both know your mommy and daddy certainly did that, didn't they?"

"Uh huh." There was a long pause; then Josie got in her final say. "Please, dear Uncle, open daddy's box so I can make sure he's okay before he goes to heaven."

Beemis racked his brain for some way out. "Besides calling you his sugarplum, do you remember anything else your daddy said before he left?"

Josie thought and thought. "Oh, I know! Daddy was so brown he said he looked like an Indian and wondered if my mommy would know him when he went to get her."

"That's it, Sugarplum! Boy, am I ever glad you remembered that because your daddy's not brown like that anymore. You know what? Well, I think you and I should remember him like the way he left here! All brown like an Indian! Yes, Sir, that's the way we're both gonna remember him! Which reminds me, what were you and Aunt Maybelle gonna do today in the kitchen before you came out here? Remember?"

Josie's eyes lit up. "Bake cookies!"

Maybelle heaved a big sigh of relief. "Come, Josie! Just as soon as I change my dress, we're going to bake cookies and you get to lick the spoon and scrape the bowls. You're the best little helper I've ever had! What say, Sugarplum?"

That night Beemis watched Josie say her prayers, then he helped Maybelle tuck her in before saying goodnight. In their bedroom, Maybelle spoke first. "That was a close call today. I knew from the way you were acting, you didn't want Josie to see Clay. Did he really look that bad? Claire looked better then we expected…"

Beemis laid his specs on the dresser, then sat down on the edge of their bed. He rubbed his eyes, then ran his hand through a mix of salt and pepper hair. "Even in my early years, scouting for the Army…never saw anything the Indians did to the settlers that could come close to what happened to Clay. He died a horrible death! His throat was slit…had so may stab wounds I quit counting. And if you think our Josie, our sugarplum, was going to see that…never, my dear woman! Not as long as I draw another breath would I let that happen!"

Maybelle sat before her vanity mirror, she started to brush out her hair, and then stopped to turn to Beemis. "Clay and Claire are finally here and together again, though certainly not in the way or place they should be. What next, Beemis Markham?"

"Two-Moons breaks camp next week to return to the country above the rim. He'll be dropping our baby Annie off. He thinks we're both getting long in the tooth to be raising a family. I told him just 'cause we're both pushin' fifty shouldn't make us too old, should it? What say, old girl, we are up to it, aren't we?'"

Now that the trail was open once more, Beemis Markham wasted no time getting to Rock Springs, looking for some answers to Clay and Claire's tragic end. He was relentless in his pursuit of information, and it didn't take him long to ferret out the kind of man who'd done the dirty work: a freight hauler who went by one name only—Tanner. His banker friend told him that Tanner had deposited a fair-sized sum of gold coins in his bank last October and that freight haulers lived from job to job and seldom have the kind of money that Tanner suddenly had. At this point, Beemis was ready to bet the ranch that Tanner's money had come from only one source: the money Claire had been paid upon the sale of her home.

The saloons painted another side of Tanner, the kind that undoubtedly explained why Claire had fled in the middle of the snowstorm, trying to save her life and that of her unborn child. Tanner had a lust for women, especially the kind he would never have, and his niece certainly filled that bill to perfection. Bartenders in two different saloons told of Tanner's heavy drinking after his return in late October, and that his taste for the women who went upstairs with him had changed dramatically along with his drinking habit. They said Tanner would only pay for whores who were small boned and had light hair. Beemis now realized why Clay had paid with his life to give Claire a chance to get away from Tanner.

One of the town's storekeepers added more information. Tanner had told him that the owners of his wagon load of household goods had welched on paying him for his services, so he had had no choice but to return to sell the goods so he'd get paid. The owner went on to say Tanner's story did sound reasonable, but that he had made Tanner wait a week for his money in case a dispute arose. When no one had showed to claim otherwise, Tanner was paid.

Beemis thanked the man and was about to leave when the man's wife appeared from the back room. He noticed she was wearing a very nice dress and that she looked to be about Claire's build. He decided to ask. "By any chance, did that very nice dress you're wearing come from any of the trunks of clothes Tanner sold you?"

"Why yes, Mr. Markham," the woman replied. "Finest sewing I've ever come across. Was going to sell all the clothes, but decided to wear them myself. If you know the lady who did this wonderful sewing, please tell her we'd like to make a deal with her to sell anything she cares to make in our store."

"I only wish with all my heart that'd be possible...You see, my niece is dead."

"Oh, I'm so sorry! Were there children?"

"Yes, two girls, whom my wife and I are trying our best to raise. One is still a baby and the other just turned five."

"Wait up, Mr. Markham! Please!"

A minute later, the woman returned from the back room with a doll. She handed it to Beemis. "I'm sure this doll would've belonged to that five-year-old. This doll had to come from back East somewhere because we don't get fine porcelain like this out here. Told my husband to take it out of our window before we set out the Christmas things or else it would've been gone for sure. To tell you the truth, I kept this doll for myself, it's so special."

A tear welled up in the old boy's eye, trying to fine a home behind his spectacles. "You.... you don't know how much this doll will mean to Sugarplum—er, that's what we call Josie. Her last Christmas was mighty lean, no mother or father around to tell her that Santa won't forget her. Fact of the matter, he did, 'cause we couldn't get out to buy her anything, had to make do with what my wife could scare up." He handed the doll back. "Would'ja mind wrappin' it up? I'm gonna tell Josie that Santa came late, that's all! Had a hard time findin' her 'cause she moved way out West!"

"I believe there's still some Christmas wrapping paper left. I'll be just a minute!"

The last call Beemis made was to the local sheriff's office to sign a warrant for Tanner's arrest. He was armed with more than enough information to provide a complete and accurate description of the man. The sheriff, a personal friend, asked, "How much reward money goes with this wanted poster, Beemis? Usually, I see three to five hundred, maybe a thousand or so for some big-time hard-case."

"Make it five thousand!"

"Say, you must want this Tanner fella pretty bad! No one's seen hide nor hair of him for months, so don't go expectin' too much for a while, at least 'til the reward notices get posted around."

"You have no idea how badly I want him! But I figure there's enough reward money to cut down some of those months he's managed to get a jump on. I'd double it in a blink if I didn't have some big ranch bills comin' up and two little girls depending on me now."

"One thing you'd better understand, Beemis, is that the kind of money you're offering is gonna attract the worst bunch of bounty hunters in the territory. They won't hesitate to shoot Tanner in the back and then tell us he tried to escape! And for sure, the right questions won't even get bothered with! This gonna be alright with you? I mean about your conscience and such?"

A peculiar smile played across Beemis' face to match the first hint of satisfaction in his eyes. "Yeah, it's more than alright with me. Was countin' on it happening just that way! Keeps me from facin' my Maybelle after I did the same thing if I ever run across the sonofabitch!"

"Auntie! Auntie! See, no hands!"

Maybelle came rushing out the kitchen door, half blinded by the apron, which managed to fly up into her face. "Annie! Annie!" she shrieked. "Grab the horse's mane and hang on! You're too young for this! Much too young!"

"I'm okay," the three-year-old answered back proudly. "Next week, Joe said I'm going to learn to throw a lariat. I'm gonna lasso fence posts! I can hardly wait!"

Maybelle reached the side of the Arabian mare, out of breath. Joe Cady stopped leading the horse. "She's fine, Mrs. Markham, really she is! Our Annie's a natural, that's all there is to it! Look how she holds her knees in and the way she tried to hook her boots under the mare's belly. 'Course she kain't reach there yet; she's got a mite more growin' up to do before that happens."

Maybelle threw up her hands. "I wished to God I'd never let Beemis talk me into this. It's going to mean an early grave for me if this keeps up much longer." She turned to Joe. "Half hour more and that's it for today!"

"Whatever you say, ma'am; you're the boss!"

"Aw gee, Auntie! Only a half hour?"

Maybelle's hands went to her hips. "Ann Marie, in case you've forgotten, your nap time is due next, so don't try to butter me up! It'll do you no good!"

"I won't sleep, Auntie! I'll just ride my pillow'n pretend it's my horse."

"Well, dear child, at least you'll be in your bedroom where you're supposed to be."

That afternoon while Ann was supposed to be taking her nap, Maybelle and Beemis had their heart-to-heart talk. Maybelle came down on Beemis— hard. "Look what's going on around here! A tiny tyke, barely three year's old, sitting on top of that great big horse while Joe leads her around! I thought Joe was our foreman. Isn't he supposed to be breaking your mares and seeing to it that the Markham ranch makes a profit?"

Beemis put his arm around Maybelle's waist. "And don't try to butter me up, Beemis Markham. Our Annie tried the same thing, and all it got her was down off that big horse and into her bedroom. Well, what have you to say about all this?"

He squeezed her. "If it'll get us down the hall into our bed for a little nap time, and maybe something else, I'm all for it!"

Maybelle's face blushed beet red. "Beemis Jay Markham, you're beyond hope or help, but I love you for saying such things. Why can't Annie be more like Josie? They're sisters, but no one would ever know it! Annie follows poor Joe around each morning 'til bedtime and then comes into our bedroom at daybreak, still in her nightgown, pestering us to go down to the stable to see if her horse is alright. Do you know any other three-year-old girl in the world who does that?"

Beemis laughed. "No, dear lady, can't say as I do. There's another side to this, so hear me out. When I hired Joe to run our horse-raising business, I had to put up with a lot of hard bark from that ornery cuss. The only reason I've kept him on all these years is that he's as good as I've ever run across. There's been more days than I care to count when Joe was about as hard to take as yesterday's left-over coffee grounds still sloshin' round in this morning's coffee pot. That's all changed now as our Annie has really mellowed him out. He'll never own up to it, but he really enjoys having her around. Even those watery, cold, grey eyes always clear a bit when he sees Annie walking toward the bunkhouse lookin' for him. And ya gotta admit his language has improved to the point it's almost tolerable, after you've told him no less than a dozen times that he'd better not be using bunkhouse words when Annie's down there."

"Guess you're right about that, and I do appreciate the time Joe spends with her…but I'm afraid our Annie is going to turn out wild and carefree like our Arabian colts are at first."

"I'm glad you made that comparison, dear, 'cause people, like horses, can be broke. Oh, they fight the bit until it fits their style, and they'd throw off the first saddle of responsibility anybody tried to throw on them, but in the end they turn out to be a pretty decent sort, kinda the way I figure our Annie will end up."

Maybelle pecked her husband's cheek. "You do have a way of putting it, Beemis. You always seem to come up with what people want to hear. One other thing, can't you do something about the way Joe looks? Since he has no teeth, he has to gum his words right along with his food. Makes him look twenty years older and his face that much thinner."

Beemis scratched his whiskers in deep thought. "I reckon Joe's about our age, but he won't own up to it one way or the other. Far as his teeth go, it'll only happen after our Annie's grown up some. By that time, they'll be such good friends, old Joe will have to buy false teeth because he won't want to be an embarrassment in front of our Annie. It'll mean he'll have to skip a few Sunday afternoon poker games for one or two paydays. Askin' him won't do it, but allow some time and let our precious little honey-blonde horseback rider do the rest."

Beemis started for the kitchen back door. Maybelle interrupted his steps. "One more thing. The other day, Josie took her dolly down off the shelf and handed it to Annie so she could play with it. Considering how much that doll means to her, I thought it was especially thoughtful of Josie to share it with her."

"Did Annie play with the doll?"

"Annie held it for a minute or two and then handed it right back. She said she might drop it or break it and if that happened, it would probably break their mother's heart because Josie said her mother was looking down on them from heaven."

The reward money for the capture and return of Tanner was claimed eighteen months after Beemis had sworn out the arrest warrant and the first poster had been tacked up. The sheriff at Rock Springs notified Beemis by mail that Tanner was apprehended in the Badlands area near the Black Hills of South Dakota. There was no mention on any of the details or circumstances surrounding his capture. The last two sentences in the good sheriff's letter summed it up nicely to Beemis' liking. It simply said, "There'll be no need to appear in my office for positive identification or to make hotel arrangements pending trial. Fugitive Tanner was shot while trying to make good his escape after being captured."

Beemis briefly mentioned to Maybelle that Tanner was dead with the understanding that further discussion on this matter would serve no purpose for either.

Joe Cady was in the twilight of his career, and just as Beemis had predicated, their Annie had mellowed him out considerably. He showed real patience with Annie, so that by the time she celebrated her sixth birthday, she was an accomplished rider and roper. No one three times her age could match her horsemanship or throw a lariat with such accuracy; she was just that good.

The Markham ranch prospered right along with the growth and maturity of Josie and Ann. Beemis rebuilt his bunkhouse and hired a full-time cook to replace his part-time horse wrangler, who had doubled before as the cook. This contributed to a much smoother operation for everyone and reduced most of the bunkhouse grumbling, which had complained, long and loud, that their old meals looked an awful lot like the horses they were working with. On the part-time cook's last day, one wrangler with a sense of humor told it like it was. He waited for the food to be dumped on his plate. "Yup," he said, "just as I expected; this slop is raw as all Billy Hell, and for damn sure it's gonna buck all the way down once I corral it long enough to get a spoon on it!"

"Whoa there! Whoa!"

The cowboy let his reins drop—the sure sign that man and beast were ready for a breather. It had been a long, hard, two-day's ride to the Crest of Zenobia Trail. He was anxious to see if the stories about the Hole were true—that a carpet of green covered most of its bottom land and that there was plenty of tall, lush grass there for the taking for his herds of cattle to graze on.

He rose up from his saddle, peering hard over his horse's head down the steep, sharp trail, hoping to glimpse a patch or two of green beckoning him on. He saw only more trail set against Douglas Mountain, the mammoth sentinel guarding his back and the Hole's south rim. Everywhere he looked, the trail offered nothing except sharp outcroppings of rock and grotesque-looking sandstone monoliths and buttes, hardly the kind of invitation he had expected or wanted.

He stepped down from his cayuse, the native horse of the West, to take a much-deserved stretch of his six-foot-plus frame. He turned his attention to the horse by petting its mane and talking to his only listener for two days. "Alright, old girl, we're getting close; time for a smoke."

Out came the tobacco pouch with its drawstring, then a small packet of brown cigarette papers. With practiced precision, he rolled a perfect cigarette between his fingers and sealed it with just the right amount of moisture off his tongue. Next, he fished a small-sized box of farmer matches out of his shirt pocket. One strike against the grain side of the box and he was in business.

Halfway through his cigarette, he spotted movement down the trail to his right. He watched the rider move with effortless ease along a wide ledge, a lariat circling over his head. The cigarette was forgotten; it was time to watch pure poetry in motion as the master and mount worked together as one.

Then he saw the reason for the exhibition: a bear cub was trying to make it to safety into a nearby thicket of buckbrush.

"Good throw, good show!" the cowboy bellowed out. "Ya got 'em!"

He hoped the rider heard him though he could plainly see the bear cub had snarled the lariat inside the thicket. Even from his distance, he heard the cub whimper and whine, thrashing about, trying to free itself from the rope.

Suddenly the next batch of praise froze on his tongue. He shouted as loud as he could. "LET THE ROPE GO! MOTHER BEAR'S CLOSE! LOOK OUT!"

Ann never heard the cowboy's compliments nor his warning, she was so intent on retrieving her rope. Only when her Arabian reared back and snorted did she realize danger was only six feet away.

The mother grizzly rose up out of the thicket, filling the air with a growl that sent shivers down the spines of two people. Ann tried to untie her rope from where she had tethered it around the saddle horn so she could ride out from harm or worse.

The bear attacked the closest thing to her: Ann's horse. One mighty swipe knocked the horse and rider down, nearly pinning Ann beneath her horse. The horse struggled to regain its footing, giving its terror-stricken rider the chance to clear both horse and saddle.

The grizzly spotted Ann sprawled on the ground and came charging.

Kerwhang! Kerwhang! Two rifle shots rang out.

The grizzly stood up on its haunches, trying to land death blows on anything that came in contact with its mighty swipes. Suddenly, the bear uttered an ear-piercing growl and folded up next to one panic-shaken young lady.

"Ma'am! Are you alright? ANSWER ME!"

He helped her up, then stood guard next to the grizzly, rifle in hand, ready to pump another round into the bear should she come to life.

Ann raced over to her horse, tears streaming down both cheeks. "NO, no, Big Boy!" She cried out, "GET UP! C'mon! You can make it! C'MON!"

Once, twice, the big Arabian tried to respond by raising its head, only to hit the ground harder and harder.

Bang! Bang! The cowboy's six-gun barked. Big Boy shuddered a few seconds, then lay dead.

Ann came straight at the cowboy, her small fists clenched, ready to take him on. "Damn you," she screamed. "What's the matter with you? Big Boy could'a made it! I know he could! Now he's dead!"

The cowboy sidestepped Ann's charge and grabbed her as she passed by. Ann felt herself being lifted for a second and then draped over a boney knee. "What in hell do you think you're doing?"

"Paddling your cute little ass, ma'am!"

"Who gave you that right?"

"You did! Anybody fool enough to rope a bear cub needs her ass blistered real bad!"

"Stop it! Stop it! Let me up!"

The cowboy was far more amused than threatened by the petite body that refused to lay still. He administered a half dozen more fatherly whacks, then politely asked, "If I let you up, will you behave yourself? Well?"

Two more whacks.

"Alright! Alright!"

The two stepped apart, each trying to size the other up. The cowboy had never seen so much spit and fire bundled up in a five-foot-six-inch package of good-looking dynamite. He even liked the way she pouted; it complimented a very pretty, round face.

Ann stooped to pick up her Stetson, then used it to help dust herself off. Her deep blue eyes stayed trained on the stranger while she ran one set of fingers quickly through her short crop of honey-gold hair before the Stetson went back on.

The cowboy extended his hand, his offer of friendship. "Shouldn't there be at least a small thank you?"

"For what?" she fumed. "Blistering my ass?"

"No, ma'am, for saving it."

"Was thinkin' of getting to it until you shot Big Boy."

Ann liked this man—this cowboy—despite the sting she still felt from having her britches thoroughly warmed. There were things about him that attracted him to her. Maybe it was because he was older, could even pass for her father's age in that respect, she thought. There were other things about him she also liked. His manners, helped along by just enough of a Texas-flavored drawl to make the words roll off his tongue with an ease she enjoyed, though several times she was tempted to tease him about leaving a few of them still on the end of his tongue, waiting to be pushed off, so he could finish his thought in order to continue their conversation to suit her rapid flow.

His dark-brown eyes said it all long before his words were heard. "You still think I should've waited on your Arabian, don't you, ma'am?"

Ann looked over at Big Boy and then back at the lanky cowboy. "Big Boy had such strength, such grace to him." Her voice dropped. "And his—"

"Back was broken, ma'am; I did the right thing. Liked the way you handled your Arabian. First I've seen in years. Such a beautiful horse...had to stop it sufferin' any longer. Got a question, ma'am."

"Yes?"

"Just wondern' if you care 'bout people the way you care about your horse? It showed the minute I watched you work your mount..."

She was pleased by what he said. This time she stuck her hand out. "Name's Ann Barnett, and I do thank you for saving me, but not for tanning my behind. And you are?"

He completed the handshake. "Hi Bernard, ma'am, at your service."

"Hi, huh? Is that short for something?"

His slow grin fit his disposition. "Hi is short for Hiram. I'm the ramrod from the Two-Bar Cattle Company down along the Yampa River, two-day's ride from here. That answer your question, ma'am?"

"So far, but call me Ann. I like Hi a whole lot better; you just don't look like a Hiram kind of man to me. I've heard my uncle talk about Two-Bar before, says they're too big for their own good...but that doesn't explain why you're up here."

"I'm up here scoutin' for my cattle herd. Understand there's plenty of open-range grass for the takin'. Plan on winterin' five, maybe ten thousand 'til beef prices on the hoof decide to come back up so I can ship 'em back East."

"You'll get plenty of argument from all the small ranchers down here. They kind of consider it their own, have for years. I know."

"Suppose your uncle is one of them, too!"

Ann laughed. "Hardly! I live with my Uncle Beemis and Aunt Maybelle Markham. We raise Arabians to ship back East, too."

Hi stroked his chin. "Reckon I'll deal with those ranchers you told me about when I cross that ditch."

Ann stood by Big Boy, and a most worried look crossed her face. "My uncle is going to be one upset man when I show up with only Big Boy's bridle and saddle. Got him on my last birthday. Told me to pick out any Arabian I wanted, so naturally I picked Big Boy. He was the best of my uncle's prize herd—worth the most too!"

"I could kinda tag along if it's okay with you, Ann, and maybe, just maybe, hearing me help you fill in some of the story would ride a bit easier on your uncle's mind and his pocketbook."

"Gee, thanks, Hi! Make sure you tell it like it happened! My uncle's a darned good judge of horses and humans, and he doesn't cotton to truth skimming, as he calls it, no matter how good the reason anyone tries to put over on him."

"I'll keep that in mind. Say, Ann, you mentioned having a birthday, but not your age."

"Take a guess, Hi!"

"At least seventeen or eighteen. Am I close?"

Ann was pleased with his guess. She puffed up her little chest, trying to add an inch or two in the right spots, and proudly proclaimed, "Not bad, Hi, not bad at all! You're a bit low, but it'll do for now. C'mon, we'll have to use your horse and rope to raise Big Boy up enough to slip the saddle off. I've heard that dead weight is twice as hard to handle."

Maybelle's scrumptious Southern cooking won a new convert that evening: Hi Bernard. The more Hi talked, the better Beemis seemed at ease, even when told about what had happened to Big Boy and Ann's brush with the mother grizzly. No sooner had Josie and Maybelle cleared the table when Beemis pushed his chair back. He motioned to Ann. "Come tell me again exactly what happened, Annie, this time in your own words. Here, sit on my knee."

Ann rose from her side of the table, blushing beet red. "Remember way back on my last birthday, dear Uncle, you said I was too grown up to be called Annie anymore?"

Beemis started to say something then changed his mind. He glanced over at Hi and then back to his niece. It was obvious that Hi had not only captured the lion's share of attention, but had also captured his niece's heart as well. He'd never seen anybody so taken, so soundly smitten as his Annie. He decided to play along for now. "So I did, Ann, so I did! Well now, I certainly hope that you're not going to remind me that I said you're far too old to be sittin' on my lap anymore. Did we discuss that or not? Can't seem to remember for sure." He turned to Hi. "See what old age will do? Plays tricks on me every once in a while! Wait'll you get up there, you'll see!"

He'd given Ann a way out since she was bound and determined to play her all-grown-up bit to the hilt, trying to impress Hi Bernard. He felt sure that Hi, too, had succumbed to Ann's wit and charm to the point where he was more than willing to take a second look despite their obvious age difference.

Only Josie stood in the way of spilling the beans concerning her younger sister's real age. She appeared in the doorway and received nothing but dagger stares for her trouble, including a couple of none-too-subtle half nods telegraphed in such a way by Ann that could only mean one thing: *Stay to hell back in the kitchen where you belong, dear Sister! Hi Bernard is not fair game; he'd better be mine!*

Josie had taken about all the silent messages she was willing to put up with. It was high time to bring her sibling sister back down to reality and earth with a hard thud. She purposely walked from the kitchen door, flaunting her charms, of which she had plenty. She glanced out of the corner of her light blue eyes and knew she had an audience of one: Hi Bernard. Her five-foot-eight-inch frame covered the distance with a grace and elegance reserved for a ballet dancer. She completely blocked out Ann by turning sideways at just the right moment, so Hi had plenty of opportunity to see how she profiled her great figure for his pleasure alone by throwing her shoulders back slightly to enhance even more her ample breasts. She topped off her performance by tossing her head in certain clever ways so that her light-brown hair parted perfectly to fall just short of her shoulders. She stood directly in front of the mesmerized cowboy, flashed her best smile from two rows of even teeth and gushed, "Mister Bernard, there's still plenty of Annie's—er, Ann's—birthday cake left. Made it myself." Then she crooked her little pinky and beckoned him to follow. "Please come with me out to the kitchen, and I'll be happy to serve you a piece."

Hi, too, touched reality. His jaw came unhinged. "I...er, Miss Josie, I...I...don't understand. Can you keep a birthday cake that long? Doesn't it dry out after such a long spell, ma'am?"

"Long time? Come now, Mister Bernard, Ann's birthday cake is only three days old!"

"But...but, but I understood...all this birthday business..."

Josie took Hi by the hand. She smiled graciously in Ann's direction and replied, "Well, when you're a young girl, three days ago can seem almost like a year."

"Young girl? I...I don't follow."

Josie tugged gently; Hi followed. "I am not sure, but let's you and I see if all the candles are there, *all fourteen of them*!"

Ann was devastated. She fled the room in a flood of tears, not even daring to steal a peek in Mister Bernard's direction or the kitchen.

Beemis did his best to keep a lid on such an emotional, explosive situation. He waited for Hi to finish his piece of cake, then tactfully suggested that everybody had had a long day and that it was time to turn in. Once he made sure all the combatants were in their rooms, he closed his own bedroom door behind him. He sat on the edge of the bed in his nightgown, mulling through the day's events, wiping his spectacles, his last official act before hitting the hay. "What a day," he said to Maybelle. "Lost the best horse I ever had, came God only knows how close to having Annie get mauled or worse by a grizzly, and then our two girls lock horns over a big cattle outfit's ramrod, old enough to be either one's father. Suppose the danged world's movin' too fast for us, old girl?"

Maybelle sat down on the bed with Beemis. She pecked his whiskered cheek. "Better wipe your specs again, old scout, so you can see what's happening right under our very noses. Josie won't be our sugarplum much longer; she's a full-grown woman, ready for courting and marriage with the proper young man, of course. And then there's our little Annie! Only she's not going to be our little Annie much longer, either. Trouble with Annie is that she's too impatient with herself, doesn't want to wait to bloom into full womanhood like Josie has."

"Annie's got a bad case of puppy love, that's all! She'll get over it!"

Maybelle rose. "Don't be so sure, Beemis. Annie's been around older men all her short life and she likes it that way. First it was you, then Joe Cady took over, and now, this Mister Bernard is staking a claim to her heart whether he wants to or not."

"But all our Annie knows about life is riding horses better than most men twice her age and ropin' the heck outta anything that stands still or tries to move."

"And older men, Beemis! Let's not forget that!"

Maybelle put on her robe.

"Now where are you goin'?"

"Our Annie needs her mother now more than ever! I'm it, so I'm going to do what I can. I may be a while, so don't wait up. You need your sleep."

Annie felt her bed dip slightly; then a sweet fragrance moved beside her, complete with two warm, gentle hands that applied a wet, cool towel to her red eyes and tear-stained cheeks.

"Thanks, Auntie...thanks for coming. That feels good."

Two minutes later, Maybelle removed the towel. Annie sat up, then pounded her pillow with both fists. "I hate her! I hate her! Gotta notion to go to her room right now! Good old Sugarplum needs a good, stiff punch in the mouth! She ruined my life!"

Maybelle waited a full minute. "Hi Bernard was asking about you..."

Ann relaxed her fists; she grabbed the towel to blot her eyes once more. "What'd he say, Auntie? What'd he say?" The excitement in her voice died. "Never mind, I know what he said; he said I should've acted my age! That's what he said, didn't he? But I'm all grown up, Auntie! Really I am! Just 'cause I'm fourteen doesn't mean I can't be much older than that! Ask Joe Cady! He'll back me up! Ask him!"

Maybelle hugged her niece. "Yes, my dear, you are grown up! Grown up enough so that I'm going to give you something that your mother left for you. Come with me!"

"Sure, Auntie! But first, what did Hi say? I can handle it, honest, Auntie!"

"Alright, here goes. Mr. Bernard said he expected to see you first thing at early breakfast. Said he wanted you to set next to him so you two could keep the conservation real private-like. He even asked me if it was alright for you two to eat ahead of the others; that way he could get an early start because he has a lot to do."

Annie nearly hugged the poor old gal to death. "Oh, I'm so glad you told me this! Oh, I'm so glad! Thank you, thank you from the bottom of my heart!"

"And I told Mr. Bernard, I'd be glad to fix breakfast early for you two. I'll even make sure your uncle and sister sleep late. How's that, my dear?"

"Oh, I love you, Auntie! You're so good to me!"

They walked down the hall to the main meeting room, each with an arm about the other. Maybelle set the lantern on the stool in front of the organ. She opened the top lid of the organ and removed a small packet of letters neatly tied up. "You're old enough to read and understand these letters from your mother to your father when he lived out here with us for eight months while she was back East trying to sell their home."

Ann took the packet. "Oh, Auntie, look at this beautiful handwriting! Have you read them?"

"Yes, before I let Sugarplum read them when she turned fourteen. Your mother and father loved each other very much as you'll see after you read them."

"Did you ever see my mother?"

"Yes, Josie and I did for a minute or two before your uncle buried her."

"What did she look like?"

Maybelle held Annie's face between both hands. "In some ways, you remind me of her—round face and blonde hair...probably close to about the same size, too. Josie favors your father's side, a little taller and thinner through the face."

"How well did you know my father?"

"Quite well! He was a wonderful man, so full of life and excitement. Read all the time." She motioned toward the library of shelves to one side of the organ. "There's no doubt in my mind he probably read most, if not all, of these books. He was a self-educated man, smart as a whip, too! Your uncle said he had a natural nose for business...would've made a success of most anything he did or tried."

"Do you know how they met?"

"Your father said they met through the church. Your mother had private lessons on the organ before her family lost everything when her father died in a hunting accident. After that, she took in sewing to help support herself and her mother. He also said your mother was such a good organist that the church asked her to play regularly for Sunday services at the tender age of sixteen. That's about all I know about your mother..."

Annie watched her aunt raise the hardwood cover over the keyboard and slide it back into its notch. She ran her fingers over some of the keys without sounding a note. "There's a wonderful story here too, Ann."

"Auntie, tell me, please!"

"Your father said playing the organ helped your mother make it through some very hard times. He had worked two jobs before they were married so he could give this organ to her on their wedding day. Said it was shipped upstate from Albany. That's way back East in New York State. It took all the money he had to pay for it, so they never had a honeymoon. And of course, it was the only stick of furniture they brought out West. For eight months, I watched your father and Josie carefully dust if off...Then he'd turn to me and say, 'Aunt Maybelle, just wait 'til Claire sits down to play. I tell you, there isn't anything she can't do with this organ. She can make it sound like a chorus of angels has gathered around her to sing God's praises or she can cut loose with the kind of music that real life is all about.'"

Maybelle closed the keyboard cover with a reverence. She looked away, so Ann never saw the mist gather in her eyes, but she heard the crack in her voice. "I waited eight long months to hear Claire's first note...which never came, and now, fourteen years later, I'm still waiting. Guess it just wasn't meant for these tired, old ears to be treated to the glorious sound of organ music."

Beemis and Maybelle let Ann's crush on Hi Bernard drag on for another four months. The fact that Hi had probably saved Ann's life loomed big in her life and obviously took a front seat in her heart. Both hoped it would play out and life would gradually return to normal at the ranch.

One day, Josie came storming in. She'd been to the bunkhouse and heard plenty. "Uncle Beemis, Annie's been pestering Joe and the boys about Hi Bernard. Dusty told me Annie's been doing this every night before she comes up here for supper."

"Pesterin'? Whataya mean, Sugarplum?"

"Joe wouldn't tell me, but Dusty did! He says Annie always asks the same question. 'Has anybody seen or heard from Hi Bernard today?'"

Beemis decided Ann's continued badgering had to stop. The question of how to stop it came to a boil one month later after he had done some investigation on his own. He waited until supper was over. "Josie, the dishes can wait; there's family business that can't, so please go to your room until this is taken care of."

Josie, along with everybody else, knew whom the family business would be about: Annie.

Ann decided to beat her uncle to the punch. "Go ahead, slide those specs down on your nose, so you'll have four eyes to dig into me! Let's get it said so I can be excused to go to my room!"

Beemis boomed right back at his niece after moving his specs down. "Not so fast, young lady, there's plenty to hash over and get settled before you jump into bed tonight."

Maybelle interrupted her husband, hoping to keep the conversation from getting out of hand. "It's come to our attention, dear, that you're spending far too much time at the bunkhouse again. You've been told about this several times before and you toss your head like those horses you ride and ignore what's best for you. Every time you stay too long, some of that bunkhouse language comes back with you! It's crude and vulgar, and not at all befitting for a young lady to be around."

"Well, at least both of you called me a young lady instead of a lovesick fourteen-year-old like Josie did today."

"Let your aunt tell how we're going to handle this after we talk about your schooling."

"What schooling?"

"Exactly our point, dear! Your schooling has taken a dreadful turn. I can't get you to go near the library anymore. When I bring books to your room or suggest you read those I've selected, you thumb your nose into the air. This cannot go on my dear! Josie has read every book on the bottom three shelves while you've barely gotten started."

"Fine, I'll read more and ride less 'til I'm caught up! That suitcha?"

Ann rose to leave; Beemis rose too. He pounded the table so hard the dishes rattled and jumped. "Sit down. We're just getting warmed up!"

Ann knew better than to test her uncle. The sign was there alright: the hard glare that always matched the redness, which somehow showed through his whiskers when he was hellbent on conducting business his way. She took her seat without daring to utter another word while he was in such an agitated frame of mind.

He stayed on his feet to better peer down at her. "Starting tonight, there'll be no more riding or anything else until you help your aunt and Josie do the housework. And when your aunt says you're done helping, you'll be doing the lessons and reading your aunt gives you. Then and only then can you ask your aunt for permission to go riding. Are you clear about this?"

Ann took her turn. Eyes blazing, their prize rebel had her say. "I hate kitchen work! I'd rather muck out the horse stalls and pitch hay any day than watch Sugarplum ride her broom around the kitchen. Please, let me work around the horses! Please, Uncle! Auntie!"

"No dice, Ann! And that's our final word on it! We got four pairs of hired hands who don't need you gettin' in their way down at the stables and horse barns. And by the way, you won't be watchin' any broom riding as you call it 'cause if there's any ridin' to do, you'll be the one doin' it! Are we clear on that score?"

"Alright! Now can I go?"

"*Sit down*, dammit! There's more!"

Ann and Maybelle had never seen Beemis so worked up. He walked around the table, trying to control his voice and his temper. When he was satisfied both were under control, he sat down and rubbed his knuckles in a most businesslike manner. "Now then, there's another matter that needs your attention."

Annie jumped the gun. "It's about Big Boy, isn't it? Been expectin' this for four months now. Why the holdup 'til now?"

Beemis opened up in his slowest, most deliberate fashion; he had to set the table for his Annie to dive in full steam with at least her knife and fork. "Responsibility is what life is all about, Ann. Some people accept it and it makes them a better person for the rest of their life; others run and hide from it until it turns them into cowards…and a coward never leaves the right kind of mark from then on." He looked at Maybelle and got an approving nod, so he continued. "We thought you had grown up to know and understand what responsibility is all about. That's why your aunt and me gave you the best horse this ranch ever raised for your birthday: Big Boy."

The mere mention of Big Boy again tugged at Ann's heart. Oh, how she loved that special horse and it showed. She fought hard, gulping and choking down the tears with such emotion. Finally, she broke down, sobbing. "Please, please, if you two only knew how I loved Big Boy…and how much I miss him. I should've taken better care, not been so foolish, done a lot better job and…and…"

"Been more responsible, Ann. That's the word you've left out."

Beemis knew his words had touched Ann's most vulnerable spot: her conscience. Now he waited for her to give him the opening he needed.

She rubbed both eyes, trying to wipe the blur from them. "I'd…I'd like to show you two that I am a responsible, grown-up person. Give me another chance. I won't let you two down again…ever!"

He stroked his whiskers, pretending to be searching for something, some way she could prove her words to them. "Well, there is something that comes to mind…"

"Just ask me! I'll do it!"

"But Annie, this might not set well; what then?"

"I'll do it anyway! Just tell me what you want me to do!"

"Your auntie and me want you to go to school for two years."

Lightning couldn't have hit harder. She rose from the table and exploded. "You slickered me! I thought you two loved me! How could you two do this to me! How?"

Maybelle went to her. "Because we do love you and care about your future. Can't you see it's really for your own good?"

"What I see is you two are in cahoots! I feel like I'm being shipped out! Just like the horses!"

"You can back out, Annie! Of course, that'll mean goin' back on your word. That what you really want to do?"

Beemis knew Ann was at the crossroads of her young life; he hoped he hadn't misjudged her true character. Ann, too, played for time while she mulled over the trap Beemis had helped her jump into. It was time to show them she could be a horse trader, too. "Alright. I won't break my word…but I want it understood that when my two years of schooling is over, I run my own life from then on! And if I decide to ask Hi Bernard to marry me, you two won't have a fit about it because you still think I'm too young! Deal?"

Maybelle hugged her feisty niece. "You have a deal!"

She accepted Maybelle's hug, then watched her uncle for his reaction. "Do you agree, Uncle? Haven't heard a peep outta you! Well?"

"I can beat that! Here's my shake on it!"

Maybelle got in the last word. "I'm so glad everything has been settled tonight. Oh, I feel so much better now! So much better! Ann, it's time to knock on your sister's door and when she opens it, tell her you're ready to help do the supper dishes."

Ann was right, up to a point, about being shipped out, but with one big difference. Unlike the prize Arabians that the Markham ranch sent back East, she would return after two years of schooling. Beemis accompanied her to Salt Lake City, Utah, where he enrolled her in a private, church-run academy operated by the sisters of St. Mary's.

Beemis returned to the ranch, feeling quite pleased with the way things had turned out. He had been assured by Sister Agnes, the academy's principal, that the time Ann was to spend there would be a good balance between educational and spiritual needs. He'd kissed his niece good-bye after getting her to promise to write regularly.

Ann's first letter arrived at the Markham ranch only after Beemis made a special trip to Vernal, Utah, as there were no mail deliveries from the Salt Lake area into the Hole from the west. Vernal was the stagecoach's closest contact point, some sixty miles from the Hole's western rim.

Maybelle opened the neatly addressed envelope and read aloud.

Dear Uncle, Auntie and Josie:

This is the first letter I've ever written, so don't be too hard on me. My knees have been sore since the day I arrived. That's because I have learned that praying and scrubbing floors both put me in the same position: on my knees.

I've been here six weeks and have made only two friends, Mary Saunders and Sister Francine. Mary is from Vernal and loves horses like I do, so we get along just fine.

Sister Agnes rides me from sunup 'til sundown. If my homework doesn't meet her approval or if I don't respond right away in class with the correct answer, she leads me out in the hallway and points to a scrub brush and a bucket of water, just waiting for me. The hall floor between my classroom and the dining room is spotless, thanks mostly to me!

I never knew how good I had it at the ranch until I checked in here. I'd give anything to smell horses again or the stables, or curry down one of the Arabians Uncle Beemis prizes so much, getting ready for shipment. I've made at least two dozen vows already that if I ever have another horse, it will never go without proper care and attention. Big Boy taught me that!

There is good news, too! By the time you'll probably get this letter, I'll be down to less than twenty-two months to go. Then, no more sore knees, for I'll be free to live my own life the way I want to. When I think about it that way, it helps me get through another day. No matter how much school work or other work they pile on me, they will never break me, because I know I will be leaving all this behind me.

I'd better close now before Sister Agnes sends somebody to look for me. You see, I'm on kitchen work all this week after class. That means I help with the serving, food preparation, and the dishes. Of course, all of us on the kitchen work list drop to our knees and give thanks to our Lord before we take on our chores. Tell Josie I won't try to avoid kitchen work anymore. She'll get a big chuckle, I'm sure.

Oh, before I forget, I'm hoping to have a big surprise for all of you once I come home. That depends on the deal I'm trying to work out with Sister Francine.

Have you folks or the bunkhouse boys seen Hi Bernard lately? If you do, please tell him I said hello.

All my love to Uncle Beemis, Aunt Maybelle and to Sugarplum, my sister.

Signed, Ann Marie Barnett
Dated this 30th day of August, 1892

Maybelle folded the letter and put it back in its envelope. "I do hope we've done the right thing, Beemis. Maybe we've been a bit too hard on her…"

Beemis calmed his wife's concern by patting her hand. "Nonsense, our Annie will buckle down and get some good outta this and come back to us all the better for it. I am surprised about one thing though."

"What's that, dear?"

"It's taken her far too long to figure out how to cut down on the sore knees! All she has to do is quite fightin' everybody and keep her homework up to snuff and be ready in class when they call on her."

Josie, too, had a worried look. "I know she needed this schooling to help her grow up, but I hope they won't break her tryin' to get some education down her throat."

Beemis' laugh turned into a chuckle. "Breakin' our Annie would be like trying to lasso the wind. Can't be done! All we can do is hope Sister Agnes and company can get a halter on her attention and lead or pull her in the right direction."

Ann's letters continued to arrive on a fairly regular basis considering the remoteness of the Markham ranch from any scheduled mail deliveries. At first, her letters were always filled with complaints about what the ladies in the grey, starched habits were making her do. They ran the gamut from when to rise, when to eat, when to pray, when to crack the books, when to wash up, and when to make her bed, to "there just isn't any time for me to do anything except follow their rules." As always though, no matter how many complaints were noted, they always ended with, "Has anybody seen or talked to Hi Bernard lately?"

Gradually, during 1893, Ann's letters took on a far better tone, being filled with more accomplishments than complaints. Beemis fairly beamed; progress had indeed been made whether their rebellious Annie would ever admit it or not. Of course, they continued to end with the usual: "Have any of you seen or talked to Hi Bernard lately?"

Early in the winter of 1894, Sister Francine handed Ann a letter. "You look somewhat surprised; most of the girls are happy to receive mail from home."

Ann took the letter, but did not rush to open it. "Just heard from Josie last month, so there can't be much going on…especially in winter. This is from Uncle Beemis; I recognize his handwriting. He usually lets Josie do the letters…"

"I should go now, so I can leave you to your letter?"

"No, please stay. I'm afraid it might be bad news or worse…"

"You, afraid? Come, come, my Ann! You could take on the devil himself and walk away the better for it. Are you sure there's not a wee bit of the Irish in you, like myself?"

Ann laughed. "Only if you put a Mc or an O in front of Barnett! Then you'd have McBarnett or O'Barnett!"

Sister Francine sat on Ann's bed and watched her friend and student fumble with the envelope. Finally, with nervous fingers to match her voice, she unfolded the single sheet.

It is with a heavy and sad heart I put pen and ink to this paper to tell you about your Aunt Maybelle passing.

Ann dropped the letter and sobbed out. "She was like a mother to me! The only mother I will ever know and…and now I'll never see her again."

Ann threw herself into Sister Francine's arms. The smell of fresh starch on cloth did nothing to hold back her tears. "There, there, my sweet, have a good cry and pick up the letter again. There are words in it that bear saying so that you'll know the full story."

Sister Francine supplied the handkerchief while Ann read on:

She had been ailing as of late, but Josie and I reckoned it was one of those afflictions old age brings on with no cure.

I got worried early one morning when your aunt broke out with the sweats and then a fever got the best of her. I rode over to Two-Moons' camp to fetch Seeabaka to tend to her. The herbal tea helped for a while, but could not save her. Your aunt passed on to her Maker on January 14.

I am grateful your sister is here to comfort me as I miss my Maybelle so very much. She was a dear, dear woman, not given to strong opinions or harsh words or actions that you may recollect as belonging to me. I mark your aunt's traits as Southern upbringing. Maybelle was deep South through and through.

I am also thankful that you have but six more months of schooling left. Josie and I look forward to your return to the ranch and to your home, where you belong.

Signed this 17 day of January, 1894
By: Beemis Jay Markham for hisself and Josephine A. Barnett

"Such a sad story! But there's a lot of love in your uncle's letter too, I'm thinking. Your aunt deserves a prayer…from us both, so let's get to it. Tonight, there'll be no homework or extra chores for you. Should Sister Agnes have other ideas, she'll have me to deal with first!"

"Annie! Annie! Over here! I'm on this side!"

The dust from the wheels of the stagecoach made it impossible for Ann to pick out her uncle amidst the half-dozen townspeople who'd gathered around with nothing more to do, it seemed, except get in her way. Once it started to settle, Ann had no problem spotting the short, stocky man, waving his hat the hardest.

Ann rushed into his arms to smother him with hugs and kisses. Beemis handled her greeting with a certain amount of pleasant embarrassment, much to the amusement of several onlookers.

"Oh, Uncle! Uncle! If you only knew how many times I wondered if this day would ever come!"

Beemis straightened out his specs. "But it did, Annie! It did!" He picked up the package he'd dropped when he saw his Annie make her charge in his direction. "Got a surprise waitin' on ya! This is part of it."

Ann accepted the brown paper-wrapped present. "Thank you so much, dear Uncle!"

"Better thank Teetaka instead, first chance you get! She still comes to the ranch each winter to ask about you. Your aunt and I owe her a lot for nursing you through that first winter."

She looked at the large-sized package. "Wonder what's in it?"

"Give ya a hint, Annie! You'll need to step inside the stagecoach house to change your duds while I round up your two trunks for the buggy ride back home."

Beemis was nearly as excited about Annie's present as she was. He tipped his hat and smiled to several townspeople while waiting for his niece's reappearance.

Ann made her grand reentry all decked out in the new riding outfit Teetaka had made for her.

"Like it, Annie?"

"Do I! Oh, Uncle, this is beyond anything I've ever seen or worn! Look at this tanned buckskin riding skirt! It's divided like men's jeans! And these pretty Indian beads match the same pattern on my leggings! Wow, this is some fancy outfit! It's too warm today to wear my matched, fringed jacket, but you can be sure I'll put it to good use when fall shows up."

"Jump in, Annie, let's clear this one-horse town."

"Shouldn't I change back?"

"If you do, you'll be spoilin' Josie's and my part'a your surprise!"

Down the street of Vernal they went, headed east toward Brown's Hole. Ann was highly amused by her uncle's description of the town. "Why'd you call this a one-horse town? I see plenty of teams and people bustling about."

"That's 'cause this is the big day of the week, the day the stagecoach rolls in! You oughta see this place any other day; you're lucky to find even one horse tied to a hitchin' rail on Main Street."

Both got a real chuckle out of Beemis' description. At the end of Main Street, Beemis held back on the reins. "Hold up! Whoa there! Whoa there!"

"Why are we stopping? I'm in a hurry to see the ranch and Josie again!"

Beemis pointed to a corral. "See those horses in the buyer's corral?"

Ann nodded.

"Well, Annie, that fancy buckskin outfit you're wearin' ain't worth much unless you got somethin' to ride! Now in that herd of horses you're lookin' at, you'll find a Markham mare. Unless you've forgotten most of what you know 'bout horses, that Arabian oughta show up better'n anything else in the corral. If you can pick her out, *she's yours!*"

Annie ran with winged feet to the corral while her uncle whooped and hollered with pure pride and pleasure. She led a beautiful Arabian mare out of the corral gate. "Oh, isn't she something! What's her name?"

"Glory! It's our way of showin' you how proud both of us are about you. We know it took real gumption and guts to hang in there through two years of sore knees and scrub brushes. Go ahead, Glory's saddled! She's sassy as all get out! Give her a good blow! Show her who's boss!"

Ann slipped into the saddle as though she'd never been out of it. She eased Glory up alongside the buggy. "You have my word on this! I'll never take anything for granted again when it comes to horses or people like you, my dear, dear Uncle. Thanks again from the bottom of my heart!"

Late that afternoon, Annie waited for her uncle to catch up. She tied Glory to the buggy and jumped in the seat beside him. "Hate to bring this up, especially after all you've done for me...but have you seen Hi Bernard lately?"

Beemis clucked hard for his team to pick up the pace a bit. "Matter of fact, I have. Want the plain story or my sugarcoated one?"

"Give it to me straight without the frosting."

"Mister Bernard stopped by three weeks ago. Said he was proud about you staying in school. I told him you'd be comin' home soon. Was thinkin' of chargin' him room and board the way he worked our rug over deciding what to say. The man didn't want to leave 'til he'd thought and thought some more. Awful careful with the words he finally let go of. Then out comes that twang of his and he says, 'Tell Ann I'm proud of what she's done...Hope she finds a fine young lad who sets a saddle as good as she does...That's what it's going to take to lasso her heart.'"

Two long, hot, dusty days later, Ann saw the second-best looking sight she'd seen in two years: the Markham ranch house. She spotted Josie waiting on the front porch for her. Beemis barely had time to slow down before Ann jumped out and hotfooted it up the plank steps into Josie's waiting arms. "Oh, Josie, Josie," she whispered between hugs, "let's try to be good friends. I'd like that more than anything else."

Josie hugged her right back. "I think we can do better than that! Let's be sisters, real sisters from now on! Stand back a minute, let's have a look at you!"

Ann stood back, all smiles, while Josie did the commenting. "You've grown at least two inches...bet you're as tall as me if we stood back to back! Beemis, too! I like the way you've let your hair grow a bit longer. No more tomboy look." Then she smiled. "And I see you've filled out nicely in at least two other places. Come, let's take a walk!"

Hand in hand, the two sisters walked out to the family plot to pay their respects to three graves. They stood before Aunt Maybelle's headstone. "The day she died, she talked bout you...said you'd come back a far different person. And you have, Sister, you have."

Later that evening, Ann helped clean the supper dishes and started washing them without being asked, a first at the ranch as far as either Josie or Beemis could remember. Josie finished drying the dishes and helped her sister put them in the cupboards. "You know, dear Sister, tonight was the first time I ever heard you say grace. I peeked a bit at our uncle when our heads were bowed. The only thing he didn't do was strut around the table, prouder than a peacock."

Ann rose early next morning before any barnyard rooster dared think about crowing. She tiptoed into Josie's room to gently wake her. "I'll make coffee this morning, Sis, so you can catch an extra forty snores. Want to say hi to Joe, then I'll be right back to help with breakfast."

She trod the more-than-familiar path to the bunkhouse, bent on surprising her old pal and longtime friend. The door creaked, giving her away. She found him in his long johns, sitting on the edge of his bunk, filling the air around him with pipe smoke.

"Oh, Annie! My Annie!"

That was all he had time to spout before Annie bowled him over on his bed with giant hugs and squeezes. Dusty, Tex, Slim, and Shorty McCallum hooted and hollered at the reception Ann gave the old bronc-buster.

"Didn't know if'n you'd care to come by," he cackled between hugs, "since we heer'd you got shipped off to that churchified school."

"The day I can't say hi to you will never come!"

"Here, gimme a hand, Annie!"

She noticed he was having a hard time sitting back up, even with her help. He saw the worried look across her pretty face. "Now Annie, don't get to frettin'. Danged roomatiz done latched onto me while you was away! Some days I get stoved-up kinda bad…Hell to git old, Annie, hell to git old!"

"Isn't there something you can do? Maybe take medicine?"

He motioned in the general direction of his crew. "Naw, kain't do much fer it, 'cept kick hell outta these sorry excuses now and then. That loosens me up some!"

Joe and Annie were greeted by another rousing round of hoots and hollers.

"Got me a surprise fer ya! Now you turn 'round so I kin be decent fer ya!"

Ann assumed he meant getting dressed, like pulling up his pants and finding his suspenders or putting on his work shirt.

She pretended to be embarrassed. "Okay, now, Joe?"

"Not yet, Annie, I'll say when! Hey, Shorty, hand 'em over! Dang you, Shorty! Told ya to leave 'em alone!"

"Now?"

"Yeah, Annie! Now!"

She turned around; he was still in his long johns, hadn't even bothered to put on his socks. "What surprise, Joe? I don't see anything different! Where, Joe?"

"Click, click, clickety click!"

"Oh, Joe! You did it! You got false teeth! Boy, you sure look different!"

"They's store-bought chompers, sent fer 'em four months ago when I heer'd you was comin' home ag'in. Ain't played a hand of Sunday poker in months, savin' to pay fer 'em. Come next payday, I'm pickin' up the cards ag'in. Ya betcha!"

"You said you sent for them. Don't tell me you had to go all the way to Rock Springs to order them?"

Dusty answered before Joe could find the words. "Naw, Miss Annie, we got us a post office right here in the west end. Startin' next week, we even get mail from Vernal, twice a month. Ain't that sumpthun'?"

Tex chipped in. "Got us a mercantile store, too! Feller by the name of John Jarvey opened it six months ago."

Shorty McCallum had his say, too. "There's talk 'bout buildin' a school house...supposed to be across Vermillion Creek purty close to the spot where Two-Moons does his winter campin'."

Ann could hardly believe the changes or her ears. "Next thing I suppose you're gonna tell me is that we have a sheriff and a jail! Right?"

"Naw, Annie, tain't likely to happen, in my day at least! Ever since that Two-Bar cattle outfit took over most of the free range land in winter, this hole's been crawlin' with no-accounts and drifters, the likes of which you've never seen before. We know there's rustlin' goin' on all the time. Your uncle says we're to steer clear of such dealin's and we sure as hell ain't about to argue with Beemis' orders!"

She still couldn't get over how much better Joe looked with teeth. "Your teeth fit your mouth just right! How in the world did you make sure your store-boughts would be the right fit?"

"Shucks, Annie, Mr. Jarvey at the store done most of the work fer me. He pulled out one of them picture books." He turned to his crew. "What'd Jarvey call that picture book ag'in?"

Tex spoke up. "Said it were a cattlelogee!"

"Yeah, that's what he done called it, alright! Anyways, Annie, he had me gum down real hard on a piece of paper, then he marked it where it was still wet and sent it along."

Ann started for the door. "I'd better get back to help Josie get breakfast."

Joe pointed to Ann's neck. "Hold on, young'un! What's that danglin' from your neck?"

Ann's cheeks blushed a pretty shade of pink. "They gave it to me for extra good conduct this year at school."

Joe mulled over Ann's remark. "Must'a been fer ridin' or ropin'! Which one, Annie?"

"The school I went to doesn't even own a plug of a horse. This medallion is for conduct, extra good conduct."

Joe thought and thought. "Reckon I never run across them kinda words before...'Zactly what do it mean, young sprout?"

Annie was pleased as punch with her answer. "It's for being extra good! Not fighting them or giving them a hard time or sassing back. Always doing what I'm told."

Joe looked at his crew, then doubled over with laughter. All poor Annie could do was cover her ears while everybody laughed 'til their sides couldn't take any more. Finally, Joe straightened up; his rheumatism had let go long enough to let him finish everybody's thought. "Damnedest story I've heer'd tell in quite a spell, Annie! We know you filched it, but don't worry your purty lil' head 'bout it! Right, fellas?"

Josie and Beemis could only shake their heads in collective agreement as their model convert continued to surprise them time and again. No matter what job Annie was asked to do or what chore she took on, it got done! Done without a complaint, sharp tongue or snide remark. Both held their breath, wondering just how long their maverick could stand to walk the straight and narrow.

Sunday morning arrived and Beemis was well into his second stack of flapjacks smothered with butter and dripping down the sides with maple syrup. Ann rose from the table and planted a dutiful kiss on the old boy's cheek. "I think it's high time we held Sunday service right here at the ranch!"

"But we don't have a preacher," said Josie. She looked down at her uncle. "I'll just bet our uncle could hand out a stern sermon or two if called upon..."

Beemis didn't take the hint. "What kinda service do you have in mind, Annie, that doesn't need a preacher?"

"I'm talking about handing out some of Mom's hymnals and singing a few selections and then closing with a prayer."

Beemis looked over at Josie. "I guess we can handle that...can't we, Josie?"

Annie started for the door. "Thought I'd saddle Glory and do some inviting for next Sunday. Any suggestions, you two?"

"Why yes," Beemis answered, "you could call on that new family that took over the old Laughlin ranch...and while you're at it, invite Sugarplum's friend, that Dreschler boy and his family."

Josie lowered her eyes, then spoke up. "Don't forget the Suttons at the 2 BAR K, and I'm sure the Grangers at the Double S would come if asked...and...and you might try the Newells, too!"

Next Sunday, Beemis stood before six families from the Hole's east side. "Now folks, we're all kinda new at this, so I'll tell you what we have in mind. Those song books Josie and Annie handed to you as you sat down came from these young ladies' mother and father who used to live back East. We thought we'd let each family pick a favorite and one from that family would stand up here in my spot to lead us in song. After each family's had their turn, Annie will close the service with a prayer. Now, after the service, there's hot coffee, cookies, and sandwiches waiting for you out in the kitchen."

One by one, a member from each family led the group in song. Each family made sure their selection would be something the others would most likely be familiar with, so all could join in. Even Beemis could now see Annie's idea was a good one; everybody seemed to be thoroughly enjoying themselves. The last refrain from "The Old Rugged Cross" had been given a boisterous working over, leaving only the Markham ranch choice remaining.

Beemis huddled with Josie and Annie. "They've cleaned me out of the ones I know, except one! Got any more in mind? I'll follow along as best I can."

"What's the one they missed?"

"Aw, Annie, it's a great song, but it needs marchin' music to do it any kind of justice."

"Well, Uncle, you put a lot of time in the Army. All you have to do is just get us started with the right step and we'll follow. What's the song?"

"Onward Christian Soldiers! Any of you know it?"

Josie's eyes lit up. "Daddy used to hold me in his arms and march around my bedroom singing it before he put me down to say my prayers. Think I still remember most of it!"

"Good! Let's do it!"

"But Annie, it still needs the kind of music your mother could get out of that organ."

"Let's see if I can get that organ to help us out."

Annie pulled the bench out as calm as a cucumber. She lifted the keyboard cover and rolled it back until she heard a click. She laced her fingers together with the palms turned out and extended her arms forward as far as they would go. That done, she sat down and ran a few scales on the keyboard to finish her limbering up exercise. She turned to her uncle, who was speechless. "Okay, Uncle, I'm ready! Uncle Beemis, do you hear me? Uncle Beemis, go ahead and lead them!"

The old soldier-scout gathered his wits about him as best he could. He fumbled with his hymnal, trying to find the right page. Josie stepped in. She turned to the group. "Number 286 in your hymnal, 'Onward Christian Soldiers.'"

A heavy mist clouded the old warrior's eyes, but he rallied beautifully. "Folks, let's all march and sing. Time to stand up for the Lord! Just follow me!"

Beemis squared his shoulders and sucked in his belly. His hymnal came to attention too, tucked at his side where in days long past he had shouldered a rifle. He cast one glance at his Annie, read her approving smile, and he stepped forward smartly, in perfect cadence to her stirring military beat.

Around the meeting room, Beemis led the group. By the time he passed Annie, everyone had joined in. On his second time around, Beemis faltered; he was so choked with emotion that Josie helped him to Annie's bench. He couldn't hold back any longer. His specs found refuge in his shirt pocket before he bawled like a baby.

The music suddenly stopped; Annie, too, was overcome with emotion. She hugged Beemis, and together they had a good cry. Josie rescued the situation when she tactfully announced, "Folks, the service is over! Follow me to the kitchen!"

The old boy rallied once more, blubbering out, "Oh, Annie, Annie! If only your Aunt Maybelle had lived to see you play…and, and your mother and father, too! How proud all of them would've been! How proud! How very proud!"

Josie returned from the kitchen to join in. She had a noticeable quiver in her voice. "So this was the big surprise you wrote about in your first letter, Sis. Boy, are you good! How long have you been playing?

Annie dried her tears. A new happiness radiated her reply. "Almost two years. I helped Sister Francine get the church ready for each Sunday service, and she taught me how to play."

Summer had come and gone, and fall had been taking a big bite out of this time of year. The Hole's residents had only to open their doors or look out their windows to see that winter would soon be hard upon them. Cold Spring and Diamond Mountain already had more than a thorough dusting of "the white stuff" as Beemis called it on their upper reaches. Soon, winter would come calling, and the three passes down into the Hole would be closed until the spring chinooks opened them once more. Several ranchers complained that the sun's rays were too feeble now to be of much use. They noted that they saw their breath hang in midair, past noon each day, barely leaving time to thaw before new frost formed shortly after sundown.

Ann followed her older sister around, peppering her with personal questions, most of which got a little too personal. On this particular Monday morning, they were in Beemis' bedroom. "Are you and Cleve Dreschler planning on getting married soon?"

Josie handed Annie one of Beemis' pillows. "What on earth makes you think that?"

Annie slipped on a fresh pillowcase. "By watching you two kiss so much. I thought when that happens, marriage must be around the corner."

Josie flung Beemis' other pillow as hard as she could at her sister. Annie had plenty of time to duck. "For your information, my snoopy sister, kissing a person doesn't mean you've set the date. We're just good friends, that's all! Nothing more, so far."

Annie saw Josie quickly sit down where the other pillow used to be. "C'mon, Sis, get back up! Let's see what you're trying to hide."

"Hide? I'm not hiding anything."

"Alright then, let's change sheets."

Josie raised up. "You're not supposed to see this whiskey bottle. Uncle Beemis has been drinking some since Aunt Maybelle died. She'd never allow him to bring whiskey into this house because she was afraid he'd set a bad example for us. She made him drink out in the horse stables or else in a saloon in town, but never here! Now that she's gone, I've peeked in his room quite a bit and found him setting on her vanity bench, holding her picture in one hand and a whiskey bottle in the other. He misses her an awful lot."

"I've been here four months now and this is the first time I've seen a bottle. How does he bring it in?"

"Whenever he says he's going to check on the horses after supper, that's when he brings a bottle in from the stables where he stashes his whiskey."

Annie handed Josie another pillowcase. "But I'm usually around when he does that. Where does he hide it?"

"When he needs a new bottle, you'll see him put on a jacket or coat, no matter what the weather is like."

Josie slipped Beemis' bottle back under his pillow. They walked on down the hall to the meeting room. Annie polished the organ while Josie started sweeping the floor.

"Sis?"

"Yeah."

"Where do the noses go when you and Cleve kiss?"

Josie stopped sweeping. "I've never thought much about it that way. You'll just have to take my word on it; everything works out fine, just fine!"

Annie started on the bookshelves. Josie busied herself by moving Beemis' big rocker to sweep under it.

"Sis?"

"What now?"

"When you're kissing, I know your bodies come together…Is that the best time to let Cleve feel your breasts?"

First the broom, then the dustpan flew in Annie's general direction. Neither came close to the frustration or exasperation Josie had on her mind. "Ann Marie Barnett, I'm not about to answer any more of your questions! You hear me? No more! Get yourself a man friend, and then, just maybe, you'll find out for yourself!"

"Since I'm free to run my own life now, that's exactly what I aim to do! Soon!"

"UNCLE BEEMIS! UNCLE BEEMIS! ANNIE'S GONE!"

Josie had shaken him out of a sound sleep. He flipped the covers back and rolled out of bed. Down the hall he went as fast as his old legs and nightgown would allow, with Josie hot on his heels, holding onto his specs. When he reached the front door, he stopped, looked up, and then heaved a big sigh of relief. "Not to worry, Josie, our Annie did the right thing."

"Whataya mean she did the right thing? Glory's missing from the stable, along with two of my pots and pans, and enough food for four or five days' worth of riding. And we both know she's headed out of here for one reason only: to see Hi Bernard!"

"This had to come sooner or later! No, I'm talkin' about takin' my rifle! See, it's missing along with a box of cartridges! She knows how to handle a rifle, just in case, so we don't need to worry."

"DON'T NEED TO WORRY! What if she marries that middle-aged man? Then what, Uncle Beemis?"

Beemis put his arm around Josie's shoulder and together they walked back down the hall. "Trust me on this, our Annie's got a hard lesson coming, probably the hardest knock she'll ever get, because Hi Bernard is gonna turn her down. She'll come back home worse than a whipped dog, and it'll be our job to help her pick up the pieces to get on with her life."

"How can you be so sure? How?"

"With about sixty-seven years' worth of smarts, Josie! When I rode scout for the Army, I learned how to stay alive! Ya gotta know your horse and you damn sure better be a pretty fair judge of people and what they'll do next! That included Whites and Indians alike! I still got my hide, so I ain't misjudged too many times. Hi Bernard ain't in no position to marry, that's the good news!"

"And the bad news?"

"Our Annie's not gonna be our sweet Annie much longer. She'll sour on us and then it'll be up to us to figure out how to sweeten her up again for the next round of life."

Ann followed the trail, cutting back and forth, keeping Ladore Canyon to her right. At times, the noise from its rush of water through the ever-narrowing walls nearly deafened her. She urged Glory on, her heart beating faster than the wings of the chicken hawk she'd spotted circling overhead. Gradually, the roar lessened, leaving her a wide expanse of rugged terrain to cross for the two-day ride south, where the Green River met the Yampa. That was where she hoped Hi Bernard would be.

Late in the afternoon of the second day, she topped a small rise on the side of a butte, shielded her eyes from the sun under her cowboy hat, and let out a war whoop. Down below, a small sliver of silver glistened in the sun. "That's it, Glory! That has to be the Yampa!"

Even before she saw the great cattle herds of the Two-Bar Cattle Company, she was made aware of their nearness. The breeze shifted slightly, filling her nostrils with a totally new stench, enough to gag her. Down, down toward the river bottom she carefully picked her way, sure that all she had to do was follow that awful smell to its source, and she'd find Hi Bernard.

Then it hit her, the unmistakable sounds of cattle milling and bawling everywhere. Two small rises were topped. There, below, was an unbelievable sight as far as she cared to strain her eyes—a seemingly endless army of hides, hoofs, heads and tails. Clouds of dust hung over the critters, waiting for a stiff breeze to carry it away so more and more and more cattle would be seen.

The ground along the river bottom looked trampled to death; there wasn't a shred of green grass anywhere, yet she noticed the cattle looked fat and well fed. Glory snorted and half stumbled as swarms of flies came at them, forcing Annie to whip out her cowboy-sized handkerchief to cover her face to keep the flies from having a feast.

She worked Glory toward one edge of the mighty, moving mass. Two cowboys wearing handkerchiefs over their faces spotted her and rode over. Ann couldn't help but notice they and their mounts were covered with layer upon layer of dust.

"Looking for Hi Bernard! Seen him?"

The nearest cowpoke raised his handkerchief. "Christ, lady, this is the last place you'd find the boss. We're drag riders!"

"Drag riders? What's that?"

The other cowboy pulled his kerchief down to speak. "Guess you don't know nuthin' 'bout cattle. Drag means the rear-end of everything. Worst damn place to be. Keep to your left, ma'am, and ride maybe seven or eight miles. When you spot the chuck wagon, you'll be up toward the head of the herd; that's where you'll find Hi Bernard."

Ann thanked them and followed the breaks above the river. A fresh breeze lifted her spirits to the point she slipped her kerchief down around her neck to breath the air. Her heart started pounding again as she neared the chuck wagon and was surprised to see two dozen or more cowboys lined up, getting fed.

Hi recognized her and helped her down off Glory. She wanted to fall into his arms and shout out her love for him, no matter how many pairs of human or animal eyes took it all in. They stood apart for an agonizing few seconds; then Hi extended his hand. "Good to see you, Ann…What brings you all the way down here?"

Again Ann fought the impulse to shout: *I love you! Shouldn't that be reason enough?* Instead, she calmly but firmly said, "Need to talk to you…when you have some time."

"Nighthawks are linin' up for chuck. Got some orders to give 'em…We can talk later."

"Sure, Hi, no problem…I can wait."

Ann pulled the saddle, saddlebag, and rifle case off Glory before hobbling her down so the mare couldn't wander too far. She heard Hi give his orders, then motion for her to come join him at the head of the line. He handed her a tin plate and cup. Two bull cooks promptly filled their plates with hot beans, a sizzling strip steak and cold biscuits to help cut the taste of burnt coffee sloshing around in their cups.

Ann used her saddle as a seat while Hi sat on her saddlebag to eat. "What are nighthawks?"

He spooned down some beans. "They're my night riders who watch the cattle, make sure nothin' spooks them…Some even sing or talk softly to them. Cattle are not like sheep, need to get them to lay down n' sleep…the rest usually follow. Have to keep 'em from gettin' too edgy or milling around crazy-like; that's when they're ready to stampede. Lose too much weight if that happens. Then all our summer grazin' goes up in smoke, and I've lost a bundle."

Ann cut into her steak. "How many in your herd?"

He mused on her question, then held his cup between both hands. "Don't rightly know…reckon between forty-five and fifty thousand."

She stopped chewing. "You mean you've never counted them?"

He turned his cup over to empty the grounds. "Ever try countin' to fifty thousand? Herds this big make it near impossible. Takes too long."

Ann thought on Hi's comment and decided he was probably right. No wonder the small ranchers in the Hole had easy pickings, rustling from the big herds that winter there. What paltry few they took would never be missed. "Plan on wintering again in the Hole?"

"Have to…prices on the hoof are down this fall. I'll up my herd in the Hole to maybe fifteen thousand this go-round."

Ann used her biscuit to help push the beans onto her spoon. "Better redo some of that figurin'. Uncle Beemis cut hay on both sides of Vermillion Creek. Had to build a new barn this summer to hold all the extra hay…even Josie and I helped haul it in."

Hi slammed his plate hard into the ground. "Damn that man! That's open range land. If he wasn't your uncle, I'd have more than a word or two with him!"

"My uncle sees it about the same way you do—first come, first served."

Hi picked his plate up again and went silent. Ann decided to change subjects. "Your herds look fat and healthy, but all I see is powder and dust where they're been. How can that be?"

The lines around his mouth softened, his jaw relaxed, and most of his hardness disappeared. He pointed with pride to his herds, using his spoon to drive home his point. "My point riders tell me there's plenty of grass all the way to Steamboat Springs. The Yampa gives us all the water we need—add good grass to good water gets me better'n twenty pounds more on each animal—and with this many, I do pretty well when we ship from Steamboat."

He stacked both plates and put the cups on top with the silverware. "Soon as I drop these off, let's mosey on over the ridge for a spell. Good place to talk."

To Ann's surprise, he held out his hand in plain sight of everybody. Her heart skipped more than a beat as she placed hers inside his big paws. Hand in hand, they walked together until they'd put a low ridge between them and the chuck wagon. Hi looked back to make sure they were out of sight.

Ann's emotion was about to go rampant. She wondered if he felt on fire too, hoping that her presence awoke the same stirring in him.

He answered her wonder by pulling Ann into him and hugging her for the longest time. He finally broke the spell. "You didn't ride all this way to hear me talk 'bout cattle, now did you, Ann?"

She looked up into those same dark-brown eyes that had captured her heart over two years before. They had to be filled with love, like hers. "I'm ready to be your wife…waited all summer for you to show. When you didn't, I decided to come down here and tell you how much I care for you…how much I love you."

Hi bent down, then tilted her chin up to put no more than seven inches between their lips. He planted a kiss, a moist, paternal one, finding only one corner of her mouth.

Ann refused to settle for that. She forced her lips all over his, making sure he nearly sucked the breath out of her. She opened her eyes to take it all in again, marveling to herself how everything worked out perfectly as Josie had said—no collision of noses whatsoever!

Her heart plummeted a second later when she felt him stiffen, then ever so gently break their embrace, keeping her from him at arm's length. "Sorry, Ann…must've been plum outta mah mind. Please let me apologize…please, dear Ann."

Ann was having none of that. She began to unbutton her work shirt to bare her breasts for his pleasure, sure that he would have to come to her, to kiss them at least, maybe do more, much more.

"Don't, Ann, please don't…I couldn't stop if you do. It'd be wrong…all wrong."

"Wrong, Hi? How could it be, when we love each other! I know you do, same as me! Don't fight it! Don't, Hi!"

She tried to rush back into his arms to make sure he felt her breasts one way or another, just so long as he did something to her. Instead, she felt his strength through both arms. He had no intention of letting down his guard.

"Listen to me, dear Ann, please do! I'm out here for weeks or months at a time. That's no life for you…sittin' back somewhere, waitin' for me. Havin' you out here won't work either. Got a hard n' fast rule: no women allowed out here. Too many lonely cowpokes…trouble sure to happen no matter what."

Ann knew he was right about his rule, but she had the answer. "Alright, what you said does make sense out here, but only out here!"

"What are you drivin' at?"

"After you ship from Steamboat, you're going to split your herd, right? Keep some out here to tough out the weather and winter, the rest in the Hole. How'm I doing?"

"Up to a point, you're right…Go on…"

Ann's confidence climbed with every word she spoke. "Well, Hi, what you're saying is that your cattle business is divided into two seasons, summer and winter. Now, I figure you'll probably leave one of your top hands to run one herd while you ramrod the other! Since you're the boss, why can't you choose to spend each winter in the Hole with me? After we get married, I'd still live at the ranch, and you could give me a baby, so when both herds are together during the summer, you'd have two waiting for you instead of just me when you come back to us each winter. And since no women are allowed out here anyway, neither of us would have reason to worry, now would we? Our marriage would be as safe and sound as the ground we're standing on! How'm I doing?"

Hi was flabbergasted by the logic and thought Ann had carefully crafted into her reply. She, indeed, had an answer, one that deserved some real soul-searching. He dropped his arms, turned away to scuff at the thin topsoil with his boots while he put his mind to work searching for just the right words.

"Well, dear, I'm waiting…"

"Now hear me out, and I think you'll see another side to this. I won't say you're too young to get married…because you're not, not after the way you've grown up…filled out all over…and you've got a good head on your shoulders. What you just said, proves that. But you are too young to be tied down with our baby, no matter how much you love me. You need to meet other men, a younger man who can spend both summer and winter with you, not just one season. You do me the greatest honor I've ever had just to think of me this way. I'll always care for you…but I've made up my mind. It must be this way between us. Perhaps if I was ten years younger…had a different way to make a livin'. Only thing I know is cattle."

He let her back into his arms to cry her poor, broken heart out. When her body-shaking sobs became small sniffles, he lifted her chin once more. "This was your first kiss, wasn't it, dear Ann?"

"Y-yes."

"Mine too…for more years than I care to count."

They came back the same way they had walked over, hand in hand. When they were still out of hearing range, Hi turned to her. "Don't worry, dear Ann, there'll be lots more kisses before the sod gets planted over you, I'm thinking. Yes, I can see it now…Probably break more'n your share of hearts too before you settle down with the right young man."

Beemis Markham hit the nail right on the head. Annie returned to the ranch an emotionally devastated young woman. She never volunteered one word about her meeting with Hi Bernard. She didn't have to, for all Beemis and Josie had to do was look at her to see how love's rejection had taken her in a totally new direction, one filled with listless days and nights, complemented by growing despair and depression.

He was convinced that time would be the great healer to her heart. The only question in his mind was, how long? Weeks became months and those same months somehow slipped into seasons with no visible change. Something had to be done, and Beemis, who was never short on action when he saw a compelling reason, was doubly sure that drastic measures were now needed to turn his Annie's world around. He was even willing to risk their relationship if it would produce the desired results—new life for his Annie.

A horse buyer from the Boston area had been invited to visit the Markham ranch to look over Beemis' prize Arabian stock. Mr. Bascom paid top dollar for five young mares and one stallion. Flush with plenty of money, Beemis now prevailed upon the man to use his influence to get Annie admitted into the most prestigious finishing school in all of New England, The Beatrice Potter School for Young Ladies in Boston, Massachusetts. He knew the mere mention of more schooling would undoubtedly bring out the fight in Annie and a lot more. The trick would be to keep it contained within reconcilable limits to allow Annie to remain part of his family.

Beemis stood by the organ while he sent Josie to bring Annie to him. She appeared in her nightgown in the middle of the afternoon, her once beautiful, honey-blond hair a tangled mess. He shook his head and the first act of war between them opened with him tactfully asking, "How long has it been since you've sat down here to play your grand music?"

Ann tossed her head as easily as she tossed out her answer. "Dunno, dear Uncle, but I'm sure you're about to tell me!"

"Over seven months ago! How long has it been since you've given Glory

96

a good ride and then brushed her down or fed her?"

He saw a bit of fire return to her eyes. "Three weeks, maybe more!" she snapped back. "Look, is there some point to all this?"

"You bet there is! In case you've forgotten, this is a working ranch, not a hotel with a riding stable! Everybody pulls his weight around here or else!"

Annie jumped into the confrontation with both feet. "Or else what? Okay, slide your specs down! Let's get it said! Then I'm going back to my room! I've had enough of this!"

"So have we, dear Annie! It's time for a change!"

"Oh yeah? I'm free! Remember our deal?"

Beemis refused to counter her charge; instead, he waited for their explosion to simmer down so he could control the charges and countercharges. In almost a subdued tone, he stuck it to her. "Josie is packing your trunk. You'd better get dressed...You're leaving with Mr. Bascomb as soon as you do. You'll be in the best finishing school for young ladies back in Boston. It'll be a whole new start. Meet new people, make new friends. I've put a lot of thought into this...It's best for you...and for us."

"Well, I haven't! I'm not going anywhere!"

"That's already been settled; you are going, Annie!"

Annie stomped her foot down hard. "Time for your checkbook, isn't it? That's how you handle everything! Ship 'em out and then write a check to cover it!"

"You should be glad I have the money to do these things for you. Your sister sure appreciates what I've done for her, given her, provided for her, most anything she needs or wants."

"Well, I'm not Sugarplum!"

Beemis slid his specs down, then cleared his throat. "No, my dear, you certainly are not! That's about all you and I agree on lately!"

"If you ship me back there, I'll run away! Maybe never come back! How'd you like that?"

Beemis took Annie's threat most seriously, yet he stuck to his decision. He looked over his specs straight into his niece's eyes and never gave an inch or an inkling of his true feelings for her. "Should you get yourself kicked out of school or decide to run away, don't bother coming back!"

Through the rest of the year 1895, Beemis and Josie lived by his "get tough with Annie decision." Month after agonizing month managed to slip by without one letter from Annie. The only contact either of them had was through the school's quarterly progress report, which as Beemis put it, "ain't hardly worth the paper or the postage." It was anything but encouraging.

Josie could only add, "Well, Uncle, the only good news is that Annie's still in school and hasn't run away."

In February 1896, Beemis received the following letter:

Dear Mister Markham:

By the time this letter reaches you with its disturbing news, your niece could well be on her way home. I have decided to write you personally instead of sending you our regular progress report, as there indeed is little, if any, progress to report.

Ann Barnett is a troubled young lady. If it was your intention to send her to our renowned school in the hope that she would profit by it, then I must sadly report that you have failed. She has made no friends here, and it is only through my personal intervention on her part that my teachers continue to spend time with her in or out of the classroom. She can do the class work assigned to her when she wants to; however, as of this writing, she puts forth only enough effort and interest to barely keep from being expelled due to poor grades. Mister Markham, every young lady here has excelled in her school work and class recitation except your niece.

Yesterday, I spent considerable time with Miss Barnett in my office, trying to understand what it is that is troubling her. Thank goodness my door was closed! Never in the thirty years of this distinguished school, have these hallowed halls or my ears heard such foul language. She has been warned by me, that one more outburst of profanity will leave me no choice but to expel her immediately for conduct unbefitting a young lady.

There is one area in Miss Barnett's education that she is, without doubt, in a class by herself. I have personally watched her in the equestrian arena, and there, she has no equal, standing head and shoulders above all in every phase of horsemanship. What a pity that she does not see any reason to transfer some of this energy or talent into the other rewarding subjects we offer.

Our goal is to provide a well-rounded education for every young lady attending our school. Being only interested in horses will not be nearly enough to grant her continued residence in my school. Should Miss Barnett somehow survive this school year under these most trying conditions, I will not extend any offer of residency for the coming school term.

Respectfully,
Beatrice M. Potter
Headmistress and Owner
Dated: 1 February, 1896

Beemis and Josie kept their fingers crossed and hoped and prayed that no more letters from Boston made their way out West. Then it happened: another letter arrived. Josie watched Beemis pick up the letter, then put it down like it was a hot potato. He wanted no part of it even though his anger and disappointment plainly showed.

"Aren't you even going to open it?"

"What's the use? Annie's been kicked out. Hope I sent her enough money last time to come home on. If not, maybe she'll write to ask for some…Leastways, then we'll finally hear from her."

Josie let things ride for another day. Finally, curiosity got the best of her, so she opened it. She came running out to the stables. "Uncle Beemis! Uncle Beemis!" she exclaimed. "The letter's not bad news! It's an invitation to attend their open house, including a social tea and horsemanship exhibition! Annie's made it! She's still in school!"

Beemis grabbed Josie and around and around they went, doing their impromptu jig until the old curmudgeon's leg went game. "Hallelujah! Hallelujah!" He panted, nearly out of breath. "Hang the cost, I'm goin' to Boston to see our Annie perform!"

Beemis showed his invitation at the finishing school's main gate, whereupon he was taken to the well-manicured grounds where the social tea was set to get underway. He quickly signed the guest registry book and was handed a small card and told to fill it out with his name and that of his niece, and give it to the announcer. He had hoped to arrive early enough to say hello to Annie and possibly mend some of the broken communication fence between them, or at the very least, fix a strand or two. Instead, he was ushered under a bright-colored tent with its sides rolled up, and he was told to wait there until his name was called.

It took only a minute of looking around for Beemis to realize he was out of his element in every respect. He could only hope that his name would not be called first, so he'd have time to watch the other couples when their names were called to spare Annie as much embarrassment or humiliation as possible. Thank God, he told himself, that Josie had had the foresight to find one of her father's library books, which said that a business suit and top hat were the dress code required of all men attending such a function. He surmised, correctly, that this would be the only thing he'd have in common with those who waited beside him.

Rubbing elbows with the best dressed and most well heeled that Boston had to offer had a humbling effect on the rancher. Yet Beemis was determined not to be undone by those, many of whom, he had no doubt, could trace their background or family lineage to the very deck of the Mayflower itself. He'd keep his manners in check and engage in meaningless, polite conversation if need be, if only his Annie would give him some attention and a little respect.

The announcer, dressed in a tuxedo, put a megaphone to his mouth.

"Abigail VanZandt, daughter of Mr. and Mrs. Arthur VanZandt."

"Priscilla VonStueben, daughter of Dr. and Mrs. Wilhelm VonStueben."

And so on and so on, the list of names called out would've put most social registers to shame; of that, Beemis had no doubt.

"Ann Barnett, niece of Beemis Jay Markham."

Beemis sprang into action, following the procedure set by others. He walked ten paces and turned sharply, ninety degrees, to face Beatrice Potter some sixty feet directly ahead. Out went his elbow as he waited for Annie to join him from a side room off to the right. He glanced out of the corner of his specs and was pleased to feel her slip her arm through his.

"Gotta talk to you, Annie, first chance we get."

"It's Ann, not Annie! From now on, leave it that way!"

Ann's cold reply stunned him. They walked side by side for another ten feet before Beemis spoke in low tones. "Pardon me, your highness, bit touchy today, aren't we?"

Halfway to Miss Potter, Ann spoke softly. "Like your cane. Good show...makes you look like you belong."

"No show, Annie...er, Ann...dang left leg went game on me."

Neither managed another word until they stood before Miss Potter, where Ann was expected to make the formal introduction. Beemis removed his top hat. Ann began, "Miss Potter, I am most pleased to present my uncle, Beemis Jay Markham. Miss Potter, Mister Markham!"

Her cold touch did nothing to improve any of the three's disposition. Beemis saw her for what she was: a woman in her late fifties, prim and proper to the last degree with a face and cold stare stripped of any emotion whatsoever. She looked at him, then shifted her eyes to Ann. "Well, this is certainly a surprise...for all of us."

Ann lowered her eyes. Beemis bailed her out. "Yes, you could say that, and since we're all here together, let's enjoy this special day."

Several hard lines around Miss Potter's mouth relaxed a bit. "Splendid comment, Mister Markham. You know, dear man, we consider anybody who lives west of Cleveland to come from such a raw, primitive land where civilization and the social graces are all but forgotten. Don't you agree, Mister Markham?"

Oh, he was sorely tempted, was he ever! *Lady, if you'll just lower that snobbish beak of yours that passes for a nose, you might discover that the people who live west of Cleveland manage to hold onto a manner or two, just in case people like you cared to venture West to find out.* He nodded his head, then smiled in her direction. "Yes, I suppose you could say that...but I understand the King of England once said the same thing about Massachusetts when it was the worst colony he ever ruled. Don't you agree, Miss Potter?"

Ann got in a curtsy, and they left before Beatrice Potter could respond to her uncle's obvious retort. Once out of hearing, she said, "You sure nailed that old biddy good! How in the world did you ever come up with that gem?"

They moved on toward the tea area. "I cracked a book or two in my younger days. It didn't all come off the walls of outhouses west of Cleveland! By the way, I sure do like that dark-blue dress you're wearin'...matches your eyes and such a pretty face, too!"

Beemis had a way with words, the kind that could thaw or melt down people he loved or cared about, of that Ann had never been more convinced. She gave him her first good, warm smile, a good sign the thaw between them had started.

They followed an attendant, who led them to a covered patio area complete with wrought-iron tables and padded chairs. Beemis, remembering his manners, seated Ann first. He tried to park both elbows on the table before Ann nudged him with her foot. "Not here, Uncle, you're not in the kitchen at the ranch."

"Danged table's hardly big enough for a decent-size steak on a plate. It'd have to hang on for dear life 'cause they build 'em so darned small back here."

"It's just the right size for small teacups and little squares of tea cake."

An attendant served them tea on a saucer and left a small plate of pastry.

Beemis looked around. He half whispered, "What do I do next?"

Ann lowered her voice. "Watch me unfold my napkin and lay it across my lap…You do the same. And remember, sip your tea and nibble your tea cake. Sip and nibble, sip and nibble, that's all there is to it."

Her uncle looked down. "Doesn't hardly seem worth doin'…I could down what's in my puny little cup in one gulp, and there ain't enough tea cake for one mouth, let alone two."

Ann's eyebrows arched before she gave him one long, exasperated look.

"Yeah, I know, sip and nibble."

She took her first sip.

"What's the matter with your little pinky? It's stickin' straight out!"

Ann had all she could do to keep from busting out with laughter. "Nothing's the matter with my little finger; that's the way you're supposed to sip tea. Now you try it."

Beemis was all thumbs trying to follow Ann's instruction. He spilled most of his tea before a drop touched his lips. He set the cup down and looked over at his niece. She knew what was coming long before Beemis got it off his chest.

"Had a bellyful of social graces for today. What say you show me around some? Maybe take in a classroom or even gander where you room and board."

They walked across the grounds to the ivy-laced, brick buildings. The first building they visited was the elaborate dining hall. Ann pointed to Miss Potter's table on an elevated platform, flanked by two others reserved for her teachers. "No one dares to pick up a napkin or touch their silverware until she is seated. Then she taps on her water glass with a spoon; that's the signal for the servers to come out of the kitchen."

Next, they briefly visited the exercise hall and several classrooms before ending the tour in front of Ann's dormitory. Ann noticed that Beemis' leg was starting to bother him, so they sat down on a bench nearby. She touched his arm to keep his mind off the leg. "Well, Uncle, what do think?"

He removed his specs, then pulled out a handkerchief. He was determined to never let Ann know that she wasn't wanted or welcome here. Wiping his specs gave him time to sort out the right words and sentences to handle it his way—the Beemis way. "You asked, so here goes! I made a terrible mistake…You don't belong here…neither do I! Suppose there's a snowball-in-hell's chance me and you could patch things up?"

Ann launched herself into his arms. "Oh, yes, yes, dear Uncle! You beat me to it, that's all! I was gonna tell you how miserable I am and ask you if I could come home. I'll never give you a hard time ever again!"

They hugged each other again and again, the bond between them never better or stronger. "There's one other thing that needs your attention, my dear. Don't think you're aware of this, but we're not too far from Herkimer County—that's in upstate New York. Your father and mother came from there, and I have the name and address of your mother's mother…She'd be your grandmother. We could swing by on the way home, if you cared to say hello."

"Did you ever write to her?"

"Only once, after I buried your mother. Told her what I figure happened and that your aunt and I would do our best to raise you and Josie."

"Did she ever write back?"

"No, can't say that she ever did."

"Then I see no reason to see her. You and Aunt Maybelle are the only family I know. You're the only father I've ever had, and I love you like you are my father. Let's leave it that way!"

"Fine by me! Thanks for all those nice things you said about your aunt and me, but I'd trade the whole shootin' match in on lettin' me call you my Annie again! Deal?"

She kissed him. "Done!"

Beemis rose. "My ears don't seem to be workin' just right. Had a real hard time catchin' the tail ends to lots of words today. Never noticed that before…back home."

Ann snickered. "Your hearing's just fine, Uncle. It's that darned Boston accent that threw you for a loop, that's all! Look, I should go now to get changed for the horsemanship exhibition. If I point you in the right direction, think you can find the arena?"

He was his old self again; Annie saw the twinkle return to his eyes, magnified by his specs. He leaned on his cane, ready to take on anything or anybody. "One thing that they can't change, even in Boston, is that good old smell of horse flesh and the stables."

Annie smiled. "Sorry, dear Uncle, even that's different back here. Miss Potter has the stable hands rub powder into each horse after they's been cooled down and curried before they're led to their stalls. Makes them smell a lot better, she says."

She pecked his cheek. "Gotta go!" She pointed to a tree-lined walk. "Follow that walk and you'll end up at the arena."

"Give 'em a good show, Annie! One they'll never forget, and we'll head back where we both belong tomorrow morning!"

Beemis managed to find a good seat high in the stands in the exhibition arena. He overheard a gentleman next to him speak to his wife. "Pay close attention to the last rider on the program. Our Abigail says she can make her horse do about anything with only a tap or brush of her quirt on the horse in several places. And not one spoken word!"

"Oh, pshaw! No one's that good!"

Another man behind Beemis spoke up. "It's true, that's why I'm here! I've seen her in practice, and even their instructor can't master his horse like she can. But her freestyle program's the best exhibition by far. Wait'll you see her rope and ride! I've seen Annie Oakley and this young lady's in her class, any day!"

Beemis' buttons on his vest were about to pop, he was so proud.

"What's her name?" asked a lady to his left.

"Ann Barnett," answered the man behind Beemis.

"Hmm...I can't seem to place the name. Maybe she's on the other social register..."

A lady in front of Beemis spoke up. "Hardly! My daughter says she comes from way out West. Lives in some hole in the ground with her uncle! Has no family background or lineage at all. No one likes her! She's a foul-mouthed little filly with no manners whatsoever."

"What's she doing in Miss Potter's school if that's the case?" questioned another lady.

Beemis was about to supply the answer with a few choice words of his own, ably supported by the tip of his cane pressed firmly at the lady's throat.

"Quiet now," said the man behind Beemis. "Here comes LePard, the riding instructor."

Master instructor, Jacques LePard, sporting a clipped mustache, paraded in front of the grandstand spectators, astride a beautiful palomino. A dapper little dandy, to be sure, he looked to be exactly what he was: the epitome of horsemanship, snobbishness and perfection all rolled into one. He was a nervous, impatient sort; nevertheless, he waited for the noise from the crowd to drop to his acceptable level before he raised his megaphone. In perfect monotone, his French-accented voice rang clear.

"Good afternoon, ladies and gentlemen. Our program will consist of two parts: a modified dressage followed by an open exhibition of all-around horsemanship. The dressage will demonstrate that our young ladies have mastered the fine art of horsemanship in splendid fashion. We ask that as each lady completes her routine, please hold your applause until after our last rider has completed her ride. In that way, there will be less distractions, for each of our ladies has worked very hard to maintain the high standards expected of her."

One by one, twenty-five ladies put their mounts through a series of moves designed to show their parents and the crowd what horsemanship was all about. Their dress consisted of bright-colored blouses that fit snugly into riding britches with dark leather riding boots. They rode sidesaddle and issued low-voice commands, barely audible, during their stops, starts, back-ups, gaited trots, and short bursts of speed. Two horses bolted, and only one gave its rider more trouble than she seemed able to cope with. All in all, a very creditable performance. They lined up to face their audience and received a well-deserved round of applause.

LePard waited for them to leave the arena, then put his megaphone to use once more! "We have a very special treat in store for you. Our last dressage rider will demonstrate what we believe is the finest exhibition of horsemanship ever seen in any arena. However, there is one condition that must be met before she will perform. We must have absolute silence! She will do all of her maneuvers in front of you at very close range. We challenge you to see her lips move or hear one spoken command. Quiet now! Please!"

Ann entered riding a big dapple grey. Instead of riding around the arena before starting her dressage, she went directly before the crowd and waited. It seemed an eternity before the whispers and shuffling stopped. At last, not a squeak or even a cough could be heard.

"Miss Barnett, if you please," LePard intoned without the megaphone.

Ann brushed her quirt; the dapple grey walked. A quick tap, her horse stopped. Another rapid brush stroke, her mount went into a gaited trot. Two taps, her horse backed. One slight boot jab, her horse did a beautiful sidestep maneuver. Two boot jabs, the dapple grey broke into an abbreviated gallop. She had her horse parade smartly back and forth before the mesmerized crowd; she was simply that good. Her last move was her crowning glory. The quirt brushed the horse on the rump, the horse dropped to its knees, whereupon she stood on the ground, the quirt between both hands while she bowed.

The crowd rose, as if on cue, to give her a thunderous standing ovation. Beemis refused to take his seat when those around him finally sat down. He raised his cane above his top hat. "YOU SHOWED 'EM, ANNIE! YES,

YOU DID! THAT'S MY ANNIE!"

The lady who had badmouthed Annie before her performance had enough of Beemis' celebration. "Sit down, you goat, whoever you are! We've all had quite enough of you!"

Beemis took her to task. "If you'll kindly keep your nose from gettin' out of joint for a second or two, I'll tell you who I am! I'm Ann Barnett's uncle, damned if I ain't! My Annie may live in a hole out West, but she sure as hell climbed outta it long enough to put a charge in your fanny, my dear!"

Ann had missed most of the fireworks in the stands between her uncle and the lady with more blue-blood credentials than she cared to count. However, the applause put a new idea and a resolve in her like never before. She was bound and determined that her final ride would be the one most remembered, one way or the other.

LePard broke up the confrontation in the stands with his megaphone announcement. "Ladies and gentlemen, take your seats, please! The last part of our exhibition will be an open or freestyle performance. Each of our ladies will be allowed to ride her mount and perform in whatever manner she chooses. As each lady completes her routine, she will raise her quirt above her head before she leaves the arena. Your most welcome applause will be appreciated at that time."

The open-ride portion of the exhibition got off to a very good start. No doubt the relaxed rules allowed each young lady to perform to her best. There were bursts of speed, pretty gaits, beautiful gallops, and balanced trots to whet any horseman's appetite, all of which received nice rounds of applause. None of the ladies had any trouble with their mounts.

LePard, too, seemed pleased, judging by the way he actually smiled, and had his mount do a bit of a curtsy. He signaled his palomino to dip down slightly in front of the crowd as he removed his top hat. The crowd responded with a hearty round of applause. He waited patiently, then brought the megaphone to his mouth. "We have saved our best for last once more. Miss Barnett will regale you with an assortment of acrobatic stunts, using the Western work or cowboy saddle. Please rest assured that the ladies' sidesaddle will continue to be the standard used here. There is no substitute for the beauty and grace the sidesaddle brings to each lovely rider. However, in this case, Miss Barnett has been granted this exception to enhance her exhibition."

He turned toward the arena entrance and pointed with his quirt. "Miss Barnett! If you please!"

Ann re-entered the arena, decked out in the fancy, split riding britches Teetaka had made for her. LePard moved near the stands so he could give a stunt-by-stunt description to the crowd.

Then it began, and everybody sat with their jaws ajar, their mouths open in awe. Annie had everybody exactly where she wanted them—spellbound. She opened up with her balancing act, standing on the dapple grey's rump, keeping her mount in a slow, deliberate gallop.

"Notice how Miss Barnett's knees bend in perfect unison with her mount's stride," LePard said. "On her next pass in front of you, she will drop the reins, but her horse will never break stride."

Everybody rose, clapping their hands.

"Next will be the famous hidden rider stunt. Miss Barnett will literally disappear before your very eyes!"

LePard's announcement brought out a smattering of guffaws from half a dozen doubting Thomas'.

Ann swung herself off the saddle and poof, disappeared right before their very eyes.

One alarmed lady shouted, "Where is she? I didn't see her fall!"

LePard waited til Ann had passed completely by. "Miss Barnett is safe on the other side! You'll see how she does it when the horse circles across from you!"

Sure enough, as her horse continued full gallop across the stands, the spectators saw Ann cling to her mount's side using only one stirrup and one handful of the horse's mane in her hand to keep her balance. The crowd rose. "Hurrah! Well done! WOW, what a performance!" echoed up and down the stands along with a steady barrage of hand clapping.

"Miss Barnett's next stunt will be her own version of cartwheels. Watch closely as she will do them in continuous motion, touching the ground only long enough to propel her upward again to complete the cartwheel. She will do them with such speed, her legs and body will appear to make one continuous circle. Please count the circles with me!"

The crowd couldn't wait to help LePard count. "One! Two! Three! Four! Five! Six! And there you have it, ladies and gentlemen, six complete cartwheels for your pleasure!"

Annie stopped directly in front of the crowd to acknowledge their standing ovation. She reached down and removed a coil of rope from the saddle horn. Gradually, ever so gradually, she worked her lariat until its rope-circle spun around her body, then up to the level of her shoulders, and finally above her cowboy hat.

"Miss Barnett's last act will be a series of rope tricks while galloping around the arena, never breaking stride. Miss Barnett! If you please!"

Annie whirled her lariat, up and down, over her horse's head without so much as brushing her mount's nose or its neck, while in full stride. For that piece of artistry, the crowd went wild. The whooping and shouting were deafening!

On her next pass, somebody shouted out what most of the crowd was thinking. "GO AHEAD! See if you can rope something! We dare you!"

Annie smiled and looked directly at LePard. Most thought it was part of the act and applauded wildly, expecting Annie to give chase. She did!

Only three people knew this was not part of the act, as LePard rode for the exit as though the mill tails of hell had suddenly remembered his name.

"LET ME PASS! PARDON ME, LADY! ANNIE! ANNIE! NO! NO! DON'T DO IT!"

Twenty feet before the exit, Annie's rope serpentined over LePard's head, ready to strike. *Wham!* Down he went, bouncing and skidding along the ground, screaming at the top of his lungs in French and English. Twice around the arena Annie dragged him, making sure he plowed through every sizeable pile of horse manure she could find. Then she released the rope and headed for the exit.

LePard slammed the stable door shut behind him. He found Annie calmly brushing down her mare.

"You cheap, dirty little slut!" he yelled at her. "Look at me! Look at me!"

Ann put her brush down and tried her best to keep a straight face. "Well, LePard," she wisecracked, "you look about right to me...all full of horse patootie! Sure do like that new color you decided to wear; it sure becomes you, that natural, all brown look."

LePard went crazy. "Should've rolled you over in the hay like I wanted to last week! I'm gonna pull your pants down and give you something to remember, too!"

Annie grabbed her quirt and glared at him. "You try to lay one hand on me, Frenchy, and I'll turn you into a gelding. That's a promise, Frenchy! I mean it!"

Beemis opened the door just as LePard made his rush at Annie. Down they went into a pile of hay next to the dapple grey. Annie scratched his face and bit him on the nose. LePard screamed out in pain and let go. Both got up at the same time. This time Annie planted a hard boot toe to LePard's crotch. Down he went, kicking and screaming in agony, grabbing his crotch.

"Let me finish him off," yelled Beemis.

And he did. Nearly out of breath, Beemis slipped the crook of his cane around the Frenchman's neck and half dragged him kicking and screaming to the open door. There, he finished him off by releasing his cane and laying one hard kick to the Frenchman's hind end before he went flying out the door.

Beemis picked up his cane and rushed back to Annie. "You alright? He didn't hurt ya, did he, Annie?"

"No, but he sure wanted to. Been trying to take liberties with me for three months now. Says he could keep me in school despite my poor grades if I was nice to him. Two weeks ago, he snuck up behind me and put his hands on my breasts and threw me down. Before I could get back up, he ran his hand down my pants, trying to feel me up—that's what he called it. I punched him in the stomach and slapped his face, damned hard!"

"Good girl! But why put up with him? Why didn't you talk to Miss Potter?"

Annie straightened out her riding outfit. "I was going to, but I realized it would be his word against mine, and you know how that would've turned out. I decided to put up with him until you got here, because I knew you'd spent an awful lot of money keeping me in school with these blue-blood snobs."

"Yeah, you're right about that…six Arabians' worth…"

Annie watched her uncle sag against the stable partition boards. He began to hold his sides; then he gave that up in favor of keeping his belly under control. When that didn't work, he let go with two minutes of belly-busting, sidesplitting laughter. He laid his cane aside so he could wipe his eyes before they smeared up his specs.

"Is this really that funny, dear Uncle?"

"Oh, Annie, I just wish you coulda seen the look on LePard's face when you dragged him through all those piles of horse biscuits. If I make it to one hundred, it was worth every damned dollar I've ever spent on you to see that French dandy covered from his head to his boots with that all-brown biscuit look!"

Annie, too, could now see the humor in what she'd put LePard through. "Horse biscuits, dear Uncle? Horse biscuits?"

He finished wiping his eyes. "Well now, you sure didn't expect me to say horse shit, now did ya?"

"Uncle Beemis! Such language! Shame on you!"

CHAPTER THREE

Old Henry said, "It was a time when a handshake beat out a piece of paper. If you welched on your promise, someone would put a bullet in you to square the deal."

Knock! Knock! Knock!

"Alright, alright, I'm coming! Hold your horses!" Ann exclaimed. She crossed the familiar, oval rag-rug in the parlor and reached for the brass knob to the front door.

The minute he saw Ann, he removed his sweat-stained slouch of a hat. Underneath a mop of the most unruly red hair she'd ever seen, the young man spoke his mind. "Name's Deke Landry," he began. "Lookin' for work and a place to bunk down."

Ann was surprised by the information the young drifter had volunteered. Rarely, if ever, did any of the hard cases who happened by give out both first and last names. She walked out on the porch with him and pointed in the direction of the bunkhouse. "Our foreman's name is Joe Cady. Tell him I said it was alright to bunk down. My uncle does all the hiring, but he's away for another three days. You can stay 'til he returns; then it's up to him. You're too late for supper down there. Tell you what, after you check in with Joe, you're welcome to come back here if you don't mind leftovers."

He flashed a big, generous smile. "Sure it won't be a bother, ma'am?

Don't wanna put you out none…"

Ann smiled back. "If it was a bother, I wouldn't've asked you in the first place."

The young man nodded in an understanding way and disappeared down the plank steps off the front porch. Ann continued to watch him from the window. Josie joined her. She shook her head. "Well, at least this one has polite manners." Then she pointed. "Look, Annie, look at that poor plug of a horse he's leading; it's nothing but skin and bones! Don't think there's another two days' ride left in him! Never seen so many drifters lookin' for work or a handout…third one in the last two weeks."

Ann summed up her thoughts. "His jeans look like they're on their last leg too…Noticed his shirt…it is about shot…and those boots. Don't think they'll last 'til next payday even if Uncle decides to keep him."

Josie smiled. She put her arm around her sister. "You kinda like this one, don'tcha? When you go to the trouble of offering to fix supper for one of these down-on-their-luck hard cases, then that means he must rate a cut above the rest. Right, Sis?"

Ann turned away from the window. "Never thought I'd ever give a tinker's damn about another man since Hi Bernard. How old would you say Deke Landry is?"

Josie followed Ann into the kitchen. "Deke Landry, huh? Not Mister Landry? I'd say he's probably somewhere between my age and yours. Besides good manners, I'd say he's got one other thing going for him."

Ann set a pot of chili beans on the Monarch range for reheating. Then she shook the coffee pot to see if a cup or two could still be sloshing around inside before setting it down next to the chili. "What's that, Sis?"

"First drifter I've seen in over six months who isn't packing some well-used hardware on his leg. No, this one isn't trying to hide his past or his name; he's probably what he looks to be: a down-on-his-luck young man looking for a second chance." She hugged Ann. "Kinda like you were in a way…until Uncle Beemis went back East to bring you back if you wanted another chance."

For the next two days, Ann watched Deke do whatever job Joe Cady handed out, grateful for the chance to lend a hand and earn his keep until Beemis returned from Rock Springs with the summer supply of flour, sugar, cured bacon, and other assorted dry-goods essentials. She liked the way he handled himself—nothing flashy, but with a sureness that told her he knew horses through and through despite his young years. Joe Cady confirmed more about Deke by telling her he'd been breaking mustangs up in Montana until he'd been cut loose when the owners sold out to some back-East company.

The boys were back in their bunkhouse, their day's work done, and as the expression goes, there was still plenty of daylight left in the barn, so Annie decided to pay Glory a visit. She was surprised to hear someone talking— talking to her horse, of all things. She walked in on Deke petting and stroking Glory between his horse talk. Glory's whinny gave Ann away. Deke turned around; his blue eyes brightened even more. "Could tell this was your mare just by the way she said hello to you. Boy, what I wouldn't give to own one like this." Then he laughed. "Guess that's purty farfetched, ma'am, me ownin' an Arabian when I ain't got a plug dollar to my name…or nuthin' else for that matter, 'cept my horse, Old Dusty, and a thick, cardboard box with a rope tied around it to keep my belongin's from fallin' out."

Annie stroked the soft flesh under Glory's chin. "Maybe that'll change when my uncle gets back. He's a darned good judge of people and horses…hasn't been wrong very often since I've known him. He did mention before leaving that he'd like to hire a good, all-around horseman, one that sees what needs to be done and goes out and does it without waiting for his or Joe's orders."

Beemis arrived and Deke was given a two-week tryout. Late one night, Beemis rapped lightly on Annie's door.

"C'mon in, Uncle, thought you'd hit the hay long ago." She motioned for him to set down. She turned around to continue brushing her hair while watching him in her mirror. He seemed deep in thought. "Deke's working out pretty well, isn't he?"

He scratched his chin. "I need your thoughts before I make up my mind about Deke."

Annie was surprised. Beemis had never asked or consulted her about anything concerning ranch business before. "You're still not sure about Deke, is that it?"

"Joe says Deke's a comer if he ever saw one! Says he knows more 'bout horses than most men twice his age, and that's good!"

Annie stopped brushing. "So, what's the problem? Hire him!"

"I will! That is, I will if you say so!"

"I…I don't understand. What do I have to do with Deke staying on?"

"Everything, my dear! Joe's so crippled up with arthritis that his days are numbered." Beemis rose. "Move over on that bench! I can talk to you better when I sit down by you."

Annie moved as far over as she could to make room for Beemis. He could see that the mere mention of Joe's disability bothered her considerably. He put his arm around her. "Now, now, Annie, what I'm about to say needs sayin,' so here goes. Joe and I talked it over today. He has a sister out in Lodi, California…She's a widow and couldn't mind havin' Joe move in with her when the time comes for Joe to say good-bye around here. Joe says he'll stay on 'til Deke takes over as my new foreman. The other boys know what's up, so there'll be no surprises. Now comes the hard part. What are your plans for the future?"

Beemis' question threw her a curve. Yes, indeed, she could now see what he was leading up to. "Since Boston, I thought I'd stay here with you and Josie…if that's alright with you, dear Uncle?"

His hug helped give her some reassurance. She needed more. "Of course, that's alright with me, but Joe and I aren't going to live forever! It's high time I knew where you stand on things around here. Would you be interested in taking over the Arabian horse business I started? I figure Josie will probably marry that Dreschler chap before long, so I can put her future to rest. It's you who's keepin' me up late at night while I talk to your aunt. No rush on this, Annie. Take your time…but don't take too long, either!"

Annie laid her brush down on the vanity. "You figure Deke will be the new foreman after Joe leaves…and I would take your place…run the ranch."

"I'd show you the ropes, break you in gradual-like…start you out by handlin' paydays around here, writin' checks, makin' sure you learn every part there is to know, 'cause I'd be lookin' over your shoulder. There's paperwork too, so it'll all take time if you're willin' to ease into it with the idea all this would be yours someday. Well, Annie, does any of this sound like this is what you'd like to do with your life? If you have other plans, I'd be obliged if you told me now."

She walked around her bedroom, deep in thought. Beemis turned around to watch her and to catch any expression that might give him an inkling, one way or the other.

"Horses have been my life…Yes, it does make sense…only if Josie gets a fair shake out of this when the time comes. How will you handle that?"

Beemis got up to join her. "My dear, that will be no problem. From now on, the Markham ranch will be divided into three shares: one for you, one for Josie, and one for me. And when I pass on, my share will go to either you or your husband, if you decide to marry. Sound fair to you?"

She held his hand. Their bond between them now that much stronger. "Yes, it's time I got on with my life…as you and Josie have been trying to tell me. Alright, since I'm handling next payday, I'm going to give Deke an advance on his wages, so he can go down to Jarveys to buy new boots. His were past putting on days ago."

Beemis broke their hand holding. "Listen to your old uncle about this and you'll never get steered wrong about the men who'll be working for you. No matter how sad their story, no matter how much hard-luck bull they throw atcha, never give any man who works for you any money before his payday! That way they learn to get along with what's paid them! Once you break that rule, they'll have you over a barrel every time they run a little short!"

Beemis saw another side to his niece, a compassionate one. "What you say, dear Uncle, is a good, hard, and fast rule to follow. However, I've seen the holes on the soles of Deke's boots. Joe told me he let Deke take a small piece of leather from our tack shed to fit inside both boots so he'd feel something besides cold ground mixing with his toes because his socks are full of holes, too! The socks will have to wait 'til payday; his boots won't."

The thing that Beemis had hoped and prayed for—and drank about in the small hours of the morning—took hold like never before. Annie accepted her new responsibilities with a reborn and redirected energy that pleased him down to his stubby toes. Beemis helped her oversee every phase of his successful operation, being careful not to push too hard or too fast. He always knew she had horse-sense smarts; now he could see the results!

Annie would rise at the crack of dawn, make coffee, then rouse her sister and her uncle, eager and excited about getting the day's work underway. No detail was too small or unimportant to escape her attention. Time and time again, she surprised the old boy with one astute observation after another, oftentimes making changes that did improve the overall ranch operation and leave him with nothing to do but beam a smile as broad as his round face would allow.

Deke, too, was beginning to pay big dividends toward improving Beemis' stock of one hundred Arabians. He no longer worried about where his next meal was coming from or if there was one coming at all! Every morning, all he had to do was rub the sleep out of his eyes, and he knew there was the best job he'd ever had waiting on him. Time and time again, he drew praise from Joe Cady and Beemis on the way he handled, broke, trained, and fed the horses. It made no difference if a horse buyer happened by with a good price or if Beemis came down to the stables with a letter and check from back East, the Arabians were always ready to ship or show.

The weather took the devil's turn. That's the way the old-timers referred to the heat wave that visited the Hole, and like an unwelcome guest, it refused to leave. Day after day, the temperatures soared, sucking the usual cool morning and evening air up and replacing it with what the old-timers called "Hades' special," more and more scorching heat. This forced the Markham ranch to divide its workday hours into an early morning and late evening schedule. The bunkhouse boys grumbled and griped about their long days, which denied them their usual time off. Beemis walked in on one such grumbling session and flatly told them they had a choice: either put up with the long days like everybody else, or use the same trail that had brought them down to the Markham ranch in the first place. None seemed overly eager to look for his grip or bedroll.

The heat wave also changed Josie's routine. Breakfast was the only hot meal of the day. Even then, every window and door was opened to let the kitchen heat escape as much as possible when she stoked the Monarch range in preparing her meal.

Deke appeared during supper late one afternoon. "Got a tender-mouthed mare that needs some work." He looked at Annie, holding a glass of lemonade. "Could stand some company, if you'd care to ride along..."

Annie's expression told it all. This was the first time Deke had invited her to ride with him. She put the glass down. "I'd like to, but I should help Josie...Haven't been pulling my weight around here lately, spending too much time down at the stables."

Beemis pushed his cold roast beef sandwich aside. "Nonsense, you've been learnin' the ropes. Go ahead, I'll give Josie a hand!"

Josie nearly feel out of her chair. Beemis willing to grab a dish towel? Since when? However, she rallied her thoughts, sure that her uncle had something up his sleeve. "Sis, you go on ahead. Uncle and I are old hands at this sort of thing...got him trained for kitchen work about as well as the way you two have been workin' those Arabians."

Annie and Deke left. Beemis stacked most of the dishes and followed Josie into the kitchen with an armload.

"Alright, Uncle, what's up?"

He scraped several plates, then looked at his niece and winked. "Never seen two people who can't find enough hours in the day for their horses. Now maybe, just maybe, if we put those two together enough times, things might work out for everybody around here. Wouldn't that be the cat's whiskers?"

Josie finished scraping the plates. "Just leave the dishes stacked up 'til morning when I heat the water." She went back to the dining room to wipe off the table. "Notice how much better lookin' Deke is these days? First time he knocked on our door, I'd a'swore that he'd never pulled a comb through that mop that lives on top of his head. Thickest hair on a man I've ever seen!"

Beemis couldn't help chuckling over Josie's description. "Speakin' of mops, Joe told me that the mop they got hangin' on their bunkhouse walls got better cloth in it than what Deke had in that beat-up cardboard box he slid under his bunk. Now look at him! Two paydays under his belt and two trips to Jarveys' have sure worked wonders on the lad."

She finished wiping off the table. "He's still wearin' that God-awful, sweat-stained thing that used to be a hat before two dozen horses trampled it to death."

Beemis tickled Josie's chin. "Not to worry, Sugarplum! Got Annie workin' on that come next payday." He mopped his brow. "Let's move out to the front porch. Could even catch a breeze or two if we're lucky. Beats sweatin' to death lyin' on top of bed sheets."

Josie perched on the top plank step while her uncle found his usual rocking chair. "You really do want them to get together, don't you?"

Beemis fanned himself with a piece of cardboard he picked off the seat. "Sure do, Sugarplum! Sure do! The pieces of our Annie's life are comin' together. If they'd learn to love each other 'bout half as much as they do horses, I'd say we'd have a match made danged close to heaven."

The shank of the evening was barely upon the two horseback riders as they really let out their mounts for a good blow. Two miles from the Markham ranch main gate, Deke called a halt. Annie, too, stopped to see what was wrong.

Deke got off the young mare and petted her. "She's still fightin' the bit. I'd better take her bridle off so her mouth won't get too sore."

Annie handed him a short length of rope from her saddle horn. "Here, use this! Make a halter for her, and you should be able to neck-rein her on the ride back."

Deke fashioned a halter in no time and slipped it over the young mare's head. He tied another short length of rope he had to use as a lead rope. "I'd better walk her for a spell, give her a chance to get used to the halter. Any place around here worth walkin' to?"

Annie pointed to her right. "Vermillion Creek's not too far. I keep forgetting you're new to this part of the Hole."

He laughed. "Yeah, the only thing I know about Brown's Hole is the trail down into it as far as your uncle's ranch and the back path to Jarvey's store."

Annie got off Glory and walked beside him. Well, Deke Landry, for your information there's a lot to see in this hole. Just follow me!"

They walked about one mile, then hobbled both horses near a big clump of cottonwoods. Deke walked along the bank of Vermillion Creek, picking up flat rocks, then trying his hand at skipping them across the water. Annie saw the fun he was having, so she joined in.

"I haven't done this in years!" she exclaimed. "You're a better thrower than I am! Mine doesn't want to skip!"

He held a flat rock for her to see. "It's in the wrist! Just make sure your wrist snaps when you throw it. Makes the rock spin so it'll skip longer."

They moved along the bank until they found an old snag. Both pulled off their boots to let their feet dangle in the water.

"Wow!" said Deke. "This water's ice cold! And behind us, everybody's cookin'!"

Annie smiled. "All this is snow fed from the mountains around here. Go down another half mile where this creek runs into the Green and your ears will go deaf on you! That's where the Green starts to funnel into Ladore Canyon."

Neither spoke for a minute; then Deke broke the silence. "Joe told me you got the best education money could buy. Them big words you just used proves that. Me? Well, I never did hanker much for book learnin'. Guess it shows, too! But I love horses! Always have!"

She didn't know why, but she touched his arm. She felt an electricity pass between them. He looked at her with an urge—a sudden urge that must be kept under control. She was the boss' niece, which meant hands off if he wanted to keep his job.

"Deke?"

"Yeah!"

"You felt something, didn't you? So did I!"

"I'd be lying if I said I didn't. Maybe we'd better get started back."

They both rose. Neither really wanted to go. Annie spoke up. "I know very little about you...Can't you at least tell me that much before we head back?"

They started walking, slowly. "Not much to tell...Followed this here trail down from Montana...all the way down here. It's really not the kind that has deep ruts into it like the stagecoaches or wagons make, but it's got good people along it. Just be honest about yourself and tell them the truth. Told 'em I was hungry and could I sleep in their barn if I done chores or worked for them to earn my keep. Most of 'em gave me a handout to keep me movin' 'til I ended up here. I did spend some time around Rock Springs...and that's about it. Pretty simple life...Nothin' like yours, I'm sure."

Glory whinnied as they approached. Deke shook his head and laughed. "Glory sure likes you. Knows you're a good, kind person. Horses know people sometimes better'n people know themselves."

Annie turned to Deke. "You're right about that. Most of that high-priced education my uncle paid for was because I didn't know what I really wanted. I thought I wanted a certain man...turns out he didn't want me nearly as much as I wanted him."

"Sure hope you're over him! Are you?"

"That's one of the reasons I rode here with you; I need to find out for myself."

Deke liked what she almost said. He felt now he had a chance, even if it turned out to be only a small one. "Wouldn't bother me none to hear one or two of them other reasons..."

The sun's scorching rays outlined her petite figure for Deke. Yet he allowed she'd be plenty of woman for the lucky man who could get next to her. He watched her take out her farmer-sized handkerchief to wipe the perspiration off her forehead before putting her cowboy hat back on. He liked the way the sweat off her body made her man's work shirt stick to her breasts, leaving very little to his imagination. He judged them to be coffee-cup size, just right for her body.

Her words broke his thoughts. "I like being around you...working with you. I like the way your blue eyes turn serious when you're all work, and yet I've seen you laugh when the day's work is over and the breaking bits and halters and saddles are stacked in the tack shed...I like that, too!"

He started toward her to sweep her up in his arms, then held up. "I've wanted to kiss your lips first day you fixed supper for me...after I thanked you proper-like, of course! I don't dare! If something goes wrong between us, there goes my job! Never had a better job...No, I don't dare!"

Annie, too, felt a surge of emotion. "Deke, kiss me! I promise no matter what happens between us, it won't cost you you're job. Beemis says you're the best! He has big plans for you! If you don't kiss me right now, I'm going to kiss you!"

They rushed into each other's arms, bent on letting their lips speak for their bodies. Deke was downright clumsy and Annie wasn't much better as they knocked each other's hats off in their haste to hold each other tight. What could've been hilarious or even a disaster finally swung in their favor as they settled down to enjoy the moment and savor their first kiss as each had wanted it to be.

Annie had only to tilt her head up slightly to feel the force of Deke's lips full upon hers. He gathered her even tighter until their bodies became a beautiful blend of sweat, sticky clothes, and heated emotion. He felt all man to her, just what she needed and wanted! Never mind that she could hardly separate the scent of Deke from his horse; both were more than welcome!

Suddenly he dropped to his knees and went after her breasts. She thought about unbuttoning her shirt to let him have them, but there wasn't time. No matter, she told herself, one thin thickness of cloth would never keep each from enjoying such sensual pleasure.

"Deke! Deke! Deke!" was all she managed to say while she held his head to her breasts.

He took it as yes, do more! So he did!

Suddenly he rose as quickly as he had dropped, his face a mixture of pleasure and embarrassment. "I...I...don't know what to say...Never done this before in my whole life. Musta been plum outta my head...Please let me apologize. Annie, it won't happen again..."

She pulled her wet shirt off her nipple, then let him stew a minute in his own predicament, thoroughly enjoying the moment. "I certainly hope you don't mean what you just said. I liked it...and so did you. Only next time, kinda give me a little idea what you have in mind so I can be ready."

He picked her up and hugged her nearly to death. "You said next time! Yes, you did! Oh, Annie, I could kiss you all over again!"

She felt her boots touch the ground once more. "Well, what's stopping you?"

All week long, Beemis and Josie got one earful after another of Deke, Deke, and more Deke. Deke's going to do this, and Deke's going to do that, and you know, Deke's really not much taller than I am, that makes Deke just about right for me, wouldn't you say?

Beemis winked at Josie, then stopped buttering his stack of flapjacks. He looked at Annie with as serious an expression as he could muster under the circumstances. "With all this talk about Deke, got only one question for you,

Annie."

She pushed her plate aside and got ready to leave. "Yes, Uncle, shoot!"
"Is there any work gettin' done down at the stables?"

The heat wave sizzled on through the third week, taking its toll on every
living thing that called Brown's Hole home. At the Markham ranch, tempers
flared up; cool heads became feisty and irritable from lack of sleep. Scuffles
broke out in the bunkhouse, down in the stables, and in the work corrals,
mostly over nothing. People purposely avoided each other in the hope that no
contact meant less chance to get into another heated argument.

Old Henry Ettleman paid Beemis a social call late one evening. Josie
brought out fresh-squeezed lemonade to both men seated on the front porch,
and then promptly excused herself. Usually, she enjoyed the old man's wit
and wisdom, often laced with some pretty hefty doses of life's hard knocks.
Tonight, she told herself, it was just too damn hot for down-home humor.

Henry, now in his late eighties, was only a whisper of the man he used to
have been. Beemis allowed that the only thing holding the frail man up had
to be spit and vinegar. The spit was the glue that kept his bones from poking
through his weather-beaten, old hide, and the vinegar was the fire that erupted
in his belly and brain, which made him spill out those pearls of wisdom every
so often, whether he wanted to or not.

Beemis opened their conversation. "Glad you came by. Was gonna have
Annie and Deke ride your way to make sure you and Etta are okay. She hasn't
had any more of them faintin' spells, has she?"

The Hole's longest living legend put a shaky hand around the lemonade
glass. He finally raised it to his lips, much to Beemis' relief. "Hell, Beemis,
ain't nuthin' wrong with Etta; she'll outlive me by at least twenty." He used
two hands to steady his glass back down on the small table beside his chair.
"What's stickin' in my craw is this here weather. Been here since thirty-six
and I'd'a swore I'd seen it all. So I figure there's only one way to explain it.
Gotta be the devil himself punishin' all us folks fer doin' something he didn't
cotton to…Trouble is, he ain't told me what he's mader'n hell about!"

The two old friends chewed the fat for another half hour. Finally, Henry
raised all ninety-six pounds of brittle bones out of his chair. A glint shone in
his dull-grey eyes. "Seen that new fella ya hired and your Annie down by that
clumpa' cottonwoods next to the creek. They seemed to be in an awful hurry
'bout somethun'. Didn't see no cane poles fer fishin'…Nope, that can't be it!
Tell Josie thanks fer the lemonade."

Josie came out on the porch to pick up the glasses. She found her uncle talking to himself at the far end of the porch. Every now and then, between mutterings, he'd grip his cane so hard Josie thought if his cane were alive, he'd have squeezed it to death long ago. "Uncle, what's bothering you? Didn't you and Henry have a good talk?"

He turned to her. "Didja ever notice how bushy old Henry's eyebrows are gettin'? Gotta be as thick as that pile of underbrush he calls a mustache. When he moves those eyebrows to talk, I had to look twice to see if his words were comin' from up there or down where them words and yarns he spins are supposed to be comin' from."

She put her arm around her uncle's expanding waistline and gave him a pretty good peck on the cheek. "Alright, this heat's got everybody edgy as all get out. It's about Deke and Annie, isn't it? Bet it was something old Henry told you. C'mon! Out with it!"

"You and me got a job to do when they get back. I know they think the world about each other, but there's limits, Sugarplum! There's limits for both of 'em to follow 'til they get hitched! I'll handle Deke and you take Annie aside and give her a good talkin' to…the same kind of woman talk your aunt gave you. I'm countin' on you to handle it!"

The same three weeks of record-setting heat that everybody in the Hole complained or cussed about only served as an elixir of love for Deke and Annie. The awkwardness that Deke had first experienced with Annie was a thing of the recent past. Annie, too, had honed up her skills in the lovemaking department, making sure she telegraphed plenty. She now could control exactly what she wanted from Deke with her alluring smile, beautiful eyes, and encouraging words that beckoned him again and again to take and taste her fruits of flesh and pleasure she'd given him so freely.

It hardly seemed to matter that what had once started out as a routine ride one late afternoon to work out a young mare's tender mouth problem had blossomed into the real thing—love. Each day, from that first time, they had left the ranch behind with its prying eyes and tough questions to engage in what their hearts desired—each other.

Deke grabbed their saddle blankets while Annie hobbled their horses. Both looked over their shoulders, surprised to see and hear a buggy pass by so close.

"Who's that?"

Annie waved. "It's old Henry Ettleman on his way back from Uncle

Beemis'. Wave to him, Deke, or else he might wonder what's going on…"

Deke waved. "Feels kinda strange…First time anybody's come this close. Next time we'd better find a different spot…give the grass time to grow back too. Heard Beemis talkin' 'bout cuttin' grass down here, come this fall."

Annie plucked a big, blue, farmer-sized handkerchief out of Deke's back pocket. "You take care of the blankets, love, while I soak our handkerchiefs in the creek."

By the time she returned, Deke had a double layer of blankets spread on the ground. They took turns wiping the perspiration off each other's faces.

"Boy, that feels good," he said. "Danged water's too cold, or else I'd strip down and jump in."

"Me too," Annie chimed in. "There's nobody around…just in case we change our minds…"

They looked at one another, each reading the same thought. Deke spoke first. "Let's do the next best thing…like we been doin'…you know…"

Each pulled off their boots in record time. Then they stood up to undress in front of each other. Their clothes went in every direction, their needs and desires in only one direction, the same one their eyes were focused on—each other.

Annie rushed into Deke's arms. He smothered her in hot kisses, matched only by the heat round their naked bodies.

Deke started to work on her neck. Annie knew what he wanted next. "Say the words, love…You know what I mean…before I let you…"

"Oh my Annie, oh my Annie."

"That's good, but you can do better! A lot better!"

"I love you! I love you!"

He said the magic words she had to hear before she let him enter her Garden of Eden to taste and take her forbidden fruit: her breasts. He worked each one gently, cupping them in his hands, feeling their firmness and then toying with their nipples until each stood straight out ready for pleasure-giving.

Annie held his head to her breasts while he gave them a good, long working over. She ran her fingers through his hair, stroking it over and over, keeping pace with the sucking sounds. "See, my love, how good it gets when you tell me how much you love me? We both get what we want and need. Oh, Deke, Deke, don't stop. I want to give you more and more each time we do this…"

She had him smouldering with want and desire. His shaft was thoroughly aroused, but she would not let him lay her down—not just yet. She moved her body away from him to allow her to kiss his nipples. It left a salty taste on her tongue and lips, which moved her to more passion.

He slid his arm under her buttocks to lay her down on the blankets. He wanted to roll her over with his body eased between her thighs so he could penetrate. Instead, she cradled him with her thighs and legs, leaving his shaft with no place to go.

"No, my love," she whispered, "no matter how much I want to feel it in me…not 'til we're married."

They held this embrace, their bodies stuck together from the passion and perspiration, neither could've slipped a blade of grass between. Then Annie reached down to guide his shaft between her thighs and buttocks.

Deke felt his shaft being eased past the fine hairs of her thatch until it found a new resting place. He had to settle for the second-best sensation of his life.

They lay that way, their bodies in perfect harmony, their lips only a kiss apart, their minds as one, working overtime with one unfulfilled ecstasy yet to be tapped.

He kissed her hard. "Annie?"

"Yes, love."

"Don't know how much more of this I can stand…without…you know."

"Just a little longer, love. Just a little longer…"

"Here they come, Uncle! It's so dark out, can just barely see them!"

Beemis rose from his favorite haunt on the front porch, his soft, deerskin-stretched rocking chair. "Here, take this lantern, leave the other one for me. When you see Deke, send him to me, NOW!"

Josie intercepted the two riders at the tack shed. She waited just long enough for Annie and Deke to remove their saddles. "Uncle Beemis wants to see you, Deke! Been waitin' on you two for over an hour! I wouldn't keep him waitin' one minute longer if I were you!"

Deke expected to see a wild man go into a rage the minute he reached the bottom plank step to the porch. Instead, he found Beemis seated in his rocker, the picture of calmness, framed by the lantern's light.

Beemis motioned for him to sit down. "I helped old Joe write a letter to his sister out in California. Soon as he gets the answer back that we expect, you'll be my new foreman."

Deke went speechless, then found some words. "So soon! Thanks, Sir, for the big promotion! What about the others?"

"Joe took care of that while you were supposed to be out ridin' this evening, breakin' in another balky mare."

"Supposed to be?"

"You heard me!" Beemis snapped back. Then he went to rocking, slowly back and forth. Deke was sure the old boy was only gathering up steam for one of his real set-to's.

"Whataya think of my Annie?"

"I love her! That's what I think of Annie!"

More rocking. Finally the old warrior rose. Down went the specs off the bridge of his nose. Deke knew this was it! "There'll be no more triflin' with my Annie, no matter how much you say you love her!" He was about to lay down some more law, then calmly changed his tone. "You claim you got serious intentions, so this would be an awful good time to let me hear 'em."

Deke rose to face his boss, the one who had just promoted him, and then turned around and took Annie's sweetness away from his arms. "Annie and me are serious about each other. Aim to propose marriage soon as I take over as foreman."

It was Beemis' turn to finish up what was still on his mind. Up came the cane, its rubber trip pressed hard against Deke's Adam's apple. "Son, just 'cause I look through spectacles doesn't mean I'm blind to what's been goin' on between you two. The later you stay, the fresher your horses look comin' back. Last two nights, they didn't even need to cool off or a rub-down. So far, your suggestions for handlin' my Arabians have paid off well. I can't think of a better time to give me another suggestion about those evenin' rides you been takin'. Make it your best one yet!"

All Deke had to do was fill in the words. He knew what Beemis was angling for. "Alright! No more rides with Annie 'til we're hitched!"

The cane tip hit the plank floor. Beemis pumped Deke's hand as though he had a hold of the handle to an outside water pump. "Now I know why we understand each other so well and get along so good. Son, you took the very same words clean outta my mouth!"

Ann knew from the tone of Josie's words to Deke that her sister was part of a family confrontation that had been three weeks in the making. Deke was undoubtedly getting dressed down by Beemis at this very moment. Now it was her turn. She laid her Indian blanket on the stack of saddle blankets. She was surprised to see Josie yank it back off the stack and then kneel on it, closely examining its beautiful Indian design.

"You've seen this blanket a hundred times, Sis! It's the one Teetaka made me two years ago! Why the fuss over it now?"

Josie pulled several blades of grass out of it, then stood up. She dropped the blades in front of Ann. "Ought to be more careful…Next time let Deke spread his blanket on the ground first…That way yours won't pick up all the grass."

Ann was mad, fighting mad. Even in the dim lantern light, Josie could see her sister's face flush to another shade. "Okay, Big Sister, what's this all about?"

They stood eyeball to eyeball, boot to boot, with Josie's lantern the silent third party to the fireworks. Josie didn't beat around the bush any longer. "I'll tell you what this is all about! I like Deke, too, but you're giving him too much—way too, too much. Save it for later…when you're married."

Annie never backed down one smidgeon. "And what makes you think Deke's gettin' anything at all? What, Josie? What?"

"I wasn't born yesterday! Two saddle blankets on the ground means only one thing: You're lettin' him go too far! Makin' it too easy for him! I'll bet you've given him everything, haven't you?"

Annie fired right back. "Stop trying to be my mother! I don't need this lecture! Not from you, anyway! Tell you what, dear Sister! You take care of Cleve Dreschler your way, and I'll take care of Deke Landry my way! How's that?"

Josie pointed her finger under Annie's nose. "You let Deke get you pregnant before you're married, and you'll break your uncle's heart! And don't you come crying to me when I catch you throwing up your breakfast some morning, either!"

"What makes you so sure I'm giving him my body?"

"I know you've been giving him your breasts for over two weeks! Checked your drawers and every brassiere you've ever owned is still there!"

"It's been too damned hot out to wear them! And I'll thank you to stop snoopin' around my things from now on, SUGARPLUM!"

Josie shook her head. "Don't lie to me; it's not your style, Ann Barnett! Bet you're not a virgin anymore, are you? How many times, Sis? C'mon, how many times?"

This time Annie couldn't wait to spill the truth. "NONE, DEAR SISTER! NOT EVEN ONCE! Now, anything else, MOTHER?"

Annie never saw the relieved look replace Josie's worried expression on her forehead. Josie grabbed the Indian blanket and placed it on top of the stack. She picked up the lantern and left Annie still standing in total darkness inside the shed.

Ann had to run to catch up with Josie. "Cut it kinda short, didn't you? Beatrice Potter tried to chew on me for over two hours. How about it, Sis? Mother?"

Josie kept her pace with the lantern leading the way toward the ranch house. She knew one more question could very well tear them apart for good—the last thing either really wanted.

"Let's all join hands in a circle and give praise to our dear Lord for the fine fellowship we've had and the good food we're about to enjoy."

Beemis' supper guest sat between Josie and Ann. He extended his arms in both directions, waited for Beemis to hold his out, then said grace. All three residents were impressed with his politeness, his articulation, and most of all, his soft-spoken sureness. They finished their meal on a high note as their guest amused them, time after time, with his keen sense of dry humor, often laced with some real down-to-earth profound statements.

"What kind of business did you say you were in, Mr. Parker?"

Parker looked across the table at Beemis. His deep-set blue eyes fairly danced. "I didn't, Mister Markham. Let's just say I'm an investor in opportunity."

Parker's statement was everything and nothing. This rankled Beemis to no end. He wasn't about to let Parker off the hook that easily. "Does that mean you're lookin' for investment opportunities here in the Hole? A ranch, perhaps?"

Parker seemed preoccupied with making sure his dark-haired cowlick stayed in place over one side of his forehead. After patting it down, he ignored Beemis' question, then directed his smile at Josie. "Let me apologize for what appears to be an honest mistake. When I knocked on your door, this charming and beautiful young lady assumed I was looking for work. As you can plainly see, I'm neither dressed for ranch work nor am I in need of any handouts. I understand that's the custom here in Brown's Hole. When Josie asked me to supper, I couldn't turn her invitation down. The offer of a home-cooked meal was just too good to pass up. What I am looking for are directions to Matt Warner's cabin on the side of Diamond Mountain. I'll be more than glad to pay for this delicious food and a bed in your bunkhouse if you'll let me stay the night."

Beemis was about to answer when Josie interrupted. "Mister Parker, we wouldn't think of asking you to pay. You've been such good company, and it's such a treat to see a well-dressed man in a business suit come to our door instead of the usual run of drifters, and Lord only knows what else! Won't you stay for dessert? It's fresh-baked huckleberry pie!"

Again, Parker was polite—almost too polite for Beemis' liking. "Why, that's my favorite, Miss Josie. Down home, my mother always saw to it there was plenty of huckleberry pie when picking time came."

"And just exactly where would that be, Mister Parker?"

Parker tossed out his answer to Beemis, but never took his eyes off Josie. "Down in Utah…southern part."

Annie joined her sister out in the kitchen to help serve. "Wow! That Mister Parker is something alright! Couldn't keep his eyes off you if he tried!"

Josie took the dish towel off the pie and began cutting it. "Don't know what you're rattlin' on about, Sis. Mister Parker was just tryin' to be polite and keep the conversation fresh and interesting, that's all! Certainly don't see many like him around."

"In a pig's eye you don't! Every time he stares holes through you, you turn every shade but green. Best dressed man I've seen in many a day…Wonder what he really does for a living?"

Josie finished dishing up the pie. "Guess your mind must've been down there in the bunkhouse with Deke. Heard him tell all of us he was an investor…in opportunity…Not too sure just exactly what that means."

"Neither does Uncle Beemis, no matter how hard he tried to worm some more information out of your Mister Parker. I'll say this about the man, has the smallest and softest hands." Annie held up one hand. "Not really much bigger than mine…but boy, are his ever strong, like Deke's! Thought he was going to squeeze the stuffin' out of mine when we held hands during grace."

Josie handed Annie two plates. She laughed. "Well, we do know one thing about George LeRoy Parker."

"Now it's George, is it? What do we know about this man for sure?"

"It's been a long time since he's gotten dirt under his fingernails! Cleanest looking nails I've ever seen on a man. Even puts Uncle Beemis' to shame!"

Annie nearly cracked up over her sister's candid remark. "Hey, Sis, we better get a move on serving this pie or else they'll think we're just getting out the pails to start picking."

Josie moved just fast enough and turned her body just right so Parker caught a quick peek of the pretty scalloped edges of her petticoat. He pretended not to notice, but Josie knew he was most pleased with what he'd been privy to. She made a special point of serving him, then reached down to remove the saddle bag next to his right leg. "Let me move this out of your way, George—er, Mister Parker. I'll just leave it by the front door, next to your Stetson and guns…"

Parker clamped his foot on the bag, pinning it against the leg of the table. For a brief moment, he caught Josie's hand on its downward path. "It's fine, Josie, right where it's at!" He caught her astonished expression. "Hope I didn't gouge your hand. I'm sorry if I did!"

Parker's actions brought more than a few puzzled looks around the dinner table from Beemis and Annie. However, he proved he was a master at conversation and diplomacy. "That was a most delicious way of preparing steak, Josie. Tell me, what did you use for seasoning?"

Josie blushed a pretty shade of pink. "I used wild onions and chopped them up into fine bits, then brushed them on with a little butter."

He turned to Beemis. "Didn't see anything but those fine Arabians when I rode in. Where do you keep your beef?"

For once Beemis held the floor against this highly intelligent stranger. "We buy our beef, contrary to what a lot of our neighbors do or what you may have heard about Brown's Hole."

A sly smile camped across Parker's pleasant face. "Yes, Mister Markham, I do believe I've heard something about small-time cattle rustling going on down here. Mostly at the expense of those big cattle companies, I'm told."

They finished their dessert without another word. The silence was deafening to Josie, who was infatuated by this sudden rush of attention heaped upon her by a man she wanted to know more about. His conversation was stimulating, so was his charm. To Beemis, this Parker had a cockiness about him that bordered on arrogance or at least its cousin, downright conceit. Yet it'd been a long time since he'd been in the company of someone who had an absolute command of what he wanted to say and when it needed saying. He had to admit this man had the special tools used by the successful men he'd come across in his lifetime. Now if he could just figure out why the man was here in the first place. He seemed to be so in tune with everybody and everything for a person who'd never set foot in Brown's Hole.

Parker interrupted everyone's thoughts. He made Beemis and Annie seem as though they weren't there, looking only at Josie. "I must be going. Wouldn't want to wear out my welcome when I've had such a charming and gracious host. Let me carry my dessert dish on my way out."

The stranger slung his saddlebag over his shoulder and then proceeded to follow Josie and Annie out to the kitchen. He handed Josie his dessert plate. "Best pie I've tasted in years, Josie. I'm just sorry about one thing."

"Oh, what's that?"

"I'm obviously too late to come calling on you socially. With all your charm and looks, to say nothing about the way you cook, there'd only be one place for me and that I'm afraid would be at the end of the line of suitors whom I'm sure must be courting you."

"Yes, you're right, Mister Parker," volunteered Annie. "Josie's got a steady now! Only thing left to do is set the date."

Josie stamped her foot. Her face beet red, she glared at her sister. "That's not so! Mister Dreschler and I are good friends! Nothing more than good friends!"

"Well, in that case, do I have your permission to come calling, Miss Josie?"

"Yes, Mister Parker," she gushed. "If you'd care to…"

"Thank you! And from now on, let's stay on a first name basis. You may call me George, just as I've been calling you Josie all evening. Now then, let me pay my respects to your uncle on my out. Give me a day or two to take care of my business; then I'll be back."

Parker held Josie's hand, then bent as though he meant to kiss it, but left his lips a scant inch away. Josie blushed all colors of the rainbow at the magnificent gesture. He stood straight once more, pleased with his own performance. He smiled at Josie, then spoke to Annie. "Nice meeting you, too."

He left the kitchen, but not in Josie's heart. Annie seized the moment to do her own mimic version of Parker kissing Josie's hand. She held out her own hand, then bent down to kiss it. "Oh, Mister Parker, you really shouldn't do this; what will Cleve Dreschler think?"

"Stop it, Annie! It's not funny! Mr. Parker…I mean, George, was just trying to be a gentleman, that's all! Why can't you see it that way, too?"

Annie turned serious. "I really do, Sis…Let me say this about you, and I do mean it from my heart: whoever does get you to say I do will be the luckiest lug in all the world because you're going to be a real catch for that certain man."

The two sisters hugged each other. "Thanks, Sis," Josie whispered. "Coming from you, that means an awful lot to me."

Annie broke their embrace. She walked around the kitchen, turning and twisting, then gave up.

"Now what do you think you're doing?"

"That swishy-swish-skirt business, when you gave George his own private peek! Didn't think I saw it, didja? Hey, Sis, it really wasn't necessary. You had him hooked the minute he laid those two peepers on you!"

Beemis walked Parker to the front parlor door. There, he handed Parker his Stetson and a brace of six shooters, two wicked looking Colt 45's. "Sorry I made you take them off, but I've had this rule for more years than I can count: No guns of any kind are allowed inside our home. Anybody walkin' 'round with 'em on makes the girls uneasy…Me too." He pointed to his old Army rifle above the doorway. "Always trusted that old rifle in my Army scouting days, never felt a handgun could do a better job!"

Parker cinched the belt buckle holding the 45's. Then with deft hands, he gathered the leather strings attached to each holster and tied them around both pant legs. "Depends on what you're taking on, wouldn't you say, Mister Markham?"

Beemis played Parker's game, ignoring his direct question. Instead, he looked at Parker's hardware and held out one hand. "Never seen wooden polished handles before…Mind if I hold one?"

Parker cleared the gun from his holster before Beemis could finish his blink. "Here, see for yourself! It's a beauty, right?"

Parker grinned while Beemis examined the six-shooter, turning it over and over in his hand, then letting it balance off his palm. "Can't get over it…perfect balance…even with the wood. Special made, I'll bet! Right?"

"Yes. In my line of work, weight is as important as speed."

Beemis saw the opening he had been looking for all evening. He pressed Parker. "And just what line would that really be, Mister Parker?"

Again, Parker skirted the question. He reached for the brass doorknob. To his surprise, the knob turned before he could grasp it. In stepped Deke. He started to say something, then changed his words when he saw Parker.

"Butch! What in heck are you doin' down here?" They shook hands. "Sure glad to see you!"

This was the only time Beemis saw Parker's complexion change a hair from its controlled demeanor.

"Always meant to thank you, Deke. You left town before I got the chance."

Now Beemis was really puzzled. Somehow, somewhere along Deke's travels down the Outlaw Trail, these two had met. He aimed his question at

Deke. "What brings you up here?"

"It's Joe! His roomatiz is real bad tonight! Could Josie and Annie please come to see if they can do something?"

Beemis picked up a lantern by the door. "Get the women, Deke! Parker, you follow me, and I'll show you where you bunk tonight. Tomorrow, I'll have one of my boys go with you part way up the trail to Warner's cabin."

Josie and Annie fussed and mothered over poor old Joe Cady until he was ready to scream uncle. The two finally got him to relax enough so he could stretch out on his bunk for the first time in hours. Towels dipped in a water bucket and then wrung out helped the most to relieve the soreness and stiffness in his back.

During all this, Beemis cast a suspicious eye over at Parker. He'd made himself at home, his suit coat hung on a nail overhead. Two things struck Beemis as rather odd. Parker never removed his gun belt as most men would when they bedded down, and he'd brought both his saddle bag and his saddle into the bunkhouse. Beemis watched him carefully tuck the bag under his range pillow and then rest his noggin on top of both. He'd cast Josie's goose-down pillow aside in favor of the hard leather. Beemis could only wonder and wonder about the man who ate at his table, avoided certain questions, knew Deke, charmed his Josie almost out of her shoes, had lightning-quick reflexes, and guarded his saddle bag like no other man he'd ever come across.

Old Joe had had enough mothering. "You all git the heck outta here," he yelled. "Thanks fer all ya done and tried to do...Now lemme be!"

Once outside the bunkhouse, the questions came hot and heavy. "Alright, Deke, you called him Butch, and all night long, he told us his name was George LeRoy Parker. Now, why'd you call him Butch?"

"'Cause that's the only name I ever knew him by up at Rock Springs. Butch spent time in the Wyoming pen, and he hired a smooth-talkin' lawyer to get the governor to let him out early if he'd promise not to do anymore holdups or robberies up in Wyoming."

Deke's admission really caught Josie off guard. "Is Butch his real name?"

Deke scratched his mop with the brim of his new Stetson. "No, not really, Miss Josie. You see, when they let him out, he had to find a new line of work. A meat cutter took him in, gave him a job cuttin' up meat while he waited fer the cowboys to come to town on paydays." Deke laughed. "Come to think on it, Butch got purty good at both—skinnin' the meat, and then skinnin' them cowboys come payday. We first called him the butcher man, but he didn't care much for that, so he shortened it to Butch. Been callin' himself that ever since."

Beemis had more questions. "Why'd he thank you? What was that all about?"

"Butch and this old rancher got to drinkin' purty heavy one night. Later, the town marshal locked him up. Said Butch robbed the old man and took his money. Shucks, I know'd Butch purty good by then; he'd never do that…didn't need to with a steady job and lots of extra money on paydays. I was swampin' out the saloon where this all was supposed to happen. Found this old man's gold, pocket watch and a wad of bills under a table. Went right to the town jail with the goods. They had to let Butch out. Boy, he was madder'n hell! Said it was a damned good thing Rock Springs was in Wyoming! I left town then, and started down this way. Butch caught up with me here…and thanked me, too! Butch never fergits a friend!"

Josie took her turn. "You said Butch was drinking heavy. I don't like that in any man, no matter how much of a gentleman he claims to be."

"Shucks, Miss Josie, Butch never really drank hard or heavy…more like a possum and fox put-on, I'd call it!"

"I don't understand. What do you mean?"

Deke went on. "Come paydays, Butch would pick out a bunch of cowboys in one of the saloons. He'd wait 'til they got oiled up purty good; then he'd buy a bottle or two and invite 'em over to his table. Before the drinkin' was over, Butch had 'em where he wanted 'em. He became a possum…pretend he was drunker than they was. Out behind one of them saloons was an old tree with a tin cup nailed to it. I'd see Butch wobble n' weave so bad in his saddle that you'd expect him to fall on his head next."

"Did he?"

"Naw, Miss Josie! Butch would circle that tree, actin' all drunked up; then he'd straighten up in the saddle just long enough to nail that cup good! Then he'd slump down in it and fall outta it on the next pass. Every stupid cowpoke would say Butch had a streaka' dumb luck and they'd have to pay up. I know'd better, never seen Butch miss once! He was too darned slick and fox-like fer them cowpunchers."

Annie had her question. "You said he called himself Butch. Did he ever go by any other name? Like a last name?"

"Yup, he sure did! Took the name of Cassidy. Heard tell he got that from his uncle, showed Butch the ropes down in Utah somewhere…That's the story I was told…"

Beemis put it all together. "So, Deke, what you're sayin' is we been hoodwinked by the best of the worst! We been entertaining the worst outlaw that ever hit the trail into the Hole. Well, I'll say this for him, he did it to us with a style that sure fits the way you talked about him, all possum- and fox-like!"

Josie broke away. Tears streaming down both cheeks, she shouted from the pain Deke had suddenly dumped upon her heart. "He's not Butch Cassidy! He can't be an outlaw! He's George Parker to me! He's too nice, too honorable, to be Butch Cassidy!"

It took less than two weeks for the Hole's worst-kept secret to leak out. The long-standing reputation of the Hole as a roost for small-time, nameless outlaws, petty cattle rustlers, and other assorted merchants of shady dealings was over. It had gone big time with its biggest and most sought-after celebrity to date: Butch Cassidy.

News of the daring bank robbery at Montpelier, Idaho, finally filtered down to the Hole some thirty days later. Beemis had no problem putting two and two together. George Parker, alias Butch Cassidy, or vice versa, had entered the Hole with the robbery take still stashed in his saddlebag. No wonder he felt attached to it, never letting it out of sight for a single moment.

Beemis wasted no time laying his law down regarding courtship rules—now for Josie as well as Annie. Only the front parlor, the front porch, and an occasional walk out to the ranch's main gate a quarter mile away would be allowed, with no exceptions. He was deeply disturbed by the way Josie had suddenly changed. Yet he allowed that Josie's common sense would return in due time once Cassidy left his new hideout for another robbery or bank holdup. Josie would have to face the cold, hard truth; no matter what alias Cassidy or Parker went by, there'd be no escaping the fact he was a wanted man on the run from the law. Until then, he'd try to be as patient with Josie as he had been with Annie and Deke.

Cassidy moved his base of operations from Matt Warner's cabin to a rocky ledge high above Charley Crouse's place on the face of Diamond Mountain. On this sandstone outcrop, he built his own cabin, protected on three sides by the ledge itself, which meant it could only be approached from one direction: down below. It could easily be defended should a lawman decide to pursue; however, none had ever ventured into the Hole at this point—a consideration, no doubt, that received Butch's careful attention and planning. His followers, made up of mostly local talent, rewarded him by calling it Cassidy Point. Though his group of admirers and hope-to-be gang members changed from time to time, one thing never changed: Butch Cassidy's absolute leadership went unchallenged.

Josie's continued relationship with George Parker took on new aspects. George was never Butch and Parker couldn't possibly be confused with Cassidy. These were two distinct, different men! One she had all the time in the world for, and the other she couldn't or wouldn't tolerate under any circumstances. This was the only way she could keep her sanity, the only way she could make peace within the bounds of her troubled soul.

They sat on the front porch; a cool breeze rustled the light skirt Josie had on, making her wonder if she was dressed warm enough. Parker turned to her with the same thought in mind. He rose from Beemis' rocker to wrap his thin jacket around Josie's shoulders. "Perhaps a walk will keep us both warm," he suggested.

Down the main road they walked, side by side, each anxious to delve into the other's heart to see what was really there, fact or fantasy. Halfway to the main gate, George held out his hand. Josie slipped hers in his as they continued on. She felt the warmth from his hand travel through hers, a sure sign, she told herself, that her just being beside him would open his heart and mind up to her with the good news she had prayed for: He'd be staying.

A full moon cast a steady stream of moonlight down on the two, shedding a soft halo of love around Josie. If only George would see it too, she thought; then he'd have to bare his heart and need for her. Then her fantasy would become fact.

He gathered her in to him under the shadow of the huge crossbeam that spanned the main gate. Always the gentlemen, he spoke before he acted. "Please, Josie…may I?"

Every emotion for a man she'd ever known suddenly took charge. She moved her body into his, hoping she'd given plenty of hint of how she really felt about him.

He sampled her lips at first, then took her to paradise when he feasted full upon them, drawing their nectar until she had no more to give.

Josie took his hand and placed it over her breast, hoping that he'd do more—much more.

"Are you sure you want me to?"

"Yes…yes, my love…"

He made sure his jacket covered her breasts before he slipped his hand up. Her thin blouse offered only a token front to the pleasure she wanted him to have. Gently, ever so gently, she felt his hand feel, then cup, then massage first one, then the other.

Josie moved in even tighter, her hips melting into his body, making sure nothing was left to chance between them. She knew now that he was hers—with the proper encouragement and the right words, of course, strengthened by that which told him this was as far as she would let him go, no matter how many times he tried. Only a marriage proposal would allow him further pleasure—up to a point.

Suddenly he finished cupping and massaging. He kissed her hard, again and again, trying to make sure she understood his needs and wants, yet trying not to hurt her lips.

She smiled to herself, knowing full well she held the key to unlock his passion.

He was breathing hard. "Josie…oh, my Josie…look what you've done to me…made me do…I didn't mean to hurt you. If I did…"

She kissed him back, tenderly. "You have something else on your mind…besides me, don't you?"

"Yes…how did you know?"

She gave him no hint or help, leaving him to his own choice.

"I've decided to stay longer than I intended…You're the reason. I'm waiting on a friend of mine—best lawyer around by far—to help me out."

"Same one you had up in Wyoming?"

"Why, yes…how did you know?"

She began to cry. She had made the connection. It would no longer be George or Butch, but George now in Butch's clothing. She felt so alone and so betrayed—by herself.

He tried to comfort her as best as he could without fully understanding the terrible turmoil churning inside her. "Was it something I said, Josie? Was it?"

She dried her tears with his handkerchief. "Maybe we'd better go now…unless you have something more to tell me?"

Josie started to walk away, hoping against hope that he'd say what she wanted to hear before she reached the front porch. Then it'd be too late—too late for her, and for him.

He caught up with her. "Listen to me," he begged. "I'm going to change…Just give me a chance to prove it…I can change."

"Is that all?"

She didn't wait for his answer; instead she walked at a rapid clip toward the ranch house.

George had to run to catch up. "Josie, Josie, hear me out! I love you! I love you! Doesn't that count for anything anymore? What about tonight?"

She turned around to face him. He'd never seen anybody so determined to get her way, so hurt, and yes, so in love. "You have this winter to prove yourself to me. If you ride out of here next spring when the chinooks come, I'll know for sure it was only Butch Cassidy playing possum again, trying to act like George Parker."

Annie snuck a peek at Butch kissing Josie goodnight on the front porch; then she walked down the hall, intent on waiting 'til morning before confronting her sister with the hard, cold truth as she saw it. On second thought, she decided the sooner the better for Josie.

Josie took off her shoes before she walked past Beemis' bedroom. Her good news concerning George Parker could wait 'til Beemis had a chance to sleep off his Aunt Maybelle nightcaps. Breakfast always brought out the best in her uncle, she reasoned. Maybe he'd even offer a word or two of encouragement once she told him how things stood between George and herself. Maybe he'd even go so far as to call him George instead of Butch, just to please her. Maybe? Maybe? Maybe?

"Oh my gosh!" she gasped. "Thought you'd hit the hay long ago when I saw Deke leave for the bunkhouse! Why, that must've been a good hour ago…"

Annie motioned for Josie to come sit with her on the edge of Josie's bed. "Is he a good kisser? Better than Cleve? Been watching you two all evening!"

"That's none of your business, Ann Barnett," Josie snapped back. "But just so you can put your mind at rest, yes, he is! You're not here to talk to me about the way George kisses; c'mon, Sis, out with it, so we can both get some sleep."

"Thought you liked your men taller. Butch can't be more than two thimbles taller than you, if that! Cleve's at least four inches above you!"

Josie was beginning to see red. "His name is George!"

"No, it's Butch Cassidy, and that's why I'm here! To talk some sense into you if you'll only take the time to listen. Will you?"

"If I do, then can we get some sleep?"

"How serious is it between you two?"

Josie stood up. The lantern's light only enhanced the sparkle in her eyes. "George told me he loves me. Gosh, Sis, isn't that the best news yet?" Then she added, "I thought it would never come…him being so polite, so careful, and so honest."

"Bet that he tells that to the first available woman he sees after he's holed up somewhere on the run from the law."

Annie's comment brought a far different answer out of Josie. "No, Sis, think about what you just said. He's too careful about things like that...not his style at all."

"Okay, I may be off a bit on that score." She rose to add emphasis to her next point. "Say he really does love you, but that doesn't change anything. Someday a lawman will outsmart him and either put him in jail or a bullet in his head. And sooner or later, once the reward money gets big enough, Butch had better watch his backside or else one of his own bunch will nail him to collect the money. Either way, that's no future for him or you!"

Josie hugged Annie to death. "Yes, there is! Yes, there is! George has promised me he's going to change!"

"He's in too deep already! He has no way out! And our uncle has told me about the gang of small-timers that hangs around him, looking to make a big name for themselves right along with Butch."

"George has a good friend, some big-name lawyer who's working to get him a pardon or some kind of amnesty deal on that Idaho hold-up. Once he gets that for George, he's home free to start a new life with me!"

Annie braced both arms against Josie's shoulders. "Uncle Beemis has been doing some checking up on your Mister George Parker. He was gonna give you the bad news at breakfast. Thought I'd try to soften the blow tonight."

Josie was near tears. "What bad news? I don't understand! There's only one mess that needs to be straightened out...only one...and George has promised me—"

"Wrong, Sis! There's a wanted poster on Butch for a bank job he pulled off at Telluride, Colorado, three years ago!"

"That only makes two! Not so many that there's no hope! Look how you've changed after you met Deke! George can do the same thing! He promised me!"

"Alright, for your sake, let's suppose Butch does change! To what? How will he make a living? Uncle figures most of that Idaho money went to that big-shot lawyer you just told me about to spring Butch's old gang buddy, Matt Warner, from a fouled-up shooting mess in Utah. That's why Butch showed up here in the first place!"

Josie shot right back. "See! See! George never forgets a friend! Look how much and how important loyalty and friendship are to him. Think what it will be when we're talking about love! His love for me!"

Annie turned away. She began smiling; then the smile turned to laughter, the kind that always brings out the tears when her sides hurt so much. "My sides are killing me…I can't help it…this is so funny…I'm sorry, Sis…really I am…"

Josie was furious. "Funny? You said funny! Love is funny?"

Annie tried to wipe away the tears. "Not love! Us, Sis! If we aren't a pair! I'm trying to straighten you out…trying my damnedest to be like you…to be your mother…like you always used to try that on me…"

Josie began to lighten up. Yes, she could see the humor in it, too. "And I was acting just like you used to whenever Uncle or I had to ride a little hard on you 'cause that's the only way we could get your attention. You're right, we sure are a pair!"

They sat down together on the bed, hugging and holding each other close.

"Josie?"

"Yeah."

"One good thing came out tonight."

"Yeah? What?"

"Shows we really do look out for each other, shows that we care…shows that our parents would've been proud of us. Shows that we'll take on the whole world if we have to…no matter what's said or who said it about us!"

"Gull-dang it! Ah ain't gonna tell ya agin! Lemme be! Dammit to hell, Deke, leave me be! The day Joe Cady kain't make twenty paces to a buggy is the day they'd better plant me fer good!"

Four people had to stand by and wait for him to take one agonizing step after another to Beemis, waiting for him in the buggy. They dared not try to help him; no matter how much they wanted to, they could only do one thing: watch in near-tearful admiration.

He moved ever so slowly, grimacing hard with each painful step. Twice, he tried to straighten up, then decided the effort took too much out of him, so the old crust, cantankerous and ornery to the bitter end, did it his way! And God help the man or woman who thought otherwise!

This was the day Annie had dreaded, the day she knew had to come. It took all she could do to keep from shouting: *Go back to the bunkhouse, Joe! There'll be no getting rid of you today or any other day.*

Halfway to the buggy, he tottered and weaved, he was so racked with pain. He blinked again and again, trying to clear his watery eyes enough so he could make the last ten paces. Annie turned away, so old Joe couldn't see her cry.

Old Joe reached the buggy and sagged against it. He used it as his prop against his back while he took a much-needed breather before gathering enough strength and gumption to force his legs to raise up high enough to make the buggy step and on into the buggy. He looked around at the three anxious people ready to rush to his side should be falter. Then he picked her out, his Annie, the one with the honey-gold hair. He put on his best face, wiped the perspiration from his forehead with his shirt sleeve, clicked his chompers to make sure they were working, and yelled out. "Well, are ya just gonna stand there? Don't I rate some kinda kiss or at least a hug fer puttin' up with ya all these years?"

Annie made a beeline straight into his arms. Her tears came down in buckets, and she didn't care who saw it or what they thought because she loved this old fossil, this twisted weed of a man, who'd taught her everything about horses since day one.

He stroked her hair. "Now, now, Annie, don't go to usin' up all yer water…Save some fer Deke on the day you two gets hitched."

She looked over at him, red eyes and all. "I'm gonna cry all I want to…and you'd better not try to stop me, either!"

Josie held her close, grateful for all the attention she gave him. Finally, half out of embarrassment, he said what was in his heart. "We sure 'nough rode a lot'a range together, small fry, didn't we?"

Her sniffles shut down. "Yes, Joe, we sure as heck did!"

"Still 'member the first time I saw you down to the horse barn…weren't a'feer'd a' nuthin'. Guess you was 'bout the size of a grasshopper—still draggin' your diaper you was—and wanted me to set you way up on top of a horse. Plum scared the liver outta your Aunt Maybelle, you did. Tried to tell her you was a natural if ever I see'd one. She never paid me no mind 'cause she was so worried 'bout you. And now look atcha! Annie, you done grow'd up on me! That's what ya done alright…ain't got no grasshopper no more! Don't need no more ridin' or ropin' lessons, neither! After your uncle see'd you back East, says there ain't none better! Nowhere!"

She kissed him. "Thank you from the bottom of my heart…not just for teaching me to ride and rope, but for all you've done for me. How can I ever thank you enough?"

He looked at her. A most serious expression mixed in with the wrinkles on his forehead and across his boney cheeks. "By bein' a good partner with Deke." Then he looked in Deke's direction. "Got somethun' that needs sayin' to you, young man. Better not hear one word 'bout you not treatin' my little Annie right, 'cause if'n I do, I'm gonna come back'n kick the Billy Hell outta you!"

Deke answered. "Don't worry, Joe, that'll never happen."

"Alright! Ya been told!"

Annie looked up at her uncle. The tears started down her cheeks again. "Please, Uncle Beemis...please let Joe stay. He won't be any trouble...I'll take care of him...please!"

Annie had thrust Beemis into the very middle of her emotional dilemma. Old Joe took her and Beemis off the hook. "Thanks fer them nice words, Annie, but my sister is 'spectin' me shortly, and if'n I don't show up, then thar's hell to pay out in Californy!"

Two days later, Josie came into Annie's bedroom. "Got an idea to get you out of the dumps since Uncle took old Joe to Rock Springs to catch the train. Now that you're the boss 'til he gets back, how about givin' Markham Ranch a day off? Do us all some good, Sis! Especially you!"

"Alright, I'll do it! What'll we do?"

"Get Deke to hitch up the two-seater and take us over to Jarvey's Mercantile. Mister Jarvey's put in a whole new line of women's things. Let's do some shopping!"

They arrived at Jarvey's Mercantile in good spirits, even Annie. The two women rushed into the store and oohed and aahed over the latest fashions from back East.

Josie held up a woman's corset. "You're lucky, Sis, with that hourglass figure of yours, it'll be years before you'll need this. What's Deke doing, standing outside with the team and buggy?"

Annie laughed. "I invited him in, but when I told him I'd be lookin' at women's unmentionables, his face turned beet red, and he said he'd rather wait outside."

Josie chided, "He's not henpecked enough, Sis, that's your fault."

"Deke's changed a lot for the better, but don't expect miracles."

Josie decided on the corset. Annie went over to the new line of pantaloons. "Look, Sis, they're cut lots shorter, even have a peek-a-boo slit up the sides. That's for me!"

They arrived back at the ranch with three boxes of unmentionables. Deke dropped them off in front of the main house, then returned to the barn to unharness and walk both mares to their stables. Seconds later, he came racing up the front steps. He walked in on both sisters getting ready to model their purchases for each other.

"Excuse me, excuse me!" he exclaimed. "Better get down to the stables, pronto! Got something to show you!"

They followed him down, wondering what on earth could've brought him on the run. Deke swung both doors wide open.

Josie gasped. "Four quarters of beef! Hanging just as neat and clean as you please! Someone even trimmed most of the fat! Wonder who?"

Deke had his say. "Not who, Josie, but why?"

Annie took her shot at the riddle. "Maybe Butch has changed, and maybe he hasn't, but it sure looks like he's gettin' in plenty of practice just in case he feels he's a mite rusty cutting up meat again!"

"Do you suppose George bought this beef before he butchered it?"

"Well now, Sis, what do you really think?"

The long winter months edged ever closer toward spring, which did little to comfort Josie. Almost without exception, whenever George Parker paid a social call on her, she would take him aside and badger him about any news concerning a federal pardon or amnesty deal. After a half-dozen or so such grillings, Parker's cool composure went on a real meltdown. His eyes spoke volumes, but he held his tongue in check. "Josie, even a high-priced lawyer like Douglas Preston has to let the system work its way. These things take time!"

To that, she snapped back. "I sure hope not 'cause you're running out of time with me, Mister Parker!"

Other things started to put a definite strain on their relationship. The more gossip she heard about what was going on at Butch's cabin, the less time she gave him. Rumor had it he was about to fly the coop. No doubt another bank or payroll had been targeted. All he was waiting for were the chinooks, and then, poof! He'd be gone, leaving Josie with nothing but fond memories and a broken heart, possibly beyond repair.

Cassidy's gang, at this point, consisted of Elza Lay and Robert Meeks. They were the only true professionals, each carefully recruited by Butch for their speciality. The other gang members were rank amateurs, cowboys or drifters who found themselves on the wrong side of the law for one reason or another. Their combined talents were no match for the threesome, and Butch treated them accordingly, as evidenced by their ever-changing numbers, coming and going.

"Stack the dishes, Sis; it's time Deke learned to dance!"

Deke rose from the supper table, a visibly shaken man. "But...but, Annie," he protested, "I ain't never been to a dance in my life! Got two left feet that gets tangled up just comin' near anything that looks or sounds like dance-hall music!"

Annie smiled at her shrinking violet. "You got a choice, dear! Either let Josie and me teach you how by the time our big basket social comes up next month or else!"

"Or else what?"

"Or else I go alone and dance with the first rancher that asks me. And if he happens to mention how nice I look or ask if I'm spoken for, I'm gon' to have to tell him the truth."

"You are spoken for! Sorta..."

"Still waitin' on that marriage proposal, Deke! Now I'll just betcha if I gave a hint or two, maybe even offered a little encouragement, I could get some lonely, good-looking rancher to pop the question. What'a you think, love?"

"Let's get to that foot stompin' you was talkin' about!"

Beemis smiled at the way his Annie was trying to hogtie Deke. One way or another, he knew she was going to be hitched before too many days passed. He picked up his coffee cup. "I'll be in the front parlor. When Deke's ready for some square-dance callin,' come get me."

"We ain't got no dance music, Annie! Now what?"

She led him by the hand to the organ. "Oh yes we have. I still remember enough chords and enough dance tunes to get you over the hump." She called back to Josie. "C'mon, Sis, you're gonna have to suffer through some stepped-on feet for a spell."

Annie rolled back the keyboard cover. Two minutes of running a few scales up and down the keyboard and she was ready to proceed. She turned to Deke and Josie. "Okay, this is a simple beat. Just listen to it for a minute, then try to move your feet with this beat. Josie will show you how to hold your dance partner. When she moves, you move with her. Got it, Deke?"

Josie showed Deke their starting stance. "Don't be so stiff, Deke! Relax and you'll start to enjoy this. Okay, Annie, try it again! Slow, real slow!"

Deke moved stiff as a board with Josie doing the guiding.

"Ouch! Ouch!" Josie yelled. "You're stepping all over my feet! Stay off them!"

Deke stopped. "I'm sorry, Josie! Tried to tell you folks, I can't dance!"

"Take your boots off! Then we'll try it again."

This time Deke stayed off Josie's feet. Two more minutes of near-misses produced some positive results. "Alright, Deke, you're doing much better…much better. Gotta loosen you more…smile at me…that should help."

They made their first complete circle around the room. "Say, I'm startin' to get the hang of this…Kinda like it…"

Annie called out. "You're still holding Josie too far from you. Let her move a bit closer…Yes, that's better…now keep your body that distance. That's called a safe, respectful distance…for both a man and a woman. Anything closer is reserved for just me and you, Deke, when we dance together. Understand what I'm driving at?"

Deke led for the first time. "Yeah, Annie, I caught your drift. Just think, when I'm dancin' with you, I get to squeeze my honey real tight! Right in front of God'n everybody! Wow! Ain't that something!"

Annie picked up the beat slightly; Deke had no trouble keeping pace. Suddenly Josie jerked away and ran out of the room.

"Annie! What'd I do wrong now? I never so much as touched her toes! I swear!"

"Not you, Deke, it's that damned Mormon! Stay put! I'll be right back!"

Annie found Josie in her bedroom, crying her heart out. Annie took a handkerchief out of the top dresser drawer, then patiently sat on the edge of the bed. Finally, Josie raised her head out of the pillow. "Oh, Sis, I'm losing him…I just know it. All I hear is rumors and more rumors about him…It's tearing me apart."

Annie handed Josie the hankie. "Go ahead, Sugarplum, give it a good blow! Hope you blow Butch right out of your life too! Give Cleve Dreschler another chance; you won't go wrong with him. Good time to start over with Cleve would be at the social. I'm sure he'll be there…A dance or two…and it'll be like old times again with him."

Josie sat up. "Did I tell you the latest about George?"

"No, but I've a feeling I'm going to hear about Mister Wonderful anyway. Shoot!"

"I've put up with an awful lot since George came to dinner that first night…but now this…Oh, Sis, it's bad, real bad! I can't take it! I won't take it!"

"Fine! Now let's get those eyes dried and get back to Deke's lessons."

"Minnie Crouse! Have you heard what she's been doin' lately?"

"Takin' sandwiches and liquor up to Butch's cabin real regular is what the gossip cows have been tellin' me…"

"That's just half of it! Heard Butch kicks that bunch of no-good riffraff out so he can be alone with her whenever he needs a woman…Guess it's been goin' on for some time…"

Annie sat awhile, deep in thought. Finally, she put her arm around Josie. "I don't have much use for Butch Cassidy—never did…never will. So what I'm about to tell you comes twice as hard from me. Never met a man who is so careful about everything, and I do mean everything! From the way he wets that cowlick down to the way he provides entertainment for his gang, including whiskey and grub. But I've never heard one story about him getting drunk as a skunk or bedding down with the nearest available whore. Oh, I know Minnie's just itching to get wedded and bedded down by Butch, but that'll never happen because there's a streak of honor and decency in him that doesn't fit the sleaze and the slime that runs with him. Like I said, he's so careful about everything, and that includes his women. That's why he picked you! Like it or lump it, the man's honorable and gets respect wherever he goes! Just think what Butch could do with his life if he ever went straight! There'd be no stopping him!"

Josie's tears showed up again. "Thanks for saying what you did about George. I never knew 'til I met him how much loving a man can hurt, but it does, all the way down to my toes."

Annie got up. "I'll tell Deke we'll practice his dance lessons another time."

"No, no, Sis, he's starting to move his feet in the right direction; there's hope! Just give me a few minutes to freshen up. Wouldn't want my new brother-in-law seeing me like this."

Annie stopped short of the bedroom door. "Deke's still a ways from being that, Sis."

"No, he isn't. He's been saving almost every dollar. Told me he hardly sits in on the Sunday afternoon poker games anymore. I helped him with a suggestion. Can't tell you any more or else it wouldn't be much of a surprise, now would it? But I can tell you, he'll be popping the question mighty soon! Mighty soon! Kinda goes along with his big surprise!"

"My goodness, Sis! What's Aunt Maybelle's good silverware and linen tablecloth doin' out?

"Gettin' ready for next Sunday's early dinner! George'll be here!"

Annie knew that in Josie's mind, it was way past showdown time—way

144

past. Two things had happened three weeks before the Hole's big social bash: its annual basket auction and dance. Most of the old-timers started jawing about the chinooks coming early this spring. It was a good sign, they told each other. The freight haulers from Rock Springs had already been down, the passes were open once more, and things were certainly on the move again.

That supposed good news had exactly the opposite effect on poor Josie. A rash of new rumors hit the Hole with the force of a late summer lightning storm. Butch Cassidy was clearing out. Butch Cassidy's federal pardon fell through. Butch Cassidy had proposed to Minnie Crouse. Butch Cassidy was already married and had a good Mormon wife and a passel of kids waiting for him over in Utah.

Saturday came and Annie went straight to her uncle for help. "Josie's in no shape to be putting on a big Sunday spread for Butch or anybody else. Go to her! Tell her you've decided against it! Make up any excuse you can think of, but don't let her do it! I lost count of the number of times I've heard her crying herself to sleep lately."

Beemis mulled over the situation. He read the deep concern in Annie's eyes and on her face. "Damn that Cassidy! He'll show up like nothin's happened. He'll unfold his napkin and tuck it right where it's supposed to be and go on bein' nice, *Mormon nice!*"

"Mormon nice? Don't think I ever heard you use that expression before."

"Didn't need to before Cassidy stared courtin' our Josie."

"Well, what does it mean?"

Beemis strutted around the parlor, trying to work up the proper tone to deliver what was most certainly on his mind ever since George Parker had said grace at his table. "Okay, Annie, here goes! Damned Mormons make you feel welcome…up to a point. Maybe even share with you…up to a point. They're always tryin' to convert you…up to a point. But neither are you goin' to be pushin' them…up to any point. That's Josie's Mister Parker or Butch Cassidy or whatever else he calls himself! He's Mormon nice…up to a point!"

George Parker was appalled the way Josie looked that Sunday afternoon, though he did his best not to show it. The months of half-truths, bald-faced lies, and circumstantial gossip, fed by fresh rounds of more of the same, had taken their toll on her. She looked thin and pale; there was no life left in her face or her eyes. Her hair was unkempt. Even her clothes didn't seem to fit or belong to her anymore.

She had aged overnight beyond her young years. It was as though Parker had held Josie's love for him hostage. He might just as well have used his gun or threat of violence. The result would've been the same: total destruction of Josie's happiness, to say nothing of her feelings or emotional stability.

Josie came out of the kitchen, carrying a fancy tray of sliced roast beef. The aroma tantalized the taste buds of everyone gathered around. Two steps from the table, she stumbled. The delicious roast hit the floor, and Aunt Maybelle's best serving tray shattered into a hundred pieces, flying all directions.

Annie rushed to help her sister. Josie sat down, right in the middle of all the mess, and looked blankly about. She seemed to be in a daze.

Annie shook her slightly, then whispered, "Sis, what are you doing?"

For what seemed like an eternity, there was no reply. Josie blinked once or twice, then snapped out of it. "I'm looking for a serving piece large enough to put George's meat back on it, so I can serve him. What's wrong with that?"

Josie slowly rose with Annie's help. Sure enough, she'd found a sliver of the tray large enough for just one slice of roast beef. Her clothes and apron were spattered with the gravy she'd poured over the meat. Slices of roast beef stuck to her, then dropped off when she moved toward Parker. "Here's your dinner, George," she calmly said. "Before you eat, there's a few questions that need answering."

Parker was startled by Josie's actions. He then realized she was on the brink of losing her sanity. "Alright, Josie, I'll do my best."

Josie didn't scream or yell or hurl accusations. It was uncanny to say the least.

"You've been making love with Minnie Crouse, haven't you, George?"

He turned around to catch Beemis' and Annie's reactions, wondering if his answer would serve any useful purpose.

"Go ahead, Parker, answer her!"

Beemis' comment left no doubt in Parker's mind that only a true confession would satisfy everybody in the dining room.

He held Josie's hand and looked her dead in the eyes. "As God as my witness, I've never slept with that woman. Minnie started that story to shake you up. Hoped you'd get mad enough to break it up between us. I'm here to tell you, I've never had any feelings for her. It's you I love, not her."

Josie released his hand, then toyed with a speck of gravy on her dress, oblivious to all the other meat and gravy stains on her apron and dress. She stopped picking at the small spot and concentrated on Parker instead. "The chinooks have come…That means you're going to leave me, aren't you, George?"

"No, no, Josie, that's not correct. I may leave later, but not now." Then he hastened to add, "I don't ever want to leave you…Do you understand what I've said?"

Josie gave no hint whatsoever that she believed or understood him. Then it became apparent that she'd rehearsed a certain set of questions over and over in her mind until they took over every waking or subconscious thought she'd had about Parker. She pulled out her chair and sat next to him, then leaned over to get even closer. "You keep telling me you've changed…Does that mean you no longer care for me or does that mean you've changed from George Parker back into Butch Cassidy again?"

Parker was in a quandary.

"Answer her!" Annie demanded of Parker. "We'd all like to hear what you have to say!"

Again he held her hands. "I've changed for the better ever since I've met you, Josie…I'll always be George Parker when I'm with you."

"And when you're not with me. Who are you then, George?"

Again Parker was in a dilemma—one of his own making. "I'm still Butch Cassidy."

Josie shook her head and blinked several times, trying to sort things out in her muddled mind. She rose quietly, still waiting for the right words to click in. She snatched the broken tray piece away. A wildness entered her eyes. Everybody saw a volcano slowly building within her. It erupted. "GET THE HELL OUT OF MY LIFE, BUTCH CASSIDY! I NEVER WANT TO SEE YOU AGAIN!"

Butch rose, dumbfounded.

"You heard her!" Beemis exclaimed. "Now go!"

Annie led Josie away from the table. "Come, Sis, let's get you cleaned up and ready for bed."

Josie broke down, sobbing her poor heart out. "Couldn't take any more, Sis! I can't handle it! Can't take any more! I know he told the truth…but they're all lies to me! Every one!"

"Is Josie going to be alright?"

Annie closed the door, then they walked down the hall. She'd never seen her uncle so worried and so agitated. "There's nothing left of her…Body next to nothing…mind just a nudge away from looking like her body. Never believed true love could do this to anyone…least of all, to Josie. She was always such a rock. Always there when I needed her. Now she needs me…more than ever. When you hear the pots and pans rattling around the kitchen, I'll be me, not Josie. I'm gonna do my best until we can get her back on her feet. Thank God, it's over between them!"

Beemis helped Annie clean up the mess. He picked up the last broken piece from the serving tray. "Good thing your aunt wasn't here to see this; we'd'a had two down the hall instead of one."

Annie came into Josie's room. "Are you sure you're ready for the basket social and dance? It's only been three weeks…No doubt Cleve will be there…good chance he will too!"

Josie turned around on her vanity stool. There was new life in her cheeks, and a fresh coating of blue shown in her eyes to match her dress. "You don't have to say 'he' anymore when you mean Butch."

"No more George? It's Butch from now on, right?"

"I haven't packed my picnic basket…had too much on my mind lately…"

Annie hugged her big sister. "Not to worry, I've already taken care of that. It won't look or taste like your food, but it'll just have to do for this time."

Charley Crouse's schoolhouse was set for a real night of socializing and dancing, Brown's Hole style. It would be a chance for some genuine toe tapping and lots of boot-stomping, in-your-face kind of music.

Beemis was perched at the entrance door in his usual chair, the official collector of all firearms, knives and assorted weaponry that each man might possess. He looked so dignified in this capacity. In front of him was a half-filled old dynamite box, a good sign that the dance was well underway with plenty of people.

"Drop your hardware, Butch! No one passes unless he's willin' to part with it. I'll see that it's returned on your way out after the basket social or if you leave before."

Beemis' order drew at least fifty pairs of eyes, each wondering if Cassidy would comply. Butch rested one boot on the corner of the box. He smiled graciously, all the while searching the crowd for one very special lady.

"She's here," Beemis growled. "You've already put her through seven seasons of hell; leave her alone."

"I only want one dance with Josie. If she won't dance with me, I'll leave."

Cassidy saw Beemis tap the box twice with his boot. "In the box, Butch, or it's no go!"

Cassidy turned around to the other two men with him. Off came his gun belt. "Do as I do; you're among friends here! This man will keep his word; you'll get your guns back when you leave."

Elza Lay scowled a bit, but followed his boss' lead by unbuckling his gun belt. Fast fingers carefully wrapped his belt around his two six-shooters as he handed them to Beemis for deposit. Lay's eyes traveled the crowd quickly; he felt naked without his trusty sidearms at his fingertips, yet he knew he'd better follow his boss' example or he'd never set foot on the dance floor.

Bob Meeks, the third member, gave the entire crowd the once-over, making sure he spotted nothing but friendly faces.

"Your guns, Sir!"

Beemis' request startled him. Butch turned around. There was no mistaking the stern look on his face as he stared at Meek. Meek's face reddened a mite; then he reached for his belt buckle. The belt dropped off his hips and fell toward the box. Quicker than lightening, Meek caught the belt in midair, stark evidence that he'd been mighty busy doing something besides rustling cattle.

"Thank you! You're new around these parts aren'tcha?"

Meeks pushed on by Beemis without an answer one way or another. Fifty mouths gave a collective sigh of relief when the three melted into the crowd. The dance got into high gear once more as the square dance caller went to work, ably supported by two fiddles, one beat-up guitar that'd seen better days, and a young lady doing her best to keep from making too many mistakes on her concertina.

Annie and Deke sashayed around the dance floor to "Turkey in the Straw."

"How'm I doing?"

She looked up and smiled. "Not bad! You're getting the hang of it, as you say."

They spotted Butch standing alone in the crowd.

"Look at him go after that cowlick. Saw him wet his hand and pat it down. Wonder why he does that all the time?"

Deke kicked up one boot and slammed it down hard, just as half a dozen other men did. "Heard tell, up in Rock Springs, that Butch got grazed by a stray bullet in his early days of horse stealin'. There ain't one drop of volunteer blood in me or anybody else here willin' to find out for sure."

The evening wore on in fine fettle as Henry Ettleman would say. The better the dance, the more petticoats that swished and swirled, and the louder the men's boots stomped on the hardwood floor. The strains of a beautiful waltz drifted out over the crowd, a signal for young and old alike to find a partner. The slow music thinned the wallflower crowd out considerably. It seemed most everybody could handle a waltz.

Butch wasted no time getting to Josie's side. "May I have this dance, Josie?"

His eyes pleaded. The magnetism between them was stronger than ever.

Cleve Dreschler took exception to what he saw. His dark-brown eyes flashed. His husky voice erupted. "Miss Barnett is with me, in case you hadn't noticed. You know, Cassidy, without your guns, you look kinda undressed! Three inches smaller, and a good twenty pounds under my hundred-eighty! You bother her again, and we might just step outside to find out what holds your pants up, your reputation or the real thing."

Josie knew it was time to head off trouble, big trouble. "It's alright, Cleve! I did promise Mister Cassidy one dance." She quickly took his hand as they threaded their way through the few remaining wallflowers to reach the dance floor.

Neither spoke a word as Butch proved he was as graceful on the floor as he was masterful off of it. He tried to hold her close; she politely, but firmly, resisted. They made a full circle around the floor, one wanting the slow body-beat to go on forever, the other wanting only one thing: to be free of the emotional tug that had torn her heart to shreds.

"Why did you call me Mister Cassidy when you know good and well it's George Parker?"

No answer for another fifty steps. "Because George Parker no longer exists. George Parker is wanted by the same law that wants Butch Cassidy. And George Parker has been robbed by Butch Cassidy, who has taken over his mind, body, and soul."

They danced on. "Did I ever tell you how beautiful you really are? That I can't leave you alone because I love you like no other woman I've ever known?"

More silence. Josie refused to answer, yet Parker knew she wanted to hear his words of love. She allowed their bodies to touch, then backed away to a respectful distance.

He moved his head closer to hers. Her perfume stirred his sense, his mind, and his lips. He whispered close to her ear. "Please marry me. Please, Josie?"

Again there came no answer, only two bodies caught in wondrous, slow motion, telegraphing their love for one another in the midst of others.

They circled past Cleve, who waited on the sideline, arms folded impatiently, tapping his boots, trying to make the slow waltz speed up, so Josie would be back with him.

"Four months, or even one month ago, I would've said yes because I believed you when you said you would change. The man I marry must be with me always. The man I marry must want a family…and when the day's work is done and our children put to bed, I want him to take his time holding me close. I want to feel his love in me…his seed, too…so that next morning when I leave my bed, I will feel proud to carry his love in me until we touch again. None of what I said sounds like either Butch Cassidy or George Parker."

They danced on, knowing this would be the last time they would ever hold each other close enough to whisper words lovers often do out on the dance floor. Their bodies, their minds and their souls danced as one—one last time.

The waltz went into its last refrain. Both felt helpless to do anything about it except look into each other's eyes to gauge once more the depth of their love for each other, despite their obvious differences.

Josie moved closer. She felt a need to feel what she had been cheated out of: everlasting happiness with this man who changed names to fit the situation. This time her lips brushed his cheek. "No woman ever loved or felt about a man the way I do about you. A thousand times, I've asked myself, why? Why did you come into my life too late to change? Why? Why tear my heart apart until I nearly lost my mind over what might have been? Why?"

George Parker, alias Butch Cassidy, had no answers either. The planner, the ultimate perfectionist, the man who could mold men into doing his bidding, couldn't even come up with one simple answer to what fate had foisted upon them.

The waltz ended. Its finality hit them with a crushing reality neither were prepared for. They walked across the floor, each looking straight ahead, neither daring to cast another glance at the other for fear their hands and their hearts would become hopelessly entangled.

Parker deposited Josie in front of Cleve. "Thank you, Miss Barnett…for the dance."

Josie watched George Parker disappear back into the crowd, but not from her heart. Beemis hailed his old friend, Henry Ettleman. "How 'bout spellin' me off for a bit? Need to see PA Jones and stop by Speck before the break."

Henry sauntered over. "Sure, Beemis, I ain't doin' nuthin' 'cept wishin' I was twenty years younger. " He pointed toward his wife, holding court with some of the other ranchers' wives. "We watched that outlaw dance with Josie…Gotta say this 'bout 'em, both shoulda paid more attention to where their feet was headin'. Nowadays, the young folks don't seem to get much kick outta dancin' the way Etta n' me used to. Guess they got other things on their minds…"

Beemis picked up his cane and disappeared out the front door with a lively polka filling his ears. He made his nature visit to the outhouse, then headed straight for a small covered wagon with its end gate dropped down for business.

"Hey, Speck, I like the way you put hinges on that rack. Now you don't have to reach back or hop inside to get my favorite whiskey!"

"Yes, Sir, Mistuh Beemis, ah got yo favorite right here!" The Negro poured Beemis a hefty shot into a tin cup, then handed it to him. "This is mah best stuff…good ol' Kaintucky mash! Saves it fo' special folks like you."

Beemis downed the whiskey, then handed the cup back. "And what do the rest of the folks get?"

Speck laughed. "Depends on who doin' the askin' and how they's treats me. Some gits purty good stuff…others git what ah calls my come-down whiskey. After two, three drinks, they's come down an awful long ways. Guts gits to actin' up somethin' terrible…"

Speck handed Beemis his cup back. "Ah knows ya got important job inside…so jus' give ya one little snort dis time. Right, Mistuh Beemis?

Beemis smiled, then drank slowly. "Boy, this sure rides a smooth trail down. Thanks again, Speck!"

The lantern's light caught the Negro's friendly face. "Ah been sittin' here all even' listenin' to all dat music goin' on inside. Yo folks gotta be havin' one heckava good time! Man, when all dem boots comes stompin' down, then ah knows there's gonna be plenty a' men comin' out soon to git Speck's whiskey. Business sho' been good tonight! Umm! Umm!"

Beemis handed him a five-dollar gold piece. "Gotta' go! Old Henry's mindin' the firearms box. Better get back; he doesn't exactly strike a whole lotta fear into any of those young hotheads inside who might suddenly think they're real naked without their sidearms."

"Mistuh Beemis?"

"What is it, Speck?"

"Dat Butch Cassidy's inside…is he a real badass like dey say?"

The Negro watched Beemis chuckle. "Naw, Speck, he's just another good Mormon farm boy gone bad! Found out he can pick a gun outta a holster a lot faster then pitchin' a fork full of hay, so he's turned to outlawin' big time! He'll catch a bullet or a knife in his back one day, and it'll all be over, except maybe his reputation!"

Charley Crouse said the magic words just as Beemis got back to his station. "Break time, folks! Break time! There's lanterns already lit inside the outhouses for your convenience!"

Josie grabbed her sister's hand. "C'mon, Annie, we can still beat the rest of the women out to see MA Jones! Got something to tell you!"

The two ran like frightened jackrabbits looking for a hole—in this case a two-holer.

Nearly out of breath, Josie closed the door to the women's outhouse and slid the wooden latch in place.

"Okay, Sis, what's so important that it couldn't wait?"

Josie squealed in pure delight. "Butch proposed to me!"

Annie lifted her dress to clear the seat boards. "Thank God, you said Butch, not George! You turned him down flatter than a flapjack, didn't you?"

Josie rearranged her rumpled dress. "Hardest decision I'll probably ever make in all my life. Did what my head told me to do…didn't listen to my heart this time."

"Good girl! Cleve's your type! No future waitin' on Butch to come back…after he keeps pullin' off one job after another. Beemis thinks Butch is way overdue…only stuck around this long…"

"Because of me! Right, Sis?"

"You said it, Sugarplum, not me!"

A not-so-dainty fist rapped soundly on the door. "Hey, you two, get off the throne! Been waitin' long enough!"

Another female voice seconded the motion. "Yeah, you two, either wipe it, cut it, or squeeze it! There's others out here, you know!"

While the ladies waited in their line, the men also lined up at Speck's rolling chuck-wagon bar. One by one, Speck remembered most of the customers' favorite whiskey and promptly served him, handing each a tin cup should the man prefer to pour instead of being a bottle baby, as the ranchers called it, when one of them drank their whiskey straight.

Bob Meeks was clearly out of sorts, being the last to be served. Butch's wiry sidekick was on the prod, having danced with one rancher's wife, who gave him plenty of reason to think she'd be willing to slip out of the dance to accommodate his needs under the pretext of paying MA Jones a visit. She pushed everything she had into his tough, lean body, including two oversized, voluptuous breasts, while he discreetly massaged them under the very nose of the woman's husband. While she wasn't exactly a looker, she wasn't a dog, either. Meeks figured some smooth spirits from the bar would help him forget her face. After all, once he prodded her, either in her own buggy or against its side, the darkness would let him concentrate on what needed doing the most.

"Don't 'member yo bottle, Sir! Would you kindly point to it?"

Meek's temper exploded. "Ain't got one, Nigger! Now gimme your best! Damned old fart inside made me drop my hardware or else I'd learn you a thing or two!"

"Dat's Mistuh Beemis, Sir, an' he ain't no old fart, neither! You talk like dat n' ol' Speck here ain't gonna serve you, no more, no how!"

Meek steadied one of the two lanterns hanging from the wagon's frame. "C'mere! Let's have a real, close look!"

Speck obeyed.

"Well, I'll be damned! A light-skinned, freckled-faced nigger! Now get this, nigger! Fetch me a bottle and be damned quick about it! Got a woman inside who needs my attention. Hop to it, nigger!"

"No, Sir, not one drink 'til Speck gets a please an' thank yo, *Sir*!"

"Alright! Alright! Please gimme a drink, *Sir*!"

Speck reached back into his stock. He handed Meek an unopened bottle.

Meek hurriedly broke the seal and raised it to his lips. "Hey, wait a minute! How come you didn't give me one of your other open bottles!"

"Dat's ma best stuff. Saves it fo' special folks…like you, Sir!"

Meek took one long, long, healthy swig.

"Yo' done had 'nuff, Sir! Deed yo has!"

"Don't tell me when I've had enough, nigger!" Meek deliberately sucked on the bottle until he had over half of it down his gullet. He looked again at Speck, who started to say something, then took another healthy swig. Finally, he handed the bottle back.

"How much, Nigger?"

Speck put the bottle back. He raised his hand. "Dat's alright! No charge! It's on the house! Time yo' get back to dat lady what wants yo!"

Meeks made his way back to the dance, carrying a pretty good jag of Speck's cheap whiskey locked hard inside his belly. Speck had taken an immediate dislike to the outlaw and served the worst rotgut he could lay his hands on instead of the smooth Kentucky mash from his own private stock. Meek, in turn, had drunk far more than he had intended to just to show up this no-account, free nigger. Speck was about to reap more than small satisfaction for serving whiskey "on the house."

High-top button-down shoes, flashes of petticoats, and swirling skirts were everywhere as Meeks tried to make up for lost time. Two steps past Beemis, he was met by a wall of warm air generated by too many bodies trying their level best to outdo each other in such close company. A wave of nausea swept over him, his knees buckled, the sweat fairly poured from his forehead all the way down his back, but he gamely held on. He clutched at his growling stomach. "Damn that nigger," he swore under his breath, realizing he'd been setup, but good.

Meek spotted her again, the rancher's wife he'd danced with, the same woman who had all but invited him outside for some extramarital activity under cover of darkness. He cut in, barely bothering with the formality of tapping the woman's husband on the shoulder.

The rancher obliged, but kept his eyes trained keenly on the couple, a cloud of suspicion gathering in his head. Meek and the woman rounded the floor, bundled up, far too tight for the husband's liking. He was about to reclaim the dance, outlaw or no outlaw.

"Meet me outside in five minutes," Meeks managed to mutter in her face.

"Alright, but don't hold me so tight...not now," she answered. "Later...when we're outside..."

Then it happened. Meeks belched in the woman's face. She broke from their embrace to get away from his blast of whiskey-laden breath. He grabbed at the nearest thing that stuck out to keep from falling flat on his face: her big breasts.

"Stop pawing me! You're drunk!" exclaimed the woman to save her own hide and reputation.

The rancher was out on the floor quick as a cat. He caught Meeks' jaw with a roundhouse right, sending the outlaw crashing to the floor in a crumpled heap. He doubled up his fists. "Get up, you sonofabitch!" he yelled. "Here's more, any time you're ready!"

The nearest couples gasped. The music stopped as if by some cue. Everybody on the floor gathered around to see the outcome. A woman's honor was at stake, and nobody was about to walk away until it was settled, one way or the other.

Meeks, groggy from the blow, staggered to his feet. Instantly, long, deft fingers slid down the inside of his boot. Out came a toad-stabber, an Arkansas special, a seven-inch knife, in the most practiced hand ever seen in the Hole. One quick feint—two at most—and it would all be over with the rancher never knowing what or how it happened.

Two couples felt a barrel push them aside. Beemis was there, all business. "Drop the knife, Mister," he called out quietly. "One move, and you're guts will be splattered all over the floor."

Everybody's eyes, except the two men's, were on the shotgun Beemis wielded with complete authority.

"Ain't gonna ask you again! Drop the knife!"

Beemis felt someone nudge his side. "He's my problem; let me handle this."

A ripple went through the crowd. Butch Cassidy had taken center stage beside the grizzled horse rancher. He talked in low tones to Beemis. "His wrists are so strong, one flick, and it's over before you can squeeze your trigger. No doubt you'll splatter him, but it'll be too late for the rancher."

Cassidy deliberately walked in front of Beemis, blocking his shot. Now it was just Butch and Meek. Butch held out his hand and moved forward, ever so slowly. "Give me the knife…We're among friends here…We need friends…you need these people…we both need these people if we're gonna have a place to stay ahead of the law…"

He now stood two feet in front of Meeks; his hand was still out. The crowd went spellbound. They'd never seen anything like this in all their born days. Ice had to be running through Cassidy's veins. Meeks shook his head to clear his glazed eyes. He handed Butch the knife.

"Now, Mister Meeks, you owe this man and his wife your apology. Let's hear it!"

Meeks blinked several times, still fighting off the effects of Speck's rotgut whiskey. "'Pologize, Sir…Ma'am…"

"Give me a twenty-dollar gold piece. I'll see to it that it's put in the school fund as your donation. Get on your horse and ride out…See you later at my cabin."

They gawked in awe while Meeks fished into a vest pocket and produced the gold coin. He gave it to Butch, then mumbled, "See you later, Butch…at the cabin."

Cassidy watched Meek leave the building. Satisfied Meeks was gone, he turned to the dance band. "Thank you for your patience. Please, dear friends, let's keep dancing!"

Josie raised both hands to her lips. "Did you see that? The way Butch handled that man?"

Annie couldn't resist her first impulse. "Yeah, he was something alright.

No more George Parker, the Mormon! Butch Cassidy doing what he does best: controlling everybody and everything!"

The dance resumed, but the crowd was abuzz with what had happened. Like it or not, Butch Cassidy was the center of attention. People went out of their way to shake his hand or speak to him, grateful that Beemis Markham hadn't had to use his shotgun.

Twenty minutes later, a new ripple took hold, especially among the single ladies. Charley Crouse stood before the crowd. "Lemme have your attention," he pleaded. He waited a full minute before continuing. "You all know what's coming' next, the basket auction. But first, John Harvey has some big news to tell all of you! Go ahead, John!"

John Jarvey stood alongside Charley Crouse. The crusty, old mercantile owner let his gravelly voice boom out over the people. "Tomorrow morning, the United States Government is gonna put Brown's Hole on the map! Tomorrow morning, there'll be a new sign under my mercantile letters. It will say United States Post Office, Brown's Park, Colorado! That's right! From now on, we're gonna be called Brown's Park, not Brown's Hole!"

The crowd turned noisy with Jarvey's announcement. Several ranchers shook their fists, obviously unhappy with the news. Others clapped their hands and stomped their boots, glad that at least there was outside recognition and progress at long last.

Jarvey waved both hands, trying to restore some order. "Folks! Folks! In case you don't know it, it's 1897 up on top of the rim! God only knows what year it is down here!"

That brought out more catcalls and a half-dozen hoots. One young buck answered for two dozen other young men gathered around him. He cupped both hands over his mouth and shouted out, "Who in hell cares what year it is! Let's get to the baskets and see these young ladies!"

Charley Crouse had no trouble getting volunteers from the crowd— especially the young men. Oil cloth, donated by Jarvey's Mercantile, was spread over rough planking, which was laid across sawhorses. These would serve as the tables. Wooden folding chairs were borrowed from the wallflower section and placed under the planks where the couples would be setting. As each basket was auctioned, the highest bidder claimed the right to eat the goodies from the basket with the single lady who had prepared it. Charley carefully counted the tables, making sure the number of tables matched the number of baskets. He counted twelve. Satisfied all was in order, he gave the signal. "Ladies, please pick up your baskets and stand in line so the auction can begin!"

The single women scurried to the back of the building to claim their baskets. Minnie Crouse got there first, so she waited for Josie to pick hers up. The two had never liked each other, and since Butch Cassidy had come into their lives, they had even less use for each other. Minnie fired the first salvo. "Butch only danced with you once! Kinda puts you outta the running, doesn't it? He danced with me, *six times!*"

Josie fired right back. "That's 'cause he felt sorry for you!"

"Sorry for me! Huh! That's a good one! We'll see how sorry he was when he bids on mine and not yours! And for good measure, I might just let him take me home. Butch's been hintin' around pretty strong that I'm what he's been lookin' for. He knows I can give him just what he needs!"

"Sure you can, Minnie! More sandwiches and whiskey for his men!"

Minnie was about to hurl her basket in Josie's direction, then thought better of it. "You're just trying to rile me up, but it won't work! Butch likes what he sees in me! Told me so just yesterday!"

"Yeah, he had to cut it down to just one word! FAT!"

Annie stepped in between the two. "Hey, hey, you two, let the auction settle this!"

Minnie glared at Josie. The only thing missing between the two was the brass knuckles. She turned to walk away before any more fireworks went off. Josie got in another parking shot. "For your information, CHUBBY, I only needed one dance to get Butch to ask me to marry him. Haven't made up my mind to say yes or turn him down!"

"That's a lie, Josie Barnett, and you damn well know it! Butch'll never marry you! He's as good as promised me! Better let your old flame, Cleve Dreschler, bid on yours 'cause that's the only action you'll get tonight!"

Minnie thumbed her nose at Josie and walked away. Annie shook her head. "Boy, there's sure no love lost between you two! Hey, Sis, you laid it on pretty thick for Minnie's sake, didn't you? I mean, you *did* turn Butch down…like you told me at MA Jones?"

An old wistful look crept into Josie's beautiful blues once more. "Yes, I did…and it still hurts…"

"And it still shows, too!"

"LET THE BIDDING BEGIN!"

John Jarvey's raspy voice ended any more discussion between the Barnett sisters. One by one, each young lady would stand beside the white-haired old gent and hold her basket high above her head, the signal for the bidding to get underway.

The crowd closed in on the twelve young ladies who were outnumbered at least four-to-one by the young, single men. It was a social measure of sorts, the kind that told the young ladies who was interested in each, and gauged that interest by the amount of competition between the eligible bachelors. The more spirited the bidding, the more suitors the lady had, and of course, the more money raised for the school.

The bidding stayed brisk as evidenced by the growing pile of gold coins in Charley Crouse's cigar box. When Minnie's turn came, she stood next to Jarvey.

"Hold your basket high, Minnie!" Jarvey exclaimed. "Boy, that fried chicken smells awful good! What else ya got?"

She picked out Butch Cassidy, standing alone on the edge of the crowd. Their eyes made contact and she directed her reply only to him. "There's my favorite, baked beans, and Johnny-cake muffins smothered in butter with clover-weed honey just waitin' to be spread over them. And for dessert, I made apple tarts…"

Jarvey licked his chops. "Boy, what wouldn't I give to be forty years younger and single!"

That brought out a roar from the married folks, and more than few hoots and hollers from the young bucks.

"What do I have?"

"Two dollars!"

"Four dollars!"

"I'll make that seven!"

Cassidy hadn't even opened his mouth before the bid reached ten dollars. "I'll give twelve!"

Minnie's brown eyes grew big as buttons. Butch had joined the bidding.

Jarvey kept the bids moving at a fast pace. "I have twenty dollars," he boomed out. "Who'll make it twenty-two?"

The bidding suddenly died. "Twenty-one! Do I hear twenty-one?" Jarvey searched the faces of the young men. "C'mon, men! Let's make it twenty-one!"

No takers. The twenty-dollar bid did not come from Cassidy. It was obvious to everyone, except poor Minnie, that Butch had entered the bidding only to spur the bids and thereby help raise the contribution. She did everything but plead with her lips. Twice she quickly brushed her eyes, pretending that something had somehow gotten into them when none of the other ladies before her had any problems with imaginary specks or real insects.

"Alright, Minnie! George Hays is the lucky fellow! Enjoy that basket of homemade goodies!"

Near tears, Minnie Crouse was escorted to the table by a smiling, jubilant George Hays.

Nine more ladies had their baskets auctioned off with high bids. Jarvey shook the cigar box. "You've done mighty good, mighty good tonight!" He turned to the remaining two young ladies and beckoned them to approach him. "Folks, we're down to two more baskets and they belong to the Barnett sisters, Josie and Annie! Now in the interest of time, I'm not going to ask what's in those baskets! But take it from me, I've been to the Markham ranch enough times to tell you there's no better food to be found anywhere! Josie, you go first! Now, what am I bid?"

Six young men shot the bidding up to twenty-five dollars. "Do I hear thirty?" asked Jarvey.

"Thirty," said one young buck.

Another raised his hand. "Make that thirty-five!"

"Forty!" yelled another.

A ripple went through the crowd at the unheard-of bid, the highest by far.

Cleve Dreschler stepped forward. He glared at his competition, letting them know in no small terms they had better drop out now or else! After he was satisfied all got his message, he raised his hand. "I bid forty-one!"

"Do I hear forty-two?"

The noise quieted considerably. "You heard me! Do I hear forty-two?"

A voice behind Cleve answered loud and clear. "I'll bid fifty!"

Cleve whirled around. Cheek muscles flexing, he wanted to see who dared to buck his bid. "Cassidy! I might've known," he growled. "That invite to step outside still stands any time you'd care to take me up on it."

Jarvey could see Cleve had a short fuse. "Mister Dreschler, this auction will be conducted fair and square. Mister Cassidy has as much right to bid as the next man."

Jarvey inadvertently gave Cleve the opening he was looking for. "Not when the money Cassidy bids on comes from that Idaho bank job he pulled! Sure, I know he can bid me up 'til the cows come home because not one person here tonight has that kind of money! What's fair and square 'bout that?"

Cleve Dreschler had made his case—a darned good one, too! Most of the crowd sided with the likeable young rancher. Josie could only stand and wonder how Butch Cassidy could possibly handle this one. This time her composure gave no hint as to what her heart and her emotions were going through—a real pounding.

Butch turned to Cleve. "May I see your hands, Sir?"

Cassidy's strange request caught Cleve completely off guard. He complied, though he hadn't the slightest idea what his rival had in mind.

"Yes, just as I thought," declared Butch, loud enough so everyone could catch his words. "Your hands tell me that you work hard and take pride in what you do."

Cleve smiled, proud as a peacock.

"Well, Mister Dreschler, I, too, worked just as hard as you to earn my money. The only difference between us is that you worked on your ranch to get yours while I worked my brains day and night to get mine. I took risks you can't possibly know, much less understand. I also did all the scouting, set the timing, and then carried my plan out to make sure no one got hurt or shot, so that the only thing taken was the money. I even rehearsed a backup plan in case something went wrong at the very last minute. When I arrived here, I paid my way, just the same as you do when you owe money. Nobody who held their hand out to get paid by me ever said, 'I'm sorry, Mister Cassidy, I can't accept your money; it could be stolen!'"

A new wave of mutterings crisscrossed the crowd. Butch, too, had made a very strong case. More than just a few had to admit to themselves, if not to their friends, that Butch's money had been welcome everywhere he traveled in the Hole—up 'til now. Why should this be any different? Why?

John Jarvey spoke his mind. "Mister Cassidy has been a frequent customer at my store…and like he said, none of us ever turned him down when it came time to pay. I say let the bidding go on!"

Cleve stomped his boots down hard in disgust. "Then count me out for any more bids. If any of you people want to cow-tow to this outlaw, so be it! But I won't!"

Jarvey stayed true to his purpose. "Any more bids? Any more bids?"

The crowd's din rose into an uproar. Some sided with Cleve, and a growing number decided that Cassidy's money was as good as anybody else's, just as Butch had contended.

Butch made his move. He took Josie's basket and led her by the hand away from John Jarvey. Josie was pleased and yet flustered by all this new attention. "You're going in the wrong direction; the table's over there!"

"No, I'm not," said the outlaw. "Three weeks ago, I said I'd never give you cause to be hurt by me again! You're too fine a person! Mister Dreschler! Mister Dreschler, wait up!"

Butch had to almost run to catch up with Cleve Dreschler. When he did, he had this to say. "Please accept my bid as your bid for Miss Barnett's basket. If I had been in your place, there's no doubt I would've done the same and probably said what you did. Enjoy the picnic basket and this wonderful lady's good company. If you don't know by now, you soon will; there is no finer lady than Josie Barnett!"

Those who stood nearby to witness what happened would gladly take an oath that George Parker, alias Butch Cassidy, had his finest hour on the dance floor that night. They saw gallantry and chivalry as it was intended to be, all in the name of true love. Those who were too far away to see exactly what happened had quite another view: Butch Cassidy would do anything, including giving up Josie Barnett, to make sure he had friends in the Hole waiting for him whenever he needed safe refuge.

Jarvey waited for the commotion to die down. "Folks, it's gettin' late, and we've kept Miss Ann Barnett waiting far too long. Our apologies to you, Miss Barnett. Now, LET THE BIDDING BEGIN!"

Five young men took turns jump-bidding each other until the bid reached fifty dollars, the same as Josie's last bid. At that point, four shook their heads and walked away. Only one stood before Jarvey and Annie.

"Well, Deke, that's an awful lot to bid, but I sure do appreciate your most generous contribution to such a worthy cause."

Deke's face reddened up a mite. "There goes my month's pay, but Annie knows it means we'll have to wait a bit longer, that's all. Figure she won't mind…"

Jarvey turned to Annie. "Do you know what this young man is talking about?"

Annie flashed her biggest smile. "I kinda do…but 'til I hear Deke's own words, I'm going to pretend my ears were plugged up real good tonight."

"Alright, last call! And I do mean last call, folks! Any more bids?"

Some of the people started to shuffle out; the bidding was over. Eleven couples were seated, enjoying their picnic baskets. Annie was ready to hand Deke her basket.

"I BID FIFTY-FIVE!"

A tall man stood apart from the retreating crowd. He was easily the most handsome man there. He looked to be exactly what he was: all polish. There was a distinct accent in these four words he'd spoken so far. Annie guessed it came from way back East—possibly Boston. He had light brown hair and bewitching hazel eyes, almost too nice for a man. Yet he was all man with a swagger about him that told the ladies, "watch out!" This man would steal your heart and your good senses and then walk away to add another notch in his belt.

"Do I know you?" Jarvey asked.

"No, I'm with Mister Cassidy. Name's Lay, Elza Lay."

Most of the crowd turned around. This they had to see.

Deke's lips twitched, the muscles on his neck rippled, he had cotton in his mouth, but he spit out the words, "Butt out, Mister, this bidding doesn't concern you!"

Elza sized up his competition. "Last man I came across with red hair like yours was a hothead! A fool who let his mouth run faster than his brains."

"Well, Mister, that's somebody else, not me. Since you're with Butch Cassidy, I'll kindly ask you to do the same thing. I'll let Mister Jarvey keep your donation, and I'll say thank you, and bid you good evening."

"Yes, Mister Lay, that was such a splendid gesture on Mister Cassidy's part. And I, too, thank you for such a generous donation. Good evening!"

"Hold on, you two! I'm still interested in bidding higher if I have to!"

Deke's face matched his hair. He turned to Jarvey. "Alright, I'll sign a paper promising to pay against next month's draw."

"Sorry, Deke, I can't accept any promises on paper."

"Well then," said Lay, "here's my donation!" He took the basket from Annie and then offered his arm to escort her to the empty table. "Time to eat a delicious picnic, and enjoy this patient little lady's fine company!"

CHAPTER FOUR

Old Henry said, "Hell, I run cattle in the Hole long a'fore
them big cattle outfits hogged up all the free-range grass."

"Say, wait a minute, Brick or Red, or whatever they call you! I'm still
talking to Miss Ann! And there's still half my sandwich and dessert that
hasn't been touched!"

Deke was in his foulest mood. Annie had never seen him so wound up!
Seething with rage and jealousy, he snatched the picnic basket in one swoop,
then lifted Annie up from the table before either she or Lay could utter
another word. "The name's Deke Landry, not Brick or Red! Social hour's
over! Time you was makin' tracks back to Butch's cabin, where you belong."

Lay rose to intercept this brash, rude man who wouldn't even let him
enjoy what he'd paid such a high price for. Instinctively, his hand traveled to
his side. He found nothing but his pant leg and more empty air. His eyes
narrowed a tad. He had an instant dislike for Deke. "Your manners need a lot
of work. Perhaps another time, another place, where we won't be bothered
with social rules..."

Deke handed the basket back to Annie. "Now's as good a time as any.
Let's just step outside for a minute or two...Annie won't mind waitin'
inside...figure that's all it'll take..."

Ann stepped between the two. "Stop it! Stop it!" Eyes blazing with disgust, she turned on Deke. "Mister Lay's right! Your manners are terrible! Apologize to him! Or do I have to do it for you?"

Deke started to double up his fists; then his fingers opened. "No, Annie, you'll do no such thing for me. There's no apology comin' from me, Mister! So git on your hay burner and ride out!"

Beemis and several others started toward the three, thinking there might be more trouble in the making. Lay handled the situation almost as tactfully as Butch would've. He smiled at Annie, then bowed his head slightly before he spoke. "You've been as delightful and charming a lady as your sister. No wonder Butch speaks highly of you, too! Goodnight, Miss Barnett!"

Lay then took leave of the situation, stopping only long enough to holster his shooting irons.

Beemis handled the team's reins on the buggy ride back to his ranch under bright moonlight. He looked around. Nobody, including himself, seemed in the mood for conversation, so he kept his thoughts to himself. He clucked for the team to pick up the pace, and they responded. He couldn't help but take a glance or two at the back of his two-seater where Deke and Annie sat. Ordinarily, they'd be snuggled up together, holding hands, and stealing a kiss or two, letting the Man-in-the-Moon wink at them while they enjoyed the shower of moonbeams he'd sent their way. But not tonight. A tall, handsome man whose words flowed like honey had driven a wedge between them. They sat as far apart as their seat allowed, looking everywhere but in each other's eyes or faces, searching for the right answers.

He'd seen Lay's type before a number of times. If he got his way with her, there'd be no "trifling," as he called it, with his Annie's affections. No, indeed, by the time he'd finished with her, she'd be worse than just "damaged goods." What bothered Beemis most was that Annie had thoroughly enjoyed his company, something up until tonight he'd been willing to bet half his ranch that no other man could come between Deke and his Annie. Now, he was not so sure.

He glanced to his right on the seat next to him. How proud he felt toward his Josie. Only three weeks ago, she had teetered on the verge of losing her mind, fighting a losing battle, trying to separate George Parker from Butch Cassidy until it had nearly done her in. Yet his Josie had asked Parker the tough questions, the right ones, and then drawn her own conclusions that Cassidy was the one in control, not the other way around. He knew Parker or Cassidy had made his move on Josie again tonight, but whatever had passed between them on that lone dance Josie had given him left her unchanged in her resolve to live the life she was cut out for—a rancher's life. Oh, there was no doubt that each time Cassidy rode away, a piece of Josie's heart would go along with him, too! Yet in the end, he felt sure that Cleve Dreschler's chances improved with each passing day because time was on his side, and that was the one thing that Cassidy could never count on with certainty, despite his careful planning, scouting, and rehearsing before each holdup or robbery.

Cassidy then took over center stage in Beemis' mind. He wondered if the very traits that keep Cassidy head and shoulders above all the outlaws and other questionable characters he'd known would in the end prove to be his undoing. He thought back to his Army days as a scout. He'd run across an outlaw or two in those days, and every one he remembered had a "short-run," as he called it, when it came right down to it. Sooner or later, fate or an unfriendly bullet snuffed out their lives, only to be buried in an unmarked grave or at best given permanent residence in some cowtown's boot hill. He also wondered when Cassidy's time was over, how history would treat him. Would he be remembered for the kind of man he really was? Maybe even rate a sentence after one of those stares, as he called it, at the bottom of a page in the middle of some Western writer's collection of colorful characters who helped to change and shape America's real Wild West.

Beemis gave Josie a little tweak on her cheek.

Josie came out of her own deep thoughts. "What was that for?"

He clucked again to his team. "Oh, nothin' special...No, I take that back! It's for bein' who you are, Josie, my sugarplum!"

"Mind if I scoot over? I need to feel close to somebody I trust...and love."

"Sure, Sugarplum! Your old uncle could sure use some close company right about now. Maybe those two in the back seat will take the hint!"

"Butch has been gone three weeks, Sis. Next time Cleve pays you a visit, the least you could do is give him the time of day."

Josie stood over the washboard, the bar of soap squeezed hard in her hand. She had yet to rub or scrub any of the stack of clothes behind her. "Darn that Mormon! I could scrub 'til this bar is nothin' but a nub in my hand, and that man would still be on my mind...and in my heart."

Annie held up one of Beemis' shirts. "Now isn't this just like a man! Three new work shirts up in his dresser drawer, and all we ever see him wear are the same old ones! Look at this one! I can see daylight through it, it's so thin! And if this one isn't put back on top of his stack after we do the ironing, he'll come down the hall wondering whatever happened to it! Then I'll have to fish it out from under his pile of new ones, and he'll say, 'Annie, don't bother puttin' it on top, leave it out so I can wear it first thing in the morning.'"

Josie had a big chuckle. "You sure do know your uncle! When are you going to add Deke's work clothes to our pile?"

Josie's question made Annie feel a bit uneasy. "I should really set our date...Deke's been wound up tighter than that pocket watch his grandfather left him. He's afraid he's losing me...afraid we're starting to drift apart..."

"Is he right? Are you two drifting apart?"

Annie separated hers and Josie's dainties from the rest of the work clothes. "No...not really. It's just that Elza does everything so different. He's so smooth...so polished...and Deke...well, he's kinda rough and crude..."

"Don't you ever doubt his feelings for you, Annie, they're pure gold!"

Annie dropped Beemis' everyday pants into the wash tub. "I love Deke...I really do. We both have so much in common...It's just that Elza does things to me...puts a different kind of excitement into me...guess you could call it a twitch or something..."

"Careful, Annie! Lay is a lady killer! If you give him a chance, any chance at all, he'll put a lot more into you than just a twitch or some different kind of excitement! You know what I'm talkin' about! The same thing Deke tried to get from you when you two played on your Indian saddle blanket under that clump of cottonwoods by Vermillion Creek!"

Sunday at the Markham ranch was a day off—a day when the wranglers could sleep in, eat or choose not to, depending on how much liquor had been drunk the night before. Above all else it was their day to do pretty much as they darned well pleased. By mid-afternoon, invariably a poker game was going on in either or both of the two bunkhouses. If it was the first Sunday after payday, the stakes were usually higher; the closer to next payday meant the winner's share of the pot had dwindled considerably—such was the life and times of the typical bunkhouse boarder.

On this particular Sunday, Deke Landry's share of the poker pot had been growing; he'd had a good run of cards. Lady Luck had smiled down on the curly haired, likeable redhead. The poker game was the social leveler, so to speak; it didn't make one whit of difference it you were the cook, a bronc buster or their foreman; once you sat in on a game, everybody was equal until either you were ground out of your money or you were the last to leave when you scooped up the winner's share.

Shorty McCallum came barging into the bunkhouse where Deke was in the midst of another hand of good cards. Even the stubble on his face couldn't hide his excitement. "Hey, Deke, guess who's driving up to the main house in one of them fancy rented buckboards?"

Deke kept his eyes focused on his pat hand. "Is he well dressed?"

"Yeah, he's duded up somethun' fierce...Got one of them cute little black hats on...brand spankin' new suit'a clothes that must'a cost a pretty gold piece or two...even got one'a those carpet bags with him..."

"Sounds an awful lot like Butch Cassidy, but he always rides a fine horse..."

Shorty cackled with glee. "Not today. It's Butch alright. Come callin' on Miss Josie again, I reckon. Got another feller with him...It's that sidekick'a his...oh shaw! Cain't 'member that name..."

Deke fanned his hand. "Sidekick? Hell, that's gotta be old slick-tongue hisself...Elza Lay...or should I say Bill McGinnis. Hell's bells, he's no Boston charmer, not by a long shot! Did some checkin' up on him; he's nothing but a Utah farm boy...another Mormon who couldn't make it pitchin' hay down on the farm or prayin', so he went to cattle rustlin' 'til Butch took him on. Got a swagger about him that goes hand in hand with those fancy words he's picked up along the way...got a way with women...They fall for all that hot air he puts out...Got no use for him."

Shorty's dry cackle sounded more like a wheeze that sprouted feathers. "Tell ya 'nuther thing that Elza fella nearly got last time 'round at that basket social...he nearly got Miss Annie away from ya...didn't he?"

Deke's eyes narrowed; his cheeks flushed beet red, matching his hair. He bolted up out of his chair, sending it sprawling behind him. Down on the table came his pat hand, the sure winner he'd been holding; his five cards went flying in all directions.

"Count me out! Got some straighten'n out to do right now!"

Old Gus, the bunkhouse cook, picked up Deke's cards. "Thought you told me you was set to marry Miss Annie and move up to the main house?"

"Sure did! Now I'm gonna set the date! Tonight!"

"Want me to play out your hand?"

Deke was a step away from the door. "Do what you like with my cards. Got other things on my mind that needs doin,' pronto!"

Shorty peered over Gus' shoulder. "We'll split Deke's share...Looks like you're gonna lick the pot clean!"

Gus turned around and snorted. "Do nuthin' of the sort! By God, who's holdin' this hand, me or you?"

The Barnett sisters assumed Butch Cassidy and Elza Lay came calling to pay their respects. The only one who viewed the two outlaws' social call with his usual neutrality was the redoubtable Beemis Markham. Yet even Beemis had to admit the two, especially Butch Cassidy, was the epitome of whatever he wanted to be—in this case a well-dressed businessman or land speculator as he later divulged in conversation, without so much as a toss of conscience one way or the other. Butch was simply that good an impersonator.

Josie was serving fresh-baked apple pie when Deke made his appearance. "Won't you join us for dessert?"

Deke was in no mood for social graces or Josie's mouth-watering pie. "No thanks, Josie, some other time." He glared at Elza, then started straight at Ann. "Step outside a minute, got some jawin' to do."

Elza sensed his competition was about to blow sky high. He seized the advantage with all the smoothness of a Rock Spring's saloon card dealer. "Can't you see Miss Ann is busy entertaining? And I see your manners haven't improved any. Are you always this crude?"

Deke turned on him, jaw set, cheek muscles tensing. Elza saw Deke's fists double up. "Only when you're around! That answer your questions?"

"Well then, I think the answer should be obvious: One of us should leave! Good day, Mister Landry!"

Butch came to everybody's rescue. His remark was a great piece of statesmanship. "Elza and I were just leaving, Deke...after we finish our coffee and this delicious pie."

Deke ate his dessert out in the kitchen, opting to wait it out until Butch and Elza left. Ann had never seen him so uptight; he was a stick of dynamite just waiting for his fuse to be lit. After what seemed forever, Ann finally made her appearance out in the kitchen. "You're going to have to be in a much better mood, dear, or else I think we'd better call off this conversation 'til tomorrow."

He came straight to the point. "Let's set our wedding date...No sense waitin' any longer."

She put her arms around him, trying to comfort and console him. What she said didn't. "Elza's got you all upset...that's why you're trying to push me. Don't do that, Deke, I won't be pushed. You should know that by now! Let me decide! I think the woman should set the date, not the man."

He kissed her lightly on the lips. "Can't help it, I love you so danged much.

Am I losin' you?"

Ann was flabbergasted. "No, no, Deke, that's not it!"

"Then why the stall?"

She broke from their embrace and walked around the kitchen, searching for just the right words to put his doubts and troubled mind to rest. "I just want to be sure, that's all. I'm pretty sure...no, better make it almost one hundred percent sure."

He gathered her up in his arms once more. "I don't know nothin' 'bout that hundred percent business. If your heart says yes, and your brain's holdin' cards as good as that or better, that's all the hundred percent I need."

She kissed him passionately and then laughed. "Been playin' poker again I see! Hope you're winning, darling! Just hang on a little longer; I'll set the date."

Ann's answer seemed to satisfy for the moment, but only the moment. "Good, but don't make it too much longer. Don't cotton to no cat'n mouse games...I ain't cut out that way...You should know that by now, don'tcha?"

"Yes, my love, I do know that about you...and a lot more."

Cassidy's recent prolonged-absence sparked more conversation than the mysterious fire that burned down the McLaughlin Ranch in the Park's east side. Not one, nosey rancher had the guts or the gumption to ask Butch where he'd been or what he'd been doing. They collectively figured, that sooner or later, the details of his latest job would filter down into the Park, much the same way the early morning sun's rays always seemed to take their time, separating dawn from daylight in the Park at this time of summer.

Beemis came rushing out to the working corral, waving a letter. "Been to the post office and look what showed up!"

Deke, Annie, Shorty, and two other wranglers stopped their work. Annie pulled off her gloves to read Beemis' letter. "Oh, Uncle, this is great! Best news yet! Your Boston horse-buyer really must like our Arabians! Wants two dozen more two-year-old mares for breeding and two more young stallions. Says he's not even coming out to pick them! Wants you to use your best judgment! Boy, that's some endorsement, Uncle! Some endorsement!"

Beemis hugged Annie. "You ain't seen the check, Annie! He upped the price three hundred more for each! Biggest order I ever got!" He looked at Deke and then over to his Annie. "Only one thing that could possibly be better news than this! Only one thing! Deke? Annie?"

Deke started to say something, then held up when he saw Annie was about to burst the seams with her own announcement.

Annie's blue eyes sparkled, her cheeks blushed a beautiful shade of lilac pink, and her cherry lips bubbled over with love and the good news. "Deke, how long would it take you to wrap that old piece of rope around your cardboard suitcase and carry it up to my bedroom?"

He jammed his leather gloves into his hind pocket. He took off his Stetson hat and sailed it out over Shorty's head. "Oh, Annie, oh, Annie! Is this what I think it is? Is it?"

Annie smiled, then played coy with him. "I told you I wanted to set the date, and now's the time! If I waited for you to ask me, I might be ready for a rocking chair before you got around to it. I'll marry you after you ship out this order! How much time do you need to get these horses ready?"

"Two weeks! No more!"

"Good! Then we'll get married the day after you get back from Rock Springs!"

Deke picked Annie up. "Yipppeeee! Oh, Annie, you've made me the happiest and proudest man in all the world! YipppEEEE!"

He hugged and whirled her around and around. Annie squealed and giggled in pure delight. Her heart told her this was the time, the right time. "I love you, Deke Landry! Now don't you ever let me down! Promise?"

He finally let Annie's boots touch the ground. "Shucks, that's the easiest thing I've ever been asked to do for the rest of our lives, Annie! Let's seal it with a kiss! A proper-like kiss!"

They embraced and kissed as though they had inherited their own private world with no bystanders or spectators whatsoever. Shorty McCallum and Beemis swore they were glued together. The other two wranglers hooted and hollered 'til Deke and Annie realized their kiss wasn't so private after all.

Beemis moved in to hug the both of them. "Tell you what! Got me an idea that'd make one heckava weddin' present. Combine a little business with a whole lot of pleasure!"

Annie couldn't imagine what was on the old boy's brain. "Alright, let's hear it!"

Beemis could hardly wait to spill it. "I'd like to send you two on your honeymoon, all the way back East! I'll give ya a list of my best customers and you two can look 'em up! Introduce yourselves…You know, tell 'em who you are and that you'll be takin' over the Markham horse business! And when you get back, Annie, I'll let you handle all the correspondin' with these folks!

That way, I've worked you and Deke into it without so much as one of my old customer's feathers gettin' ruffled! Now, how's that for mixin' business with pleasure?"

"Fine by me," said Deke. "Ain't never rode a train…"

Annie forced her lips through Beemis' grizzled beard to find his cheek. "Oh, Uncle, that's a great idea! Can we afford it?"

Beemis waved the letter in front of them. "We sure can now! And believe you me, it'll pay off in the long run for you two!"

"But what about Josie? Where does she fit in in all of this?"

"Not to worry, Annie! Soon as you two get back, I'm going to put our money into three accounts…like I told you before. Once a year, we'll hold a little meetin' and go over the expenses we've paid out, and then we'll divvy up what's leftover into those accounts, so every one of us gets a fair shake. Later on, you and Deke can buy Josie out, if she agrees, or you could leave her as one-third owner if that suits everybody. And you and I have already talked about what happens to my share…after I'm gone…"

"Please, please, Uncle, no more talk about that! Not on such a day like this!"

Beemis couldn't be more pleased. "When you're in Rock Springs, Deke, I'll have you drop by the bank and see my old friend, Dirk Snyder, the president. Tell him I'll be in later to get all what we've discussed down on paper so it's all legal-like. That way, there's no ifs, ands, or buts comin' up, down the road."

The upcoming horse shipment, along with Annie and Deke's marriage, moved Markham Ranch into high gear. Everybody pulled together without so much as even a mild complaint or bellyache about the amount of work that had to be done in such short time. Once the young mares were selected, Deke had his crew immediately harness them in tandem with older mares to "gentle them down," as he called it. Each day, the same two would be harnessed together and worked around several holding corrals. By the end of the first week, the results were amazing. No more spooked or skittish young mares. They no longer fought the traces; indeed, they were gentle enough so any of the hands could approach them without any bucking or kicking or rearing up. Nervousness was a thing of the immediate past.

Beemis watched Deke work one of the pairs. "There'll be no skinned-up knees this time when that train slams into our cattle car. Don't believe the steam belching from the engine will bother 'em much either. Best calmed-down shipment we've ever had, Deke! Even Old Joe Cady never tried this! You sure got a way with horses, my good man!"

Annie stepped down off one of the fence rails, pleased by her uncle's compliments. "That's why he never had any trouble filling Joe's shoes. And that's just another good reason why the Markham ranch is doing better than ever! Deke has new ideas and he's not afraid to try 'em out, either!" She blew Deke a kiss. "I'd better help Josie fix supper. You're expected too…soon as you're through this afternoon."

Deke's broad smile nearly matched the wide brim of his Stetson. "Thanks, Annie! Sure do like all those invites I've been gettin' lately. Guess marryin' the boss' niece sure don't hurt none."

"And that's just for starters, son," Beemis added. "You'll be a regular 'round Josie's table just as soon as we get all those I do's out of the way!"

That evening, Deke went out onto the front porch to take a breather, while he waited for Annie to help Josie with the dishes. He sat down on the top step, then sucked in a big gob of fresh air. He stretched his arms out and exhaled slowly, letting air escape slowly through his teeth, making a soft whistling sound. "Yes, Sir, Deke, my good man, you got the world by the tail," he told himself. "Sure as heck beats the way things used to be. Broke, out of work…no gal to love…no woman who cared a hoot about you. Boy, has this all changed…ever since Annie came into your life…ever since Beemis started treatin' you like a son. Yes, Sir, Deke…ya got a lot to be thankful for…and it's just gonna get better n' better."

He watched the first, long shadows of twilight cast their darkening shades across the ranch, striking the two bunkhouses first, then the horse stables and barns, finally ending up on the opposite side of the porch he was sitting on. It had been the kind of day he said went smooth as salve. Then he saw Shorty McCallum emerge from out of the gathering darkness. He already guessed what brought him up the well-trod path to the main house: the day's only fly in the ointment, old Gus, the bunkhouse cook.

Deke towered by at least eight inches over Shorty as he rose to hear what calamity Gus had dumped upon the bunkhouse boys.

Shorty removed his slouch of a Stetson to show respect for his new foreman and boss. A balding head of silver-grey hair, supported by two elf-sized ears, made the man almost look comical, yet his deep-set eyes held their purpose. "Deke, Deke," he began, "sumpthun's gotta be done! We can't take no more!"

"Alright, Shorty, what now?"

173

Shorty put his Stetson back on, rocked on the balls of his feet inside his boots to look as tall as possible, then exploded. "Dang good thing you ain't been chowin' down with us, lately! 'Cause if'n ya had, you'd'a had the runs tonight, just like what hit us! Old Gus burnt the hell outta everythin'! Had to throw my biscuits n' gravy into the slop bucket, that's how bad it's got! Now whataya figure on doin' 'bout it?

"Did Tex, Slim, and the others have the same problem?"

"Boy, did they! I got cleaned out first, so they elected me to come up here! This keeps up, an' we're gonna have ta' dig a new home fer Pa Jones, 'cause the old one's fillin' up fast!"

"That bad, huh?"

"Jus' the start of it, Deke! Jus' the start!"

"Tex told me old Gus never takes the big wash tub down off the wall no more! Says he ain't had a bath in over a month…"

"Ya, an', an' he never washes them dirty-lookin' hands no more neither! Even when he's out to Pa Jones! I know 'cause I been checkin' on him every time he's out there!"

"Alright, I'm gonna do something 'bout old Gus! You and me got company with us when we drive those young mares to Rock Springs. Beemis put me in charge, so I'm gonna make a change. Dang it to hell, anyways!"

"Why? What's wrong now, Deke?"

"It'll mean another day or two up there 'til you and me can find a new cook! That's pushin' my weddin' day back just that much more! And Annie ain't gonna be too happy waitin' more days than we figured on…neither an I."

"I'm sorry to be upsettin' your weddin' day, Deke, but like I said, we can't take no more!"

"I understand…it's just that the timin' is bad…but you go back and spread the word that old Gus is history come next week! I'll tell him myself before I bunk down tonight."

Annie appeared just then. "Oh, hi, Shorty! What brings you up here this evening?"

Shorty shifted, first on one leg, then the other. "Deke's handlin' it just fine, Miss Annie." He started to walk away. "You're a good man, Deke! Dang, good man!"

Annie waited 'til Shorty was out of hearing range. She slipped her arm around Deke's waist. "What was that all about?"

"Old Gus. It's a toss-up!"

"Toss-up? I don't understand…fill me in."

"Right now, I can't figure out which is worse, his cookin' or his smell!"
Annie roared. "Yeah, I see what you mean. You're going to replace him,
aren't you?"

"Yes, he's goin' with Shorty and me next week when we drive those mares
up to Rock Springs." He turned to her, his eyes flashed what was on his mind,
in his heart, and in his body—his need for his Annie.

She moved into him, letting him feel her breasts rub up against him,
leaving no doubt he was most definitely on her mind, too. She let him slide his
arms down from her small waist until he used her buttocks to draw her petite
body that much closer into his.

They held that embrace for the longest time, each on fire, searching the
other out, their clothes no longer much of an obstacle to what they both
wanted: each other's body.

"Annie, Annie," he breathed softly into her ear, "I can't hold out much
longer…You feel so close…I can almost feel it…me, into you…Good thing
I'm puttin' in long hours. Want you so bad…that's all I think about lately."

She kissed him with a passion reserved for the bedroom. "I know, I know,
love…you don't know how many times I've dreamed about our first time—
how it will feel—hoping it will last forever…and what I can do after so I can
get you ready again…so we can make love over and over…"

He moved away from his Annie to make himself cool down, so he could
think of other things. "Never been in a woman's bedroom before…always
wondered what your bedroom looks like. Bet it smells a lot like you do…all
lavender-lilac-like…probably full of fluffy, frilly things with lots of geegaw
and purties, too!"

"Deke, what's a geegaw?"

"It's a word I made up for all those things that I'm sure you probably
have…you know…woman kind of things…"

"Well, you're right, I probably do have lots of geegaws around in my
bedroom just waitin' on you to look at them, touch them, maybe even sniff
them 'cause they're so dainty and thin and fine…"

"Could I maybe take a peek? Now?"

"Deke, if I let you into my bedroom before our wedding night…well,
somehow my door would get closed and you know what would happen
next—spoil everything—make us sayin' our vows seem kinda second-rate
instead of first-class all the way. That what you want? Really want?"

"Naw, not really, since you put it that way. I only know one thing, them

175

young mares are gonna make it to Rock Springs at least a half-day early, even if I have to yank old Gus outta the chuck wagon. I'll set him on top of the team, hand him a fryin' pan to beat on and tell him to yell like hell!"

Annie squeezed his hand. "I promise, Deke, the wait will be well worth it...for both of us!"

"Okay, Shorty! Move 'em out! They're ready as they'll ever be!"

Deke's words put a jump in Beemis' heart and a small lump in Annie's throat. Two weeks or more of not seeing that familiar mop of unruly red hair going through his paces, giving his crew orders, and then showing them how it should be done in case they needed some help. That was Deke Landry, through and through. He was the epitome of what horse wrangling was all about!

Beemis, Annie, and Josie rushed out to say good-bye and see them off. Beemis shook Deke's hand. "Remember now, you got three things to do up in Rock Springs. Load the mares and make sure you put a wooden gate between them and the two stallions in the cattle car. There's extra wire and pliers and boards in the back of the chuck wagon in case ya need them. Then stop off to see my banker."

"That's two, Beemis! What's the third!"

"Hurry back to your waitin' bride!"

"Okay, Shorty, move 'em out! They're ready as they'll ever be!"

Deke's words had a finality about them—and a beginning, too! It was the culmination of two long weeks of hard work, making sure most of the traits young mares usually have had been "put to rest," so to speak. They were as gentle as they were going to be, considering the fact that they'd never been driven off of Beemis' range land or loaded at a stockyard with a steam engine's belching and banging while it was being coupled to the cattle cars.

It also signaled the start of at least two weeks or more of separation between Deke and Annie. Yet there was an excitement or rush of adrenalin about this, too! True, the young lovers would not see, hear, or touch one another for fourteen days or more, but each understood that the reward for this forced absence was what made their hearts skip a beat: their upcoming marriage. If absence truly made the heart grow fonder, then this was made to order for both of them.

Beemis, Annie, and Josie waited by the main gate to see Deke off. Shorty McCallum came by first; he tipped his hat, smiled big as life, and then rode on.

Annie cupped both hands over her mouth. "Have a good trip, Shorty! Come back safe and sound!"

Shorty acknowledged Annie's words by turning around in his saddle to wave back at her. Beemis also waved at the small-sized man. "Damned good man," he said, "even if his boot heels are twice as thick as everybody else's. Always tryin' his best to figure out ways to look taller!"

The main herd of mares passed by. Josie spoke up. "There's something about these Arabians that I never tire looking at. They always have such beauty, such poise, and yes, I believe, such pride!" She turned to Beemis. "They have pride, too, don't they?"

Beemis put his arm around Josie. "You bet they do! They're a lot smarter, too, than most people give them credit for."

The horse's hooves had kicked up quite a cloud of dust, raised from the dry ground that lay between the two main gate posts. "Tomorrow, I'll have Tex bring in several loads of gravel to spread it around. Should settle most of the dust from now on," added Beemis.

"Here comes Deke bringin' up the rear and old Gus drivin' the chuck wagon. Gus looks like he's lost his last friend! What a sourpuss!"

Josie smiled at her sister's candid remarks. "I wonder if he really had any friends from the way they all talked about him. Shorty told me last week they put a bar of soap next to the washbasin with his name on the wrapper. As of yesterday, the wrapper was still on!"

Deke rode over to the threesome. Beemis stepped out to shake his hand. "You're a little late gettin' started...Any trouble?"

"Gus lay in his bunk this morning,...wouldn't get up to fix breakfast. I had Shorty and Tex tip his bunk over. He got up mad as hell. I told him to get his butt out in the chuck wagon and be damned quick about it! I had the boys gather up his smelly, old clothes n' such. I gave them to him so we could get started."

"Then none of you had breakfast this morning? Right?"

"It's okay, Josie. I wasn't about to bring him in to slam the dishes and pots and pans around and then end up throwin' his food out 'cause none of us could stomach it!"

"After you leave, I'm going right down there to fix breakfast. Uncle Beemis, from now on, until Deke gets back with a new cook, we're all going to have our breakfasts in the bunkhouse!"

"Thanks, Josie, the boys will sure appreciate it!"

"Count me in, too! I can help!"

Beemis gave him his last minute orders. "Ya already know 'bout those three things that needs doin' up in Rock Springs. When you stop off to see my friend, Dirk Snyder, the bank president, tell him I'll be in next trip to sign partnership papers for Annie, Josie, and myself. Remember now, it's called a partnership! He'll know what papers to get ready."

"And the last thing, Beemis?"

"Find a new cook, no matter how long it takes. I figure with you and Annie waitin' to get hitched, you'll scare one up somewhere! And make sure he can cook! Don't want any more repeat deals like we had!"

"I can handle those three things! Anything else?"

Beemis winked. "Got a purty little blond behind me that claims you owe her a good-bye kiss. Better lean way down or else she just might pull you clean outta that saddle."

"Whoa, Thunder! Easy boy!"

Annie rushed into his arms to smother him with good-bye kisses. "Remember what we talked about the other night? Hurry back, so neither of us has to wait an extra day! I love you! Always remember that, my love!"

The two lovers finally let go. Deke looked at Josie. "Don't I get a good-bye hug or something?"

"Sure, Deke, since you're going to be my new brother-in-law."

She gave him a big hug, then stepped back. "And don't forget what you and I talked about...your surprise for Annie..."

"Giddyup, Thunder! Let's go!"

They watched Deke, the back of the chuck wagon, and herd gradually grow smaller in the distance. Beemis put both arms around his two girls. "Best damned horseman I've ever seen...and he'll be part of my family when he gets back. Lord, do I feel blessed! Gonna have a new son-in-law, and I got the two best-lookin' gals this hole's ever seen for my daughters. Got money in the bank and plenty of Markham Arabians mares ready to build up our stock! How in the world can anybody beat that?"

Annie shielded her eyes from the sun and squinted hard to catch the last, faint glimpse of Deke on Thunder. When the two specks melted into one, she turned to Beemis and Josie. "The only thing that could beat the pat hand your holding, my dear Uncle, is when I see that mop of red hair pass through the main gate, heading straight into my arms."

"Amen, Sis! Amen!"

"Think Mom and Dad would've approved of the way our lives have gone so far?"

Josie's question startled Annie; she had thought she was alone during her visit to the family cemetery. She mused a minute. "Yes, for the most part." She turned to look at her sister. "Do you remember much about either of them?"

Josie moved closer to Clay's and Claire's headstones. She touched the twisted, scrub-cedar marker at the head of their father's grave. "I remember our dad best…because of the long train ride to Rock Springs. He had a great sense of humor, and so sharp, too…always kidded me whenever I told him how much I missed our mother. He'd make up games to keep me amused…told me lots of stories about the West…and then he lived those very same stories after we got out here. Just being around him made me think I could do anything. Uncle Beemis used to kid him…said he turned Indian overnight. Brownest looking White man he said he ever saw…except for his blue eyes, which gave him away…a lot like mine."

"And mother? Anything special you remember about her?"

Josie took her sister's hand and patted it lovingly. "Don't remember too much about her…except she liked to hug me and kiss me all the time. Had real fair skin…beautiful hair…a lot like your complexion and your hair, too! That's about all I remember…about either of them. Sorry, I'm not much help when it comes to remembering them."

They walked over to Maybelle's marker. "Think Beemis will ever remarry?"

Josie's question caught Annie off-guard. "No…not likely. All he ever talks about is what he calls his last mission in life. When Deke showed up on our front porch and took over, I finally figured out what he's been talking about all these years. He'll never admit this, but in the back of his mind, he figures the good Lord left him a job to do and that is, and was, to see to it that we're safely married and leading good, respectful lives. Deke is my part of that job, and when you marry Cleve, then Beemis will rest easy, as he calls it."

"But I haven't settled my mind on Cleve for sure."

"Yes, you have, Sis! You just don't see it as clear as Beemis, me, or Deke see it, that's all! Butch Cassidy has clouded up your usual good sense. Now that you know him for what he really is, you do realize that Mormon was never good husband material."

"I hate to bring this up, but neither is Elza Lay! So get him outta your head, too, Annie! He's just like Butch…both cut by the same pair of scissors!"

"C'mere, Sugarplum, there's a small thread hanging from your new dress!

179

Let me get it!"

Josie moved into Annie's bedroom. Annie dropped to her knees, lifted the hem, and gave a quick jerk. "There now, you look fine as a fiddle! And remember, give Cleve more than his usual two dances. Who knows, you two might just start to hit it off again!"

"Aren't you coming, Sis?"

"Guess you've forgotten, I'm a promised woman! Wouldn't look too great if I went to the dance without Deke, now would it?"

"If you behave yourself, I don't see any harm! Besides, it'll help pass the time 'til Deke gets back. Better than sittin' around here like you've been doing for the last ten days, mooning over something that won't change until your redhead shows up!"

"Gosh, I miss him! No, you go on ahead! Beemis is ready, and you're all gussied-up, and I'm still in my men's workshirt and jeans."

"We'll wait!"

Beemis and his two nieces arrived at Brown's Park's social center in fine fettle. Both sisters sported stunning, new deep-blue dresses and black, high-top, high button-down shoes. Charley Crouse's schoolhouse had a different look that particular Saturday night. Money raised from the basket social and auction had been put to work—namely, a new school bell, housed within its steeple, now set perched atop the roof thanks to a weekend of volunteer labor from three ranch families.

Things were different, too, inside. Two rows of new school desks were stacked at one end of the building up against the blackboard. The blackboard got everybody's attention as they entered. Someone had printed in foot-high letters "School Arrives Next Week! Send your outlaws!"

That message held a special meaning for the park's families. There was no doubt a lot of arm twisting would be required before any of the ranch family's young mavericks or outlaws would listen to the ringing of the school bell or even begin to think about setting foot inside the building to gather some sort of schooling. Just because Charley Crouse said they needed an education didn't mean in their minds that they were about to get one.

Nevertheless, Charley's concerns were pushed aside, temporarily, in favor of laughter, good times, fiddle music, and a snort or two of whiskey at Speck's chuck-wagon bar. A general, all-around, boot-stomping, knee-slapping, butt-kicking social hour was in store for all who ventured past Beemis' box of unbuckled side arms, knives, and various sundry outlaw and rancher hardware.

The evening got off to a very good start—no fist fights, arguments or snide remarks between ranchers' wives. Indeed, love-thy-neighbor had bounced beautifully around the building from all four walls; it promised to be just that kind of a social success.

Halfway through the third graceful waltz, Butch Cassidy and Elza Lay paid their respects to Beemis and politely unbuckled their six-shooters for safekeeping. The music stopped—nobody seemed to know why, but it stopped nonetheless. Forty sets of eyes followed the dapper pair. Every single woman's heart fluttered a bit at the tall, handsome man next to Cassidy—he commanded that kind of presence. Every motion he made oozed with charm and a bit of swagger, too, thrown in for good measure. There was no mistaking the man; he had it all: looks, a great build, a devilish take-your-chances-with-me-lady captivating smile that complimented the man from head to toe. Lord, he was something to see, and he sure as hell knew it!

Butch, ever the diplomat, bubbled over with his distinctive style of dry humor. "I've held up a few things in my day, but never a dance. Please, please, my good people, let's get back to dancing!"

That bit of double-edged wit received at least a dozen hoots and snickers, particularly among the men. One young buck remarked, "Wonder who or what he held up this time to pay for them spiffy duds?"

Another seconded the motion. "Hell, by the time we find out, Butch'll be long gone. That kinda' news don't exactly travel pony express down here."

One of the young, unattached females spoke for the dozen single ladies. She never took her eyes off Elza while she gushed, "He's so damned good lookin,' kinda makes you wonder what he's busy doin' when he's not using his six-shooter."

It was too good a question not to deserve another young buck's loaded reply. He turned to the young lady with the stars still in her eyes. "Well now, I'll just be there's more'n a few women who found out his hips ain't the only place Mister Lay can shoot from...probably got another six-shooter down there, too!"

That sewed up most of the thoughts about one Elza Lay. If you're a bank loaded with money, better post an extra guard or two! If you're a lady with time to spare—look out!

The fiddle music broke up the crowd and their caustic remarks and thoughts for the time being. Butch managed a couple of dances with several of the ranchers' wives, then concentrated on renewing his friendship with Josie with a dance or two after tactfully assuring Cleve Dreschler that was all he had in mind.

The dancing moved on through the evening at a good pace, when at last, the head fiddler called out, "Last dance! Last dance! Find your true love'n make it count! Last dance!"

There was a scurry and a bustle; no one wanted to be left out. Elza wasted no time getting Ann into his arms. He was so light and graceful on his feet, the man was polished perfection in every sense. Around the floor they circled, kicking up their heels and toes to the polka strains coming from the squeeze box, the Italian concertina, ably supported by the whine, twang, and saw from the husband-and-wife fiddle team.

Elza and Ann ended up in front of Beemis when the polka came to a resounding halt. Lay stooped low to whisper something in her ear. Josie saw it from twenty feet away. Beemis was so close, he felt he should've been part of the conversation.

"Come, Annie, Josie," he called out, "time to head back home!"

"Ann," Elza blurted out, "I didn't get a chance to finish—"

Beemis sawed Elza's eloquent thought in two. "Got a rule out at our ranch: Whoever comes with me to the dance goes back the same way—with me!"

Elza's eyes pleaded for more time; his lips spoke the words. "Mister Markham, surely you could make an exception, just this once." He turned to Ann. "I assure you, I'll deliver you back home in my buckboard, safe and sound."

"Good-night, Mister Lay!"

"But, but…Ann?"

"One last time, *good-night*!"

Beemis Markham was probably the only person in the entire West who ever got in the last word on Elza Lay. For all his charm and social manners, it took an old-crust Army scout to put him in his place—at least, for this night.

There was a noticeable lack of conversation between Josie, Beemis, and Annie all the way back to the ranch. They drove under the main gate, and to both women's surprise, Beemis let them off at the plank steps leading to the front veranda of the ranch house. "Uncle, why don't you let me drive to the horse barn? I'll unhitch the team; you've had a long day."

Beemis refused to hand over the reins or step down. "Thanks, Josie, but I need to do this…'cause if I don't, I'm likely as hell to say something that might upset a certain young lady I used to think an awful lot of."

The women stepped down. Beemis snapped the buggy whip over the team's rumps, and they were off in the moonlight headed to the horse barn.

Josie waited a full two minutes; then she really tore into her sister. "I never thought I'd see the day! What the hell came over you tonight? You didn't dance, hell, you fell into his arms like some cheap slut who rubs her body all over him! You—"

"You'd better shut up, Sister!"

"Don't tell me what to do; I wasn't the one who invited him on and on. It's a good thing Deke wasn't here tonight; there'd be all hell to pay if he'd a' seen what Beemis and I saw."

"Oh, yeah! And just what do you and my dear uncle think you saw? I'll tell you! Nothing! All I did was kick up my heels and have some fun! So I did, and now I'm being roasted for it!"

They started down the hall toward their bedrooms. Josie wasn't through. Up shot her warning finger in Annie's face. She waved it back and forth, so close Annie was sorely tempted to take a bite out of it! Anything at all, to change the subject. "It was disgusting, the way you threw yourself at him! Hogging up all those dances with him! You're supposed to be a promised woman! Why couldn't you at least act like one?"

Annie tried to break away from the accusations. Josie moved even closer to cut off any possible movement toward her bedroom. She felt pinned against the wall. "Well, Mother, I've had about all I can take from you tonight. Get the hell outta my way!"

"Not 'til you come to your senses, dear Sister! Well, have you?"

Annie let her temper cool down. Then she calmly said what was on her mind. "I let most of what Elza said to me go in one ear and out the other! Even when he whispered in my ear as the last dance ended! He knows how much I like horses, so he invited me to go riding with him in the morning. But the way you and Uncle are carrying on, you'd'a thought he asked me to lie down with him right on the dance floor."

"Do you honestly think all he has on his mind is riding with you tomorrow? C'mon, Annie, surely you can do better than that."

This time Annie did the finger pointing. "You know, Sister, you'd better clean up your mind! I wasn't going to do one damned thing about Elza Lay tomorrow. Now, I will! Just to show you and Uncle how wrong you two are!"

Annie shoved her sister out of the way and moved down the hall. Josie followed hot on her heels. Annie beat her to the door. *Slam!* Then Josie heard the door latch click!

Josie was furious. She knocked on the door soundly. "I'm not through with you yet! Let me in! Annie! Do you hear me? Let me in!"

She stood alone in the hallway outside of Annie's bedroom door. She thought about knocking again and again, but decided that sore knuckles was about all she'd get for her trouble. "Alright, Annie, if you're so damned bent on going riding, you'd better make damned good n' sure that the only thing Elza Lay rides is his horse!"

Annie sat alone on her bed, a very angry young lady. She felt betrayed by the very two persons whom she loved dearly. Were her actions with Elza Lay really that bad or disgusting? True, she'd flirted with him most of the evening, but it was just that, nothing more. She was sure he understood that it was just a harmless game she'd drawn him into, more out of a sense of loneliness, because she felt so empty and alone without Deke being by her side. Lord, how she missed him!

She gave herself a good pep talk. "Hey, Annie, you're in control! Look at the way you kept Deke from getting what he wanted! Boy, did you ever shut him down when he thought he was all but in! And Mister Lay, just in case you try anything on me, I'll really shut you down! You'll never get within a foot of where Deke's been because I love him, not you! And…and you know what, Mister Lay? As soon as Deke comes back, I'll be married, and you'll be where you belong: with Butch Cassidy!"

Ann slept in, finally letting her fitful sleep have its way. She arose and put on her split riding skirt. She decided not to drop by the bunkhouse for breakfast so that neither Beemis or Josie would get a chance to jump on her all over again about last night. She went to the kitchen, sliced two pieces of bread, spread each with a quarter-inch layer of Josie's berry jam, and headed back to her wash basin in her room. There she transformed herself into what she really was: a most attractive, desirable young woman. The last thing she put on was her new Stetson hat, a present from Deke after his last payday. She slipped the hat's leather string under her chin to keep the wind from knocking it off her head—one of Deke's suggestions that always worked, for in his mind if anything was new, he'd do his doggonedest to make sure it stayed that way as long as possible. Going without for years had, indeed, left Deke with a down-to-earth attitude and approach about most everything, including money.

Out toward the stable, Ann strode again, hoping she wouldn't have to come face to face with either Beemis or Josie. Her spirits rose by the time she set foot inside the tack shed. Again it was clear sailing.

Glory let out a whinny long before her master opened the gate to her stall.

Annie set the Indian-weaved blanket and the saddle down. She stroked the mare's chin. "Well, old girl, time to get outside...enjoy this beautiful day." She moved on, petting her round belly. "Say, say, what have we here?"

The mare whinnied again as if they were on the same language level. "Boy, are you ever fat!...I know! I know! Been neglectin' you, haven't I? No more, Glory, that's a promise! And we both know I do keep my promises! 'Course, there's a couple of people around here that might think otherwise, but we'll show 'em, won't we?"

Ann needed to be in the saddle again, letting Glory have her head, blowing out some of the fat and feed as her powerful legs stroked in unison, kicking up thin wafers of dust on the trail once they passed the gravel at the main gate. They veered sharply to the right, heading toward Crouse's ranch and Butch Cassidy's cabin perched high above on a rocky point up the face of Diamond Mountain.

She choose the easier of two paths to the Crouse Ranch, passing by stream-fed meadows so rich with tall, green grass that it tickled the belly of Glory at times. She called out to Glory. "Boy, won't Beemis lick his chops when he sees this."

Just to the west of Crouse's ranch, the lower trail rose sharply, zigzagging back and forth until it joined the upper trail. She urged Glory on, her heart pounding with every stride her horse took, wondering why she felt torn between two conflicting desires. One, getting stronger by the minute as though there was a magnetism drawing her toward a man who would surely try to live up to his reputation. The other singed and burned at her conscience and good sense, telling her she was risking everything by keeping a promise made to a stranger, who'd held her far too close on a dance floor.

The steep trail forced Glory to slow her pace, giving Annie time to hope that Elza wouldn't be there. If, by chance, they should meet again, she would truthfully say she kept her promise, then toss out a quick good-bye, and be rid of the entire infatuated mess.

Glory topped the last rise and her heart hit rock bottom. There stood Butch's cabin with its front door wide open. In the open doorway sat Elza Lay on a chair tilted back against one side so his long legs could accommodate the open space. He looked to be the picture of what he was, a devilish dandy, taking in the view and the sunshine, just waiting for a certain woman to walk into his web of seduction.

He rose to hail her. "Your uncle never gave me a chance to mention the hour, so I figured I'd better wait it out, in case you kept your promise. Now that you have, thanks for coming."

Annie felt nervous being alone with him. She looked around. "Where's Butch? This is his cabin; why isn't he here?"

Elza helped her off of Glory. "Easy, easy now. I won't bite, I promise!" He smiled at Annie, then kissed her hand. His sudden attention caught her off-guard. "Told you, I don't bite." His second smile cut her heart in two. "Butch won't be back for some time...give us plenty of time to get acquainted, maybe do some riding...later."

"I...I came up just for the ride! That's all!"

Suddenly Elza turned his back to her and nearly doubled over with laughter.

Annie was furious. "I don't see one thing funny about me keeping my promise!'

He turned around to face her. "No, not you, Ann! It's Butch!"

Now Annie was stumped. "What's so funny about Butch?"

The laughter kept on coming nonstop. Tears welled up in the corners of the most gorgeous pair of eyes Annie had ever seen on a man. Elza finally wiped most of the moisture away with his shirt sleeve.

"Well, are you gonna tell what's so funny or not?

Her question was made to order for the most handsome man she had ever laid eyes on. He shook his head and regained his composure. "Butch said to this lawman, who stopped him on the street, 'You have a good day, Sir!' Right after we cleaned the payroll out, right under his very nose! That's what's so funny!"

"How come this lawman didn't get suspicious? I don't understand!"

Elza motioned for Annie to sit in his chair. He waited until he was sure he had her full attention. "I'd better back up a bit. Don't see any harm in telling you; we'll be long-gone by the time this hole would've gotten the news anyway! Ever hear about the Castle Gate Coal Mine over in Utah? Near a town called Price?"

"No, can't say as I have! Why?"

"Butch knows that country better than the back of his hand. They have more than two hundred men workin' the coal mine over there. There's been a lot of outlaw activity around Price, so their paydays are staggered; that way, nobody knows for sure when the payroll from Salt Lake City will show up. And that's why they've never been cleaned out, 'til Butch beat 'em at their own game!"

"Alright, I'll bite. How'd he do it?"

The gleam in Elza's eyes said a lot. The grin on his face said even more. His lips did the rest. "For two weeks, Butch rode down to the depot to meet the train from Salt Lake City. Got so everybody knew him and waved to him. He kept track, so he had a pretty good idea when the next payroll wad was due. Now all he needed to make sure of his getaway was a fast horse. One that had been seen around town so nobody would think anything about him or the horse. He blended into the town's goings-on like he belonged, like he'd always been there."

"Where'd he find such a fast horse?

"Ann, this is the next to the best part. Bob Meeks' cousin, Joe, has the fastest horse by far in those parts. When he's not part of the local sheriff's posse, he races the big grey for money. Does pretty well, too, from what we heard. Anyways, Butch talks Joe Meek into loaning him that horse. You know what a good talker old Butch is! Always the right words at the right time to cover the right situation."

"Do I! My sister swallowed so much of his bull, it's a wonder she kept her sanity. It was a mighty close call, two months ago!"

"Alright, everything's set for Butch's big surprise. The train from Salt Lake rolls in, and as usual, he's down there to greet it. Only this time, he guessed right! Sure enough, the paymaster and two guards get off the train and start walking up the street to the coal company's office above a store, say about seventy-five yards or so away. Now get this, old Butch even helps clear the way for the paymaster. 'Let me give you a hand,' he tells the paymaster. 'Didn't see any strangers hanging around, but you never can tell!'"

"I don't believe it! What brass!"

"Well, when the paymaster and the two guards reach the stairs, I and Meeks step out from under it to relieve them of those heavy payroll bags. 'Better do as they say,' Butch tells them. 'They look like they mean business! No sense gettin' killed over somebody else's money!'"

"Then what?"

"We cold-cocked the three to keep them from yelling for help, and Butch rolls up the biggest and heaviest payroll bag in a blanket, ties it behind his saddle, and meanders, slow as you please, down Main Street. He tips his hat to the ladies and stops to chat with the sheriff's deputy. He looks up the street, catches my signal, and says to the deputy, 'You have a good day, Sir!'"

"You mean, nobody saw anything in broad daylight?"

"That's right! Right under their noses! Leave it to old Butch to figure all the angles and come up with something different. Pretty soon, the paymaster and the guards come to, and they go screaming and yelling down Main Street. 'We've been robbed! We've been held up!' They shout at the top of their lungs. Meeks and I hide out in the livery stables with the two small payroll bags until we see the deputy find Joe Meeks and a couple of others. He deputizes them, then says to Joe, 'Where's that fast horse of yours? There's still time to catch those payroll robbers! They can't be far away!' Joe has a sheepish look plastered all over his face. 'Ain't got my fast horse…loaned it couple'a weeks ago to a cowboy…friend of my cousin.'"

"So, how did you and Bob Meeks slip outta town so quick?"

"We didn't! We stashed the rest of the payroll in our saddle bags, hid the bags under some hay, and stepped in at a local saloon for a couple of drinks. We knew they'd never catch Butch, not on that fast horse! Once he reached his first relay, that fresh mount would take care of any posse chasing for good!"

"Weren't you afraid that the paymaster and his two guards would recognize you two?"

"Butch had that figured out, too! He knew first thing they'd do was run to the telegraph office to send for the sheriff. Butch had Meeks cut the wire, so he knew there'd be no outside lawmen chasing him, only the local deputy and his sworn-in posse. And he also knew that these men were still on duty for the mine, which means that there'd be no drinking on company time! All we had to do was make sure we left town the opposite way the posse left. That way, we wouldn't run the risk of ever meeting up with them!"

Annie got up from the chair. "Butch'll get caught someday. He'll outsmart himself, make one mistake too many, and it'll all be over for the three of you!"

"Where are you going, Ann?

"In case you forgot, I came up here to ride with you, so let's do it!"

Annie headed for Glory. Elza's long stride beat her to the horse. "Here, let me give you a hand; then I'll tend to the reins."

She placed the toe of her boot into the foot stirrup, fully expecting Elza would do the gentlemanly thing by helping her on up. She felt his strong arms encircle her waist. He helped her alright, all the way down into his arms.

Startled by his sudden impulse, she tried to slap his face. He caught her hand off the side of his head before she could deliver enough sting to leave a lasting mark.

"Put me down! Put me down!" she screamed.

Elza ignored her outbursts and her flailing arms. He seemed possessed with something she'd never run up against with either Hi Bernard or Deke

Landry: polished, fluid motion that bordered on perfection.

Annie felt light as a feather in his arms, despite her attempts to wriggle loose, only to find herself carried through the doorway. She had the distinct sensation that he accomplished three things in the same motion, though she didn't know how that could be possible. He moved toward the bed, used one boot heel to catch the door, and never broke stride.

He laid her down oh so gently and continued to kiss her lips while his fingers went into perpetual motion. About the time his lips left hers, she went into near shock at the way he'd undressed her upper body. Her men's work shirt was wide open, and her brassiere had all but flown away, naked testimony that she'd been easy prey to the fastest fingers in the West. He dropped his head down and continued his fluid assault, feasting on her nipples until he received the response he obviously was looking for: her sexual arousal.

"Don't, don't, please don't," she offered, trying her best not to let him know how much she liked what he'd done up 'til that very moment.

She watched him work her nipples over, helpless to do anything more about it. The only thing she refused to do was help hold his head in place as she'd done so many times Deke.

Elza sensed he'd found her most vulnerable spot, her breasts. He went after them, polishing his tongue over her nipples until she moaned out in sheer pleasure. Lord, how he did work them over! By the time he'd let up some, he had her exactly where he wanted her: ready for what he'd been preparing her for—penetration.

How he raised her up enough to slide her pants down and get her boots off, poor Annie never fully knew the way he did it. She only knew that somehow he'd worked his fluid magic on her once more.

He never bothered to straddle her as Deke had done countless times before. Instead, he opened her up and moved inside, his shaft erect for instant insertion. She remembered only one thing; she winced with pain.

He smiled, overjoyed by his discovery. "Oh," he said, "I'll try to take it as easy as I can."

Annie felt him push again, wondering how in the world she could possibly accommodate such a big, thick shaft. To her surprise, somehow he managed to sink every inch he had into her. Lord, he was deep, oh so deep!

She was amazed by a new sensation—a fullness that seemed to overwhelm her, despite her tightness around his shaft.

He kept most of his weight off her, except where they were joined at the hips. Gradually, ever so gradually, he moved his shaft in and out, trying to get into some kind of body rhythm, she believed.

"Meet me," he whispered in low tones. "You can do it…"

She lay back and let him do the work. After all, less than two minutes ago, she had still been a virgin. She could only look into those beautiful eyes of his and wish she knew what in the world he was trying to tell her.

"Meet me," he pleaded again. "Push up when I stroke…it'll feel a lot better each time you do…"

Up 'til now, Annie had felt cheated, keenly disappointed by what was happening to her. She lay back and let him do all the work, her mind on remembering the times Deke had tried to make her and she'd held him off at the last instant—for this?

"C'mon, help me," he pleaded again, bringing her back to them, to the now.

Alright, she told herself, might just as well give it a go. She concentrated with both mind and body, trying to meet him, as he called it. At first, she mistimed everything. Then suddenly, it happened, not once, twice, but almost every time. The more she met his strokes, the better if felt. Then, she realized what was happening; her own wetness was lubricating his big shaft. An eagerness came over her; now she wanted more and more of this great feeling mixed with pure pleasure.

Annie was on fire, and Elza sensed it. Now, he really poured it to her, raising her to one level after another of pure sexual ecstacy. Every fantasy she had ever had now was being more than fulfilled by beautiful body motion.

She started pushing up hard, barely giving him time to re-stroke. Lord, what pleasure! What a feeling! She wondered how long they could keep this up, wanting more, and wishing it could go on until each wore the other out.

Annie felt Elza break their perfect harmony. All he seemed to want to do was push harder and harder into her. Lord, she thought, what more could he possibly what? He was as deep as he could get into her. She noticed other changes, too, coming in a hurry. She felt his breath on her face, coming in erratic bursts, matching his hit-or-miss strokes. Judging by the way he acted, she was sure he must be in some kind of exquisite pain, though there was still plenty of pleasure still left on his face.

He jerked and jerked. All of a sudden, she felt a series of rapid pulsations going on deep within her. He was coating her with something that felt hot! No, not just hot, but lukewarm, then somewhere in between! Exhausted, he lay on top of her, his body spent. Now, she had the answer to just how long he could give her this special kind of pleasure.

They lay together, savoring the moment, each aware that it was over yet bonded together by what had happened between them. The hardness of his shaft changed dramatically; it felt soft and limp as it seemed to withdraw from her without much effort on his part.

Elza rolled off her to get dressed again. Annie still did not remember him undressing before he had seduced her. That part was still a blur in her memory, part of his fluid motion, which bedazzled her beyond comprehension or recognition. She only knew one thing: He had, indeed, had his way with her. The wetness between her thighs didn't lie.

Annie sat up and turned her back to him, now angry and ashamed how easy it must've been for him to make her. She reached for her brassiere. The pangs of her guilt and cheapness stabbed her worse than a knife in the back. There'd been no love or passionate embrace between them, only physical attraction that she had allowed to go too far—way too far!

He must've read her mind. By the time she pulled her pants up she heard him say, "That clod you're hooked up with sure has been missing out on the best piece of tail I've had in a long, long time! Considering you were a virgin, I'd say your performance was first rate! Yes, Ann, it was first rate!"

She buttoned up her shirt, then exploded. "I don't need your report card on me to know I've made the biggest mistake in my life! Go to hell, Mister Lay!"

He smiled, oblivious to her anger or disgust. "Look, he doesn't have to know, now does he? Go ahead, marry him! Tell him he was your first; he'll believe you! If he gets to wondering later on, tell him what a lot of women say."

"Oh yeah? And what would that be?"

"Why, dear Ann, I'm surprised at you. Just tell him a lot of hard riding broke your cherry. Any man who rides a horse will fall for that. Happens quite a bit of the time, so I'm told."

Annie pulled on her boots. Her question confirmed what she already knew. "You've had a lot of women...Doesn't that bother you at all?"

His smile became a gloat as he boasted. "Yes, I've had my share...better make it more than my share. I look at it this way: Some preacher's wife or some rancher or storekeeper's wife will not get the chance to really feel fulfilled. They'll have to go on through life feeling they've missed out on something."

"You egotistical bastard! How come you left out the saloon sluts or whores off your list?"

He stepped forward and bowed. "Ann, Ann, look at me! Now, do I look like the kind of man who needs them? I've never had to pay for a piece of ass in my life. The women I take good care of all come to me! Like you!"

Annie finished pulling on her boots. As she stormed by Elza, he opened the door for her and put a little extra effort into his most graceful bow. "Then I take it you won't be back for any more horseback riding. Pity, though, because I'll still be here for at least three more days…in case you should change your mind."

"You got that right, Mister Lay! GO TO HELL!"

Annie rode back, slowly, toward the Markham ranch, her heart and her mind in torment beyond anything she'd ever experienced. She felt ashamed and disgusted with herself. Over and over, she asked the question, how could she have done such a thing to herself? To Deke? To them? She felt like vomiting, and earnestly wished she could if somehow that would bring up the sordid affair she'd had with Elza Lay and leave it on the ground where it belonged. Instead, she felt lower than a saloon slut. At least they charged their customers for going through the physical motions with the agreed-upon price left on some bedside table or night stand before they lay on their backs.

She barely remembered reaching Vermillion Creek, her mind a kaleidoscope of hurt, anger, and self-incrimination. Glory snorted and jerked the reins out of her hands. Annie just sat on her mount, oblivious to anything moving around her, even the ice-cold, rippling waters that always fascinated her and refreshed her mind as well as her spirit, and often times, her body.

Her body began to jerk into convulsive sobs, so she got down off her mount and held Glory's reins in her hands while the mare drank. There on the creek bank, she had the cry of her life, hoping and wishing, somehow, the waters would refresh her heart and carry her troubles downstream for good. When the sobbing finally stopped, she dipped her handkerchief and held it against her reddened eyes and swollen cheeks.

"Isn't there something I can do to help, Sis?"

Josie started to hand Annie the food tray, then decided against it. "I'll take this out to Beemis; I'm running a little late this morning. You know how our uncle expects his lunch to be served on time. Do you suppose when we get to be his age we'll do the same?"

Annie laughed. Oh, how good it felt to laugh! "Well, Sis, guess it all depends on who'll be left in our lives to wait on us! Sure there isn't something I can do to help?"

Josie placed the tray back in Annie's hands. "Be careful when you walk; I filled his glass of milk too full! Might spill over on his sandwich."

Annie started for the front porch. To her surprise, Josie followed right behind. "Where are you going?"

"Out to curry down old Jerome!"

A lump the size of a crab apple lodged in Annie's throat. "You...you went riding this morning?"

"Sure did! Oh, I meant to ask you, how'd your ride with Mister Wonderful go?"

Annie tossed out her reply. "Oh, we rode around some, no particular place, mostly just here and there. Where'd you go?"

"Oh, I followed you, and like you said, I went to about the same places you and Lay rode to, here and there!"

Josie's bedroom door barely closed before the two sisters had it out. She jerked Annie around and slapped her face. "You stupid, stupid woman," she hissed, trying hard not to turn their confrontation into a shouting match, so Beemis could be kept out for the time being. "I saw your Mister Wonderful carry you into Butch's cabin. Don't you dare lie to me and tell me nothing happened!"

Annie tried to rush into Josie's arms before her tears took over. Josie was not about to offer a sympathetic shoulder or anything else except more scorn. "Don't you want to hear my side, Sis? Don't you? Bet you let Butch go a lot farther than you first intended, didn't you?"

"Butch Cassidy never got between my legs and you damn well know it!" Josie dropped her voice. "You let that man screw you! Yes, my dear Sister, you just screwed yourself outta most everything that used to count in your life! I sure hope you enjoyed it, 'cause that's about all that's left in your life, one real screwing that'll burn on your conscience 'til hell freezes over!"

Annie dropped to her knees and pleaded for understanding. "Please, please, Sis, don't say anything to Beemis or Deke when he gets back! Please, don't!"

"Get off your knees! You'll get no sympathy from me or anyone else, once they find out what you've done!"

"I'll lie if I have to! It's your word against mine! Deke will believe me, not you! Uncle Beemis, too!"

Josie grabbed Annie by the shirt collar. "Oh really? Think about this while you're tryin' to save your precious little hide! Why would I dare say such a terrible thing if there wasn't something to tell? Why, Sis? Why?"

Annie was boxed into a corner with no way out, and she knew it, yet she rallied with her only hope: reasoning. "I'll tell Deke what happened and promise I'll never let it happen again, and it won't! I will be the best wife that ever said I do from now on."

"Still don't know a damned thing about men, do you, Sis? You'd have a better chance with Deke or Beemis by asking them not to take another breath, then going ahead with something that'll never gain one grain of respect back from either!"

Annie's puzzled look said it all. "Whataya mean?"

"Next to life itself, the one thing Deke wants to take to his wedding bed is the fact that he knows he will be your first and only! Now, he gets neither! No matter how many times you tell him it will never happen with another man, no matter how many times you try to make love with him, what you've robbed him of, what you've cheated him out of, will haunt both of you 'til your dying days!"

"I love him too much! I can't let him go! He won't, once I tell him again and again how much he means to me!"

"You should've thought of that before you agreed to go riding with Lay!"

Again Josie's point cut the very heart out of her sister. Tears welled in Annie's eyes, but she fought back. "Give me at least a chance to talk to Deke when he gets back!"

"Then get ready to lose him and get on with your life as best you can, Annie! There's no way out for you!"

The next two days were a nightmare in slow motion for Annie. She lost sleep, looked terrible, and had little or nothing to say to either her uncle or sister. Whenever they tried to talk to her, she seemed lost in time. Her work ethic evaporated into thin air. She ran the gamut of lame excuses to get away from them so she could close the door to her bedroom on a problem that wouldn't let her rest or leave her alone. Each agonizing day, only putt off the inevitable, her showdown with a hard-nosed horse wrangler, who'd captured her heart and soul, and who was undoubtedly on his way back to the ranch.

Beemis watched Annie head back to the main house from the horse corrals. "Yesterday, it was headaches, the day before, said she had an upset stomach. Keeps this up, she'll look worse than me on her wedding day! What in the world's wrong with our Annie?"

Josie started to say something, then changed her thought. "When did you say you were planning on seeing that friend of yours in the bank?"

"Thought I'd take the two-seater the day after Deke and Annie get hitched. We could drive up to Rock Springs together, and I'd put them on the train to start their honeymoon back East! Why?"

"Better look for a new foreman while you're in Rock Springs, Uncle. I'll let Annie fill you in after Deke gets back."

Beemis leaned hard against the rail. "Has to do with Annie ridin' out that mornin' after the dance to meet up with Cassidy's right-arm, that bucket of sticky flypaper who calls himself Elza Lay! Right?"

Elza Lay finished strapping his bedroll behind his saddle. He double-checked his rifle in its scabbard, then opened one of his saddlebags to make sure two boxes of rifle cartridges were there—just in case. His trained ear caught the sound of hooves clattering across the hard, shale outcropping that led up to Butch's cabin. Someone was coming, and coming fast.

Instinctively, his practiced hand went to his six-gun—just in case. He moved behind his mount and waited for the rider to appear, so he could make his move, one way or the other. He strained both eyes; then his jaw dropped a full inch. The rider was the last person on earth he expected to see.

Annie arrived almost as much out of wind as Glory. Elza never got a chance to help her down. "Take me with you," she gasped, trying to catch her second wind.

Elza played coy. "Who says I'm going anywhere? Last time I saw you, I got your famous go-to-hell speech! Why the sudden change?"

Annie tied Glory to the rail. "Couldn't face some people…and I see you are going somewhere!" she pointed repeatedly to his mount. "Your roll's extra thick! Your saddlebags are bulging; you're going somewhere, alright!"

Elza loved the predicament Annie was in. "Couldn't tell your clod, right? How bad do you really want to go?"

"I'm a better rider than either you or Butch! I can handle a rifle better than most men, too! If you need anything done with a rope, there's none better! Now, what do you say?"

He held her at arm's length, then looked at Glory. "My, my, my! Rifle stickin' out the side of your horse, and I see you're packin' a six-shooter, too! Got us a real, live Annie Oakley! Darned if we don't! How bad did you say you wanted to go with me?"

Annie swallowed hard. She'd left her pride and most of her common sense back at the ranch. She knew Elza's question probably had a double edge. "I—

I'll do anything, if you'll just take me with you!"

Elza released his hold. "Well then, Ann, we'd better get to it before Butch shows up! Hole-in-the-Wall bunch broke up! Butch and me are going to meet most of them. Butch's got a whole new plan, better pickings for those he chooses to form our new association." He started to lead Annie toward the cabin.

"Whataja think you're doing? I'm ready to ride!"

Annie's predicament was made to order for Elza Lay. He wasn't about to pass up another chance to bed her down, Cassidy or no Cassidy! A devilish gleam shone in his eyes that complimented his charm, along with plenty of smugness and arrogance. He pulled on her arm. "Well, now, let's see if we can't improve on the last time you were inside."

Annie looked at the bed again in despair. "I'm really not in the mood for this, Elza. Maybe some other time, after we're camped for the night, away from here…"

He kissed the back of her neck, then turned her around and began unbuttoning her work shirt, slowly and deliberately. There'd be no need for his slight-of-hand, fluid motion. "Why don't you leave that up to me? I think I can get you in the mood."

Elza bedded her down and worked her body over from head to toe. Annie would've taken an oath that every part of her body was either touched, kissed, massaged, or stimulated beyond anything she thought possible. He had her so hot, so ready, that by the time he entered, she exploded on his penetration and gasped out in sheer delight and dug her fingernails into his back. She was all over him, urging him on, wanting him to give her more, and more and still more.

He started to push hard again. This time, she knew what was coming, what to expect. Suddenly, he stopped in the midst of their most intense moment.

"What's the matter?" she whispered, still pushing to meet his piston-like strokes.

Annie saw lightning strike in the fingers of Elza Lay. He stayed on her, his six-gun cocked, ready to spew death in an instant. "Somebody's coming; it should be Butch—keep going—I'll watch the door…just in case…"

She heard it too, the unmistakable sound of a horse approaching. She continued her body motion until she'd milked him dry.

"Elza! Elza! It's me, Butch! Who's in there with you?"

"Just a minute more, Butch, we'll be through! Don't come in!"

Annie heard several horses whinny. Glory was saying hi to Butch's mount. Then she thought she heard a horse stomp and start, and stomp some more. Butch must be impatient.

"C'mon, Elza, kick your whore outta the fart sack now! There'll be women where we're going...probably better stuff, too! I see you were ready to go...What changed your mind?"

"Best I've had lately...too good to pass up!"

"Send her out here, let's have a look at her!"

Annie was fit to be tied. How dare they talk about her like she was some old whore, ready to lay down at the first jingle from a gold coin or two! "Get off me," she snarled. "I'll show that Mormon a thing or two!"

Elza warned Butch. "She's coming out, and she's madder than hell! Packin' a gun, too!"

Annie opened the door and stepped out into the sunshine. All she saw was a blur before her eyes.

"Drop it, Annie! You won't stand a chance! Don't make me use this! Sorry about inside...Saw your Arabian, but didn't figure it could be you. Still can hardly believe what I see—never cared much for surprises either...try to avoid them every chance I get."

"I'm joining up with you, so I'll let what you said about me pass for now." She pointed to Glory. "I'm ready to ride, too, so I won't be holding us up any! Where are we going?"

Butch looked at Elza. He didn't get a signal one way or the other. "Didn't Elza tell you? No woman rides with me! Hard and fast rule! Saves a lot of trouble when I have other more important things that need all my attention! Sorry, Annie!"

Eyes blazing red hot, Annie turned on Elza. "You low-down bastard! You dirty sonofabitch! You used me!"

Elza answered back, "Never said I'd take you. I never used you, only screwed you, that's all! And I might add, you sure acted like you enjoyed it!"

Three riders rode, single file, down the steep part of the trail from Cassidy Point to where it branched out about Charley Crouse's ranch. When they came to the fork that joined the lower trail, Butch dropped back to wait for Annie. He could see the agony etched in the honey-blonde's pretty face. She avoided eye contact with him, ashamed no doubt that the word whore he'd used had taken on real meaning after what had happened a second time in three days at his cabin.

Butch broke their stone-cold silence. "Go back and start over, Annie! You can! I can't! If my pardon had come through, I really believe Josie would've married me!"

Annie's eyes glassed over with moisture. "You'd'a never made it, trying to settle down. Your reputation wouldn't let you, same as mine, now!"

He held his mount's reins steady, giving him time to digest Annie's words. "You're wrong; you still have time, once this gets behind you."

"And after it does, I've lost the only man I truly loved. He'll never pardon me for what I've done. Can't really blame him…if the boot was on the other foot."

Butch held out his hand. "Time will tell, Annie! Time will tell! This is good-bye."

They shook hands. "You mean for now 'til you and that good-looking bastard and your knife-throwing sidekick pay us a visit again."

"No, Annie, this is good-bye for good! We're on our way to a little meeting. If things pan out the way I figure, Brown's Hole has seen the last of us! I'm going to be making a big change! You can do the same thing, too!"

Annie held their handshake. She still marveled at the strength he had in such small hands for a man. For the first time, she saw some of what Josie had always seen in him—more than just his usual ring of sincerity! Here was a man who had the brains to be anything he wanted to be: imposter, rancher, meat cutter, land speculator, holdup man, bank robber, churchgoer, and of course, the best in the business, the undisputed king of the outlaws. The title seemed justified now more than ever.

"Anything you'd care to pass along?"

He had a wistful look about him, one of the many shades of Butch Cassidy. "Tell Josie to get on with her life…maybe marry that Cleve fella…that rancher. Pretty decent sort when you come down to it. Tell her I hope she raises a family…" He swallowed a second. "Always wanted a wife and family…From where I'm headed to…that will never be a part of my life."

Butch and Elza rode away, leaving Annie alone with her thoughts and her troubles. Suddenly, Butch turned around in his saddle. "Tell Beemis good-bye, too! Best man I've ever run across, anywhere! Annie?"

"Yeah, Butch!"

"Josie always bragged on you. Said that finishing school back in Boston made you the equal or better of any man, on any subject you'd care to talk about! After those words you used today, don't you think it's time to show her she's absolutely right?"

Annie never let on that day that she was privy to a new era in the making. Butch Cassidy and Elza Lay rode east out of Brown's Park to a meeting at Power Springs, Wyoming, which will forever be called the start and planning for the greatest string of railroad express-car holdups and robberies the West would ever know. From the breakup of the Hole-in-the-Wall Gang, he carefully selected a gang of professionals, unmatched anywhere, anytime. Call it coincidence, dumb luck, or just plain good timing and good fortune. No matter what the call, Butch's Wild Bunch ceased to be! In their place emerged Butch Cassidy at his smartest and best, in absolute control of the Train Robbers Syndicate, a.k.a. Butch Cassidy's train professionals. His new recruits included George Curry, Lonny and Harvey Logan, and Harry Longabaugh, better known as the "Sundance Kid." None of the new members were afraid of gunplay or dynamiting railroad cars, the requisites that Butch needed in order to be successful in his new venture in such a lucrative and promising field of railroad outlawing.

Josie saw Annie riding back under the main gate, so she waited for Annie out at the horse stables. She watched Annie turn Glory loose. "My, my! What have we here! Ann Barnett, the would-be outlaw, who got screwed again and turned down by Butch! How'm I doin', Sis? C'mon, tell me!"

"Shut up! Had about all I can take from you!" She tried to push past her sister.

Out came the folded piece of paper from Josie's apron. She opened it, then tore it into little pieces in front of Annie. "This note you left doesn't begin to cover the hurt you laid on everybody around here! Beemis is mad enough to scald a chicken! And what does his little Annie do? Let me tell you! She rode off like some thief in the night to join up with Butch Cassidy! But as usual, she played her stupid woman part to the hilt! No doubt you let Elza screw you again, and Butch said no to you joining him! I coulda saved you this stupid trip and another screwin' if you'd've told me what you were planning on doing! Butch told me months ago that he would never let any woman ride with him. Said they're nothing but trouble!"

Annie doubled up her fists and took a swing at Josie's jaw. Fortunately for both, she missed. Josie grabbed Ann after her miss and shook her hand. "Better pull yourself together, Sis. This must be your day, alright! Time for you to play stupid twice in the same day! Deke's back!"

Annie ran like the wind toward the ranch house with Josie hot on her heels. She washed her face, put on a touch of lipstick, combed her hair, then changed into her best blue dress. She snapped at Josie. "Since you're not doin' a damn thing but watchin' and gettin' in the way, how 'bout going to your room to find that good pair of scissors?"

Josie shook her head, then disappeared. A minute later, she reappeared with the scissors.

Annie held up her dress. "You're better with scissors than me, Sis! Go ahead, cut all the netting out from the bustline on up!"

Josie did as she was told. When she was through, she handed the dress back. "Don't see what showing Deke more of your breasts is supposed to do! What he needs to hear is the truth from you, not look down at your tits and wish his head was there!"

Annie walked the well-trod path from the front porch of the main house to Deke's bunkhouse. She was determined to play it any way she had to so long as Deke remained at Markham Ranch. If she could get him to stay, no matter what she'd done, she was sure that, in time, he'd come around, and then she'd have the chance to make amends, to prove to him that true love could win out if given a chance.

She didn't necessarily buy into the old wives' saying, "damaged goods can't be repaired." No, she had a better phrase: "Give the right man what he wants when he thinks he needs it, and a woman's past will soon fade into history."

Fifty feet away from the open door of the bunkhouse told her that Shorty McCallum was holding court. She stood in the doorway, saw Deke with his back to her, shaving, while the diminutive Shorty had the other seven hands in stitches with one hilarious story after another.

Annie pressed a finger to her lips, her signal for Shorty to continue. He smiled at Annie, shoved his slouch of a battered hat further back on his elf-sized ears and let go. "I tell ya, there ain't nothun' worse than a danged gandy dancer! Good thing I spotted that Chinaman first day in Rock Springs or else we'd still be lookin' fer a cook! Right, Deke?"

Deke worked his brush around the shaving mug and lathered up one side of his face. "Yeah, Shorty's right!"

"Took Deke n' me two afternoons at the Painted Lady Saloon to loosen that gull-danged gandy dancer foreman enough to find out if he had a money belt or not! Ain't that so, Deke?"

"Yup!"

"How'd you spot his money belt anyways?"

200

"Well, Tex, I got pretty hard up a few years back! Yup, I worked on the railroad fer a spell 'til I heer'd Markham Ranch was hirin'. All them railroad foremen carry payday money in a belt round their belly, so ah know'd he had one. Trouble was, this one was so damned fat, I had a hard time pickin' out which was his belt from all them rolls of blubber he had 'round him!"

That brought the house down. They hooted and hollered and stomped their boots. When the commotion quieted down, Shorty called over to Deke. "Of course, after I spotted his belt, you poured a few drinks of cheap rotgut down his guzzler, so he'd pay off the Chinaman, so we could leave town! And then, would'ja believe it, that foreman tried to cheat the Chinee 'til Deke made him pay up every dollar owed him! Tell ya 'nother thing, Deke n' me got to sample his grub on the way back! Comes 'bout as close to Josie's cookin' as you guys will ever git! Ain't that a fact, Deke?"

Deke shifted his stance. Then he spotted her in the mirror. Lord, what a pretty sight! He tried to blow her a kiss. Instead, two wads of shaving lather left his mouth, landing a few feet in front of him. Everybody roared and roared, and roared some more. Even Annie sagged against the doorway, trying to keep from doubling over with laughter.

Deke pulled the towel off his shoulder. "Alright! Alright! That's enough!" He wiped enough lather so he could finish his orders. "All of you, listen up! Me and this pretty little lady ain't had a chance for a proper hello for quite a spell! Shorty, you lead 'em over to the cook shack and have 'em meet up with Mister Chang Lee, our new, genuine Chinaman cook! And stay over there 'cause you're gonna get early supper tonight! And Shorty, how 'bout closin' that door when you leave?"

The door latch barely had time to click before Annie was in his arms, forcing her lips through more lather, feasting on his. "Oh, Deke, Deke, my love, how I've missed you! Never forget how much I love you! Never forget!"

Deke moved into her and Annie responded like never before. She left nothing to chance, pouring every inch of her dress into any fraction of space between them, from her hips right on up to her breasts, which formed their own bond to his chest.

"Annie, oh, my Annie," he kept repeating over and over again. "I started to shave…was about to take a bath…hope you don't mind…must smell stronger than a billy goat…wanted to get cleaned up before I came up to see you first, then Beemis…"

"I don't care how bad you smell. I only care about you! That you're back! That you're here with me again! Do you have any idea how much I love you?

Do you?"

He held her at arm's length finally to get another look at his Annie. To see what he'd been missing for twelve long days. "You look different, somehow…thinner too…that you don't need. Have you been cryin' a lot or worryin'…'bout me?"

Annie's face flushed beet red. "Yes, my love…you have no idea how I've missed you! How much I want to spend every day with you from now on…"

Deke's excitement overflowed. "Annie! Annie! I got good news! And I got better news! Which do you wanta hear first?"

His excitement spread to her. "Alright, let's have the good news first!"

He held up the forefinger of each hand to emphasize. "Preacher's on his way with the license…be here day after tomorrow! Hope that's soon enough! Even got one of them picture-takin' fellers from Rock Springs to come with him! We're gonna do this up right! After all, only figure on gettin' hitched once! Someday, we'll look at our weddin' picture and say, 'What a day it was! What a wonderful day we had!' Before I left, Josie said she'd bake our weddin' cake! Got two days to do it! Hope that don't cut her too short!"

Annie looked away, fighting hard to control her emotions and her tears.

"Hey, hey, little lady! Are you sure you're alright? Thought I saw the makin's of a tear or two! I know! Must be what they call tears of happiness! Or is that tears of joy? Think both probably are right…"

He watched his Annie put on her best poker face—not one hint of the impending disaster that lurked in her mind or heart. "That's great news, Deke…and about the better news?"

"Come, take my hand!"

He lead her to his bunk. There, she could only stare at a large, white cardboard box with its pretty pink ribbon. She gasped out, knowing full well what must be inside.

"Annie, it's for you! Open it!"

She sank to her knees, then sobbed out her hurt, her pain. "I can't, Deke…I can't…Oh God, what have I done…I can't…I can't…don't you see?"

He dropped beside her and took her in his arms to comfort her. "It's the only one in Rock Springs…saw it in a window…shoulda seen me go right in that store. I told the lady, size eight—that's what Josie told me to say. It's the most beautiful wedding dress I've ever seen…Truth is, it's the only one I've ever seen! Here, let me take the ribbon off, but you have to lift the top off! Hold it up to you…you know, like when you and Josie go over to Jarveys to try on new dresses…you always hold up one you like first!"

Annie waited for Deke to untie the ribbon. He was all fingers and thumbs, so he finally had to settle on sliding the ribbon off. Then he watched her, the excitement coupled with such anticipation glowing in his eyes and across his face.

She folded back two layers of tissue paper and carefully lifted the garment out. There was a daintiness about the exquisite dress; its white lace and beadwork, especially from the bodice on up, left her speechless.

"Ain't she something? Aint's she, Annie?"

"Oh! Oh! Oh!" she gasped out. "It's so beautiful, Deke!"

"Wait'll I see you with it on! Now I understand! Yes, Sir, now I see what Josie was tryin' to tell me!"

Annie held it to her, being careful it didn't touch the plank floor. "What was Josie trying to tell you, love?"

"Josie said that color, that white color is something special to the woman what puts on a white weddin' dress. It means she's pure…you know, innocent-like, 'cause if she wears it, it means there's never been another man before him…that he'll always be her first and only! Never thought I'd say this, Annie, but now I'm glad we didn't. All those times down by the creek…on that Indian saddle blanket…when I wanted to…and you wouldn't quite let me. Now it all kinda makes sense…Yup! It sure does!"

Deke watched his Annie, puzzled by her reluctance to try it on.

"Ain'tcha gonna try it on, Annie? Shucks, I'll even turn my back…pretend I never seen you in your birthday suit—touched and kissed all them special places you got—if that'll help."

Annie carefully folded the wedding dress and laid it back in the box before her tears nearly blinded her. She sank to her knees, her sobs so severe, her body shook, again and again.

Deke knelt beside her. He tried to comfort her. She pushed him away. "Annie, Annie, it's okay! We didn't make love! You got as much right to wear this dress as anybody! Close doesn't count!"

She sobbed out her hurt. She cried out her pain, then mumbled a few words.

Deke bent close to Annie once more. "What's that you're sayin'? Sounds like you said somethun' 'bout not bein' pure…but Annie, that can't be! I should know! That can't be!"

She mumbled again between sobs, her words still unrecognizable to Deke. Then she rose and started for the door.

Deke caught up. He spun her around. "What's goin' on, Annie? Isn't that dress good 'nuff for you? Paid damned good money for it, and I can't take it back! C'mon, spill it! What's goin' on! How come you changed your mind? Won't even try it on?"

Her lips quivered, her body shook, and finally she spoke clear enough. "Promise me, whatever happens, you won't leave here! Promise me! Deke?"

Now he was confused and upset. He was still trying to get a read on her. "I ain't goin' nowhere, Annie! You know that! Got the best job, best boss I ever had. What's wrong, Annie? Why am I gettin' the dodge?"

She fell into his arms and buried her face in his chest, too ashamed to look up to face him with the truth. "You're not going to be my first...or only...not anymore."

For a full minute, they stayed together, Deke holding his Annie, trying his best to comfort her while he sorted through her words, over and over. Then he exploded. He shook her again and again. Her head whipped to one side, then the other; she was a real-life rag doll that'd gone limp! "Gotta be old slick himself!" he yelled out to vent his anger and hurt. "Elza, wasn't it?"

"Yes..."

"I don't understand! I don't understand! How? When? You're a promised woman! How could you?"

Annie gave no answer, at least not fast enough for Deke's liking. He raised his hand to backhand her face until she was willing to talk. He started, then held up. Instead, he kicked at his bunk bed, then ran over to tip it back up. He changed his mind and punched the hell outta the wall. He had to hit something, anything, to get some of the hurt and anger out.

Annie screamed and went running to him. "Deke! Deke! You're hurt! Your hand's bleeding! Let me help!"

"Stay away from me! Come one step closer, I'm liable to beat you to death! Think you was Elza for a minute!"

Annie ran to the wash basin and grabbed his shaving towel. She dipped it into the water pail and rushed back. Afraid Deke would turn on her, she tossed the towel. "Wrap it around your hand, tight. Should help stop the bleeding..."

He followed her instructions. He sat on his bunk bed, strangely calm, holding the towel around his skinned-up knuckles. Annie kept her distance, standing on the opposite side, not sure if he was ready to explode again or talk. "When, Annie?"

"Three days ago. Supposed to go riding with him after I promised him the night before...at the dance. One thing lead to another...Still don't know exactly what happened...but it did..."

The silence between them was deafening. He broke it. "All those times…you made me wait…for what? So he could be first? He only wanted one thing from you…couldn't you see that? How could you fall for him? How? How, Annie?"

"I've asked myself that at least a million times…You're right…doesn't make sense."

Again the conversation died. Each was afraid to say more for fear the damage would be too great, the hurt too deep, the anger lasting too long for them ever to get past this. Annie still thought there was a chance, a way to hold onto him. "I know you'll find this hard to believe…but I love you, now, more than ever. I realize this now…Please, for your sake and mine. I know the wedding's off—it should be—but stay on for Beemis' sake, even if you can't stand me anymore. Don't take it out on him for the mistake I've made. You're still the best horseman Markham Ranch ever had…"

Deke rose from his bunk and went to the washbasin. He soaked his hand in the water. The bleeding had stopped, but his right hand was terribly bruised and swollen. "I'd like to…but it'd never work, Annie…"

Annie came to him. She even dared to rest an arm on his shoulder. "Why won't it work, love? Why?"

"Every time you'd be around me, I'd want you…never stop thinkin' 'bout you…what we had, what used to be. Pretty soon, Beemis would see me slackin' off…my mind hardly on my job anymore. He'd have to let me go…'cause I'd never be worth much to him, or to you, for that matter…Nope! Never work!"

"Tell you what, give it two months! Then if you still feel it won't work, I'll go to Beemis myself and tell him to let you go. That's fair, isn't it?"

Annie's suggestion did make sense, even Deke could see that. He stewed and stewed over it. Annie could see he was coming around to her way of thinking. A new surge of hope entered her heart; there was still a chance for them. She only knew one thing: If he stayed another two months, she'd see to it that wedding dress would not be a wasted purchase, not if she had anything to do about it.

Deke left her side and walked slowly back to his bunk, the towel wrapped snugly around his hand. He stood there at the foot of his bunk, steeped in though. He glanced back at Annie, still the picture of everything in the world he ever wanted and almost had. He stooped over, and with his good hand, he began fishing beneath the blanket hanging low off the side of his bunk.

An alarm went off in Annie's head. She rushed over just as he pulled on an old piece of rope. Out came his battered, heavy, cardboard box.

"What are you doing? You agreed to stay for two months!"

He turned to her, his eyes so deep with hurt, his voice a snarl of anger and hate. "It's eatin' me up inside already! I can't take it! I'm likely to come at you! Hit you again and again 'cause I'd be outa' my mind over you! Over what you'd done!"

"Listen to me, Deke! Listen good! I promise, if you'll stick by me, you'll never regret it! I'll be the best wife a husband ever had! Give yourself a chance! Give us a chance!"

Deke exploded. "You promised me, Annie! And how many days did your last promise last? C'mon, tell me!"

"Nine days, the first time."

He caught her slip of the tongue. The towel dropped to the floor. He grabbed her with both hands and shook the living hell out of his Annie. "Whata'ya mean, the first time? I'm waitin', Annie! Better come clean! NOW!"

She tried to jerk away from his grasp. A stick of dynamite wouldn't have done any good. Deke's arms became bands of steel. He was going to get the rest of the sordid mess out of her, even if he had to squeeze it out! She began to cry. "If I tell you, you'll never understand…you'll hurt me! Maybe even kill me! Please don't make me! Please, Deke! It's not important! Not anymore!"

"I'm waitin'! Let's get it all said!"

"Josie followed me up to Butch's cabin. That's where it happened…both times. We had it out, back here, after I came back from the first time. Please Deke! No more!"

"The rest, Annie! All of it!"

She tried to look away from his hard, cold stare. She saw his jaw set, the neck chords ripple up and down. "You won't understand…"

"TRY ME!"

"I felt so low, so ashamed about what I'd let Elza do to me…I couldn't face you…so I went back again. I tried to join up with Butch's gang. Elza used me…got what he wanted, then laughed in my face 'cause he knew Butch'd never let me ride with him…"

Annie's second, stunning revelation sucked the life out of Deke. He seemed frozen in time, yet his grip never relaxed one iota. His words had a hollowness about them. "Since you let him do it to you twice…well, how was it?"

"Don't, Deke! Please don't make me answer that. You might get even madder if I tell you…"

"HELL, I'm as made as I can get! Can't be any worse! Let's hear it, Annie!"

"I…I…kind of liked it." She saw his face turn crimson. "Better make that, I did like it. But…but Deke, with us, it'll be better, better than it ever was with him…honest! I promise, Deke! It will!"

He slapped her—hard. "Yeah, sure it will! One little problem, Annie. I ain't gonna be around to find out! Well, let's hear the rest! When did it happen again?"

"Please, please, don't ask! Please…"

"I'm havin' one hellava time gettin' all the truth outta you. Keep gettin' this sick feelin' in the pit of my stomach that if Josie hadn't caught you, none of this would be leakin' out! Care to have a go at my thoughts?"

"You got it all wrong, Deke. I would've told you before our wedding. Honest, Deke!"

"Yeah, sure! You'd'a given me the same runaround old slick gave you when you two went at it again! Right, Annie? Now let's hear when this second time happened before what little patience I got left for you gets used up."

Deke relaxed his ironclad grip for an instant. Annie ducked out and made a run for the door. Deke jerked her up by the belt, leaving her kicking nothing but bunkhouse air. "Now, by God, spill it! WHEN?"

She screamed out her answer. "THIS MORNING! SATISFIED?"

Her shoes touched the floor just as he released her. She never knew what hit her or how many backhanded slaps. When he finished wearing his one good hand out, she crumpled to the floor, screaming and crying. He towered over her, one leg straddled on each side of her body.

"Please, no more! Don't hit me any more! Just let me go! Please!"

"You got two things to do, Annie, before I let you go! NUMBER ONE, GIT UP!"

She quit rubbing her eyes or feeling the welts on her cheeks. "Don't hit me…don't hit me…I know I deserved it…Please, Deke, don't…"

"Then you'd better get back up before I forget you used to be a lady…MY LADY."

He helped her up without raising his hand to her. For that, she seemed genuinely grateful. "Okay…I'm up…now what?"

"Lift up your dress, turn around, and bend over while you pull your pants down!"

"I WILL DO NO SUCH THING!" she screamed out. "No matter what you think of me, I won't do it!"

"Okay, then I will!"

Deke jerked her dress up and stuffed it into both armpits, then made her clamp both arms down to keep her dress high. Next, he pulled her pants down 'til she was hobbled by the white panties around her ankles. Then he made her bend over.

"Yup! It's there alright! Had to be! No other way to figure it!"

Annie was furious. "Of course it's there, alright! All of me! Now can I pull up my pants and drop my dress?"

He shrugged both shoulders. "Fine by me! Still got your head up your ass instead of keepin' it on your shoulders where it oughta be. That explains a lot to me! No wonder you ain't been doin' any straight thinkin' lately!"

"You can't talk to me like this! How dare you!"

"Next time you use a washcloth on your face, better give your ears some more attention 'cause I just did!"

Deke blocked the door and pointed to his bunk. "Fetch your weddin' dress, Annie, and stand right next to the stove. I'll meet you there!"

This time Annie knew exactly what Deke had in mind. "No, no, Deke! Not that! Please, let me save the dress! I know now I'll never get the chance to wear it, but don't destroy this beautiful wedding dress! Please, Deke! Please!"

"When I get through with you today, I'm going to make you a promise that'll stay with you every day you draw breath. This will be a day you'll never forget! The day you destroyed yourself and me right with it! NOW, BY GOD, PICK UP YOUR WEDDING DRESS!"

Annie had never seen so much hurt and hate in another human being, nor so much determination to see it through, no matter what. She picked up the dress and did as she was told. She waited for him to approach. Deke saw the tears show up again.

"Wipe those tears on your wedding dress, Annie! GO AHEAD! DO IT!"

Again, Deke gave Annie no choice but obey. She pressed the delicate garment to her body, then kissed it, literally and figuratively, good-bye.

Deke supplied a farmer match and shoved it in her trembling fingers. "Go ahead, strike the match and hold it under your dress! Go ahead! DO IT!"

Annie's first strike against the cast-iron stove failed. She turned to Deke.

"Strike it, Annie!"

In a matter of seconds, flames consumed the bottom of the dress. Deke opened the lid to the stove. "Now drop it, Annie!"

Both stood by the open stove lid, watching the flames lick their way through Annie's wedding dress. There came a ball of fire, then a flicker or two, and the dress was no more.

Deke quietly walked back to his bunk to begin packing. He took down a jacket, then a work shirt off several nails, which served as pegs. From the top two drawers of a night stand, he took socks, shorts, and several pairs of long johns. Under his pillow, he fished out a beat-up copy of a dime-western novel, a Ned Butline saga. He raised his mattress high enough to remove two pairs of work jeans that he'd left there to smooth out the wrinkles before he'd left for Rock Springs. The last thing he did was return to the wash basin to pick up a comb, hair brush, razor, and his shaving mug and brush. He looked around to see if he'd missed anything. To his surprise, Annie stood in the open doorway. Evidently, she had watched the entire packing process.

He tied his rope around the makeshift box and headed toward Annie. She looked worse than a Saturday night drunk with a Sunday morning hangover.

She touched his arm, her cherry lips quivered, but the words came nonetheless. "Aren't you even going to say anything? Maybe good-bye?"

He removed his Stetson and used it to scratch his mop of unruly, red hair. "I'm just a poor, dumb, Montana mustanger, Annie...but no man could ever love a woman more than I did you. Guess that wasn't enough...guess you wanted something more...something I never got a chance to give you..."

"That's it? That's all you have to say?"

"Since you put it that way. I'm going to tell you this: If I never hear about Markham Ranch or the name Ann Barnett again, that'll be two days too soon for me!"

CHAPTER FIVE

Old Henry claimed, "Fastest way to get into the cattle business is to strip the critter's skin—then burn your brand on the hide and you're respectable!"

Josie stood by the stove, waving a flapjack turner in her hand. "Last call for pancakes! The griddle's still hot; anyone for more bacon and scrambled eggs?"

Annie looked directly across the breakfast table at her uncle. Beemis cast his eyes everywhere but on her. "Sis, tell that old goat who used to be my favorite person to pass the maple syrup."

Beemis responded with his own brand of sarcasm. "Sugarplum, tell that young lady who left her brains in her riding britches that she still has two good legs! If she wants the syrup, all she has to do is get up off her hinder and come get it herself!"

Josie's turner hit the breakfast table. "Alright, you two, I've had it up to here with the way you're actin'! Either you learn to get along or you can forget about me doing any more cookin' or washin' or anything else connected with this ranch house."

Beemis let a few choice words filter their way between his whiskers. Again, Josie's turner hit the table. "Stop mumbling, Uncle! That's all I've heard for—"

Annie cut her off. "For one month, two weeks and three days! That's how long Deke's been gone!"

"Best damn horseman this ranch will ever see! And you went n' pulled a boner like that! Still don't see how you managed to screw everything up royally!"

Annie snapped right back. "And I suppose you never made a mistake in your life? Right, Uncle Perfect?"

"Yeah, I've made a few! Who hasn't? But none'a them could hold a candle to what you pulled off! Or down!"

Josie threw up her hands. "That's it! Get out of this kitchen! Now! Had a speck of good news 'bout somebody you both know, but we're all going to forget that! Unless you two start treating each other like family once more, I'm going to have a long spell of forgetfulness!"

Annie rushed over to Josie. "It's about Deke, isn't it! Where is he? What's he doing?"

Beemis, too, suddenly became interested. "Where'd you see him? Did he mention he might think 'bout comin' back?"

"You two had better find a way to give each other a big hug or it's no go!"

They stumbled into each other's arms. It was a bit awkward, but the healing process finally got started between two people who once were inseparable.

Josie watched with a certain amount of matronly approval. "That's better, much better."

Both Beemis and Annie turned to Josie. "Alright, here goes. When I was in Jarvey's yesterday, one of the Hoy brothers was there. Heard him mention that they'd taken on a new hand over a month ago. Jarvey asked Hoy how he's workin' out."

Annie's eyes shone bright for the first time. "It was Deke, wasn't it? C'mon, Sis, don't hold back! Please!"

Josie was the only one who stayed calm. "Now don't read more into this than there is, but yes, Deke's punchin' cows at Hoy's! That's all I know."

Beemis' mouth opened about the same distance his jaw dropped. "Hell, he don't know nothin' 'bout cowboyin'; he's a horseman, through and through! I'm surprised they've kept him on!"

Annie mused a minute before letting her thoughts out into the open. "That last day Deke was here, I heard Shorty McCallum say he once worked on the railroad section gang. He called it gandy dancing! Said he was hard up, so he hired on until he heard Markham Ranch was hiring. Maybe…just maybe

Deke's doin' the same thing…"

The young cowboy rode up to Hi Bernard's tent. He dismounted and poked his head past the canvas flap. "There's a buggy comin,' boss! Small man wearing the dangest lookin' hat I ever seen! Got pitch-black eyes, too! The kind that put holes clean through a person. Who in heck is he? What's he doing way out here?"

Hi put his coffee cup down and opened his saddle bag. He pulled out a full bottle of Irish whiskey. He cracked the seal, then answered the cowboy. "Name's Ora Haley! Owns cattle herds in three states…made millions and wants to make more! Nothing stops him from doin' whatever he pleases. He either buys 'em out, hires 'em out, or if need be, drives 'em out!"

Hi ambled outside his tent, bottle in hand, and waited for Ora to pick the least bumpy path to him. When the buggy stopped pitching and weaving, he motioned with the bottle. "Good to see you, Ora! You're a month early! Let's cut a little trail dust outta our throats!"

Ora removed his derby and the two men went back inside the tent. Hi produced two fold-up canvas chairs, and the two men clinked their tin cups together over Hi's small, wooden table with collapsible legs.

Hi's boss exhaled. "Pour me another! You're the farthest from Laramie! Should be a half-bottle trip down here, at least!"

Hi filled Ora's cup to the brim. Ora rinsed it around in his mouth, then swallowed. "Ahh, that's good stuff! You always have a bottle or two ready, Hi! Always thinkin' ahead! I like that in my ramrods! Other two I got never keep the best money can buy! That's just one more thing I like about you! I never drink alone, Hi! Come join me!"

They worked their cups down, and Ora did the honors this time by pouring. His Irish slipped through in fine style as he held the bottle high. "See, my good man, I shoulda been a prophet; the bottle's half gone already!"

Hi knew his stout-chested boss could drink him under the table anytime he choose. So he did the obvious: ask questions to keep from falling on his face. "You must have something pretty important on your mind to bring you down here…What is it?"

"Been running the numbers, Hi! And as always, they tell me the truth!" He gave his range boss a friendly slap on the shoulder. "You have the biggest herd to ramrod, and you have the hardest winters by far to get through! And as always, your herd comes out on top, each and every time, man! You have a good nose and head for what needs doin,' it's as plain as salt to see!"

"Thank you, Ora, but what's all this leading up to?"

Ora fiddled with his cup, then came straight to the point. "The handwritin's on the wall for anybody who'd care to read it! The days of the Longhorns are numbered, aye, that they are! I'm shipping two hundred head of young Hereford bulls to Colorado Springs to meet up with you when you arrive. Next spring, your cows will be droppin' calves that won't be growing much horn, but they'll be puttin' on more weight, twice as fast, and it'll stay with them! That's what Herefords do! I've already begun to change my herds over in Wyoming and Nebraska. Yours is the last to begin the change."

"Anything else, boss?"

"I wish there was something to be done 'bout the winter kill! True, we always lose our share to the small-time rustlers and poachers. That can't he helped with so many thousands to keep an eye on. If only your winter kill could be lowered..."

Hi thought a minute. "Something can be done. Depends on how far you're willing to go."

"Just tell me or show me, and I'll see to it! You've known me long enough to know something's worth doin,' by God, I'll do it! And as you surely know, I'll spare no expense if it'll get the right results! Whata'ya have in mind, my good man?"

Hi leaned forward off his chair. "Been winterin' a few thousand in Brown's Hole. Plenty of grass and water to see 'em through...even add a few pounds 'cause the grass is so good..."

"So, what's the problem, man? Move all ya can! It's free range, isn't it?

Hi stood up. "Yes and no. It's a sticky situation..."

"You have my ears; let's hear the words, man!"

"Most of the free-range land is in the middle, surrounded by a lot of small cattle ranchers who think of it as bein' theirs 'cause they've been used to such an arrangement for years. In order to drive such a large herd as I have, we'd have to cross private property go get to the range land."

"I'll buy out a couple of those ranches; then we'd have plenty of right of way! Just point out what ones you have in mind, and I'll take care of it!"

"That's the rub, Ora! You've never run up against a bunch like these! They're a tough lot! Think nothing of stealing you blind with all their small-time rustling and brand changing. But they hang together thicker than thieves, they do! Most of 'em are old-timers! Got a lot of hard crust coverin' their hides, and they can be cantankerous as hell!"

Ora, too, was deep in thought. "Well, now wouldja say that a bit'a hard leanin' on them would turn the trick?"

"What do you have in mind?"

"First, we hold a public meetin' and make those that come a fair offer. I'll give you a free hand to name their price! Within reason, of course!"

"And if buyin' doesn't do it, what next?"

"If buyin' doesn't do it, we run so damn many head right across their land that there won't be one blade of grass left for them. They gotta move or else starve to death! There'll be some damages to pay when I settle up with them, but we'll have 'em one way or the other! A small price to pay for complete control, I'd say!"

"You're going to really appreciate this, Ora! There's no law whatsoever in the Hole! And by the time they send for an outside sheriff or deputy, we'll be firmly entrenched with everything under our thumbs."

"My good man, what are we waitin' for? Let's do it!"

Hi held up one finger. "One small problem! The Hoy brothers out in the west end of the Hole are starting to do the same thing. And if push comes to shove, you can figure that they'd rather deal with them than us. We're the outsiders, not them!"

Ora's eyes shone like oversized marbles. His deep frown turned to a most pleasant disposition. "If it's a money war we're talkin' 'bout, those Hoy brothers better tear up their bed sheets and wave 'em as surrender flags! They've never bucked the likes of me!"

Hi walked out with the dapper Irishman to his buggy. One of Hi's bull cooks had been holding the reins to his spirited team of blacks. Hi helped the average-sized man up into the buggy. When Ora seated himself, he leaned over with a final word. "When this business in the Hole gets taken care of, I have a promotion waitin' on you. I'm thinking of turning over my entire operation to you. You'll be my righthand man! I dare say, you've eaten more than your fair share of cold biscuits, burnt coffee, and rewarmed beans, covered with so many cow flies or mosquitos, that you either ate them together, or you didn't eat at all. And then there's cockleburs and prickly nettles you pick outta your bedroll, so you'll have a clear spot to untie your bedroll. Hi, your gypsy-tent days are about over! Man, you've earned the finest home in Laramie that I'm going to build for you. And my wife has already been looking over the crop of available ladies for you to pick and settle down. There's some fine ones around Laramie, I'm told."

Hi pumped Ora's hand. "Being boss over your herds in three states is a great honor and responsibility. I thank you for such trust!"

"Man, you've earned it! Time to suck up some of the good life you've helped me to!"

"About the Hole, Sir, there's a horse rancher down there I aim to keep outta this. He's not tied-in with the bunch I told you about. We've become friends…His operation won't hurt us one way or the other."

Ora's Irish curiosity got the best of him. "Might there also be another reason sparin' this rancher? Say, a daughter who's taken a shine to you?"

"Got two nieces, who are some lookers, I'm tellin' you! Youngest one rode all the way down to the Yampa to propose marriage to me a few years back. Had to say no…but now I'm going to be in the best position in my life to offer her something besides lonely nights and empty arms."

Ora picked up the team's reins. "Then, my good man, tis time I'm thinkin' for you to find out if she's taken or not! One last thing, when you start makin' offers, keep the price low…No point damagin' my checkbook any more than need be! They'll be seein' more money on the table than most of 'em have a right to! They're used to scratchin' for a living; let's try to keep it that way!"

"I'll post a thirty-day notice and send you a copy. Give you plenty of time to take the train to Rock Springs and rent a buggy to come on down, if you've a mind to."

"Good idea! I'll slip in at the back of the meetin'. You're free, as always, to run the show your way. Give me the chance to see for myself what keeps these small-time ranchers going, rustling some of my cattle or an honest day's work every now and then!"

Hi waved to Ora and waited for his boss to disappear over the first rise before returning to his tent. A short distance away, a few of his cowpunchers had gathered to admire the classy team of blacks Ora had driven and to talk about the stranger with the funny little derby hat. One of his bull cooks pulled out a beat-up novel and began reading.

"When you're through, don't throw it away," said Hi. "Give me a crack at it."

"Not worth the bother," the bull cook answered. "Some Eastern writer must've wrote this…doesn't know beans 'bout the real West! Keeps talkin' 'bout some big cattle baron. Hell, there ain't no such a thing! Have you ever heard of one or seen such an animal?"

Hi smiled. "Better tell your kids and grandchildren some day you saw the genuine article! That man who just left here fits that description better than any man I've ever known!"

"You mean he's a real cattle baron?"

"Sure is! He could buy and sell Colorado and have plenty of change left to handle Wyoming and Nebraska at the same time!"

"Ever see where he lives?"

"Lives in the biggest house I've ever seen in Laramie, Wyoming. Folks there call it a mansion. I'd call it a castle!"

Hi Bernard's notice was posted in the two most conspicuous places Brown's Park had to offer: Jarvey's Mercantile and Charley Crouse's schoolhouse. To say that it generated more than its fair share of controversy and wrangling would be the understatement of the decade. Old-timers gathered in front of both doors where the notices were posted and either shook their fists at such out-and-out audacity or cackled and laughed at the craziness the Two-Bar Cattle Company had in mind. Either way, many vowed, right then and there, it'd take more persuasion than even Butch Cassidy could possibly muster with ten Wild Bunches lined up behind him with pistols drawn to oust any of them. A small war was in the making, and if Two-Bar wanted in, then by cracky, they'd be more than willing to accommodate them with a big war! The battle lines were drawn a good two weeks before Hi Bernard's scheduled appearance. The only thing in question: Who'd fire the first shot?

The Markham ranch tried to take such a notice in stride. Over coffee, Beemis had his say. "This is cattle business, and it doesn't concern us. Let's leave it that way!"

Josie poured another refill. "Then you think Two-Bar really is talking to the cattle ranchers, not us?"

Beemis stirred in some sugar. "That's the way I see it! Besides, soon as I hire another foreman, I'm here for the long haul, with or without Two-Bar bein' our neighbor!"

Annie had remained quiet. Several thoughts ran through her mind. One was about Deke. Would he be there at the meeting? Give her a chance to apologize, maybe even get a read on his hurt? See how deep it really was? Her other thought centered on Hi Bernard. Would any of her old feelings still be there after she saw him once again?

She got up from the table. "You two can stay away from the meeting, but I'm going!"

"Don't do it, Annie!" Beemis continued. "It's not our fight!"

Annie's reply was ready made for just such a statement. "Well, Uncle, don't you think our ranch should be represented? One of us needs to be there…just in case."

They waited for Annie to get out of hearing range. Josie spoke up. "Why'd you do that? You know darned good n' well if you say no, Annie will break her neck to find a reason to say yes."

Beemis smiled, then patted her hand. "Sugarplum, two of the first things I learned scoutin' for the Army was there's always going to be someone to report to, and there's a way to get what you want by either doin' or sayin' just the opposite of what you really want. The Army's full of small men who'd like to show you they have a little authority, so whenever I wanted something, I'd let them exercise all the authority they had, and I'd usually wind up getting what I wanted in the first place!"

Josie laughed. "So you let on to Annie that nobody from Markham Ranch would be going, knowing full well she'd find a reason to go! Right?"

"You got it! But Annie did make one good point; somebody should be representing our side too! She also had two other good reasons to go: one of them is called Deke Landry, and the other is called Hi Bernard. It's time our Annie straightened her life out, one way or the other."

Josie started picking up the breakfast dishes. "Do you honestly think Annie will ever get Deke to take her back?"

Beemis scratched his beard. "That's a hard one…Put yourself in Deke's boots. Our Annie butchered the heart and soul right outta that man. It'd take an awful lot of soul searchin' to go along with more forgiveness than most men have to cross over all the hurt he's got festerin' deep inside just to come back, no matter how much he loves her…"

"Oh, Deke loves her alright! Deke's one of those men who only find one woman, and when he does, he locks onto her with everything he's got. Sure wish our Annie had the same kind of ingredients."

"Time will tell, Sugarplum! Time will tell!"

Ora Haley reached Charley Crouse's schoolhouse a good hour before the two o'clock meeting. He had in mind to briefly go over the bidding strategy with Hi, and then retire to the back row of seats and let Hi carry on. To his surprise, he found the building surrounded by buckboards, buggies, and horses of every possible size and description. Everything took on a circus sideshow atmosphere; the only thing missing was the popcorn and lemonade.

One young, enterprising lad approached the cattle baron. "Ain't no hitching rail's left, Mister. I'll hold your team's reins for a dollar!"

Ora did not like anything he saw. His Irish superstition surfaced, telling him it was a bad omen to ever venture inside; yet his good business sense told him he must find a seat, no matter how much it would cost him.

He fished into his vest pocket and handed the boy a silver dollar. "Mind ya now, this team's a bit high spirited, so hang onto the reins tightly."

"I will, Mister," replied the lad. "Say, what kinda accent is that?"

Ora was tickled. "Well, lad, 'tis the best kind a man can possibly have! It came all the way from the Emerald Isle with my father and mother."

"Gee, all that way, huh! Never heard'a no Emerald Isle…Is that anywhere near Denver?"

"Oh, it's a bit farther, I'd say. Remember, now, hang onto the reins!"

"Don't worry, Mister, your team's in good hands."

Ora made his way through the maze of empty carriages parked every which way. Something told him to turn around to check on his hired help. The young man had tied his team's reins to the closest rig and had disappeared. Another bad omen, he surmised.

"Excuse me, Sir, but wouldja consider giving up your chair for a price?"

"Mister, I dunno who'n hell you think you are, but my chair ain't for sale at any price! Came to hear what this cattle company's got to offer; then I'm gonna spit in their face and tell 'em to go to hell!"

Ora moved on. This time he picked on an old gent, who looked to be hard of hearing. Every time somebody spoke, he leaned forward and cupped a boney hand around his ear, probably his one good one.

Ora stood directly in front of the old-timer. "Excuse me, Mister."

"Eh? Wha'dja say? Speak up! You're talkin' kinda soft! You'll haft'a do better!"

Ora mouthed his words ever so carefully and boomed them out. "How much for your chair?"

"How much, you say? Hell, I kain't make out nuthin'! Here, take it! Was 'bout to leave anyhow…damned Two-Bar outfit ain't got 'nuff money ta interest me, no how! They're a bunch'a pikers! Meetin' ain't gonna mean one damned thing!"

Ora settled in on the back row among the rowdiest, most cantankerous group of crusty old-timers and ranchers he'd ever run across. He shook his head at what he saw. Most of them couldn't possibly rub two twenty-dollar gold pieces together and call them their own. Yet here they were, belligerent to the bone, ready to take on anybody at the drop of a hat, no matter how good or poor the offer might be. He pitied Hi Bernard; they'd surely tear him apart from limb to limb either with their mouths or their hands or both!

John Jarvey surveyed the ever-rising din the crowd made. He motioned for Hi Bernard to approach him. "Dang near got us a mob on our hands. No point in waitin' another half hour 'til two. There isn't an empty seat to be had, so I'm gonna call this meeting to order. Stay up here, beside me, and I'll introduce you, then turn it over to you."

For two solid minutes, Jarvey held both hands above his head, pleading and begging the unruly ranchers to give him their attention. Finally, two ranchers in the crowd had to stand up and holler as loud as they could. "Shut up! Shut up! Give Jarvey the floor!"

Amidst some background grumblings, Jarvey opened the meeting. "Folks, thank you for your kind attention. I hereby open this meeting! The man to my right is Mister Hi Bernard. He represents the Two-Bar Cattle Company! Let's show him that we can be a good audience and let him have his say. When he's through, there'll be plenty of time for questions and answers." He turned to Hi. "Mister Bernard, the floor is yours!"

Hi Bernard looked like he'd much rather try to take on a cattle stampede than try to face what was assembled before him. To his credit, he tried.

"Folks, the Two-Bar Cattle Company is here, ready to make you a fair offer for your spread—"

"Speak up, we can't hear you from back here!"

"Yeah, either speak up or shut up!"

That last remark drew whistles, catcalls, and plenty of boot stomping. Jarvey stood up beside Hi and whispered. "Gotta talk louder or else you can forget it." He raised one hand this time. "Folks, Mr. Bernard will talk louder this time! Let's all give him a chance! Go ahead, Mister Bernard!"

Again the mob quieted down enough so Hi could speak once more. "Thank you all! Like I said, I came to buy!"

"What's your offer?"

"One thousand dollars for your land; we don't want or need your buildings!"

One rancher in the front row took violent exception to the offer. He stood up, shook his fist at Hi. "That ain't near enough! I ain't sellin'!"

That brought the house down. Everybody tried to speak at the same time. The meeting had degenerated into pure bedlam. Hi waved and waved his hands, trying to be heard above the roar. He shouted himself hoarse, but it was no use. His soft voice was strained—almost beyond repair.

Bang! Bang!

Everybody turned toward the noise. The entrance door was open. There, amidst the swirling smoke, stood Ora Haley, his black derby in one hand, his smoking revolver in the other. Every eye followed him as he made his way forward. When he reached Hi, he handed his derby to him. "You've done your best, man! Let me go a round or two with 'em!"

He pointed his six-shooter into the air with a menacing move. That got everybody's attention. Most thought sure this stranger was about to blow a hole through the ceiling. Ora's dark eyes slowly roamed over the crowd, daring anybody to open his yap for fear he'd point and squeeze in the poor culprit's direction. Finally, Ora slipped his gun inside his thick, black belt, making sure most of the handle was in plain sight—just in case.

His theatrics about over, Ora's slow smile had a bedeviling quality about it. He bowed to Hi. "Thank you for tryin' to put up with these hooligans. See you later."

One old geezer in the second row stood up. He chomped down hard on his toothless gums, then opened his mouth wide. "And who might you be, all dressed up in them fancy black duds? The devil hisself?"

The crowd went nuts. Ora stood the gaff of laughter amazingly well, then pulled out the revolver again and pointed it at the old man. The noise died down quickly. Ora's smile came into play. "Well, now, my good man, there's some who would agree with you, but let me introduce myself. My name is Ora Haley! I own the Two-Bar Cattle Company! Take my thousand-dollar offer! It's the only one you're going to get!"

The crowd went quiet. Ora pressed his advantage to the hilt. He directed his attention and question to the same old man who'd called him the devil. "You, Sir! Yes, you! Have you ever seen a thousand dollars? Speak up!"

"Not all at once…"

"There now! My offer's a pretty darned good one!" He turned to the man closest to him. "And you, Sir! Have you ever had a thousand dollars look you in the eye? Have you?"

"No…can't say as I have…but my place is worth more than that. Been workin' it for better'n twenty years…"

"Sir! Sir! You're place is only worth what other people are willin' to pay for it! I'm willin' to pay you one thousand dollars, and I haven't even seen it! Now it could be nothing but a shack or two, or it might be worth somewhat more! The point is, you have my standing offer of one thousand dollars, right now! How can anyone possibly beat that?"

"I can!"

A ripple ran through the crowd. A medium-sized man stood up to be acknowledged. Ora turned in his direction. "And who might you be, Sir?"

"Name's Adam Hoy, and I will better your thousand by one hundred dollars! These people are my neighbors, and I'm sure they'd rather deal with me instead of some big-shot cattle company owner!"

A sprinkling of applause made its way forward from several rows deep. Everybody strained their eyes and ears, wondering just how Mister Two-Bar would handle this competition. The wheels in Ora's head clicked in. They didn't have long to wait. He walked over to one side of the room to address the man, still standing.

"Sir...Mister Hoy, I'm not here to get into a bidding war with you! But if I were, you'd never win! You could raise your price a hundred dollars an hour, and Sir, meaning no disrespect, you'd never live long enough to outbid me!"

One could almost hear the deflated air escape out the school's front door. Ora had made his point, the kind that'd netted him millions off the free-range grasslands in three states. Ora seized his hard-won point and decided to drive it home. "I have two questions for you, Mister Hoy! And I'm sure all these good folks would appreciate a fair and honest answer from you. My first question is, how high are you prepared to go on everybody's land? My second question is, if you're in the land buying business, why haven't you held a public meeting like I have instead of waiting for me to make the first move?" He gestured to Adam Hoy. "The floor is yours, Mister Hoy; we'd all like to hear what you have to say!"

Adam Hoy had never met a man the caliber of Ora Haley. He suddenly realized he'd come up against a man who literally lived and ate numbers! The kind that turned grass-chewing cuds into pounds on the hoof, which in turn produced the millions of dollars that fed his ego and his cattle empire. "I can go to eleven hundred...that's my best offer...but only on twenty or so ranches until I get some more backing."

"And the meeting?"

"I waited 'til I seen what you were going to do..."

"Thank you, Mister Hoy, for your straight answers." Ora brandished the revolver again in the grandest of one mighty-grand performance. He had the crowd where he'd angled to get them—seeing things from his point of view. "Well, now, my good folks, I would top your neighbor's offer by ten dollars and that would be the end of it! But I'm in a most generous mood! I've taken a liking to ya! Yes, I have! Two-Bar is prepared to pay twelve hundred dollars for your land, sight unseen! And I'll buy anybody's spread! There'll be no limit of twenty ranches or so! I'll guarantee to buy anyone's ranch who signs up now! Just write or print your name on the notice posted outside on the door and see me after the meetin'! For those of you who can't read or write, you'll get the same consideration! See me after the meetin'!"

Ora felt he had them in his hip pocket. His pitch had been well received. After all the fist pumping and shaking, along with all the disruptive hoots, hollers, and assorted catcalls, had all but disappeared. He was sure he had melted a good share of the hard-core resistance. Now it was time to do what he did best: conduct his kind of business. He was about to say, "This meeting tis over, follow me outside!"

One old coot stood up to break Ora's spell. "How long we got to sign up or sell?"

"You have thirty days, my good man! Any other last questions?"

Another in the back row had his say. "And if we don't sell, Mister Two-Bar, what then?"

Ora had been stopped dead in his tracks by the same question that nagged at least seventy-five percent of those attending. His composure never waffled in the slightest. He was still master of his own situation. "That's a fair question, my good man! Before I answer, let me ask you this. How many head of cattle do you own, Sir?"

The rancher scratched his chin. "Let's see…milkin' six cows, two's comin' fresh in 'bout three weeks, that's four more. Got one bull and eight steers…"

"Then you'll have nineteen in three weeks, correct?"

"If you say so…"

That brought out a few snickers, mostly because Ora was so quick with the count while the rancher was still in the recollectin' process.

Ora walked over to one side of the room. "And you, Sir, how many head of cattle do you own?"

This rancher couldn't wait to get his answer out. "Fifty-two!"

Ora pointed to another old boy. "How about you, Sir?"

The old man gave Ora his best tobacco-stained smile. "My missus been ailin' lately, so I sold off part'a my herd, so I could take care'a her. I'm down to fifteen…"

He walked back and forth, making sure every eye remained riveted on him. "Anyone here own one hundred head or more?"

Two ranchers raised their hands.

"How about five hundred? Anybody?"

Ora had only one taker: Adam Hoy. "Thank you, Mister Hoy!" He stood again in the center of the room. "Let me tell you what's goin' to happen if I don't get enough ranchers to sell. There's better than fifty thousand head of cattle that will be comin' in here, either with or without your say so. Just to give you an idea of how many that really is, let me tell you folks this! Come next spring, my cows will drop move calves from birthin' in the first hour than all the cattle you good folks have ever seen together in your lifetime! Now do you kinda get what I'm tryin' to tell you?"

Ora's numbers staggered the imaginations and minds of everyone there, with the possible exception of Annie.

Another old codger rose. Ora acknowledge him. "Yes, Sir! You have something to say?"

"Don't know how many fifty thousand really is. Can you put it some other way?"

Ora paced a bit, trying to change fifty thousand into the kind of terms and words that everybody could fully understand just how many cattle he was going to bring in. He stopped before the same man who had raised the question. "Aye, that I can, Sir! Try this on for size! Tell your woman not to hang her wash out anymore because it will be torn down and trampled and eaten up long before it has a chance to dry. And don't open your front door anymore unless you're invitin' my cattle to bed down with ya. And there's one other thing; you'll have to consider when you need to make a run to the outhouse! Man, there'll be so many milling around, you best hold it 'til you see a clear path, and then you'll have to run like a jackrabbit in order to make it! And after you've done your business, only open the door a wee bit, or else you'll have plenty of company! Now, do you see how many fifty thousand will be?"

Ora had delivered one powerful description and how! The room became still, no shuffling or shifting in the chairs, and no mumbling or grumbling in the back. He had tamed the mob! His sharp eyes finally picked out one who hadn't gotten his message fully or who still doubted his word. He snapped his fingers. "You there? Yes, you! If you have something that needs sayin', let's hear it!"

The middle-aged man had been singled out, perhaps even unfairly. Now, every head turned in his direction. He shifted uneasily, mute testimony that he hated being the center of attention. A defiant, ugly curl formed around his mouth. He did, indeed, have something to say. "Dang tootin,' I got somethun' to say, Mister Big-Shot! Dang tootin'! Just 'cause you show up with all them cattle don't mean all fifty thousand is gonna make it back out of the hole! Catch my meanin'?"

The crowd stirred again. Their neighbor had touched on the one forbidden subject.

"I do, indeed, catch your meanin', Sir! The first man I catch tryin' to rustle one head of my beef will be shot on sight! Just so there's no misunderstanding, let me say that I'm going to give my hands five-hundred-dollar rewards for every damned nestler they shoot! Now, do you catch my meanin'?"

"What'd you call me?"

"I didn't, Sir, I was only speakin' in general! There's nothing lower than a Nestler! He's a small-time nester who steals and rustles on the side to put food on the table. He can't make a decent living doin' an honest day's work, so he rustles from me and every other big cattle company that comes into the Hole! Those days are over! I'm warning each and every one here and now! Now, do you catch my meanin', Sir!"

"'Peers like to me, you as much as called me that name from what you just said a nestler is…Why that's a whole lot worse than bein' an S.O.B. in any man's talk. You either take that name back, Mister Big-Shot, or else you've bought yourself something else besides ranches! Now, do you get my drift, Mister Big-Shot?"

Ora's Irish would never let him back down, even if he wanted to. "I stand by what I've just said! EVERY DAMNED WORD!"

The meeting was in shambles! An uproar rippled from one end of the room to the other. Ranchers pumped their fists high in the air as symbols of their defiance. Ora had stepped into a quagmire of hostility, the likes of which he'd never seen or experienced with hard-core, small-time ranchers, who felt he'd hung a label on them for all times. Two young ranchers made a special point of returning through the outraged mob just to tear up his public notice into bits and pieces in front of the cattle baron. Three others returned just to hurl every imaginable insult they could think of! They called him names that would've put an Irish bartender to shame! To his credit, Ora took all this verbal abuse without so much as one inkling as to the boiler room of emotion and disgust that was churning inside him behind the silver-plated belt buckle that'd caught more than a few stares minutes ago.

Annie remained in her seat, waiting for the mob to empty out. She looked around and saw five others doing the same thing. She noticed that Ora had moved off to one side to converse with Hi Bernard in low tones. Two thoughts entered her mind: Had Ora coined the word nestler in the heat of his verbal exchanges with the rancher? Or was this the culmination of all those many years of the petty cattle rustling he had been forced to absorb as owner of the Two-Bar? She concluded either way, there would certainly be hell to pay before this was all over.

"Are you lost?"

Hi's question startled her. "I know you're probably wondering what I'm doing here."

"My voice is pretty hoarse…had a lot more I wanted to say when I spotted you."

"They gave you a pretty rough reception. Your boss sure put the buggy whip to them…until that last incident. Now, it's all-out war, isn't it?"

Hi pulled up a chair and straddled it before he sat down. "Went to special pains to keep Markham Ranch out of this…told Ora again, just now. Stay out of this…gonna turn ugly before Ora runs them out. He's not about to back down."

"And neither will the ranchers." She tried to change subjects. "You've grown a mustache! Looks good on you."

"Thanks, Annie. Back to business…you're probably the only person who really knows what fifty thousand head looks like. Seems like a million years ago when you rode down to the Yampa to see me…Remember our first kiss?"

"Sure do…and all the dust clouds, too. These ranchers don't have a clue as to what I saw…to what this hole will look like when Ora gets through with them. They really don't understand, do they?"

"Not really, even though Ora did his best. Back about us…things have changed; soon as this business has been settled, I'll be in a much better position to offer you something except loneliness. I only hope your feelings toward me haven't changed."

She thought a minute, then gave him her most charming smile. "Things have changed for me, too; I was all set to marry a young man. Beemis hired him as our foreman. I made a terrible mistake…wedding got called off because of that. He's working for one of the ranchers who stood up to Ora."

Hi liked what he saw. He noticed how her maturity had taken hold, filled her out in all the right places. She was even prettier than he'd remembered. "If things don't work out between you two…I'd sure like to come callin' after this business is taken care of. And it will be, Annie! It will!"

Annie got up. They shook hands. "I'll keep what you said in mind…after Ora moves in. Take care of that sore throat. Gargling with Epsom salt should help."

Hi touched his throat. "Remember, stay out of this."

Annie shuffled on out the door. She had at least one answer. Hi still made her heart miss a beat, but only slightly. Just wishing Deke had been there made her heart do cartwheels. She walked over to the handrail. Glory had a friend, an old, familiar friend, who could stroke her chin like no other! Annie's wish had come true.

Both acted as though they wanted to forget the past and leap into each other's arms. For Annie, some harsh remembrances rolled off her tongue too quickly. "Thought you never wanted to see me! Oh yes, how'd that go? 'If I never see you, that'll be two days too soon!'"

Annie's barb sank deep into his heart. "No problem! I can sure take care of that! Just turn your head, and I'll be gone!"

He started to walk away. Annie ran to catch up. "Please, Deke, don't go! Talk to me! Don't know why I said that!"

He turned to face her. "I do! Had to get it said before you figured I'd do the same to you!"

"Why can't we say what's really in our hearts? Like how much we still miss one another? Or that we still love each other? Why?"

He looked down at his Annie, his pretty Annie. "You're makin' it too easy for me to answer. 'Cause you threw it all away. I'm tryin' hard to keep my tongue and my head together, Annie. Was gonna use the word screw instead of threw…"

They kept a civil tongue, each toying with the other's feelings and emotions, always taking care to sidestep the one big hurdle that stood between them: Annie's big mistake. Deke switched thoughts first. "Still surprised to see you here…This is cattleman's doings."

"Hi Bernard as much as said the same thing just a few minutes ago inside."

"Well, what are you doing here?"

Annie smiled. "Told Beemis someone from our ranch better go, so I volunteered!"

"That the only reason?"

"No."

Annie's admission made Deke feel good. He knew her feelings for him were still oh-so-much alive! "Danged near rode over to your uncle's ranch the other day to ask for my old job back…I ain't no cow-waddy! Never was! Never will be!"

She touched his hand. He drew back like he'd been snake-bitten. "Why didn't you, Deke? Beemis would hire you in a minute! And I'd take you back quicker than that!"

He went into his old routine once more, using the brim of his Stetson to work his mop of hair over again and again, his way of thinking hard or deep. "Wouldn't work, Annie! I'd see your blonde hair and say to myself, 'Used to put my nose in that…always smelled cleaner and sweeter than fresh-mowed hay.' Then I'd move on down a bit and look into your eyes and…and I'd say, 'They're so deep and so blue…like a new day that's bein' born every mornin' at sunup! Next thing I'd want to do is work your lips over 'cause they're so soft and nice like.' Never knew lips could be like cherries…but yours are. Then I'd think 'bout the touching…maybe even feel your breasts—if you'd let me—then I'd get to rememberin' if you wanted me to work 'em over, you'd only fasten two buttons on your work shirt…make it easy for me to get to 'em."

"Oh, Deke…don't stop; you've never talked like this to me—ever!"

"That's 'cause I got all day to sit atop my horse when I'm cow punchin'. I chase a few strays back into the herd; then my mind settles on you the rest of the time. Never done so much daydreamin' in all my life!"

Annie was turned on, no doubt about it. Her eyes had a special glow, the kind lovers only see and understand. "Anything more, love?"

He put on his sweat-stained Stetson. "Couple more thoughts keep chasin' around in my head. I'd get off my horse, pick up a blade or two of grass, stick 'em between my teeth and walk a spell to work the kinks outta my legs. Next thing that grass always reminded me of was lyin' down on our saddle blankets with you. Then the grass would kinda stick to my teeth like our bodies used to stick together…Lord, oh Lord, Annie, those were such special times."

"They can be again, Deke! They can, I promise! Just come back!"

He looked away, then winced like he'd just bitten his tongue. "Yeah, I know, you promised you'd wait for me and look what it got me! A two-time cheater!"

"Can't you let that go? I can! Why can't you?"

"That's the trouble between us, Annie! You talk like it almost never happened! I can only talk like it's still there! Like it will most likely be the rest of my natural life. Gotta go now! Tell Beemis and Josie hi for me!"

He walked away from her, his Annie, a mist gathering in both eyes. Annie chased him down. "Don't you dare walk away from me! Not after the way you talked about me! All those special, nice things you said…you still love me! It's in your eyes, your expressions…and most certainly in your words, Deke

Landry!"

"Speakin' of words, Annie, I got something for you. Lots of printed ones!"

"I…I don't understand. What printed ones?"

Deke reached into his saddlebag. To her surprise, he pulled out two badly crumpled up newspaper clippings. He gave her one, then pointed to it.

"Clipped it out of the Denver newspaper. Recognize the picture, Annie?"

She tried to straighten out several wrinkles. "Looks a lot like…like Elza Lay."

Deke poked his finger through the clipping. "Whataya mean it looks a lot like Elza Lay? It's old slick hisself! 'Course the name under this picture calls him William McGinnis, but it's him alright! Save ya the bother'a readin'! He got nailed down in New Mexico, trying to rob a train! No mention of Butch Cassidy, but you can bet next payday, Butch was close by somewhere! You know Butch has been pretty busy…what with them two big train holdups in Wyoming…and now this."

"Thought you told me Butch got out of the pen in Wyoming after he promised the governor he wouldn't do any holdups or robberies. He's a liar! He broke his word!"

"Ya got it all wrong, Annie; Butch did keep his word! I got those clippings, too! Not one word 'bout anybody spotting him during those two jobs! But you know, he did the plannin,' and most of the scoutin' too, right along with that dry-run he always does before his train robbers' bunch follows his plan."

"What happened in New Mexico?"

"Old slick gunned down a local sheriff! Got caught and got life in the pen!"

Annie handed the clipping back. "Josie will rest a bit easier when I tell her about this. Won't admit it, but she's still carrying the torch for Mister Mormon Nice!"

Deke spoke his mind. "Yeah, Butch Cassidy and his gang sure raised heck with a lot of folks…especially two sisters."

Deke handed Annie the other clipping. "This is about old slick, too…but there's a big word in there…never heard of such a word before. There's no look-up book in my bunkhouse at Hoy's."

"You mean a dictionary, don't you, Deke?"

"Yeah, that's it! Anyways, you go ahead, read it! See what you make of it."

Annie read the clipping. "Okay, Deke, this says that starting in August the warden at the New Mexico Penitentiary is going to allow conjugal visits..."

"That's it! That's that big word! What does it mean?"

"Well, if I understand the rest, it says that women will be allowed to visit the men in prison. They'll even allow them to spend time together...even provide a bed for them to be alone without anybody looking on...when they're together. It's not really about Elza in particular. Deke, it's about all the prison population."

"Sure it is, don'tcha see it? It's a natural fer old slick and yourself!"

Annie didn't care for Deke's insinuation in the least. She tried to give him the benefit. Perhaps, he was mixed up. "I don't like where this is going...perhaps you'd better explain it to me."

"How can it get any better for you two? When you visit him, they're even going to give you two a bed and leave you two alone, so you can keep right on doing what you did up here! Even get the warden's blessings for doin' it!"

She slapped him hard—twice—before he knew what hit him! "Damn you, Deke Landry! You can't leave it alone, can you?"

He touched the two red welts Annie had left on the side of his face. "Never, Annie! Never! You try'un have a good day now! Ya hear!"

She watched him ride away, but not out of her heart. Her eyes gathered a mist, and her heart ached oh so much!

Beemis met Annie at the front porch. He seemed more than just a bit interested. "Well, how'd things go?"

Annie stood on the top plank. "I saw a man, rich and powerful beyond imagination, get turned down...and I saw in his eyes what's going to happen to this hole. He's going to change everything and everybody, and there isn't one darned thing you or I can do about it. That answer your question?"

Annie started for the door. Beemis' cane hit the planks right behind her. "Anybody else there?"

She turned to him. "I saw Hi Bernard. They nearly ran him out of the meeting before Ora Haley took over...Mister Two-Bar himself."

"Anybody else? Like Deke, maybe?"

"Yes, he was there. Said some of the nicest things to me I've ever heard...then he said some of the worst things, too." She hugged Beemis. "Isn't it ever going to stop? I love him so much—can't he see that?"

Beemis rested his cane against the door and held his Annie in his arms. "I think now, my dear, you're just beginning to realize what you've really done. He came to that meeting for only one reason: to show you how deep the hurt really is between you two!"

They stayed in their embrace, each comforting the other. Finally, Beemis broke the spell. "What are we gonna do about Hi's boss? You called him Ora Haley, I believe…"

"There's only one thing a cow respects: barbed wire! Forget about breaking horses or stud service! Better put our hands to work stringing barbed wire and digging fence posts or it's all over for us, too! The Park's never seen what I've already seen down on the Yampa…what Ora tried to tell them. He'll move so many cattle down here, there won't be enough hours in the day to count them, let alone stop them!"

The old man's face turned ash-white. "You're damned serious 'bout this, ain't you?"

"Never more serious in my life, dear Uncle! Never more serious!"

The next morning, Beemis was down at the bunk house at the crack of dawn. He opened the door, stepped inside, and thumped his cane hard upon the nearest bunk. "Up and at 'em boys! After you finish breakfast, you'll find a stack of leather-faced gloves outside on the steps! My advice is, use 'em! Shorty, you and Tex hitch up the wagons and get on over to Jarvey's! Buy every roll of barbed wire you can lay your hands on! From now on, all I want to see is butts bending over and elbows workin' them shovels! You boys can straighten up when every foot of Markham Ranch land is fenced! Any questions?"

For ten straight days, Beemis' neighbors, from near and far, came by buggy, wagon, or horseback to see what the old boy was up to. The idea of putting up a fence of any kind was totally foreign to them. One old neighbor, a man named Ulrich, found Beemis dumping fence posts out of his wagon. Ulrich approached Beemis. "Hey, Beemis," he called out, "they said you were a couple'a cards short of a full deck! What in heck do ya think you're doin'?"

Beemis mopped his brow. "Tryin' to save my ranch land from gettin' run over by fifty thousand head of Two-Bar cattle! If you and the rest of my neighbors had a lick of sense, you'd be out doin' the same thing."

Ulrich shook his head and smiled. "That Two-Bar outfit is all bluff and no bite. We've always let our stock run pretty much where they please."

Beemis pulled down his red suspenders to remove his sweat-soaked work shirt. "Ever see how much space fifty thousand head take up?"

"Saw ten or twelve thousand head in the holding pens at Steam Boat Springs once, years ago, just after a big roundup…"

"Well, what'd you think of that? Did their size impress you at all?"

"Come to think of it, the loading boss said some kids opened the gates and let those cattle out…took 'em four days to round 'em all up." Ulrich laughed. "You're not gonna believe this, but that boss told me they save money by payin' them kids to stay away! Can you beat that?"

"Now try fifty thousand doin' the same thing down here! Get the picture?"

Annie picked up the flatiron off the range. She put a wet finger to it, was satisfied it was hot enough, so she began to iron one of Beemis' shirts.

Josie came into the kitchen, carrying a big stack of clothes taken off the clothesline. "Sure miss not seein' Deke's work shirts, underwear and pants in with Beemis' clothes. Wonder how he's making' out over at the Hoy ranch?"

Annie turned the shirt over and began ironing its collars. "I miss what used to walk inside those clothes a heckuva lot more…"

Josie went to the kitchen window. "Never seen Beemis work this hard in years! He's loadin' up the last load of fence posts…said they'd be through with the fence line, clean around our ranch, sometime tomorrow." She turned to Annie. "Are you sure all this work and fencin' are worth it?"

Annie hung the ironed shirt over the back of a kitchen chair. "What you're really asking me is, did I really see fifty-thousand head of Two-Bar cattle down on the Yampa? That's what it all boils down to, isn't it?"

Josie hugged her sister. "Don't mean to doubt your word…it's just that fifty thousand is an awful lot of cattle. I'll be honest with you, I can't begin to imagine what that many really is…or looks like."

"Shoulda took in the meeting with me. Mister Two-Bar himself tried to tell these knot-headed, stubborn jackasses exactly the same thing. He had 'em pretty well sold, ready to sign up, until he called them nestlers! Boy, did that ever put the starch into their underwear! Thought sure a fistfight or two was gonna break out any second."

"What kept it from happening?"

"Ora Haley himself! Never saw a man more in command of himself and those around him than Mister Two-Bar!"

"Didn't you say he was Irish? Sis, the Irish are notorious for short tempers…for flyin' off the handle at most anything that disturbs them."

Annie picked up another shirt from the stack Josie laid down on the table. "This one's got better things to do with his time, like run an empire."

Josie motioned for Annie to sit down. "Here, let me iron for a while."

Annie poured herself a cup of coffee and stood at the window. "There goes Beemis. Once the fence is put up, he'll go back to raising his fine Arabians." She turned to watch Josie pull the shirt sleeve over the small end of the ironing board. "And you, dear Sis, you'll go right on raising poor Cleve Dreschler's hopes, all the while still wishing your Mormon would come calling once more.

"Yes, Annie, everybody's raisin' something around here except you." Josie put down her iron. "And from what you've told me about your first meeting with Deke...I'd say there's small chance of him ever raising your hopes once more."

Annie set her cup on the drainboard next to the sink. She gave a big sigh. "Yes, I think you're probably right...so there's only one thing left for me to do."

"What's that, Sis?"

"Raise a little hell! See if there's something or some way to stop Ora Haley from swallowing up this hole!"

Up shot Josie's warning finger. "You heard your uncle, loud and clear! Stay out of this! Hi Bernard told you, too, and so did Deke, in his way!"

Annie's hands flew to her hips. She had the most determined look Josie had ever seen. Jaw set, eyes blazing, she had fight written all over her face. "I'm getting a little sick and tired of hearing all this so-called good advice!"

"So, what are you going to do?"

"Call a meeting, Sugarplum! Call a meeting!"

"But we're not in the cattle business! We raise horses! Remember?"

Annie snapped right back. "Yes, but we're all ranchers, Josie! Or has that slipped your mind, too?"

Beemis' thoughts were to nip Annie's idea in the bud and put a stop to such nonsense, as he first called it. Yet he had to admire her insomuch as she was willing to gather the ranchers and maybe, just maybe, a few collective heads could come up with something that would set the cattle baron back on his heels, at least temporarily, until a long-term solution could be found.

Three days later, the ranchers began to arrive. Most who came were surprised that a horse rancher of all things was playing host to them. It was in this spirit and attitude that twenty-one curious ranchers finally passed through the main gate at Markham Ranch.

Annie opened the meeting while Beemis and Josie remained in the background, waiting to see if anything of a positive nature might be forthcoming. So far, all they heard was a lot of grumbling among those seated in the front parlor.

"Gentlemen," she began, "the purpose of this meeting is to form an association. From this association, we hope to come up with both a short-term and long-term solution to counter the Two-Bar plans to take over all the grazing land in this hole. Make no mistake about this! Two-Bar will be here in about two weeks unless we come up with something in a hurry! That's when our thirty days run out! And that's when all hell will break loose unless we come up with something! At this point, I'd like to turn the meeting over to my neighbor, a cattle rancher, the same as you! Gentlemen, Mister Matt Rash!"

Rash, although a Texan, was the complete opposite of Hi Bernard, and it didn't take him but a few minutes to show his true colors. He was a natural leader, one who could direct with authority before his peers, with or without their permission. "First thing we gotta do is get organized," he said, "show the Two-Bar we mean business."

"How do we do that?" piped up Henry Ettlemen, the Park's oldest and most respected rancher.

Matt let his silver tongue do the talking. "By sending Ora Haley a letter telling him we've formed an association and will meet force with force if it comes to a showdown with Two-Bar!"

Another rancher stood up. "Wup! Wup! Hold it! None of us are gunslingers. All Two-Bar has to do is hire the best money can buy, and we're outta business! Besides, what are we gonna tell Ora Haley that ain't already been said at his meeting?"

That brought out a few murmurs of agreement. Angus McLaren rose. "Let's get the law down here! By George, it's the law's job to protect us!"

Old Henry waited for Angus' words to settle. "What law? Hell, none of us has ever seen a tin star in this hole, let alone see who's standing behind it! Any of you folks know who our lawman is?"

"I do! His name's Charley Neiman! He used to work here in the Hole..."

Everybody turned around to see who spoke up behind them. Beemis stepped forward. "You folks got another problem! Like it or not, Two-Bar has as much right to that free-range land as we do! Until they break the law, there isn't a thing we can do! But I believe there is a way to keep their stay down here mighty short!"

Annie saw where he was going with his thought. "Uncle Beemis is talking about there being nothing for fifty-thousand head to feed on once they get here! You are all cattlemen! What's the one thing that nibbles the grass so short, there's nothing left to eat?"

The room was abuzz. Everybody shied away from ever saying such a word, let alone the mere thought. They looked at one another, collectively, as if such a thing was totally unthinkable. The one thing that was worse then being called a Nestler!

Old Henry finally rose. He waved both arms for quiet. "Listen up! All of you! Took a horse rancher to put some sense in our heads, but by George, he wasn't afraid to think it! Neither am I! Now I'm gonna say it! SHEEP!"

Everybody tried to talk at once. Matt Rash whistled and shouted and stomped the floor, trying to get some attention. The tall Texan stood a better chance talking to the wind with about the same success. Josie rushed in from the kitchen with her dishpan and a big mixing spoon. She held it up for everybody to see, then began beating on it like a drum. Josie finally won out; her loud banging drowned out the others.

At last some semblance of order was restored. Rash took charge once more. "Thank you, Josie. Now then, I know where we can get all the sheep we need. There's two Welshmen runnin' sheep just above the rim, east of the Irish Canyon Trail. If we let them move their sheep down here for free, I'm sure they'd come!"

Angus had his say. "And what are we going to feed our own cattle on, the northwest wind? There won't be a blade of grass left for any of us?"

McLaren's remark sparked another hot round of debate. Those that saw the merit to bringing sheep in also saw the problem of no grass left for them. What to do? What to do?

"Well, then," spoke up Beemis, "you ranchers better do what I've been doin'! Cut enough hay and stack it to see you through 'til next year when the grass grows back!"

Matt raised his arm. His brown eyes flashed; he could see a way out. "Beemis is right! Beemis is right! None of us has a very large herd, except the Hoy Brothers! Too bad they weren't here to take this in! I'll contact them and tell 'em what we're up to and ask them to join our association. That'll make our position just that much stronger. There's still time if we act now!"

Matt's words put some solidarity into the backbones of the ranchers. They could see a way out, a way to outfox the cattle baron and beat him at his own game. A rancher named Larsen put into words what everybody was thinking. "Oh, I'd sure like to be there…see the smugness disappear clean off the face of Mister High n' Mighty when he finds out there ain't nothun' to eat for all them bawling beefsteaks! That Irish mug'a his is sure due for a sudden change! A mighty big change! He'll think twice before he calls us nestlers next time!"

Matt Rash adjourned the meeting. The ranchers emptied out of Beemis' living room with more than a smile on their faces. They had a plan, a winnable one, provided each put up enough hay to tide their small herds over until next spring.

Matt approached Annie. "You were there at Ora's meeting. Do you think he'll wait the full thirty days?"

Ann rethought Rash's question. "Yes, he'll have to. After all, he's still counting on seeing some signatures up on the other posted notice at Jarvey's."

"Won't he be surprised? No signers and no grass!"

Both smiled, but neither laughed. Annie came straight to the point. "A man like Haley is not going to let one setback beat him. I look for him to do most anything to still try to take over! I don't know the man well enough to venture a guess on what he'll do next…or how far he's willing to push."

"Glad you brought up the point about not knowing him well enough. You know, Ann, we've been neighbors for better than five years, and I'm in about the same boat. Now that we're good neighbors and association members, I'd like to get to know you better. Any chance of that happening?"

This was really the first time Ann had really taken a long, hard look at her neighbor, who lived directly across Vermillion Creek from Markham Ranch. In height, he stood about as tall as Hi Bernard, and his build was similar to Hi's—lean and lanky. But there, the similarities ended. Matt was the epitome of what Hi was not. Matt was assertive in character, almost to the point of being overly aggressive. He had a flair for dramatics, always found a way to be the center of attention, whether deserved or not. He was a polished speaker who knew what to say and when to say it. His dark brown eyes drank in Ann's beauty, yet his eyes never seemed to tell the whole story. And he was better looking than Hi and certainly a lot younger—twenty years, perhaps.

"I'm still very serious about another man. There are some problems between us. I'm hopeful they can be worked out…" She flashed two rows of pearly white teeth behind her smile. "But thanks for your consideration…Matt."

Matt was not disappointed in the least. He was attracted to what he saw and liked: a pretty honey-blonde who spoke her mind and had the smarts to back it up. He sensed Annie's true love had traveled a rocky road, and if he stayed in contact using their membership in the newly formed association as his reason to be there, things could break his way. "We'll probably be seeing quite a lot of each other through association business, of course, so let's be good friends, Ann! What do you say?"

Ann shook hands. "Let's leave it at being just friends. You have a good trip back to your ranch, Matt."

He also decided he would play it slow, bide his time, get to know his competition, and then take charge as he'd done today. He shook her hand. "Fine, we'll be good friends...for now."

Matt Rash barely had time to close the parlor door behind him before Josie confronted her sister. Up came the familiar finger with more than just a significant wave under her nose. "Stay with just the handshake, Sis; you'll be farther ahead in the long run. Texans are bad news for you. The first was too old and this one, too slick! He's no drifter by any means, but Deke's worth ten like him! Did you notice the way he took charge? Nobody voted him in, but he sure didn't wait around for any of the other ranchers to nominate him. He's got a lot of brass about him, and all he's waiting for is someone like you to help him rub some of that shine."

Annie realized that Josie was deep into her motherhood act for one reason only: for her benefit. "Alright, Mother Dear, I hear you! Anything else?"

Josie led Annie by the hand to the kitchen. "Let's take Old Henry and Uncle Beemis out some fresh, hand-squeezed lemonade. You've been missing out on some pretty good stuff; time both us payed attention to the old boy. He seems to know a lot 'bout Matt Rash..."

"Such as?"

"Help squeeze these lemons, and we'll both find out."

The two sisters soon returned with a big pitcher of lemonade and four glasses. Old Henry's eyes danced a jig the minute Josie placed the refreshing drink in his gnarled hands. "Thanks, Josie! You're sure a dear! No wonder your uncle says he's gonna hate to lose you."

Josie's eyebrows arched. "I'm not going anywhere...not for a while, at least. We missed most of what you said about Matt Rash...Would you mind starting over?"

Henry took a long sip. Annie was sure he must have a hollow leg the way he drank and drank and drank some more. Finally, he moved the glass from his weather-beaten, cracked, old lips. "Was tellin' your uncle, Matt Rash worked for a big cattle outfit up in Wyoming. The name was Middlesex. The owners live in England...did a terrible job of managing over on this side of the ocean. Things got so bad that they sent one of them bean-counter fellas—"

"You mean like a bookkeeper or an accountant?"

Henry's eyes lit up. "Yeah, that's it, Annie! See what all that back-East, fancy education has done fer ya? I could no more come up with those names—"

"Alright, go on, Henry," said Beemis, slightly annoyed. "Let's hear the rest!"

Henry waited for Josie to refill his glass. "Thanks, Josie. Now, where was I?"

"The English owners sent over a man from their company to do an actual count of their cattle herd."

"Yes, Annie, that's exactly what happened! Never heard tell of such a thing bein' done before...and never have since, neither!"

"I've been down on the Yampa...saw somewheres between forty-five and fifty thousand head of Two-Bar cattle. How in the world can one person say he can give the exact count?"

Old Henry got to his answer in short order. "This bean-counter fella made the cow punchers and the range ramrod run every cow, calf, steer and bull through a long holding pen with an open chute on one end. Cowboys at the open chute made sure none of 'em doubled back to the main herd so as not to get counted twice. That's how they done it!"

"So, how's Matt Rash figure into this, Henry?"

The old boy rose and pointed down to his clothes. "I'll git to that in a minute, Beemis. Now, I got my best pair'a pants and near-new shoes on. Didja see how Matt Rash was dressed? Why, his spiffy duds make my best look like rags—"

"Oh, I see what you're drivin' at! Matt Rash dresses a whole lot better than his circumstances would dare to suggest. Isn't that about it?"

Old Henry scratched his one small wisp of hair. "Annie, them's the biggest words I've ever heard! But yes, that's about the size of it! And I got better than a strong inklin' how it gits done..."

"Cattle rustlin', that how it gets done! Right, Henry?"

"Ya done took them words clear off'a my tongue, Beemis!"

Josie spoke up. "You said there's a tie-in between the cattle count and Matt Rash. What is it?"

No man in the park enjoyed his role any better than did Old Henry. As the official unofficial historian of Brown's Park, he knew every quirk and kink of all the Hole's residents. He swelled up his chest and let go. "The day that bean-counter fella finished up his count is the very same day Matt Rash got fired! How's that fer 'taters in your stew?"

"You've as much as said Matt Rash got fired because they suspected what he was doin' all along, but couldn't prove it! Right?"

"Couldn't'a put it any better if I'da tried, Josie! A'course, stories about the why and the where-for popped up thicker than a batch of my Etta's best popcorn! But there's no doubt, Rash's goose was cooked as far as that cattle company was concerned!" He raised a boney finger. "There's another part to this that bears tellin' too…" He turned to Annie. "What's that big word…aw, shucks, I know you've heard it…it's when two things happen purty darned close together, and they might be hooked to one another or maybe not?"

Annie smiled. "I think the word you want is called coincidence!"

Old Henry's eyes lit up. "That's it, Annie! That's it! Now I'm gonna be a mite careful when I use that big word, but here goes anyway. 'Bout five years ago, Matt Rash shows up down here in the Hole with near two-hundred-eighty head'a cattle. Guess what the tally was short up in Wyoming? He slowly mouthed the word with all the pucker his drawn cheeks could muster. "Any'a ya think it might be just a co-in-ci-dence?"

All four had a good chuckle. Finally, Beemis raised his specs a trifle to clean out a bit of water that'd gathered in his eyes. Then he put a perspective on Old Henry's story. "Hell's bells, Matt Rash just elected himself president of our association. Near as I can figure, that's 'bout the same as askin' the fox to guard the chicken coop!"

Despite Old Henry's cautionary warning about Matt Rash's suspicious background, the ranchers went ahead with their haying operations. The smell of fresh-cut hay was everywhere. It filled the nostrils of every rancher on the park's east side. Within a week, haystacks dotted the countryside, looking for all the world like fresh-baked loaves of bread, hot out of the oven. This was a monumental first for the park's ranchers—pulling together.

This beehive of activity did not go unnoticed by the other non-members in the park. They gathered in the west end at the Hoy brother's ranch to discuss the pros and cons of joining the fledgling association. Someone hung the tag "The Eastern Park Association" on Matt Rash as he tried to persuade them to join up. They refused his best efforts, saying that if and when Two-Bar tried to take over, they'd handle the problem in their own way. Disappointed and disgusted, Rash asked Beemis to make a second try.

Beemis realized this split between Park residents was no accident—far from it. He also knew that without the participation of the west-end ranchers, they were all in a much more vulnerable position for a Two-Bar takeover. One evening, he and Annie rode over in Beemis' buggy to pay a surprise call on Adam Hoy.

Adam seemed a pleasant enough fellow alright as he invited the two inside.

Beemis came right to the point. "Look, Adam, we all stand a much better chance if we stand together in dealing with the Two-Bar outfit. Come join us; it'll make our position that much stronger!"

Adam itched away at one of his sideburns before giving his answer. "If it was anybody but Matt Rash in charge, we'd consider joining up! What's got me puzzled is that you, above all the other ranchers, have been taken in by Rash. I always had a lot of respect for you...until now."

Beemis came unglued. Face red with anger, the stout old gent sallied forth by pressing the tip of his cane hard against a startled Adam Hoy's throat. "Dammit, Adam," he barked out, "I'm in this thing as much for the likes of you as well as myself! Try'n see it that way!"

Poor Adam finally persuaded Beemis to lower his cane. "Alright, alright! Maybe I misjudged you and Annie here, but it'll take more than just a few sticks of dynamite to change my mind on Matt Rash. He's bad news and he's your president, and those are two pretty darned good reasons not to join. Good day, Beemis! And you too, Ann! You know the way out!"

Beemis was still foaming around the gills at Adam Hoy's attack on his character, something he'd never encountered in all his born days either as an Army scout or horse rancher. Muttering obscenities half under his breath, the old boy missed the footstep on the side of the buggy.

Annie's alertness saved Beemis from possible serious injury. She caught him just in time. "Think I'd better drive," she said. "Adam has you too riled up for your own good."

Annie cracked the whip over the teams' flanks.

"Idiots, the whole damned bunch of 'em!" Beemis continued to wave his hands, half talking to himself and half to Annie. "When this business gets hashed out, and it will, Annie, I'm gonna make a special point of having another little chat with Adam, tell him what's on my mind, what I really think of him..."

Annie refused comment, hoping that would quiet him down. It'd been a long spell since she'd seen him in such an agitated state. An attack on Beemis' character, which she could more than vouch for, was not the way to deal with her uncle.

It took another two miles before Beemis finally cooled off. He looked over the countryside they were passing by, then held his gaze on Annie without uttering a word.

She read his mind. "Was kinda hoping we'd run into Deke. Guess we both had more than one reason to make the trip over here…"

"My words could've waited, Annie. It's your words that Deke needed to hear."

They stopped while Beemis lit the lantern before continuing on. Darkness had overtaken them by the time they crossed Vermillion Creek on their way to the ranch. Soon, they passed beneath the huge, overhead timber that stretched across the main gate, marking the boundary to the Markham ranch. The lantern gave off just enough light so that they could see the reflection bounce off the barbed-wire strands on both sides of the main gate. Both gave out a sigh of relief. It felt good to be back on home soil.

Annie drove right on up to the main porch to drop Beemis off. She helped him down, then drove back to the horse barn. There, she unhitched the team and walked to the tack shed with an armload of harness, reins, and the buggy whip. She looked up at the moonless sky. She was glad, in a way, that there would be no lover's moon out tonight. What good was such a moon, she reasoned, if the one you loved wouldn't be with you to share it?

She leaned her back against the tack shed door, hoping it wasn't latched so that it wouldn't be necessary to unload to free her hands to grasp the latch handle. To her surprise, the door swung open—too easily.

The inky blackness inside blinded her temporarily as she felt two strong arms relieve her of her load. She heard the harness hit the floor with a thud; then those same two arms found her again—this time for good!

"Deke, Deke," she cried out, "you almost scared the pants off me!"

This was no time for words. All that mattered to each was the fact that they were in each other's arms once more. Their bodies melted into one, forcing their lips to do the same thing: come in contact. They kissed so hard and so long, each not about to let the other stray more than a whisper's width apart. Such hunger, such desire, such want! And such love!

"Lord, oh Lord, how I've missed you, Annie. I still love you, but oh God, how it hurts!"

Annie forced herself into Deke even harder, resurrecting such strong, sweet memories. "Please, love, let me take some of that hurt away. You know what I mean…you know what needs to be done…now, do it, my love."

Her eyes became accustomed to the dark as he carried her. "Use the blankets, love—you know where the stack is."

Both were bent on a mission: Deke to satisfy his need to be deep within his Annie; she to make up some of what another had cheated him out of. Deke's boot found the stack. He wasn't about to take the time to sort or spread them out to cushion their bodies. He knelt and laid her on top of several blankets kicked every which way.

How each managed to undress enough to accommodate the other's needs was a marvel in itself. Annie had one boot on, one boot off, and her pantaloons were down, dropped around the one boot in a hopeless maze of twisted, white material. How she was able to slip one leg free was as much a mystery to her as it was to Deke.

Deke didn't fare much better. He opened his pants to slide them down to his boot tops, then decided against taking the time to pull everything off. He was hobbled by his own haste to claim what was rightfully his: his Annie. He crouched between her legs with his pants severely hampering his freedom.

"Hurry, love," she pleaded with him, "let me help you. You're bound up too tight...move closer, so I can help..."

Slap! Slap! Deke delivered the two telling blows to Annie's face. "Is that what you said to him? Let me help!"

She screamed out in pain. "No, no, Deke! I swear, I never said those words before! Only to you! I swear!"

Somehow, Deke raised up. "The only thing missing is your promise! C'mon, Annie! Say it! Say 'I promise I never said those words to him!' SAY IT!"

She began to whimper, then broke into a crying jag. He caught only an occasional word or two between the sobs and body jerks. She sat up, then used her shirt sleeve to clear her eyes to pick him out of the wall of black that hung over her. "If I say I promise...Deke...you'll say my promises don't mean a damn thing...and...and then it'll start all over between us. The hurt will be back...I can't take that...and you neither...that's why I won't say it...only that I love you—always will. Shouldn't that be good enough? For now?"

Annie heard him move away from her. He half-stumbled over something on the floor. She guessed he was tucking his shirt back into his pants after pulling them back up. "I can now understand how you might'a made one mistake. Know I'd never do that to somebody I truly loved. Maybe in time I could forgive you for that...but two times! Never!"

She heard footsteps toward the open door. She strained her eyes to pick him out, wanting desperately for the moon to be out, to shine down on him so she could see every feature about him she dearly loved. Now, she had to settle for a faint shadow of the real thing she'd felt with her arms, her lips, and her body a few minutes ago. She called out. "Why'd you come over here tonight? To hurt me? To say you'll never forgive me? To make me cry when we should be making love?"

There came silence, the kind that served no purpose for either. He cleared his throat twice. His voice seemed so close, yet so far away. "Been hearin' things 'bout you and Matt Rash...He's spendin' way too much time over here. At first, I figured it was that new association thing...Now, I'm not so sure."

"Damn you, Deke Landry! Damn you! You won't forgive me, but you don't want me to get on with my life! Is that it? That's it, isn't it?"

Her faint shadow sprouted arms once more; Deke came back to grab her, to lift her up, and to feel her closeness one more time. He pinned her shoulders back to drive home his point, but good! "Stay away from him! And stay outta his arms, too, 'cause you're too good for that no-account cattle rustler! Now you been warned! Best advice you'll ever get! Take it!"

Had Deke strained his eyeballs a mite longer, he would've seen a wry smile work wonders across his Annie's face. "You do care, don'tcha? Oh, I know you got a mound of hurt and pride high as a haystack built up inside you, but once you pitch that aside, it's still there...like it's always been between us, like it will always most likely be between us. What are we gonna do about it, Deke, let it rot in the field and never harvest it?"

He refused to answer. He shrugged both shoulders. "Time to say good-night...and I think good-bye, too." Deke paused. "Sweet, sweet Annie."

Ann's phantom lover of the dark left the way he had come, merging into the night with no visible trace he'd even been in her arms, tasted love's nectar from her lips or felt the fire from their bodies excite 'til she was wet from want with no release whatsoever. One visible scar remained, worse than the stab wound he'd put to her heart when he withdrew from her, his final act of denial. His final way of saying without words how much he hated the mere thought another had been there before him—twice!

She trudged slowly back to the ranch house, her mind and heart weighted down by an albatross of her own making: her own stupid mistakes. She entered through the back door to the kitchen, trying her best to avoid contact with either Beemis or Josie.

Josie saw Annie try to slip by. "There's hot coffee still on the range; come join me for a cup!"

Annie sat down at the kitchen table. Josie noticed her red eyes and the raised welt on one side of her cheek, but decided against asking any questions. "You should've seen Beemis! Didn't even stop by the kitchen! When he does that, things aren't going too good! You can still hear him talking to himself in his bedroom! What the heck happened, Sis?"

Annie toyed with the sugar spoon. "Adam Hoy says he's lost all respect for our uncle since he joined the association. Should'a seen Beemis use his cane on Adam! If it'd been a sword, poor Adam would've got it run clean through his throat! It didn't go well over at the Hoy ranch…"

Josie was about to add, *And by your looks, Sis, things aren't much better in the tack shed, either!* She skirted that thought in favor of another question. "Did either you or Beemis see Deke while you were there?"

Annie's answer gave herself away. "No…neither of us saw him…there."

"Too bad…was hoping you two would run into each other, maybe try to work things out. Another time, right, Sis?"

Annie swallowed hard. She sipped her coffee. Neither spoke. Josie waited for Annie to finally confide in her.

"You're probably wondering why there's a red mark on the side of my face. Truth is, I didn't bother to light the lantern in the tack shed…thought I could find the pegs in the dark. Ran right into one! Hurt so bad…made me cry a bit."

Josie got up to pour herself another cup. She shook the pot, heard the sloshing sound, and refilled her cup. "You know, Deke said about the same thing a while back. Said there's an extra big peg stickin' out from the wall. Remember him sayin,' that when he ran into it one night, the darned thing might just as well sprouted arms 'cause it slapped him up somethin' awful! Must've been the same peg you ran into!"

Ora Haley's scowl mirrored what had gone wrong. Hi Bernard's appearance only confirmed what he suspected. "Don't suppose there's any point in askin,' but is there at least a John Henry or two on the notice?"

Hi waved the blank signature column in front of his face. "None, Ora! Not one single rancher signed!"

Ora's eyes blazed. "Well, then, my good man, time's a'wastin'. That bunch of rattlesnakes is due for a lesson or two, I'm thinkin'! I'm gonna run 'em out! When I'm finished with 'em, they'll be begging me for the loan of a team and a wagon, aye…that they will! MOVE 'EM OUT!"

Ora's composure changed dramatically. A fiendish glee pranced and danced out of his coal-black eyes. For the first time, he actually seemed to enjoy the predicament his ultimatum had put himself in. "Wouldn't miss it for the world, my good man! Not for the world! Move 'em out! All of 'em! Every last four-legged critter that can walk!"

Clouds of dust swirled up from the ground, choking and gagging every living thing that got in the way of fifty-thousand head of Two-Bar range cattle. Grizzled old-timers along the herd trail in northwestern Colorado scratched their heads and mopped their weather-beaten brows; they'd never seen anything like it in all their born days. For miles, as far as any dust-laden eyes could possibly see, there was nothing but a wall of hooves, hides, and horns, complete with an unmistakable stench that emptied those with squeamish stomachs who dared to get a closer look.

Two weeks later, three of Hi Bernard's point riders rode toward him as hard and fast as their foam-lathered mounts would take them. "Sheep! Sheep ahead! Everywhere in Brown's Park! Nuthin' but woollies all over the place! Ain't a blade of grass left to be ate anywhere!" Hi couldn't believe his ears.

Ora Haley saw the point riders meet with his range boss amidst a chorus of wild hat waving and pointing toward the front of the herd. He reached for his buggy whip and put it to good use over the rumps of his team of blacks. His buggy dipped and bounced over the rough ground, but Ora gripped the reins all the tighter. He was going to find out what the delay was all about in short order, even it meant being thrown out of his buggy by his spirited team. "What's the holdup?" he yelled. "Should be in the Park come sundown! What's the holdup?"

Hi dismounted and walked over to the buggy. "My point riders say the Park is crawlin' with sheep, Sir!"

"Sheep?"

"You heard right, Sir! Sheep!"

"Can't be!" Ora yelled out. "I was on the committee that drafted the original agreement with the sheep men back in '80! No sheep south of the Wyoming-Colorado border above Brown's Park! That's the agreement! Always has been since then! No sheepman has ever dared to break the agreement! I was there, I made sure this could never happen! I was there!"

Hi saw Ora cuss 'til he was sure the stocky Irishman had exhausted every swear word in his most extensive vocabulary. Ora climbed down from his rig, the buggy whip in hand raised high above his head. He whipped and beat and whipped and beat the ground around him 'til his arms grew weary and ached;

still the Irishman flailed way 'til at last he sagged to his knees and leaned against the buggy wheel, drained of the energy and strength to continue. His cuss words, now a mixture of incoherent Irish bar-room brogue had long since left him.

Hi waited two more minutes, just in case. He approached Ora. "What do we do now, Sir?"

Hi's question didn't raise any response out of Ora. Finally, Ora's eyes focused on his range boss. The wheels began to turn. Hi helped him up.

"Do? Do, didja say? Aye, that you did, and aye, it shall be done, or I'll damn soon go out of this world a'tryin' 'til I've spent my last dollar and taken my last breath! I'm thinkin' tonight will be a night those nestlers will not soon forget! Come the daylight, every Nestler will know what real fear is! Aye, he will never again get another full night's rest—never again 'til he's met his Maker! Aye, that's a promise I'll make n' keep, or me name's not Ora Haley!"

Ora walked around to the back of his buggy. He returned to Hi, carrying a loaded shotgun. "Get your ten best shots and follow me! There's work to be done before sunrise tomorrow! That's an order! Any man who disobeys, I'll shoot him myself!"

An eerie autumn chill saturated the Park under a full October moon. Ten handpicked men followed their masked leader down into the Hole, their rifle barrels glistening in the moonlight. Never was death more determined than ever to visit. In their leader's mind, the unthinkable had happened, the unpardonable had been done, so it must be righted. It must be avenged 'til retribution was fully and rightfully vested. Their leader realized it would be at least a year before the lush, green grass would again carpet the Hole. Until then, this night would become the nightmare, the constant reminder to any nestler who dared oppose, who dared to think otherwise, or who dared to bring more sheep next year.

Silently, they swooped down upon the first sheepherder they could find.

"String him up," ordered their leader. "Hang him from the wagon tongue and then tie a rope to it and raise both over the wagon!"

The sheepherder was jerked skyward, screaming and yelling and kicking. When his boots stopped moving, the leader gave another order. "Kill five sheep! Throw them in the wagon and then burn everything!"

Within minutes, the woolen hides fed the funeral pyre. They gathered around on their mounts, waiting for the flames to consume everything. No one said a word while they waited for the flames to eat at the wagon tongue. Minutes later, the tongue buckled and collapsed, plunging the sheepherder's body down into the fiery inferno.

The leader rode out among the sheep and pointed with his shotgun. "Use your rifle butts! Kill one thousand! Make all the noise you can! I want every damned Nestler to see, hear, and smell death!"

The clubbings, the beatings, and the bleatings continued for a solid hour. One man rode back to his leader. "I personally counted; it's a thousand!"

"Good! Time to get the next one! If he tries to run, don't shoot! Make sure he's alive n' kicking when we string him up!"

Beemis, Josie and Ann watched in shocked horror as they counted three fires off in the distance. They went out to the front porch to continue watching, knowing full well they were helpless to do anything about it. Finally, Beemis coughed and sputtered. "Never knew burned wool would smell this bad. Lord, it's awful!"

Ann spoke her fear. "Sure that's all that's burning?"

The old warrior gathered the two women close to him. "Don't think we need to find out tonight. Tomorrow'll be plenty soon enough!"

CHAPTER SIX

Old Henry says, "I'm too old to diddle; guess I'll just sit right here and try to fiddle!"

Those ranchers who dared to rise early in the Park's east end saw something totally new in their lives. The sun rose over the eastern rim of the mountains, but its rays couldn't penetrate the thick, heavy layer of the foulest stench imaginable. The smell of burnt sheep flesh and wool hung over them like an impending disaster already in the making. Even for these ranchers accustomed through the years to shootings, newly dug graves, and unexplained disappearances, last night's orgy of hangings, beatings, and screams left them in shock. They now realized Ora Haley meant business; he had more than left his calling card.

Some stood out on front porches, or in the fields, or next to their barns, their eyes still focused on three smoldering fires off in the distance. Those closest to the embers were treated to a totally new, repulsive odor: barbequed human flesh.

Matt Rash stood in the open doorway of his log cabin. In typical bachelor fashion, he banged his coffee pot against the cabin's side to loosen the thick layer of grounds. Satisfied he'd left enough outside, he looked up in the sky. A whiff from the layer of stench caught him full face. His stomach churned and gave off strange sounds, daring him to put some food down it. He clutched at it, thankful he hadn't eaten any breakfast.

Two riders rode hard in his direction. He decided he could better face them sitting down behind his table, waiting for a fresh pot of coffee to brew. He was glad he'd closed the door. At least most of the smell was kept outside.

Both riders forgot the formality of knocking on Rash's door in their haste to confront him. The older brother nearly yanked the door off its hinges, trying to get to him first. He pounded his big fist on Rash's table. "Where's the law? Where's those night riders you promised so this wouldn't happen?"

The younger brother never waited for Matt's answer. He pounded the table even harder to vent his anger. "You gave us free pasture, but it sure as hell ain't worth it! Not at this price! We're gettin' the heck outta this hellhole!"

Matt made eye contact with both Griffith brothers, but he made his pitch to the oldest. "We have an agreement, gentlemen. You move your sheep out, and we all lose."

The older Griffith put some real muscle into his arm. He jerked Matt up out of his chair in nothing flat. "Is your nose plugged up? Just 'cause you didn't see what happened don't mean you can't smell what happened! We're outta here! Pronto!"

By dusk, the Griffith brothers had moved the remnants of their forty-thousand sheep out of the park. Now the Park's association was left on its own to deal with Ora Haley as best they could.

Beemis was the first to take action. He fired off a letter to Routt County Sheriff Charley Neiman asking for an immediate investigation into the triple hangings and sheep slaughter. One week, then two, and finally three weeks passed with no response from Sheriff Neiman.

Another shockwave rocked the park. Deke Landry found John Jarvey's body floating in the Green River. Deke waded out into the swift current to pull Jarvey's body away from a snag. Jarvey was the victim of more foul play; both hands and feet were bound together. This time, the Hoy brothers joined Beemis in demanding that an investigation be launched at once!

"Hey, no need to knock the door down! I'm coming! I'm coming!"

Josie dried her hands on her apron and scurried toward the front parlor door. Whoever was on the other side of Beemis' prize hardwood either had poor manner or big knuckles, and she was about to find out which. She opened the door. Her jaw dropped.

The burly built man followed her wide-open stare all the way down to his open jacket. "You act like you've never seen a badge before!"

Josie's surprise stayed with her eyes while her sweet lips returned to normal. "I haven't!" she exclaimed. "Well, what I mean is, not down here!"

The man took one step inside before removing his hat. "Name's Charley Neiman! I'm the sheriff of this county! Lookin' for Beemis Markham!"

Josie pointed toward the smallest of four buildings. "You'll find my uncle in the tack shed, oiling down the leather. He's been waitin' forever for you to show up! He's pretty edgy about the time you've taken, so I'd be on my best behavior if I were you!"

Neiman chuckled. "That old warhorse and me go back more than just a few years. Beemis took me in when I was a drifter, kept me from straddling both sides of the law. Got me to see it his way...even helped get me elected first go-round."

The sheriff poked his head in the open door of the shed. Beemis had his back to him, laying out harnesses, bridles, and halters on a table. He quietly stepped inside, then let his Stetson go sailing past Beemis' head. It landed on the floor beside his old friend.

Beemis never bothered to turn around. He picked up a rag, then dipped it into a small pan of linseed oil. "Damn you, Charley Neiman," he growled. "I'm gonna ream your ass out before I hug you and shake hands! 'Cause you sure got' a good reamin' a' comin'! What in tarnation took you so long? Didn't you get the two letters I sent?"

Charley turned the old gent around. Beemis forgot his built-up hostility for a full minute while they hugged each other and shook hands.

Neiman stepped back. "Same old warhorse! Gettin' a roll 'round your middle. Heard you lost Maybelle some time ago..."

Beemis pinched his side. "You can blame this on my niece, Josie. I'd stack her cookin' up against anybody's, anywhere. Maybelle's good old Southern cookin' never went to waste. Gave Josie plenty a'pointers before she passed on."

"That must be the young lady who pointed me in the right direction. Say, she's some looker!"

"She's got a younger sister, too, who needs a horse quirt to keep 'em at a respectable distance. Got mixed up with one of Butch Cassidy's Wild Bunch...cost her a damned good man...best foreman I ever had. Don't know if it'll ever work out for either of them."

Neiman reached inside his jacket. He produced three letters. "I know this is gonna sound like a pretty limp excuse, but I came up here from Rifle. Had to leave one deputy in town to sort out a big shooting. Four dead, and nobody can figure out what really happened! Probably some bad blood mixed in with a lot of misunderstanding. Had to leave my only other deputy at my office to hold down the fort!" He opened both hands to emphasize his point. "I'm spread too thin, tryin' to cover too much ground! Routt County is bigger than two or three of them back-East states that used to be colonies! Now do you see what I'm up against?"

"Yeah, Charley, might just as well bark at the moon as expect any help from the law! We got us one helluva mess here! Three Mexican sheepherders got strung up on the tongues of their wagons, and then those night riders tossed some sheep into the wagons and set fire to the whole deal. We had one helluva bonfire, I'll tell you, goin' on at three different places! And to top that off, near as I can figure, better'n a thousand head'a sheep got clubbed to death around each of them bonfires! I waited two weeks and then I sifted through the ashes...put what bones I could find into a blanket and gave 'em a Christian burial. Most of the smell finally left the Hole last week!"

"Got any feeling who's behind this?"

"Sure, Two-Bar! Ain't got a lick'a proof, though!"

"I've spent all day trying to talk to all the ranchers closest to the fires. Never seen a bunch like this; they're ready to jump outta their boots, they're so scared! Everywhere I went, nobody knows anything, nobody saw anything, and nobody bothered one scrap of information. Using a crowbar to pry their mouths open wouldn't've done a lick of good! Beemis, give me or get me something solid to use, and I'll do my job! What you and I think won't hold up in court; I gotta have something I can bite into and hold onto. When I get more help, I'll get here quicker, it's as simple as that!"

Beemis didn't like what Charley told him. "You know, Charley, it's all those little folks, like us, that keeps gettin' you elected, not Ora Haley! If this keeps up, you're gonna find yourself askin' the next sheriff if he'll take you on as his new deputy 'cause you'll be out of a job!"

Charley put his arm on his old friend's shoulder. "Look, there's nothun' I'd like better than to nail the biggest of the big! I've got a peg on my wall just outta reach from behind the bars in my jail. That's where I just love to see that special black derby that Ora thinks so much of hangin' there, day after day, while he's waitin' trial."

"That'll never happen, and we both know it! Ora has too much money and too many friends in just the right places to keep him from roostin' even one

250

night in your jail."

Beemis covered the linseed oil pan and started out the door. Charley followed.

"Where ya goin'? Let me give you a hand with the oiling."

The old scout pointed to his new hay barn. "This time of year when the sun gets level with the top of that roof, I know Josie's in the kitchen fixin' supper! C'mon?"

Charley tagged along. "Can't remember the last time I ate at your table, Beemis, but if Josie's cookin' is anything like Maybelle's, I'm in hog heaven!"

Beemis' cane never broke stride. "Better get ready to do some oinkin', Charley!"

Charley Neiman had a hard time leaving room in his mouth and still complimenting Josie on her chicken and dumplings at the same time. Both received more than a fair share of his attention.

Beemis thoroughly enjoyed Charley's company, despite their differences concerning what the law could and could not do. After the supper dishes were stacked, they pushed their chairs back over fresh refills of coffee. Charley opened the conversation. His blue eyes were still full of respect for the man who'd taken him in over twenty-five years ago. "The John Jarvey murder is another puzzler. Talked to one of Adam Hoy's cow punchers, man by the name of Deke Landry. He's the one who found Jarvey. From what I heard nosing around, Jarvey was very well respected, and it doesn't figure he had very many enemies. Landry said whoever did the dirty work used sheepshank knots on Jarvey's hands and feet and then tossed him into the river. Didn't even bother sinkin' him down."

"Did you hear anything about who's going to take over the store? I know his wife doesn't want to stay on...not after what happened."

Charley shook his head. "Have no idea, Josie." He scratched at a week's worth of stubble on his round face. "This man Landry...interesting sort of a man...seems to know a lot more about horses than cattle. Can't figure out why he's wastin' his time over there. I'd'a thought he'd be a natural for your type of business, Beemis! Do you know him by chance?"

Beemis' face changed colors, Annie's too! Only Josie remained calm.

Charley put two and two together. He smiled easily. "Guess I solved that one. Sorry, Annie, Beemis...didn't mean to step on family feelin's or toes."

Beemis sipped his coffee, making a slurping sound, much to everyone's amusement. Then he held the cup in his hands, letting its heat penetrate his hands while he looked across the table at Josie. He knew she'd never bring up the one question she was dying to ask. He turned to Charley. "Since you're in the law business, have you run across Mister Mormon, Butch Cassidy, or any of his bunch?"

Josie colored as Charley picked up on it right away. "So you're the reason Butch tried to get a pardon, so he could change his life and settle down. Never put much stock in that story 'til now…Yes, I can see why he'd want to change. No offense, Josie, but I doubt it would've worked. A big reputation like he had…well, you'da ended up fightin' the same odds he'da brought to the marriage—slim and none!"

He let his words settle across Josie's face before he continued. "Butch Cassidy is living on borrowed time! Don't worry, Josie, there are too many crack railroad detectives, and Pinkerton men, and U.S. Marshalls hot on his trail for me to waste my time. They all make a mistake sooner or later, and Butch made a big one down in Texas!"

Josie gasped, fearing the worst.

"He's still alive, Josie, but the handwriting's on the wall for him! After he had that picture taken with his train robber bunch, the law got a hold of it. Now they know exactly who they were lookin' for and what they looked like. Since then, every one of his gang has been killed or captured and put behind bars, except Butch and his sidekick, the Sundance Kid! Things are gettin' so hot, Butch doesn't have time to hole up and celebrate like he used to."

"So, you think it's only a question of time before they nail him?"

Charley mused on Beemis' question while he scratched at a week's worth of beard on his round face. "I traveled on the wrong side of the law for a spell before your uncle turned my life around. If I was Butch…I'd hit a bank or two now; they're a lot easier pickings than those railroad express cars since the railroads wised up by hooking those rolling posse cars on every train that's carryin' big sums of money."

"Rolling posse cars? What the heck is that?"

Charley could see he was covering new territory. "When Butch first started hitting those express cars, they were sittin' ducks, and no protection, whatsoever, 'cept maybe one guard behind a locked door and a safe. Butch solved that real quick. Then the railroad came up with its own version of Butch's relay system by spendin' thousands of dollars to fix up special cars that have the side doors drop like cattle loadin' chutes. If the train gets stopped, they drop those doors and the chase is on with fresh horses. They're so close, Butch and his blow-up artists ain't even got time to hardly tie the money sacks on their mounts anymore. Funny thing though…just thought of something…"

Beemis moved to the edge of his chair. "What hit you sudden-like, Charley?"

Charley sipped his coffee. "You know old Butch did some pretty sharp thinkin' and plannin' too! Far as I know, in all his robberies and holdups, nobody's been shot or crippled! So, if he does get caught, they can only sentence him for grand theft…Beats murder charges all to heck!"

Three people gathered around the table exchanged glances at Charley Neiman's latest information. Two of the three grudgingly had to admit to themselves that no matter what they personally thought of Butch Cassidy, he'd obviously done more than just careful planning, execution, and thorough scouting. He had indeed covered all the corners!

Josie felt relieved—somewhat. "You said he's running out of time…Isn't there something he can do?"

Charley saw the worry lines deepen around Josie's most handsome face. "Like I said, Josie, if I were in his boots, I'd hit a couple of soft touches and then leave the country with goin'-South money, as they say…That'd give me plenty of money to set up somewhere else. Maybe then he could really start all over."

Beemis rose. "It's been a long day, what say we all turn in?"

Everybody seemed to follow Beemis' lead. Josie and Annie picked up the stacked dishes and headed for the kitchen.

"Two more things I'd like to cover before we all turn in." He called out. "Josie! Annie! Would you two mind lettin' me jaw a bit more?"

The two sisters came back into the dining room.

"Okay, you have our attention, now what, Charley?"

"I stopped by to look up your association president. Nobody was home! Years ago, I ran into a fellow up in Wyoming by the name of Rash. Could this be the same bird?"

Annie volunteered. "Yes, I'm pretty sure Matt Rash used to work up that way, why?"

"The man I met was a real sharp talker. Had a way with his words…kept smoothin' his way outta one scrape after another. Had a rovin' eye for the ladies, too. Anyway, this Rash was there when Ora Haley and six or seven big cattle spreads all got together; they signed an agreement with the local sheep men—two Welsh brothers as I remember—"

Beemis jumped in with both feet. "You mean to tell us that there was an agreement on the books and Rash knew about this?"

"Sure do, Beemis, if this is the same man! Tomorrow, I aim to find out why he let those sheep in down here when he knew he was in violation of a standing agreement!"

"That still doesn't excuse murdering three people!"

"You're right, Annie, it doesn't! But I've got a gut feeling there's more here than meets the eye! Matt Rash had his own reasons; he just didn't let you folks and other association members in on it!"

Beemis was feeling used. He started to do a slow boil. "Alright, maybe Two-Bar had their reasons, too…but as Annie says, murder is still murder, no matter what!"

"Now to the other bit of information regarding the Jarvey murder. Mister Landry found Jarvey's body in the Utah end of the park. I could've told the Hoy brothers and Deke to call in the law from Vernal, but I figured the law over there is spread out pretty thin, same as we are here. So I filled out my report and sent a copy to them through your local post office. We're all tryin' to cover too much!"

Beemis couldn't wait to vent his feelings. "Couldn't agree with you more, Charley! So from now on, instead of waitin' forever for you or your deputy to show up, we'll do our own investigation, and I'll make sure we send you a copy!"

Charley Neiman didn't care for Beemis' comments in the slightest. Yet he had to admit, his longtime friend did have a valid point. "Alright, if you do any snooping around, make sure you're in charge, not Matt Rash! I trust you, not Rash!"

The sheriff came away from the supper table with a draw. Beemis had left no doubt; he no longer was going to stand by and let Two-Bar roll over him or his neighbors! Not if he could help it! The two stood alone, sizing each other up, their friendship strained but still intact. Charley saw a chance to lighten their mutual respect for each other up a bit. "Say, Beemis, stand straight up, if you can! And quit leanin' on your cane so much! You used to be an inch or two taller than me! What happened?"

The old sage wasn't about to let someone thirty years younger get the best of him. He left Charley with a real gem. "All these years, tryin' to keep the likes of you from strayin' too much has caught up with me. Hell, if I wasn't loaded down with everyone's troubles, I'd probably be three inches taller by now!"

Annie waited and waited for Josie to start washing the dishes. Her hands were deep into the suds, but her mind was definitely someplace else. Annie flicked her drying towel around, letting it rest first on one shoulder, then the other. Finally, more out of futility than anything else, she laid the towel on the counter and touched her sister's shoulder.

Josie jumped a mile. "Don't do that! Can't you see I'm busy?"

"Yes, so I've noticed. You're so busy, your dishrag looks about wore out! Any more thrashing around in that dishpan, and I'll have to look for another dishrag for you!"

Suddenly, the tears came down Josie's cheeks. She needed a shoulder to cry on. Annie obliged, knowing full well what had brought on the latest downpour.

"I've been doing pretty well, Sis, until tonight. All that talk about Butch again…can't seem to get him out of my mind."

Annie played big sister. "Or out of your heart. You know, we're really a pair! We both know what we want and who'll make us happy, and we're both alone, more than ever now."

Josie picked a handkerchief out of her apron pocket. She wiped her eyes, then blew her nose. "You had the chance to do something about it…and you let it slip away…I never had the same kind of chance you did or…"

"Or what, Sis?"

"Or I would've never let him slip away."

Annie left her sister's side. She picked up the dish towel and waited. "That's the difference between us. I'm probably the last person to see Butch before he pulled up stakes for good outta here. The one thing that was most on his mind , the one thing he tried to impress upon me was to make sure you got on with your life. Well, Sis, from what I see, including tonight, you're sure not doing much about it."

Josie attacked the dishes with a vengeance. Any food particles left on the plates never had a chance, not the way she worked the dishes over. "You must be blind, Sis! Can't you see, I don't dare get on with life until I make sure you don't screw up again?"

Deke, too, tried to get on with his life. Ah, but there was that rub! The big rub! He was still haunted by Annie's presence, bitten by her charm, and overwhelmed by her pixie-like beauty. Whether he cared to admit it or not, love's torch smoldered and burned deep within. What to do? What to do?

He did know one thing for sure! Herding four-legged moo-machines gave him far too much time to think about Annie. Dealing with horses kept him busy and happy, something that he'd give his right arm to be doing again. Ah, but there was that rub again! The Markham ranch was the only place that raised horses! What to do? What to do?

Then it happened, a break in Deke's same old monotonous routine. He was out nursemaiding a bunch of strays from the Hoy ranch. By the time he'd rounded them up, they'd stumbled upon a patch of grass somehow overlooked by the Griffith brothers' aborted stay in the park. He topped a small rise, which gave him a good, overall view of his stragglers, who were contentedly munching away on the lush grass missed by the sheep.

He picked out a horse and rider chasing another spirited horse—an Arabian gelding! It was Annie aboard Glory in hot pursuit. Two quick spurs into his Indian Paint produced a short burst of speed. Forget the cows! Here was a chance to do what he loved best, helping Annie!

It was like old times again as he rode hard into the gelding's side, forcing the Arabian to break its stride. This hazing gave Annie the break she needed. Once, twice, the lariat circled over her head; then the rope shot out, true to its mark, settling gently over the frightened Arabian's head.

Two minutes later, the young gelding was snubbed close to Glory, a rope halter doing the trick. Deke dismounted and came up to the frightened animal. "Easy…easy now." He spoke in low, soft tones again as he gradually drew closer and closer. "Easy…easy." He touched the horse's nose and let the animal smell his hand. Then he moved his hand under its nose and stroked the soft skin just on the underside of its mouth. He kept that up while he busied his other hand gently rubbing its neck. "There…there now…that's not so bad. There…there…oh, that feels so good…yes, it does."

"Nobody, and I mean nobody, can talk to horses like you can, Deke. You have such a gift…such a natural way around them. They'll let you do things to them that I've never seen anyone even come close to, scared or not!"

He liked her compliment and enjoyed her company even more. "Thanks, Annie…sure don't get any compliments around here…'course I ain't exactly in love with those cow-pie droppin' machines I watch over." He smiled up at her. "Sure was good workin' with you again. Nobody lays a rope easier or gentler over a frightened animal's head than you do, Annie."

Annie, too, liked the compliment, especially coming from Deke. "We sure do work well together. That's one of the things I miss…since you left."

"Anything else you miss?" he asked.

"You! You, Deke!"

He stopped petting the horse. "How'd this horse come to get so far west?

That never happened when I was runnin' the show."

Annie didn't hide the truth, nor did she want to. "This gelding's name is Blaze. Don't you think he'd make a fine present...to somebody real special?"

Deke was taken in. "Boy, do I! All my life I've always wanted to own a horse like this!" He looked away. "Came close once...mighty close."

"Blaze is yours, love. He's pretty spirited—a lot like you are—so when he broke loose, I ran him over here...hoping I'd run into you...The rest you know."

"Gee, Annie, I don't know what to say."

"A small thank-you will do for now. There are no strings attached...only my love for you."

He looked at her. Lord, she was something, he thought. Even from this distance, he could smell her perfume. He saw her lightly painted lips and wished he could taste them. Her men's work shirt never did hide her breasts very well...especially when she wanted him to notice them, when she pulled her shoulders back like she was doing now. Her body, so slim and trim, yet just wide enough at the hips to hold him and give him a pleasure he always wanted, but never quite got.

Annie broke his train of thought. "Miss me?"

The shine in his deep-blue eyes told it all. "Yeah, be lying to my face if I said I didn't...and you?"

"Goes double for me."

Ann dismounted. She rushed into his arms. "Come back! Come back, please, Deke!"

Deke kissed her hand. He meant to hurt her. Instead, she seemed to sense he was doing this to release some of the deep hurt. His way of hitting without striking her.

She forced the tug of war going on between them. "This is your last chance, love. I can't take any more of this...seeing you only once in a while, meeting you by chance and then having to go home, no closer or farther than before. I'm going to get on with my life...one way or the other."

"Been hearing more and more about you and that Matt Rash. Most of what I hear I don't care for one bit..."

She kissed him. "Then come back, and you'll never hear another thing! I promise!"

"Yup, we're back to that, aren't we?"

"Back to what?"

"You makin' promises you never keep! Or have you forgotten already?"

Her anger festered. "Just can't leave it alone, can you? I made one mistake, Deke! Not a hundred!"

Now it was his turn to explode. "Better hold up two fingers, not one! Too bad with all the fancy schoolin' your uncle paid for, you never learned to count!"

"Alright! Alright, two times! Now are you satisfied? One last time, Deke, are you coming back?"

"For what? Another shoutin' match, day after day? No thank you!"

Annie stomped away from Deke. She mounted up.

"Blaze needs more work! See that he gets it!"

Annie jerked Glory's reins. "Won't have time to."

"Why not? You got plenty'a time! What's the big hurry?"

She started to ride way. "I know somebody who'll be tickled pink to get him!"

Deke cupped both hands around his mouth. "Yeah, Matt Rash! Stay away from that snake-oil peddler, he's bad news!"

Annie turned around in her saddle. "Can't be all bad! Found out the other day he's a nephew of Davy Crockett!"

She was almost out of shouting distance before Deke answered back. "Don't believe everything you hear, Annie…and only half of what you see!"

Deke's rejection of Ann's last-ditch effort to patch things up between them propelled her straight into the arms of Matt Rash. It provided lots of fodder for the gossip cows in the Park to chew on. Even Deke followed the whereabouts of the Park's latest lovebirds through the society column of the Craig, Colorado, newspaper, *The Craig Courier*. Though it made interesting reading, he still doubted Ann's real sincerity and true love interest in the self-oiling spokesman for the Park's Cattlemen's Association. There was something about Matt Rash that just didn't ring true to his way of reckoning.

Shorty McCallum gave Beemis his true feelings late Sunday afternoon. "Look, Beemis, I ain't no Deke Landry! Told'ja before, I'll do my best 'til ya come up with somebody to take over. Now when kin I expect that to happen?"

Beemis rested his cane over one of the top rails in the horse barn. "Got an ad runnin' for six months now up in Rock Springs. No takers! I also got an ad in that newspaper in Vernal, and so far nobody's made the trip over here. That answer your question?"

Shorty was about to say something when he heard horses coming. He turned to Beemis and changed subjects. "Annie and Matt Rash are comin' back after their Sunday ride. He sure don't handle that horse Annie gave him very well. Deke'd have him gentle 'nuff for a Sunday school teacher to ride..."

"That ain't all he doesn't handle very well..."

They waited for Annie to dismount. Shorty took Glory's reins to lead her down to her stall.

"Thanks, Shorty," Annie said. "I should be getting up to the main house to give Josie a hand. You're invited for supper, Matt. I'm sure Josie fixed extra, being it's Sunday."

Annie let Matt plant a kiss on her cheek. "Make it another time, Annie. Got something that needs my attention."

She started toward the door and then turned around. "See you Wednesday evening at our meeting. Make sure when you cross Vermillion that you ease Blaze into the water straight; don't let him step on all those flat rocks along the bank! That's when all the noise makes him skittish!"

"I will, Annie! I will! Take care, love! See you Wednesday!"

Beemis didn't even wait for Annie to get out of hearing range. "I've got a question or two, Matt, that could stand your attention...NOW!"

They faced each other. One, never more sure of himself, the other, full of questions that needed answers with more than a little dislike coated over for now.

"Okay, Beemis, what's on your mind?"

"Two weeks ago, a tin star tried to look you up! A good friend of mine! Name's Charley Neiman. Did he find you?"

"No, we missed each other somehow."

"About bringing those sheep into the Hole. Sheriff Neiman said there was a signed agreement between Ora Haley and a couple other big outfits with the sheepman. They weren't supposed to run sheep down here! How come when Annie came up with the sheep idea you didn't step in and tell us about it? Charley said he was sure you must've known about it since you was workin' for one of those big outfits that signed on! Well?"

Matt Rash never raised an eyebrow—even a tad. "Yes, I knew about it, but you have to look at the big picture, Beemis!"

"Whataya mean, the big picture?"

"I'm glad you brought this up! You're stealing some of my thunder for Wednesday's meeting, but since we're such good friends, I don't mind! No, I don't mind at all!" Rash went to an open doorway and motioned for Beemis to come.

Beemis stood in the doorway. "Alright, I'm here! Now what?"

"Look around you, Beemis! Not one Two-Bar brand or cow in sight! We've stopped Ora Haley dead in his tracks! The sheep did it, Beemis! Isn't it something?"

Beemis raised his cane and pointed it at the tall Texan with the light-brown hair. "Don't claim to be no cattleman, but I do know a thing or two 'bout what makes big men tick! Haley ain't gonna take this lyin' down! Better enjoy all this quiet while we can 'cause Two-Bar will be down here, one way or another! Now 'bout this big picture, I'm still waitin'!"

"I feel bad about losing those three Mexicans! Really, I do! But sometimes you have to sacrifice a little to gain a lot! It's called doing something for the greater good! Now do you see it? The big picture?"

"Wonder if you'd'a asked those three that got strung up if they'd'a said, 'Sure! Go ahead! We don't mind, 'cause we see the big picture!'"

"You really don't like me very much, do you Mister Markham? Bet it has a lot to do with you losing your top hand. That Montana mustanger who took a shine to your niece, and now, I'm her steady friend!"

Beemis lowered his cane. "Let's not get started on that 'cause you'd come out on the short end every time! Let's just let it go for now by saying Deke Landry probably forgot more about handling horses than you'll ever learn in two lifetimes! As far as what I think about you...far as I'm concerned, the jury on you is still out!"

"Sit still, Uncle! How in the world am I supposed to trim up your whiskers if you keep on wriggling?"

"Can't help it, Sugarplum! Women wavin' sharp scissors around makes me more than a bit nervous! Your Aunt Maybelle gave me the same feeling when she used to do up my beard!"

Josie had Beemis sit out on the front porch with her apron tied around his neck to keep the loose hairs from itching down his neck and back. "Here, you hold this mirror up, and tell me where to take off a little as I work around."

Beemis did his best to quit moving. "What if Shorty or the others see me like this? And you just had to wear the frilliest apron you could find! Makes me feel like some housewife who pulled up her apron and dress just 'cause she spotted a mouse!"

Josie laughed and laughed. "Don't worry, dear Uncle, no one would ever mistake you for a housewife! Now, I'm going to trim out over your ears, so watch me in the mirror!"

"Just think, in a year or two…maybe three, you could be doing this to your own little boy. Then who'll give me a trim?"

Snip! Snip! An inch of Beemis' hair fell on Josie's apron. "Hold still now…not much salt and pepper color any more. Mostly salt…getting thinner, too. Yes, some day I'll give my son his first haircut…and he'll wiggle around just like his great uncle." *Snip! Snip!* "If I live close by, I could still stop by with my son…and he could watch me trim you up."

"Cleve Dreschler's ranch isn't that far away…Think he'd make purty good father material."

"Who said anything about Cleve Dreschler fathering my children?"

"Looks like this is gonna take a while! That chair inside the door in the front room would make it a lot easier with you sittin' on it while you work on me. Save all that bendin' and stoopin'."

Josie returned with the chair. "Now, what's next?"

Beemis moved the mirror around. "On my left cheek…fuzz is stickin' straight out, won't lay down…Get that."

Josie followed his directions. "You're worried about Annie falling for Matt Rash, aren't you?"

"See that patch of bristles stickin' up like buck brush next to my chin? Take a little off there. Glad you mentioned it, Sugarplum! How do you see it?"

Josie combed the patch out, then cut away. "Not to worry…Annie's just goin' through the motions. She's a heckava lot better rider than she is actor. Only person getting serious is Matt."

Beemis moved his mirror again. "You're sure 'bout this? I hear Rash thinks he's another Elza Lay…and you know how that turned out—take a little off my top…near my forehead, will ya?"

Josie measured Beemis' hair through her fingers and went to snipping. "Annie's too impetuous at times…acts on impulse too often. That's what got her into trouble; she's paying an awful price for that mistake…that'll never happen again. Wish Deke would believe her…save a lot of ups and downs in both their lives."

"I've seen 'em kissing! Rash drools over Annie like he's in heat!"

Josie's smile broke out into full laughter. "Oh, Uncle, the way you put things. Don't worry, when Matt kisses her, she goes into her pretend life…pretending it's Deke all over again. How about me trimming those eyebrows? They get any thicker, one of our barn swallows will start lookin' for a new home."

Beemis closed his eyes while Josie carefully trimmed his eyebrows. "There now, done! Take a look!"

The old scout moved his mirror from left to right and back again. He was pleased. "Lord, I'm gonna miss you when you move out. And you will, Josie, you will! Mark these words!"

Josie hugged the old boy and gave him a resounding smack. "Not for a while, not for a while! We both have a job to do: get our Annie to keep on the straight and narrow."

"Oh, oh! I hear Annie rattlin' the dishes way out here! Must mean she's got the table set and wants you to come join her in the kitchen."

Josie untied her apron around Beemis' neck. "Here, you shake this while I make sure Annie's baking-powder biscuit dough's ready for the oven. It's her one claim to fame in the kitchen, and I certainly don't want to discourage her."

"Bet you're sorry your Mister Rash wasn't here! He missed out on one heckava meal! Add in Annie's powder biscuits for soppin' up the gravy and ya got a meal fit for a king! How come Matt had to skedaddle, anyhow?"

Annie answered as best she could. "Said something about he had to see Isom Dart." She paused, still deep in thought. "Still don't understand…those two never get along. Matt never has a kind word for Isom; yet Matt keeps him hangin' round the ranch along with that new fella, that dark, Mexican-lookin' cowpuncher by the name of Hicks. Don't trust that Hicks! Something's not right there…can't exactly figure out what, but I got a gut feeling Hicks is hiding something."

"Probably his past, Sis, just like nine out of ten others who come drifting in with their hard-times, hard-luck stories and new names to fit, so they won't look back over their shoulder quite so much."

Beemis finished sponging off the gravy on his plate with the last of Annie's biscuits. "Heard Matt say the other day he's got some brandin' to do. Maybe that's why he keeps Isom around. Understand he's good with an iron."

Annie was still deep in thought. "Matt says Isom's been a lot of places, done a lot of things. Worked on a cotton plantation as a slave, darned good all-around roper, cowboy and horse wrangler, too! Even was a wrestler for a while in some travelin' carnival…says he never lets the color of his skin bother him since he was a runaway slave during the war."

Josie started to clear the table. "Isom's got the build to be a wrestler, never seen a better built man, black or white."

"You've been over to his ranch enough times; how many head does Matt own?"

Annie sensed her uncle's question was double-barreled. "Well, Old Henry said Matt arrived here with about two-hundred-eighty head, all rustled! And Deke claims Matt's been adding more rustled cattle all along, mostly Two-Bar, that stray down the trails into the park. Matt's story is that these were mavericks and that he has as much right to them as the next rancher. He's just beating them to the punch, that's all."

"Who'd ya believe, Deke or Matt?"

Annie got up to help Josie. "Don't do this to me, Uncle! You're tryin' to make me choose, and I won't answer you one way or another. And don't you dare say what else you're thinkin,' even if you're right."

"What I was gonna say was—"

"Don't! It's about Deke bein' a better man than Matt, isn't it?"

"Annie, Annie! Listen to yourself! Them's your words, not mine!"

Matt Rash was in a foul mood. He paused only long enough at his ranch to be joined by the dark, swarthy-complexioned man who called himself Tom Hicks. He rode hard and he rode fast, leaving Hicks lagging back to either catch up or fall behind as he didn't seem to care one way or the other. When they reached the cabin at Summit Spring, they paused behind the cabin long enough to sample the thirst-quenching water that spewed out between two large boulders.

Hicks could see his boss had other things on his mind. "What's the hurry, Matt? Can't it wait 'til tomorrow?"

Matt discharged the ice-cold water out the side of his mouth. "He's a stupid, stupid man…but he's the best damned hair-brand man I've ever come across! There's none better! That's why I put up with him!"

Hicks took the cup from Matt and promptly held it under the stream until it overflowed. He raised it to his lips, drank half, then turned to the impatient Rash. "Maybe I shouldn't have tagged along if this is between you two."

"You're my backup, just in case! Don't trust that damned nigger one minute past now! Met him down in Texas when he run off with a herd of horses he rustled from the cotton plantation he was born a slave to. Been an uppity nigger ever since! Thinks he's free and White, no matter what his skin keeps tellin' him! Now ain't that something?"

Hicks returned the cup to its usual resting place: a rusty nail sticking out of an old fence post. A minute later, they were off in a westerly direction, across the lower face of Cold Spring Mountain. Ten minutes more of saddle time brought the two riders to their destination, a deep-pocket draw sandwiched in between a ravine, well out of the range of any prying eyes that might get a bad case of moral curiosity.

Hicks saw two dozen young steers milling about in a makeshift rope corral tied between three scraggly looking Juniper trees. Not fifty feet to the right stood the biggest and most powerfully built Negro he'd ever seen. Next to the Negro, he spotted a small wisp of a man who made Isom Dart look like a giant.

Matt's polished boot hit the dirt. Isom tore into him. He raised the branding iron straight at Hicks. "Who's he?" he demanded. "Weren't 'sposed to bring anyone! You was to come alone!"

Matt spoke for Tom. "Name's Hicks; he's been helpin' out at the ranch. He's damn good with a gun...thought you oughta know."

Rash's answer seemed to satisfy Isom for the moment. He addressed the stranger. "Thought you was a Mex, at first...now I see that's not so! Done any brandin'?"

Hicks climbed off his mount. He hobbled his horse, then walked toward the muscular man. "Done my share down in Arizona...worked for a man named John Slaughter near Prescott."

"Good! See you know horses, too! You three do the ropin' and holdin' down while I run the iron. Get through faster that way."

Matt was in charge or so he thought. "Hold it! How come we're brandin' today? That was supposed to happen next week after I make a deal with Jessy Wiggins at the mercantile."

Dart dropped the branding iron into the hot coals. He shook one hammer-sized fist at Matt. "Well, Mista Smart Mouth, you sure done it up real good this time! I got no cash money to buy hay to feed these critters since you done let all them sheep in. There ain't no grass left behind my cabin! Billy 'n me been stealin' hay from Old Henry's haystacks at night just 'cause of you! Ah cain't keep pressin' my luck outta my rabbit's foot much more, so I done the best I could."

Matt edged closer to Isom, fire flashing from his eyes. "Whata'ya mean you done the best you could?"

"I done made a deal with Jessy already, so you don't need to smooth-mouth him none."

Matt's hatred for Dart was ready to boil over. "How much, you stupid nigger? How much are we getting for these Two-Bar steers?"

"Twenty dollar a head after they're branded." Isom loaded up another fist in front of Matt. "Next time you call me stupid or a nigger, I'm gonna hold out five dollars for every steer from your cut."

Now it came Matt's turn. "You dumb, stupid nigger! I coulda got forty from Jessy! You let him screw us outta twenty a head! That's four hundred eighty dollars we been screwed out of!"

Isom made a quick grab for the red-hot branding iron. In a flash, Hicks saw what was about to happen. Matt was too close, far too close to escape being branded. Each man heard the unmistakable click from Hick's revolver.

"Raise that iron, Mister, and it'll be the last one you'll ever raise!"

Isom eyed Rash's sidekick with enough hate to brand every piece of exposed flesh.

"Stay outta this, Mex," Dart warned, "or you might just forget 'bout wakin' up some morning."

Hicks motioned with his cocked revolver toward Billy Styles, who'd been conspicuously quiet during the confrontation. "Tell you what, gentlemen, I'm gonna keep my gun on all three of ya 'til this brandin' gets done! That's right, gentlemen, it's time we all worked together. There's money to be made, so the sooner we get this little brandin' operation over, the sooner we all get paid."

There was no doubt Hicks brandished his peacemaker over the strangest brand-changing episode ever pulled off in Brown's Park. There was also little doubt, that Hick's trained eye and trained gun probably prevented at least one or possibly two murders, such had the hatred built up between Dart and Rash, longtime companions in the art of cattle rustling and changing brands. What Hicks couldn't stop was the continual bickering and arguing between the two. He could only shake his head in astonishment as every aspect of their previous shady dealing was washed and hung out to dry for all to hear. Fortunately, each witness was also a participant.

As far as Billy Styles was concerned, he remained Isom Dart's silent partner during the whole brand-changing operation. No sooner was the last steer allowed to regain its feet than Rash got in another parting shot as further evidence of the bad blood between them. In obvious reference to Billy, he blurted out the following: "No way in hell am I gonna divide any part of my share to help pay for your friend here."

The smell of burnt hair hung heavy in the ravine. Isom started kicking a small pile of loose dirt into the fire hole covering the last dying embers. He tramped and stomped on it until he'd completely snuffed it out. Then he looked at his longtime partner in crime. "Same goes for you, too! Damned if'n

I'm gonna give one dollah to your Mex! You brung him with you, you pay him outta your cut! Now, alla'yah get the hell outta my sight!"

Isom waited one week to make sure his wagon-wheel brand had been applied just right. One by one, he inspected his handiwork on the steers. Each marking looked uniform, a clear indication his new brand had seared just deep enough to hold the re-brand, but not too deep, through the animal's hide. Anything less would've left a faint blurred impression, the very thing an expert brand changer, like Dart, strove diligently to avoid.

The new owners of John Jarvey's Mercantile were Jessy and Delores Wiggins. How they took over was as much a story in the park as the new class of customers they catered to—the park's riffraff!

Gone were the good stocks of dry goods, the new line of women's fashions, and barrel after barrel of apples, flour, chunks of cheese, hard candy, and roasted peanuts. Gone, too, were the hardware items that Jarvey had introduced to the local ranchers to keep them from making those long supply trips so that he'd have virtually all their business. Prices shot sky high on the ever dwindling supply of items until Beemis and the other more respectable ranch families, angered by what had happened, made those long treks to Utah or Wyoming to get their supplies once more.

Behind Jarvey's old mercantile, Jessy had added a stock-holding corral and stand-shed; he had become a buyer of sorts. Rumor had it that Wiggins was dealing in everything from bootleg whiskey to stolen cattle. In short, if there was any way to turn a dollar, count Jessy and Delores Wiggins in on it!

With the thought of cash money jingling in their heads, Isom Dart, Styles, and Hicks proceeded to drive the herd of steers from their hiding place to Jessy Wiggins' store. Isom was upset and still angry that Hicks had accompanied them on the drive instead of Matt Rash. "What's the matter, Matt, too good to be seen with me?"

Hicks replied as straight as possible. "Matt's got other things on his mind these days. He left me in charge to look out for his cut."

"Ever since he done took up with that Miss Annie, he ain't been worth spit! He still owes me from our last deal…tried his smooth-mouth lies on me! Told me he only got twenty-five dollars for each head. Jessy's wife let the cat outta the bag—he done got thirty dollars! Told me so last week!"

A half mile from Wiggins' store, Billy Styles' eyes and brain came alive in his head. He turned his mount around and galloped back to Isom, who was trailing the herd to make sure none bolted back. "How come we ain't driving our herd up to Rock Springs? Heard they're payin' fifty dollars a head up there!"

Isom put his question to bed immediately. "There's Two-Bar people camped on all three trails, checkin' every critter with four legs that leaves this park! Damned if'n I'm gonna buck 'em just now! Get back up front!"

Jessy counted heads and tails as the threesome drove the herd into his holding pen. He examined Isom's artwork on the rumps of several steers. Satisfied the wagon wheel brand was the only brand showing, he smiled at the big bulge of a man. "Good job! Good job all the way. Mind waitin' outside while I get your money?"

Isom shrugged his massive shoulders. "Fine by me! I'm gonna bite them gold pieces you pay me, Jessy. Just wanna make sure they's gen-u-wine!"

The three rustlers waited outside for payday. When the door finally opened, all were surprised to see Delores Wiggins appear instead of the string-bean build of her husband. Her pasty smile and cheap perfume reeked of hard saloon days barely gone by. The once handsome-faced woman still possessed a figure worth a second look, but that was about all; everything else had been used and abused way too often.

"Where's Jessy?" snapped Isom, uneasy about the prospect of dealing with a woman.

Delores cocked one leg high upon the hitching rail, letting Isom get a clean look, almost all the way up. She thrust a small handful of good coins into Isom's hand. "We're a bit short today. Jessy's expectin' more money by tomorrow. Come back then!"

Hicks had had enough. A lightning-quick reflex produced one cocked six-shooter ready for business. The other hand motioned Dart to hand over what few gold pieces he had. "My boss gets paid today! You and Billy can wait for yours tomorrow!"

Isom knew Hicks was in no mood for further discussion. Muttering profanities under his breath, he reluctantly handed over the coins. Hicks quickly counted out Matt's share, then gave Dart back four coins. Delores, Isom, and Billy watched Hicks ride off, his gun still drawn should either Dart or Styles develop a bad case of nervous fingers. Isom turned to Delores. "Get Jessy out here, pronto!"

Delores stood toe to toe with him. "Jessy's got other business inside. Told me to take care of you two outside!"

At first, Isom didn't catch Delores' drift; then a know-it-all smile crossed his lips. He took another look at this dark-haired woman. His eyes left the hard lines of her face in favor of the size of her breasts and the width of her hips. She could accommodate him alright, he was more than sure. He asked, just to make sure. "Jus' what you got in mind?"

"Figured maybe we could work off part or most of what's owed."

The bold frankness of her proposition interested Isom. It'd been quite a spell since he'd bedded down a woman or felt her soft flesh yielding under him. "What 'bout Jessy? Ain't he your husband?"

Delores walked over to the door of the storage shed next to the store. She fiddled with a ring of keys, then found one that turned inside an old, rusty-looking lock. "Got lots'a blankets in there…Jessy takes care of business up front. I take care'a business out back! Comin'?"

Billy beat Isom to the door. Delores stuck her head outside. "Wait a minute! Wait a minute! Jessy don't owe 'nough for two, just one! Make up your mind who's comin' in!"

Shorty came running over to Beemis, waving his arms wildly. "They took 'em durin' the night! That's what he said!" He exclaimed, "Yes, Sir, they done it!"

Beemis had no idea what in the world Shorty was so excited about. "Who took what durin' the night?"

"Matt Rash and Isom Dart! Chained 'em up like hogs and throwed 'em in the back of a wagon! That's what they done! Yes, Sir! Ain't that sumpthun'?"

Beemis stopped mending one of the harnesses. "Who told you this?"

"One of Matt's hired hands rode over just now! He's down at the bunkhouse! Says Charley Neiman and one of his deputies came bustin' in! Rousted both of 'em before either got near a six gun! Never give 'em a chance to draw!"

Now Beemis was excited. "Did Matt's hired hand say what they got run in for?"

"Cattle rustlin'! Cattle rustlin'!"

Beemis grinned from ear to ear. "Well, Charley Neiman! Somebody must've put a cocklebur where it done you the most good! In the seat of your pants!"

"Ya want me to run up to the main house to tell Annie? Bet she's gonna be mighty upset about all'a this!"

"Never mind, Shorty, I'll do the tellin'!"

Shorty McCallum had most of the facts right, at least the ones that interested Beemis the most. A warrant for Rash and Dart had been issued on the charge of cattle rustling. Rustling was a felony, which carried with it no less than twenty years hard prison time, if convicted. What Shorty failed to mention was that a hearing on these charges was going to be held at Hahn's Peak, some sixty miles east of the Park. The fact that the law had finally showed up and done something for a change, instead of file the usual report and then disappear, had the park ranchers perk up their ears. Many who had dabbled in this business had been indirectly warned that their turn could come next. Twenty years hard time was no laughing matter, so everybody who was anybody decided to see for themselves just how far the law was willing to go and who was pushing it for all it was worth!

Beemis was tickled about the shocking and sudden turn of events. He figured he knew who was behind this, but there were enough questions left unanswered that being a spectator probably was the best way to fill in the blanks. After all, like it or not, Annie's friendship with Matt Rash was also on trial. Now wouldn't it be something if the law solved everybody's problems by doing its job for a change? Just the mere prospect of that actually happening made the old boy wet his whiskers down. He looked twice in Maybelle's old vanity mirror. He thought he caught a glimpse of what Maybelle once saw in him, lo, those many years they'd spent together. A man who squeezed every minute of life out of each day and then was so humbled by that experience, he felt compelled to thank the Lord for it!

Beemis hitched up the team to the two-seater and called out for Annie and Josie to come join him for the two-day trek to Hahn's Peak. Late afternoon of the second day, they entered the old gold mining community. They passed old buildings so dilapidated it was hard to believe that there had ever been a glory day or two in the old town. Josie shook her head. "There must be more ghosts here than people. Why don't they just let this old town die?"

"Can't, Sugarplum," replied Beemis. "This town still has two things in it: a jail and a justice of the peace! And then, of course, there's still some old crusts hangin' on, expectin' somebody to find a new vein or two or a better way to work the old diggings over again to reclaim more gold ore."

Annie had little to add to the conversation. Her mind was on Matt Rash. They passed down what was left of Main Street. Most of the old business houses were boarded up, stark evidence that the wind and the weather, not people, made the old plank boardwalks creak and moan. Finally, Beemis pulled up in front of the town's only hotel. Two minutes later, he reappeared. "Hotel's filled up, believe it or not! Hotel manager said this hasn't happened in over twenty years. Told me to try our luck back where we came by. Says there's a lady who's takin' in roomers just for the hearing. Think we'd better look her up right now or else we'll be camped out under the stars tonight."

"Where's the jail? That's all I'm interested in!"

Beemis pointed on down Main Street. "That last building on your left! That's it!"

"You two take care of our rooms; I'm going to find Matt!"

Annie stepped down out of the buggy before Josie could utter a word.

"Let her go," cautioned Beemis. "Annie's got another hard lesson about life comin' up tomorrow morning, unless I miss my guess. Think we both should be thankful that Charley Neiman did his job. Save some heartache later on!"

Matt spotted his lady visitor coming down the hall. He wasted no time getting to the rusty bars that separated him from freedom. They touched hands through the bars.

"Big mistake, Ann! Big mistake! I'll straighten it out first thing in the morning when I see the judge!"

She puckered up slightly, then blew him a kiss. "I'm so glad to hear you say it, dear. Told Beemis on the way over, Charley Neiman's looking for an excuse, any at all, to show us up since we all but told him the law's about as useless at tits on a boar!"

"You got that right, hon." He turned to Isom, who was sitting up on his bunk, watching the two. "Ain't that right, Isom? Said the very same thing just today."

"Then you're not worried about these rustling charges?"

"Me worried? No chance! Like I said, soon as I explain, they'll have to drop the charges." Again he turned to the Negro for support. "Ain't that right, Isom?"

Isom glared at Matt, then turned around on his bunk to stare at the wall.

Ann and Matt continued their private conversation in low tones. Satisfied Matt had everything under control, she bid him goodnight.

"Before you leave, dear, you wouldn't happen to have a piece of paper in your purse?"

She rummaged through her purse and came up with a small writing pad. She handed it to Matt. "This is all I have, dear...Looks a bit old and wrinkled; hope this will do."

"Couldn't be better, Annie. Tell Beemis and Josie to sleep well; I'll be out of this mess first thing in the morning."

"Don't you mean you and Isom'll be out?"

"Sure, sure, Annie, just a slip of the tongue. Goodnight now."

Isom waited until he heard the loud clank of the entrance door to their cell block. Like a caged cat, he sprang off his bunk and grabbed Matt by the shirt collar. "You smooth-talkin' sonofabitch! So you ain't worried, huh? And the way you're sugar-coatin' everythin' with Miss Annie—she...she's too good for you, you no-account white trash!"

"Take your dirty paws off a me, Nigger! You come near me again, and I'll forget to save your shiny black ass come morning!"

Isom relaxed his grip. "What you gonna do? The sheriff done got us but good an' you knows it! No sugar coatin' is gonna get us outta dis, Mista' Smooth Mouth!"

Josie blew the dust off the seat before she sat down in the chair. "Better use your handkerchief to dust off before you sit down," she warned Beemis and Annie. "This courtroom looks an awful lot like the rest of the town...on its last leg!"

Beemis put his farmer-sized handkerchief to good use, using it as a dust cloth on the two chairs next to Josie. After he finished, he looked around the small room already filling up fast. "Good thing we decided to come early or else we'd be standing for sure. Don't think there's been this much activity in town since gold fever hit here thirty years ago."

Annie was dressed to the hilt. A full-length, powder-blue dress with just a hint of a bustle hidden in the pleats of the garment complimented her from head to toe. Her blue eyes came alive with anticipation of how the proceedings were sure to go. She exuded an air of confidence that bordered on smugness, she was that sure of the outcome. She turned to Josie. "Matt said this is all one big misunderstanding. Don't worry, he'll straighten this out! These are trumped-up charges! You'll see!"

Josie and Beemis exchanged far different glances. Finally, Beemis put out his thoughts. "I know Charley Neiman wouldn't bother letting Rash and Dart roost in jail unless he felt pretty sure of the outcome—"

Josie put two fingers to her lips. "Sssh! Here comes a man with a robe on...Must be the justice or judge or whatever they call him."

The honorable Thomas P. Gooding stood beside his bench to address the overflowing crowd. "Before we get underway, let me remind each and every one of you that this is a hearing, not a trial! It will be my job to judge both the evidence presented and the sworn testimony given. Based only upon that will

I render my decision. Cattle rustling is a serious charge, and it is my sworn duty to determine if there is sufficient evidence gathered here today to warrant binding the two accused for criminal prosecution. If not, then it is also my duty to dismiss these charges. Now before we proceed, any disturbance to these proceedings will not be tolerated! Are we clear about this?"

The entire room was filled with an undertow of electricity. Gooding searched the crowd for any potential troublemakers. Satisfied that none had made any overt actions, the white-haired man seated himself on a high chair behind his bench. Then before God and all those assembled, he laid two things out in plain sight: his gavel and a six-shooter. His voice boomed out. "This hearing is officially in session! First order of business is to ascertain the documents to determine if they are proper and legal." He held up a document. "I have before me a warrant for the arrest of Madison Rash and Isom Dart on the charge of cattle rustling. The warrant is signed by Ora B. Haley, owner of the Two-Bar Cattle Company. I also have a copy of the list of the registered brands in Colorado. The Two-Bar is on that list. Is Mister Haley or his representative here today?"

There was a murmur and a lot of foot shuffling. Finally, a voice emerged from the back of the room. "Mister Haley could not attend; however, I am his official representative."

Gooding raised his eyebrows 'til they nearly met. "I know Mister Haley personally, and you're right, you're not that man! Do you have proof that you speak for the Two-Bar Cattle Company?"

"Yes, Sir, I do!"

Annie nudged Beemis. "That's that man who calls himself Hicks! He works for Matt! What's he doing here?"

"Sssh! Let's find out who he really is…"

Josie's caution had Annie on the edge of her chair.

The dark-complexioned man of medium height and build stood before Gooding while he examined the paper just handed him. "Yes…yes, your paper seems to be in order. This says you're a stock detective working for Two-Bar. Well, Mister Tom Hicks, or should I say, Mister Tom Horn, your reputation as the best in the business is certainly well known and well deserved!"

A stick of dynamite tossed into the crowd would've had about the same effect as Gooding's pronouncement that Haley had hired the best! Tom Horn! Super sleuth! Super stock detective!

Beemis nudged Annie. "This ain't no misunderstanding…not when Horn shows up! You can bet Horn's done his homework…"

Gooding banged his gavel to quiet the crowd. "Order! Order, I say! Shut up! Everybody! Sheriff Neiman, bring in the accused!"

Beemis, Josie, and Annie watched Charley Neiman leave the room. Josie waited for the din to die down so she wouldn't have to shout. "Well, Sis, what have you to say about all this?"

Annie turned white as a sheet. She knew now that Matt and Isom were in trouble, deep trouble. She tossed her head in defiance anyway. "Matt knows what he's doing."

Neiman brought Rash and Dart in and seated them under a table. Rash's mouth opened wide enough to can cucumbers when he realized who was going to represent Two-Bar, his newfound sidekick, Tom Hicks, alias Tom Horn.

Dart scowled and kicked Rash under the table. "Your Mex friend is gonna try to cook our goose…What you got ta say to that, Mister Smooth Talker? Huh?"

Rash returned the kick. "Shut up, damn you…this ain't over yet…"

Tom Horn definitely was in his element. Call him a bounty hunter, call him a trail guide, call him a stock detective, call him a Pinkerton man or anything else that comes to mind, but every living, breathing soul there had to call him for what he was: a professional. Driven by an insatiable ego, the man did his job with a vengeance. He opened up his saddle bags and withdrew two pieces of hide bearing the wagon-wheel brand. He cast a sharp, penetrating glance at Rash and Dart, then told Gooding to examine the hides along with him. "This first piece is one of the best hair-brands I've ever run across. The brand is deep enough to hold, but not too deep." Then he turned it over and pointed. "But you see on the underside, the hide still shows the original brand, the Double Bar or Two-Bar, which is registered in Colorado by my boss, Ora Haley."

"Yes…yes, go on."

Horn then picked up the second piece of cowhide off the justice's bench. "This one, Sir, is a sloppy job of runnin' a hair-brand." Twice he drove his forefinger into the hide to emphasize his point. "Look at this! The hair-brand didn't take! You can see the Two-Bar already startin' to show through! Don't even have to turn it over to see the original brand, the Two-Bar!"

The crowd stirred. Horn had done his job, there was no getting around it.

Matt cupped one hand over his mouth, so no one could read his lips. He whispered to Dart. "I told you to take more time, but you just had to hurry, damn you! Too damn much cash money rattlin' 'round your head."

Dart, too, was a professional, probably the best brand-change artist that ever was hauled into a hearing. He nudged Rash under the table and mumbled. "Shut up, damn you…if I go down, you go down with me."

Gooding put both pieces of evidence to one side, then asked the all-important question. "Can you prove that Mister Matt Rash and Isom Dart changed these two brands?"

"I'll need only a minute, Sir! My proof is waitin' outside!"

Every pair of eyes followed the stock detective's easy gait out the front door. A minute later, he escorted Jessy Wiggins up to the justice's bench.

Rash never bothered to shield his lips. "What in hell is he doin' here?"

Isom lowered his voice and muttered, "What you 'spect? He's here to help Horn cook our goose, dat's what."

"We got some settlin' up with Jessy…soon as we're outta here."

"What you mean, settlin' up? We's gonna be old and all wrinkled up when we gets out…twenty years hard time lookin' us square in the face."

Horn introduced Jessy. "This man is Jessy Wiggins, Sir! He will swear before you that he sold me back two dozen head of cattle that were originally branded Two-Bar and that he personally watched me cut the two samples of cowhide that I showed you as evidence."

Gooding looked down at the string-bean of a man who stared down at the floor. "That right, Mister Wiggins? Well, speak up!"

Jessy raised his head. He looked over in Rash and Dart's direction, then back at Gooding.

Horn nudged him hard, a not-so-gentle reminder that he was here to sew up the case for him.

"Yes, yes…what Horn says is right…your Honor."

Ann's face turned to a pasty white, her color drained of life again. Beemis spoke his mind. "Horn's got Rash and Dart now, for good! There's more years starin' both of them than I'd care to count. Let's go! It's all over!"

Josie tugged at the old boy's arm. Perhaps it was the mother in her, or maybe it was the protective older sister trying to show by example where Ann's affection and feelings had strayed once again. "Let's stay 'til this is over. We came this far. Ann needs…we all need to see this through."

Gooding, like Horn, was a man possessed with a mission. He never regarded himself as some political hack or an appointee, who merely went through the motions of office. No, indeed, this man lived and dispensed justice by the very law he had sworn to uphold. Jessy Wiggins bothered him considerably. In his estimation, this man was barely a cut above the two men he was about to render a guilty decision on. He had always held a high disdain for most of the Hole's residents because of their dubious dealings and association with the lawless. Here was his golden opportunity to lay it to them in no uncertain terms. "Mister Wiggins, you will stand before this bench. I have some remarks that you and most of those who traveled over from Brown's Park need to hear."

Poor Jessy Wiggins thought Gooding was about to lay at least ten years hard time on him. "Yes, your honor," Jessy mumbled, scared out of his wits that Gooding was about to lump him in with Rash and Dart and then throw the book at all three.

Suddenly, the high drama shifted from Rash and Dart to the pitiful figure standing before Justice Gooding. Gooding thoroughly enjoyed the moment, letting Wiggins soak up more silent abuse before he tore into him. "You're a very lucky man, Mister Wiggins. The only thing that has kept you from spending time in jail as an accomplice to cattle rustling is the fact that you turned in the evidence Mister Horn needed to complete his investigation and presentation. Let me go on record, here and now, that should you ever come before me again, I will not hesitate to do all I can to see that you spend hard time in the penitentiary. There is no doubt, Mister Wiggins, no doubt whatsoever, that you have been in cahoots with Mister Rash and Mister Dart regarding this cattle rustling business. You have been forewarned! Now go! Make sure your name or your presence never comes before me again, or I'll show you a side of the law that you'll never forget!"

Jessy Wiggins meekly left the room, a whipped dog, done in by a justice of the peace, who had no time for his kind. Gooding let the room quiet down before directing his attention to Rash and Dart once more. He waited and waited, choosing the perfect moment before he spoke again.

"I have reached my decision. Do either of you have anything to say before I make my announcement?"

No one gave Rash or Dart a snowball's chance in hell of beating the odds now. Yet, Matt Rash, too, had a flair for attention, and the high stakes played out before the packed room. He rose and a smirk crossed his handsome face; he did indeed wish to be heard. He turned toward the crowd, extended both arms out toward them in a pleading manner, and opened his palms up. He let a crumpled piece of paper float down to the tabletop. It was theater at its best! "Mister Dart and I have never taken issue with Tom Horn's contention that we've switched brands! Why should we? That piece of paper you saw floating down is a bill of sale! It's legal anywhere, anytime!"

Rash's theatrics dropped a bombshell in the midst of a certain recommendation against him and Dart. The crowd hooted and hollered and stomped their feet. Gooding used his gavel again and again without success, trying to restore some semblance of order.

Annie gasped as she rose, trying to get Gooding's attention. When she failed, she sat down, a badly shaken young woman.

Horn was more than upset at being upstaged by Rash. He grabbed the crumpled piece of paper and rushed up to Gooding's bench. "This is a fake!" he shouted in Gooding's ear. "It has to be!"

Gooding laid down his gavel. He motioned for Sheriff Neiman to approach. "Open the damn door, and fire four rounds out into the street! Maybe then we can get to the bottom of this!"

Bam! Bam! Bam! Bam!

When the smoke cleared, Gooding had what he wanted most: tolerable peace and quiet. He stood up behind his bench, gavel in his hand, and folded his arms, waiting for the noise to stop entirely. Five minutes later, he had won. "Mister Horn has challenged the legality of the bill of sale Matt Rash has produced. Please! Please! Everybody keep quiet while I examine this!"

Josie and Beemis tried to get a true read on Annie while Gooding and Horn were in heated debate over Matt Rash's bill of sale. Josie noticed something strange in light of the latest development. "Look at Dart," she said. "He's acting like he's as surprised as anybody over Matt's sudden bill of sale."

Beemis voiced his thoughts. "Looks like Rash sure pulled a fast one! Even his partner in crime acts like he never saw the rabbit coming." He turned to Annie. "Why'd you stand up to get Gooding's attention and then suddenly sit down?"

Bang! Bang! Bang! Gooding used his gavel hard before Annie could clear her mind or her conscience. His deep voice boomed. "Anyone here know of or seen a Mister William G. Styles?"

Gooding's question ricocheted from one end of the room to the other. No one seemed to know of such a person. Gooding was about to ask again.

"I do."

Everybody turned toward the back of the room, trying to see who the voice belonged to.

It was Josie's turn to gasp. "It's Hi Bernard!"

Gooding banged his gavel hard. "I recognize Mister Bernard of the Two-Bar. Please approach the bench!"

Horn, Gooding, and Bernard huddled while everybody else wondered what possible connection Bernard could have in the hearing. What struck most of the spectators as odd was the way Horn and Bernard were jawing at one another with Gooding doing his best to keep the conversations from getting out of hand.

Bang! Bang! Bang! Gooding pointed with his gavel for Horn and Bernard to leave the bench. Both retreated to opposite sides of the room. Horn was angry. Bernard showed little or no emotion.

"A new development has come to my attention," Gooding stated. "Mister Bernard of the Two-Bar Cattle Company has shed some new light on the bill of sale situation. He volunteered two statements and is willing to swear to both. His first statement is that he did employ a William G. Styles for a short period of time as one of his nighthawks. However, Mister Styles was promptly fired as he was suspected of rustling cattle during his watch. The second statement is that to Mister Bernard's knowledge, Styles could neither read nor write!"

"FAKE! FAKE BILL OF SALE!"

"STRING 'EM UP!"

"DO YOUR JOB, GOODING!"

Bang! Bang! Bang! Gooding worked his gavel 'til his arm grew weary trying to quiet the commotion. Neiman drew his pistol and threatened to use it if necessary to bring order to the hearing. Gradually the racket died down.

Gooding cleared his throat. No one was more upset over what he was forced to say than Gooding himself. "This hearing has left me a quandary. On the one hand, Mister Horn has produced overwhelming evidence that Mister Rash and Mister Dart are guilty of cattle rustling. Yet Mister Bernard, of the same company, has left open the possibility that Styles did, indeed, rustle the cattle in question and then sold them to Rash and Dart with the bill of sale Mister Rash claims Styles gave him. Such a bill of sale would allow him to re-brand. Since Mister Styles is not here to confirm or deny the bill of sale, I am left with no choice, but to dismiss the charges." He banged his gavel. "This hearing is declared over!"

Isom Dart knocked over the table in his haste to leave the room for fear Gooding would gavel new evidence that could convict him.

Matt Rash righted the table and tried to pick Annie out of the throng milling around. He looked none the worse for going through such a harrowing ordeal. Beemis marveled at the man, who in his estimation was guilty as sin. Somehow, he felt Annie held the key. He didn't know why or how, he just had that sinking feeling.

"Well, let's go!" exclaimed Josie. She, too, had a similar feeling. She looked directly at her sister. "Matt Rash and Isom Dart are the two luckiest people alive! Right, Sis?"

Annie refused to answer. She started for the door.

"Ann! Ann! Wait up!"

Matt Rash had threaded his way through until he caught up with her. He turned her around. "Look, I know what you're thinking, but don't say a word 'til we can be alone… 'til I can explain my side… I can do a whole lot more for the association and for us."

Beemis and Josie saw the color return to Annie's face. "You mean you can do a lot more if you're on the outside of prison instead of sitting behind bars. Right, Matt?"

Rash's face gave him away. "That's not the way I'd put it… but you have a point."

"Yes, we both know I do. Now here's something else I'm going to leave you with—"

Matt cut her off. "What's that, love?"

Slap! Slap! Annie dished out two vicious blows to Rash's right cheek. A large welt rose instantly. "You didn't let me finish, so here goes! GO TO HELL! I've made one mistake I can't take back! I'm not about to make it two!"

With that, Annie pushed her way past Matt, Beemis, and Josie. Rash tested his jaw and found it to be in working order. "Just a lovers spat… a little misunderstanding, Beemis… Josie. She'll be her old self in a few days. I'll come around then to straighten this all out."

Beemis' cane found Rash's jugular. "Unless my Annie says she wants to see you again, don't bother to come around anymore! I think she made it pretty plain how things stand between you two."

"You got this all wrong, Beemis! I swear! It's all wrong!"

"Have I? Not from what I saw! Good day, Mister Rash!"

Rash turned to walk away before Beemis could really say what he thought. Charley Neiman spotted his old friend. "Hey, Beemis, hold it!"

The sheriff looked quite pleased with himself despite the sudden outcome. "Horn had those two nailed, but good, 'til Rash managed to wiggle off the hook. How'd you see it, old friend?"

The old sage's words came tumbling out pure as spring-brook water. "Anytime ya gotta travel sixty miles to see the law fail again, it's high time we in the Park took care of our own problems."

Charley Neiman knew better than to try to rebut the truth. He shook his head at Josie, looking for sympathy. He got none, so he walked away, a sadder but wiser man.

Josie saw something else that bordered on the unreal. "Look, Uncle! Rash and Horn are together. See, they're even shaking hands!"

Beemis turned around. "Too bad Annie's not here to see this. Matt's a damned fool if he thinks Horn is gonna let this pass. He's livin' on borrowed time unless I miss my guess. Horn's got a reputation that won't go away...nor does he want it to. He'll get the job done next time...There'll be no hearing to wiggle out of. Horn will turn killer if he has..."

Horn and Rash's handshake had all the markings of a finality between the two. Horn's cold, hard stare was never more at home as he sized up Rash. "Shoulda taken the twenty...now I gotta do this all over again. Only next time, it will be different, I promise you."

Rash, too, basked in his minute of infamy. "Shoulda told me who you really was when I took you in, gave you a job, and made you my sidekick. All that yarn you spun about lookin' for a spread to buy...all horse manure and you know it!"

"Yeah," Horn admitted, "it smelled 'bout as bad as that bill of sale you came up with to save your hide. You leave me only one thing left to do."

"What's that?"

Horn gave Rash a look no man would ever forget. "Time to get you acquainted with what I'm really cut for...time to let you meet up with my new system."

Matt took the bait. "And what system would that be?"

"The one that never fails!"

CHAPTER SEVEN

Old Henry says, "The old cowboy's smile didn't do much for his looks; he was toothless, and his disposition matched his smile."

"I tell ya, Beemis, we're the laughin' stock of all the Colorado Cattle Associations. The idea, the very idea of a man like Rash as our head man don't make a lick'a sense! Told my Etta the other day, even a'fore this Hahn's Peak mess come up, we gotta get rid'a this fella. Held off doin' somethun' 'bout it on account of you, Beemis."

Old Henry spat another mighty wad of chewing tobacco. Beemis watched it barely clear the new top rail on the porch. "Didja hear what I said?" the old codger asked. "Said I held off gettin' rid'a Rash mostly on your account."

Beemis checked the tobacco-stained lips on his friend. The large pouch on one side of his cheek was gone. It was safe now to carry on the conversation. "There was never no need to hold back, Henry. Whata'ja jawin' 'bout?"

"Your Annie! That's what I was jawin' 'bout! I see'd the way she slapped him up! Quick as a cat, I turned to Etta. 'Now's the time,' I says to her. A'fore he tries to put the charm back on her. Now's the time! And it is!"

Beemis seemed a lot more worried whether Old Henry was about to thumb another potent load of chewing tobacco in his cheek than Annie's welfare.

"Josie's been ridin' tight herd on Annie…They were mostly friends, nothin' more…so you can rest easy on that. Far as taken a new vote on Rash to get rid'a him, that's already taken care of."

Henry watched Beemis rock slowly back and forth. He did what Beemis was worried about—thumbed another plug into his cheek. He worked the plug back in the same spot. A puzzled frown strayed across his weather-beaten brow. "Yeah, Beemis? How?"

This time Henry's wad fell short. Beemis rose from his rocker to inspect the latest hit, spattered beneath the bottom rail. "Tom Horn's gonna save us all the bother a' takin' a fresh vote."

"Don't see how you figure that!"

"Didn't you see what I saw after the hearin'? My old scoutin' days taught me that men like Horn don't get shortchanged very often. They always get their pound of flesh, and it don't matter much to them how it gets done. It could come out the end of a riffle barrel, or maybe a six-shooter, or even a buffalo skinning knife. Point is, it will get done!"

Old Henry stood next to Beemis. He saw what concerned Beemis, his bad miss. "I'll get Josie to give me a rag to clean it up! Sorry, Beemis! Now 'bout this new vote business! We got a bunch in our association who think that bill a' sale is the genuine thing! They must think Rash is related to Jesus somehow in order for that to happen. A'course there's those, like us, who know better! Now, we outnumber the miracle believers, two-to-one! What if Horn doesn't do like you think?"

A slow smile worked its way out from under his whiskers. A fresh glint coupled with it to make two watery, faded blue eyes a tad brighter. "Well then, Henry, I'm down to what I do best: raisin' fine Arabians!"

Matt Rash's newly gained freedom had come at a very dear price. He'd lost the one thing he wanted most: Annie's friendship. He missed the fiery blonde's company, and her alluring smile, and her fetching blue eyes that always seemed to say, "All my passion and all my love are locked up, deep in my heart for safekeeping." For two weeks, he stewed over what had happened at Hahn's Peak. Now, he decided to take matters into his own hands. It was time to call on Annie. It was time to turn on the old Matt Rash charm. It was time to live up to the reputation he's garnered over the past years concerning the opposite sex. It was time to be Matt Rash!

Josie came waltzing into the kitchen to find Annie deep into baking cookies, her one domestic love. Cookie dough was everywhere, complete with flour, a basket of eggs, a pitcher of milk, and a rolling pin. "Guess who's waiting out in the front parlor?"

Annie looked up. She pushed a strand of hair aside that insisted on hanging down in front of her eyes. "Can't you see I'm baking cookies? I don't give a fiddler's fiddle who's waitin' on me! Let it be the Pope himself, I don't care!"

Josie sprinkled a little flour on top of the dough for her sister. "Better sprinkle some flour over the rollin' pin, too! Keeps it from sticking to the dough. I'll take over, give you a break! Matt's here! New boots, new Stetson, new clothes! Everything about the man looks brand new! Even stopped to pick you a fresh bouquet of wild daisies."

Annie wiped her hands on her apron. "Thanks, Sis! Guess I could use a little break. Matt sure has a short memory! Believe you me, I do know what I'm talking about!"

Josie stopped rolling out the dough. "You know something about that miracle bill of sale, don't you?"

Annie skirted Josie's question. "Bill of sale or not, Matt Rash is a cattle rustler! He knows it, and I know it!"

"Go see him, Sis! Chance to see what the best-dressed cattle rustler in Brown's Park is wearing now days! Then shoo him out and tell him to be on his way!"

Ann was all business when she stepped into the front parlor. Gone were any feelings she used to harbor for the tall, handsome Texan. In their place was total disgust. She had no use for his disarming smile or his way with words or the way he seemed to secondguess her many thoughts.

He rose, tipped his hat, and bowed gracefully as he tried to hand her the flowers. "A beautiful bouquet for a beautiful lady," he began.

She pushed the flowers aside. "Skip it, Matt!" came her cold reply. "We both know you're lucky to be here at all!"

He tried to hand her the flowers again. "You're missing the big picture! The greater good I can do for our association by staying out of prison! Doesn't that mean anything to you anymore? Let's not be forgettin' that bill of sale means I'll be free to stop Two-Bar from takin' over. And it sure stopped that double-crosser, Horn, from puttin' me away!"

"Always thinkin' of saving your own hide, Matt! Not one word about Isom Dart, as usual!"

Rash tried his patented charm on her. "C'mon now, Annie, admit it! Our friendship has meant as much to you as it did to me! Remember, you gave

Blaze to me? That's gott'a count for an awful lot between us."

Annie let Matt's words roll right on by. "Speaking of Blaze, I want him back, right now! That was a big mistake!"

Matt hurled the flowers. Eyes snapping, he exploded. "You're a damned Indian giver, that's what you are! Gave me Blaze and now you actually got the guts to want him back! Alright, alright, c'mon over to the ranch and pick up your horse! See if I give a damn!"

"Fine! Soon as I change into my riding duds, I'll ride over with you to bring him back!"

The ride over to Matt's ranch to get Blaze was an exercise in anger for Matt Rash. He whipped his team of blacks, repeatedly, until their rumps turned to froth and they blew their noses nonstop, trying to clear their nostrils to keep the torrid pace Rash had demanded.

"Stop it! Stop it!" screamed Annie, seeing how Matt was handling his prize blacks. "Take it out on me if you have to, but leave the team alone!"

Rash only whipped them all the harder! The more chuckholes he hit, the more he used his whip. He acted like a madman, bent on driving them all into the ground before his ranch appeared. Finally, the grove of willows shot by, and his ranch appeared as the buggy pitched and swayed crazily.

The buggy careened to a stop sideways before Annie could release her white-knuckled grip. Rash leaped across his startled passenger. Down on his knees, he knelt in the settling dust. "Please, Annie," he begged. "Don't do this to me! To us! I love you! I want to marry you! I want—"

Annie cut him short. "I only want my horse, Blaze! Now get up off your knees 'cause you've got company!"

Rash whirled around. "Where? I don't see anybody!"

She pointed toward his front door. "Somebody left you a message! See, it's tacked to your door!"

The transformation before Annie was unreal. Gone was Matt's arrogance that oozed with self-confidence and dripped with conceit and seduction. His knees buckled. It took every ounce of his vanity to force himself to face the piece of paper. Cold sweat broke out on his forehead. His face, a pasty white mess!

"It's only a piece of paper, Matt! Aren't you going to see what's on it?"

Gun drawn, he slowly approached the door with the paper tacked to it. He looked this way, then that way, then gingerly tried the doorknob. He jumped to one side, expecting someone or somebody to materialize before him, guns blazing away. When that didn't happen, he realized he looked like a fool or an idiot. He put on the best bravado performance he could muster and ripped the paper off the door.

Annie called out to him. "Well, what does it say?"

Rash mumbled something.

Annie was exasperated. "Do I have to get out and come over to read it for you? Last time! What does it say?"

"Thirty days!"

"Put the gun down Matt, there's nobody here but us!"

"It's him! I know it is! Gave me thirty days to clear out!"

Annie got out of the buggy and walked over to Matt. Rash stood there, his eyes glued to the paper. "Who, Matt? Who?"

"Horn! Tom Horn! Did the same thing up in Wyoming! Now, he's on the rampage down here!"

Annie took the note from him. "It's unsigned, Matt! Why…why, it could be mostly anybody behind this! Maybe from the association! Even old Henry's tryin' to get you voted out!"

Rash took the note back and tore it into two dozen tiny bits.

"That's not going to change anything! Thirty days still means thirty days for whatever reason!"

"I know! I know!" Rash acknowledged. "But damned if I'm going to look at it any longer."

Annie started back toward the buggy.

"Where are you going?"

She turned around. "In case you forgot, I came over here with you to ride Blaze back to the ranch. That is, if my saddle, bridle, and blanket are still in the buggy. After the way you drove your team, who knows?"

Matt caught up with her. "Don't take Blaze just now! Please! I know I told you to come get him…but Annie, if you do, I'll have no excuse to come calling. I'll have no one to see who I care about…no one at all! Please, Annie! Please, let me keep him a little longer!"

She didn't have the heart to refuse him just now. "Okay, Matt, you can keep Blaze a little while longer. Now I'm going back to the ranch, so what can I ride?"

"Take Ginger, my dapple grey! I won't need her anymore if I can get you to let me keep Blaze…at least for a while longer…please, Annie!"

Matt helped Annie saddle up Ginger. Every minute or so, he would turn to look back over his shoulder, fully expecting to see somebody lurking, ready to snuff out his life.

Annie had never seen such a pitiful hunk of man turn to jelly. "Tell me, Matt, with all the stories I've heard about you since Hahn's Peak, there's one that I'd truly appreciate a straight answer to."

He handed Ginger's reins up to her. "Hell, I've heard so many, I'm beginning to half believe them myself! Which one, dear?"

"That one about you and some Indian girl named Mincy...down in Oklahoma, I believe. Isn't that where all that bad blood between you and Dart got started?"

Matt looked away, and suddenly, he was most certainly himself once more. The transformation was remarkable. He was God's gift to all the love-starved, unappreciated women on the Western Frontier. He was the answer to some neglected rancher's wife stuck away hopelessly on some Godforsaken piece of homestead that never produced anything but more kids and no money. "She wasn't a girl by any means, Ann...she was all woman and I mean that in every sense. Isom said she was too young."

He was his old indomitable, charming self once more, ready to gloat, ready to boast of his conquest and his prowess with women. "I charmed the pants right off that little Indian gal...had her begging me for it when I got through with her. Had to oblige, she wanted it so bad...'Course I brought along some firewater to help ease some of the pain and discomfort. I was her first. Niggers and Indians are like that, you know. Use 'em any way you can because they're good for only one thing; you throw 'em out like an old shoe when you're done with them."

Ann had heard enough. "And you don't call that using a woman and dumping her out?"

"No, Ann, you got it all wrong! Next town we come to, Mincy looks up this preacher, see, and... and when I told her to forget about seein' him, she up and tried to pull a knife on me. That's the honest truth, I swear! Just goes to show you can't trust an Indian...or a nigger, too, for that matter! Me, marry an Indian? Me, a squaw man? C'mon, Ann, you know me better than that! It just isn't me! It's not my style!"

She was fed up with him and thoroughly disgusted with what he'd said and the way he'd said it. "Tell you what, Matt, I'll keep Ginger for thirty days or so 'til you come riding Blaze over and then..."

He jumped at her unfinished conclusion. "And then what, Ann? Then what? C'mon say it, Ann! Say it!"

"I'll tell you same as I did at Hahn's Peak! Go to hell!" Ann jabbed

Ginger's flanks and was off, leaving Matt speechless, his mouth open wide enough to start a natural fly trap.

July eighth was a scorcher as hot summer days go; even the birds and the crickets had little to chirp about, or so it seemed. Matt Rash had been in the saddle before sunup, visiting several ranchers who might have hay to spare for his own herd. He halted a scant half mile from his cabin to take a breather and to take stock of his own situation. With the latest "go to hell" from Annie still ringing in his ears, he'd come to the realization that he'd have been far better off spending valuable time and energy putting up more hay instead of trying to romance the diminutive package of blonde dynamite. He thought about the two times he'd come close to unlocking her passion, only to have her pull away from him, vowing never to let another man touch her until she carried his wedding band on the proper finger.

Matt was not the marrying kind. His reputation as a roving ladies man had been built solidly on that premise. And yet, Ann Barnett had too much charm and too much personality to leave her alone. He thought he saw a way to get to her, even if it included a marriage proposal or two along the way. He'd been a past master at wearing stubborn ladies down before in order to bed them down. In his estimation, all Annie needed was the proper charm along with the right inducement, and she'd be his, any way he wanted her.

He yanked off the bandana that hung around his neck. He used it to wipe the heavy perspiration that lined the inside sweatband of his Stetson. His stomach started to growl, a sure sign he'd skipped breakfast, and it was high time to do something about it. True, he'd broken the Ten Commandments, some, more than just a few times. But in Matt's life, the Eleventh Commandment loomed larger than life itself, and he obeyed it religiously. It said, "Thou shalt fill thy stomach before thy neighbors so that thou can sally forth to break the other ten."

Matt rode the short distance and dismounted from Blaze. He left the door wipe open, and in the sweltering heat, he decided to start a fire in his cast-iron range. He banged the coffeepot, dislodging an inch of coffee grounds in favor of a fresh batch. Twenty minutes later, the coffeepot was perking and he had a strip steak sizzling in the heavy-clad spider. All that remained to do was cut up some potatoes and drop them alongside his steak, and he'd have the makings of a typical bachelor meal.

Blaze whinnied, so he went to the open door to see if he had company. He saw no one. The only thing that caught his attention was the sky. Its usual turquoise color had turned to a greenish-tinged blue. Even Mother Nature was telling him it was damned hot out.

He turned his back to the open doorway. Suddenly, the hairs on the back of his neck stood erect! He wheeled around just in time to catch one blast, then two, then three!

Matt fell back against the range. He staggered, then pitched sideways, trying to make his way toward his bunk. He fell upon it, his hands clutching his chest that had been ripped apart by the three shots fired at such close range. Blood spurting everywhere, somehow he managed to find a piece of paper. Once, twice, he tried to use his own blood to write the name of his killer on the paper. His body shook violently, racked by a series of convulsions. His eyes rolled around in his head; then his writing finger stopped. Matt Rash lay murdered without naming his killer.

Blaze went crazy when the three shots were fired. He pulled and jerked until he'd managed to yank part of the hitching rail out of the ground. He pawed the air, trying to break free.

Blam! Blam! Two shots put the horse down for good.

Two days later, a neighbor and his son happened by, searching for a strayed cow and her calf. They noticed the bloated belly on the horse lying near the hitching rail, and they noticed the door wide open to Matt's cabin. Flies, swarms of flies were everywhere. The father stepped inside, gun drawn. The neighbor got his first whiff of the terrible stench. His stomach churned to convulsive jelly; he upchucked before he had time to warn his son.

"Dad, Dad!" The boy screamed, "What's the matter?"

"Don't come in here, son! It's bad! Real bad!"

The murder of Madison (Matt) Rash galvanized Brown's Park ranchers into one thing: fear. Fear of reprisals at the hands of Ora Haley, and fear of his threatened takeover, and most of all, fear that each would be next on Tom Horn's list. Matt's murder and Tom Horn's name were on everyone's lips, liking the two closer than Siamese twins. Yet for all the suspicion cast upon Horn, not one shred of evidence surfaced to point the finger of guilt at him. A week later, Tom Horn appeared in the park as carefree as you please. When told of Rash's murder, he only smiled. "Shoulda let me put him away," he said. "That way he'd still be breathing!"

Ann was beside herself with heartfelt grief. She worked over several hankies 'til they were wet and soggy, then had the audacity to ask her sister if she had an extra one or two in her bedroom. Never one to disappoint her sister's requests, Josie promptly produced a fresh stack for Ann to go through, along with her not-so-nice observation. "Sis, I hate to break it to you this way, but you're carryin' on like you were gonna marry Matt tomorrow morning and that just ain't so. Heck, for all I know, you're probably cryin' harder for Blaze than for Rash. Far as I'm concerned, Blaze was worth ten Matt Rash's."

Annie cut loose with a fresh torrent of tears. "That's not so, Josie, and you know it! You never liked Matt, and that's a fact!"

Josie had had about all the boo-hooing she could stand for one day. "You've been a chaser of lost causes and losers and you damned well know it! If you're ever gonna smarten up, now's as good a time as any. Couldn't get Deke to come back so you spent Lord knows how many worthless hours on Rash, who couldn't begin to fill one of Deke's old boots when it comes to being a man. And I haven't even started to talk about fillin' Deke's worn-out jeans."

"Don't!" Ann snapped back. "Why do you always stick up for Deke?"

"'Cause, my dear sister, he's the best thing that you ever latched onto, and you screwed it all away! Or have you forgotten Elza Lay?"

The two sisters were at odds again with each other and always about the same person: Deke Landry. Both knew it was time to button up or else hurt feelings and hurt pride would put them at each other's throats, something neither wanted. So the sore subject of Deke was put to bed, or at least allowed to rest in favor of more important, pressing matters, namely what to do about the murder of Matt Rash. This worried Josie, too, because she knew her sister was impulsive at times with a penchant for getting involved before all the facts were gathered. Her latest prime example—bringing sheep into Brown's Park to thwart Ora Haley's takeover. The cost: three hung sheepherders.

Etta Ettlemen had good ears and good eyes despite her age. The small, frail woman stood at the window and peered out into the gathering dusk. She strained her eyes and finally declared. "Henry, we got company comin'! Too dark to make 'em out! Sounds like one'a those big freighters…Didja order anything from Rock Springs lately?"

Old Henry was a bit hard of hearing with poor eyesight to match. He struggled to get out of his rocking chair to join his mate at the window. "No, I didn't order nuthin'…couldn't. Our cookie jar's low on cash…and I ain't sold the calves yet. Nobody's paid us fer all the hay they been stealin' at night.

Danged parks full'a low-counts and no-accounts these days."

"Just the same, I'd better change outta this patched-up cotton dress. Gotta look decent…could be those new neighbors comin' to call on us. Didja say their name was Staylee or Straylee?"

No answer.

"Henry? Staylee or Straylee?"

"Staylee, I think…"

"Just the same, you meet 'em at the door while I change. Tell 'em there's oatmeal cookies and hot cinnamon tea comin' in a minute! And don't go to scarin' 'em with all your wild stories 'bout missin' people and fresh-dug graves 'n such. That's enough to scare the livers outta most respectable folks."

"Just the same, I'd like to see some hard, cold cash under a bucket next to our haystack…like what happened last year when some of our hay sprouted legs during the night."

Henry sauntered toward the door. He wanted to give Etta plenty of time to change before he opened it. Suddenly, the door exploded in front of his face. Three men wearing bandanas covering their faces forced their way inside. Guns drawn, the closest one grabbed old Henry. The second intruder stuck a bill of sale under Henry's nose. "Sign here, old man, or we'll dry gulch ya now!"

The third masked man shoved old Henry into the wall—hard. "Ya do know what dry gulchin' is don'tcha, you old, wrinkled-up fart!"

Shook up, old Henry answered as best he could. "'Course I do…you…you aim to leave my bones bleachin' in the sun somewhere?"

"Sign the bill of sale, and we'll spare ya the bother!"

Etta called out from the bedroom. "Henry, are you alright? Thought I heard somethin' like scufflin' goin' on…Henry?"

One of the masked men waited beside the bedroom door. The minute Etta scurried out to see what was going on, he grabbed her. "Tell your old man to sign NOW!"

Old Henry was no match for such roughhousing by the night riders. Tears watered both eyes. His cheeks quivered and his throat went dry. He took one look at the only woman he'd ever loved and signed.

"Alright, old man," growled the first night rider. "Ya got ten minutes to decide what you want to take with you 'cause the rest is goin' up in flames!"

Etta wandered through the house, trying to decide what to take. She settled on their bed, a goose-down feather tick, a few dishes and a handmade table and chest of drawers. She touched the table and chest with loving care. "Can't leave these behind; they were my wedding presents...handmade they were...from my Henry, my husband of sixty years...back in old Kentucky."

They backed the team and wagon to the door and loaded up Etta's prize possessions in nothing flat. Two night riders lifted Henry and Etta into the driver's seat none too gently while the third turned two kerosene lanterns up as high as their wicks would go.

The leader shoved a small sack of coins into Etta's trembling hands. "Here's two hundred dollars. Don't come back, or we'll feed botha'ya to the buzzards!" Then he shoved the team's reins into Henry's hands. "Sure you can still handle a team, old man?"

Old Henry shook a fist in front of the leader's masked face, his last defiant act. "When I was your age, two'aya couldn't't'a whipped me in a fair tussle! I've forgotten more about bein' a real man than the three'aya put together!"

The leader said nothing; instead, he whacked the team's rumps with a quirt.

The team bolted, nearly pulling poor Henry out of his seat as he refused to let go of the reins. The three night riders laughed and shouted. One called out. "Hey, old man, you better let your old lady grab the reins! She's more a man than you are!"

Proud down to his last ounce of flesh and bone, old Henry left Brown's Park the way he had first entered the Hole: with his Etta at his side. They picked their way slowly up the trail with the help of the two lanterns shedding their light. They rounded a curve over the bumpy, rock-strewn trail. It was their last chance to look back. Far below, they saw flame-ridden sparks shoot high into the night.

Henry tried to comfort Etta. "Now, now, old girl...it was just a two-room shack. Never did finish the foundation. And...and those two barns...good stiff breeze rattled their sideboards somethun' awful. Always said those two sheds sounded like they caught cold whenever the wind whistled through."

Etta remembered only the years of back-breaking hard work, the years of struggling to just get by, and the years of doing without, all going up in flames. "Sixty years," she sobbed out. "Sixty years, Henry!" She opened the sack and dumped the loose coins into her lap. "Sixty years and all we got to show fer it is two hundred dollars! Two hundred dollars, Henry!"

He comforted her the way he'd always done it, with just the right amount of tenderness, along with some carefully chosen words. He took his bride of sixty-five years and held her close, kissing her wet cheeks and feeling her frail body through her starched cotton dress—her best dress. He tried to put his thoughts in motion, but choked on them when he remembered how it used to be between them at a time such as this. He nuzzled his nose under one of her earlobes. "Lord, what wouldn't I give to be sixty-five again. Why…why, I'd take you in my arms—like this—and…and I'd tell you that you're gettin' better lookin' every day…and by the time you hit eighty, you'll be so darned good lookin' that there's only one thing left for me to do…"

She'd heard these same words before, but never tired of their meaning or the way he said them. She found his lips and kissed them. "That one thing you said that was left to do…tell me again…I'd sure like to hear it from you, Henry."

"Why, I'd whisper in your ear and say, 'I'd sure like to lay you down…gently, now, gently, mind you…'"

"Oh, Henry, you're right…sayin' it sure helps heaps, but gettin' back those twenty years would be even better."

He planted another wet kiss. "Guess we'd better move on and count our blessings."

Etta broke from their embrace. The whole impact of reality hit hard. "But, Henry, where will we go? What will we do? We've outlived all our friends and relatives back in Kentucky! We have nowhere to go!"

He patted her hands. "Sure we do! Sure we do! There's good folks about this rim…outta this hole. And I still got the best judge of folks right here beside me! We'll drive a spell, and when we meet some folks, all I have to do is say, 'Etta, are these the kind of folks we'd like to have as neighbors?' And if they are, you'll push back your sunbonnet off your head and say, 'Henry, help me down, let's visit a spell!'"

Etta took great comfort in his words. She reached back and found a small blanket in the chest of drawers behind her. She wrapped it around her and laid her head on his shoulder. "Leastways, we got our hides still coverin' our bones…that's more than those three sheepherders got!"

Night after night, the reign of terror and forced sales visited the park's hard-core ranchers. As always, after each visit, the night riders left their calling card: ranch buildings being put to the torch once they had the bill of sale in their hands. Those who watched and smelled such proceedings could only count their blessings as the ghosts of vengeance passed by their premises. They could only take solace in one fact: They had been spared for the time being.

The day Beemis heard about Henry and Etta Ettlemen's "quick sale" was the day he fired off a letter to the governor of Colorado, asking for immediate help. Thirty days later, he received an official response to his urgent request. Annie and Josie gathered around while their uncle read:

> "While I can and do appreciate your concern, the governor's office feels this is strictly a matter for local law investigation and resolution. I strongly urge you to contact your county sheriff, as he is most qualified to deal with such matters."

Beemis was outraged by the political rhetoric contained in the official reply. He wadded up the letter and hurled it like a baseball into his fireplace. "Two-Bar's taken over the whole Park and Haley hasn't even had to drive one damned, smelly old steer down the trail! There's ten quick sales already, and more on the way! If we wait for Neiman to make the rounds, we'll all be pushin' up daisies!"

"Well, dear Uncle, what can we do?"

Josie's question prompted the old scout to motion for his two nieces to gather round him. "Time for a family pow-pow," he said. "I've had enough! First off, I owe you two an awful lot of sorrys. I'm sorry I didn't do more about raisin' you two when you was little. Instead, I dumped most of it on your Aunt Maybelle! Look what it got her! An early grave! And I'm sorry, most of all, for keepin' you two around." He hugged Josie. "I'm a greedy old cuss! You shoulda been married and outta this house long ago! Your cookin's too damned good, that's why I kept ya around!" He slid his spectacles down from the bridge of his nose to give himself his "so-called stern look." "And when that Mormon highwayman took a special shine to you, Lord, how I wished it was Cleve Dreschler 'cause you're the settle-down type! Butch Cassidy is a smart man! Had to be to stay alive this long! But he left his brains on one of them trains he robbed, when he passed you over, 'cause you deserved better, and that's a fact! Any chance you and Cleve might hook up?"

Josie hugged Beemis back. "Soon as this mess is over with the Two-Bar people, I'm gonna say yes to Cleve!"

"Good! Don't put if off! Far as this mess bein' over, it is! First chance I get to talk to Haley, I'm gonna sell this ranch!"

Annie couldn't believe her ears. "No, no, don't sell! You can't!"

Josie seconded her sister. "Please don't! Keep the ranch!"

Beemis got the answers he expected, but he charged on ahead. He patted Annie on her head. "And you, my Annie Oakley, my horseback-ridin' and lovin' gal, any chance, any chance a'tall, you and Deke might find a way to patch things up between ya?"

Reluctantly, Annie voiced her gut feeling. "No, Deke will never forgive me long enough to take me back! Can't really blame him…once I look at what I've done from inside his boots."

"Okay, then it's settled! The ranch goes first chance I get! Was still hangin' on, hoping Deke might have a change of heart! I can plainly see now that's out the back door along with Saturday night's bath water!"

A loud knock startled the three. Beemis moved like his feet found wings. He picked his rifle off its mount and cocked its lever. Then he motioned for Josie and Annie to step back. He approached the door, ready for anything or anybody. "Better speak up! Who is it? There's a loaded rifle waitin' to greet you!"

A voice from the other side answered. "It's Isom Dart…come to speak with you good folks. Don't shoot!"

The three exchanged astonished looks. Beemis gripped the polished brass knob. "Alright, I'm gonna open this door! Remember, my finger is just a squeeze away from meanin' business!"

The door swung open slowly, and there stood a huge, black genie. His massive frame sucked up the space around the doorway. He looked like the gods had chiseled him out of ebony. In one ham-sized hand, he held a piece of white paper. Eyes rolling wildly from side to side, Isom was anything but what he appeared. "The devil's after me, Mistah Beemis! He won't let go! Horn done latched onto me and won't leave me be 'til I gonna be dead like Matt! Kin you good folks help me?"

Annie stepped forward as Isom handed her the note. "This is the same note I saw tacked to Matt's door! Says the same thing, 'Thirty days!' Even the handwriting's the same!"

No one expected Isom to drop to his knees to beg. "Please, Mistah Beemis, leave me stay with you all! Please! I got nowhere to go! I kin build fences, break horses, cook, ride, rope…do most anything. I'll pull my weight! Jus' let me bunk down with your boys!" He motioned with his head toward the open doorway. "Horn gonna kill me if he get me alone…same like he done to Matt."

Beemis was in a quandary. Here was Rash's rustling partner looking for his protection. He tried to forget Dart's past in order to do the humane thing.

"Alright, you can stay! But I gotta warn ya, I'm gonna sell if I can get a decent price from Haley! See Shorty McCallum down at my bunkhouse! He'll put you to work 'til I sell!"

Isom's powerful shoulders moved as though he'd dumped the world off of them. He made the rounds to all three, his hands swallowing theirs as he shook theirs.

"Thank ya! Thank ya! Thank ya!" he kept repeating over and over.

Dart disappeared out into the pitch blackness as easily as he had appeared. Josie wasted no time venting her feelings. "He's no better than Rash was, or Horn or those hired Two-Bar night riders who do Haley's dirty work! They've all done their share of stealin,' killin,' rustlin' and Lord only knows what else! How come we're mixed up in this anyhow?"

Beemis looked at Annie for the explanation, the right one to sooth Josie's good point. "In case you've forgotten how this all started, dear Sister, this is our home; we belong here! Not somewhere else!"

"Not for long! You heard Uncle, we're all clearin' out soon as he sells!"

"I'm staying and no Tom Horn or any hired night men are gonna run me outta here as long as I can draw another breath."

Beemis put his arm around Ann's petite waist. "Matt Rash would dearly pay most anything to argue that point...but he's plumb outta breath last I heard. How you gonna ride herd on this when nobody else can get a handle on what's goin' on?"

"That's what bothers me...but I'll find a way...for you, dear Uncle...for Josie and for myself...and maybe, just maybe, for an unforgiving, hot-headed redhead by the name of Deke Landry."

Annie rose early, her heart laden with problems that had no solutions or answers that seemed ready made. She needed a release, some way to escape, so she did the only thing that brought her a measure of relief: going for a ride.

This particular morning, she chose to ride Glory to the far eastern boundaries of the Park. This was still the area where wild game was abundant, particularly, the wily pronghorn antelope. She wanted to be alone with her thoughts and away from people. To her surprise, she came upon a middle-aged man crouched low behind a berm, a small rise in the numerous breaks that dotted this section of the park.

He caught her movement and signaled for her to dismount and be quiet. Annie hobbled Glory and crawled forward behind the berm. She was fascinated by the drama about to unfold before her.

Two hundred yards ahead, a pronghorn buck stood atop a low rise, standing guard for his herd, grazing another one hundred yards away. The pronghorn's keen eyesight told him Glory posed no danger, so he did not take flight. Gradually, ever so gradually, he circled and came closer. What in the world kept drawing him closer, Annie wondered.

Then she saw what had provoked the animal's innate curiosity: a small red ribbon tied to a wooden stake. A gentle breeze made the ribbon wave and ripple, just enough to draw the buck even closer.

Click!

At that instant, the four-legged ghost of the grassland put on a burst of speed that left two spectators in awe.

"Nice shot! Nice shot!" Annie called out to the man. "Never saw that trick tried before!"

Both stood up while the man began to roll up the string he'd tied to the camera and tripod hidden in a tuft of tall grass fifty yards ahead.

He turned to her. "Thanks for not spooking my shot. Took me most of the morning to get set up." He extended his hand. "My name's Andrew Wallihan. I photograph both the two-legged and four-legged variety. Most folks call me Wally."

Annie completed their handshake. "Name's Ann Barnett. When will you know if your shot was worth getting?"

"Tonight," Wally replied. He pointed toward a clump of cottonwoods a good half mile away. "My wagon and team are hidden there. I do my own developing each night, so if the shot doesn't turn out, I'm usually close by so I can set up and try again."

Annie walked with him to his equipment. "You mentioned the two-legged variety. What was one of your favorite people shots?"

Wally folded up his tripod. "There've been a couple! Years ago, before I became a wildlife photographer, the Army hired me to be one of their official photographers. Back in Washington, D.C. Barracks, I took Colonel Teddy Roosevelt's picture. He made a surprise inspection visit—always liked to be around frontier-type people—had him pose with a couple of Army scouts."

Annie couldn't believe her good fortune. "I'll bet you took the very picture my uncle thinks the world of! He'd rather lose a leg than part with that picture of Roosevelt standing next to him! And he was an Army scout stationed at the capitol for a while. At least that's the story Uncle Beemis has told me!"

Wally, too, became interested. "What's your uncle's name?"

"Beemis Markham!"

Now Wally was excited. He shook his head and his blue-grey eyes lit up like Christmas candles. "Well, Ann, it really is a small world, isn't it? Yes, yes, there can be only one Beemis Markham! Let me think back…your uncle was some character…darned good scout, too. Heard he later served with distinction out West…New Mexico Indian campaigns as I recall. But there's a story about that, too! Now I remember! Your uncle got into hot water with some Army top brass…told 'em what he thought…didn't set too well, so they had him transferred out West! Figured they'd never hear from him again. Boy, were they ever wrong! He served with distinction and was cited for bravery on several occasions!"

Annie had a good laugh. "That's my Uncle Beemis alright! He's slowed down a peg or two, but don't you dare tell him that! Not if you plan on eating at his table or bunking down!"

Wally hoisted his tripod over his shoulder, rifle fashion. He pointed to his camera. "Now if you'll kindly hand me my black magic box, I'll be heading back to my wagon."

"Let me give you a hand," said Annie.

Together, they started toward Wally's wagon with Annie carrying the camera and leading Glory. By the time they covered the distance, they'd become good friends. "Say, I've got an idea! How about coming to the ranch as my guest? Give you and Uncle Beemis a chance to renew old times and my sister's cookin' can't be beat! There is one condition tied to my invite: If you do come, please call me Annie! Well?"

How could he refuse? "You're on, Annie! It'll be good to break bread with your uncle once more…and to tell you the truth, my cookin's nothing to get very excited about! And if your sister's cookin' is half as good as you say…"

"It is! Just wait 'til you sink your teeth into it! You'll have to wait your turn on seconds, though! Uncle Beemis has first claim there!"

Over the best supper Andrew Wallihan could ever remember, the subject of Tom Horn came up. Beemis tried to shy away from mentioning it, but Wally jumped in with both feet. "Took Horn's picture down in the Arizona Territory six years ago. You know, he was a darned good tracker and scout, too…like Beemis, here! Horn had a lot to do with the capture of a couple renegade Apache chiefs that gave the Army fits down there. Besides that, he worked outta the Pinkerton Agency in Denver for a while. Turned to rodeoin' while he was down there—darned good rider, roper too— and always put on his best performance when he could smell first-place-prize money comin' his way. When Horn stayed sober and on the job, I've never seen none better! When he got drunk and turned mean and ornery, there was none worse than Horn! He'd turn killer if he had to! He always made sure he had a plan, so if anything backfired, he had a way out! The man is a sidewinder, any way you look at it! That's why I never cared for him! Got an ego big as a washtub, too!"

"Did you ever see him win top money down there?"

Wally turned to Annie. "Plenty of times! After he collected his money, Horn would turn to hard drinkin'. Some said he did it to forget the past. The liquor always seemed to loosen his tongue…turn him into a braggart…dared all comers to take him on."

"Did they?"

"No, Josie, nobody had the guts to go up against him, drunk or sober! That's when his reputation spread like a wild fire! Someday, it'll catch up with him, and then all those dime-novel Western writers will ask me for pictures of him. They'll make him into a legend, and I'll make plenty of money, too! Got an old drawer half full of Horn's pictures back in my house in Denver, just waitin' on his obituary!"

Beemis downed his last swallow of coffee. "I'm sure in your travels you've heard of Ora Haley and his Two-Bar cattle empire…"

Wally nodded.

"Well, Mister Two-Bar isn't happy with the millions he's made! He wants more! Got us folks in the Hole in more ways than one! We formed an association and ran sheep down here to keep his cattle out. Two-Bar strings up three sheepherders and slaughters a good many sheep to teach us a lesson. Then they send their night riders out to shove a bill of sale down our throats on a take-the-two-hundred-dollars-or-else deal! In the meantime, our association president, with dubious past cattle rustling deals, beats his court hearing but gets murdered anyway. Most everybody figures Tom Horn turned killer to keep that big reputation you mentioned alive and kicking! Of course, none of what I've just told you can be proved!"

Wally rose from the table. He moved his small frame around the dining room, deep in thought. He was caught between two choices, neither of which he liked. "When was your association president murdered?"

"On July eighth, near as anybody can figure! Why?"

Wally answered Annie's question. "I keep a journal in my wagon. Write in it every day. On last July eighth, I was behind a duck blind, shooting some Canadian Honkers on that backwater that feeds off of Talamentes Creek before it empties into Vermillion. Saw Horn, but I'm sure he didn't see me. Horn has a peculiar way of jabbing his mount when he wants to move out…uses the pointed toe of his boot like a spur instead of the heel like most riders do. First noticed that down in Arizona when I shot my first set of his pictures. Yup, it was him alright! He still does that! Had his back to me, making tracks over a low ridge, trying to keep outta sight!"

Annie was all ears. "Have you ever seen Horn write or his signature?"

"Lots of times! That's part of that big ego I was tellin' you folks about. Why do you ask?

"Before Matt was murdered, Horn left his calling card on Matt's door. Gave him thirty days to clear out or else! Matt's partner, a Negro by the name of Isom Dart, got the same warning! Both those handwritings match!"

Wally knew what Annie was leading up to. "You're saying that if you saw Horn's signature now, you'd know for sure if he was the killer. Getting his signature would be no problem; he's holed up at your local mercantile…or should I say cantina. Was in there yesterday! Shady character by the name of Wiggins and his wife are playing host! I assume from what's been said, nobody actually saw Horn murder your association president, so even if those signatures matched, you'd only have circumstantial evidence."

Josie also knew what her sister had on her mind. "No, Annie, you're not going to tempt Tom Horn into giving you his signature!"

Now Beemis was concerned. "It's not worth the risk, Annie! The man could turn killer at the drop of a hat! Even Wally will back me up on that!"

"Horn's here! Now can any of you think of a better way to know for sure?"

Four people rode in Beemis' two-seater to Jessy Wiggins' establishment. Only one had a definite plan in her head in case Horn's signature did match Isom Dart's notice. The other three were more than just a bit apprehensive about taking on Tom Horn, liquored up or not! They were Annie's protection committee, formed at the last minute when Annie told them she was going regardless of the risk involved!

Josie was the first to notice something very different when they approached the so-called mercantile. "There isn't one buggy out front! That means there's no women or families inside doing any buying! What kind of a place is this?"

Beemis supplied the answer. "Nothing but drifters and no-accounts inside! This place only attracts one kind: the worst! That's why we do our buyin' up in Rock Springs!"

Wally added his thoughts, too. "Remember, if Horn's inside, you're going to see a very different man than the one who showed up with the evidence at that hearing you told me about. Do not provoke Horn in any way! Take it from me, I know what I'm talking about!"

Beemis stepped down to help Annie and Josie out of the buggy. "Remember, you two, you're going to get lots of stares from hard cases who'd just as soon put a knife to your throat and take you out to that back room for some dirty flesh business, so be on guard! I've been in dives like this before I met your Aunt Maybelle. I ain't forgot what can go on when there's two darned-good-lookin' women and too many men who have the same thing on their minds. If I have to draw my gun, both of you make a beeline for the door and don't come back lookin' for me! I'll be alright! It's you two I'm worried about! Now let's go inside and see how good our chances stack up! Remember, if I draw, out you go! There won't be time for anything else!"

Wally led the way, followed by Annie and Josie with Beemis bringing up the rear. They found a tipped-over table in one corner, so Beemis righted it while Wally scrounged up four beat-up wooden chairs so they could all sit down together.

Amidst some of the hardest and longest stares the two women had ever gotten, Delores Wiggins took their drink order.

"Wow," Josie whispered, "she smells almost as bad as she looks. What's the matter with her?"

Wally cupped his hand over his mouth. "Too many men entertained in the back room and not enough soap and water in between all that entertainment..."

Beemis smiled knowingly. "Spent some time in New Orleans...her kind just dab on more perfume and look for another man."

Annie summed up the situation pretty well. "If John Jarvey could see what's happened to his mercantile, he'd roll over in his grave from shock. There's hardly anything left on the shelves to sell, and what's left has at least a half inch of dust covering it..."

"Yeah, I noticed that when I came in two days ago. Only two kinds of selling going on here: cheap rotgut whiskey and business out back!"

"Where's Horn? I don't see him!"

Wally moved his chair and nodded with his head to answer Annie's question. "Look just past that last drifter at the bar. You'll have to wait for some of that smoke and smell to clear, but he's there...same place I saw him two days ago."

Delores returned with the drinks on her tray. She eyed the four suspiciously, then served their drinks. "Never served sarsaparilla before; everybody orders beer or the hard stuff! Sure you wouldn't wanna try those? Had to look hard underneath a lot of stuff piled up to find these…They're our last four!"

Beemis fished out a five-dollar gold piece. "Sarsaparilla will do just fine!"

"Delores! Delores! Get over here! I need you! Now!"

"Just a minute, honey! Can't you see I'm busy with my new customers?"

Horn's voice cut through the smell and the smoke in nothing flat. "I said now! Get your ass over here, pronto!"

Everybody in the room watched Delores drop her tray on the counter and move her feet like they were fastened to hot coals.

"Did you see that?" whispered Josie. "She tucked her blouse in any tighter, her breasts would pop out! Only thing covered now are her nipples."

"Look at the way she walked," Annie added. "No doubt what she's selling…and it's not more French perfume either. How can her husband stand by and let this go on?"

Beemis beat Wally to the answer. "It's called runnin' scared! Unless I miss my guess, Horn has 'em all buffalo'd! He's king of the hill and Lord help the man or her husband who thinks otherwise!" He turned to Annie. "Well, whataya think? Had enough? Let's go home where we belong!"

"Not so fast, Uncle! We came to do something and from the sound of it, Horn is just drunk enough to let us get away with it! Time to get that signature!"

A couple of the hard cases had their fill of Jessy Wiggins' hospitality and rotgut, so they cleared out. Beemis and company now had an unobstructed view of the infamous stock detective at his worst. Even through the smoke-laden haze, Horn presented a picture none of them were apt to forget. Eyes bloodshot and glazed, the dark-complexioned and dark-haired man was in a foul mood. He hoisted a half-empty whiskey bottle to his lips, took a swig, spit out part of it, and cursed everything and everybody in a mixture of Mexican and English profanities. He tried to slam the bottle down hard to direct everybody's attention to what he was doing. Instead, he hit his plate of half-eaten, greasy-smelling food. That infuriated him all the more!

He knocked the plate off the table with a vicious half swing, then let out a bellow that started out as a laugh. "Damned food," he sneered, "ain't fit for hog slop! DELORES! Fix me some more! No slop this time!"

Delores stood behind him, then leaned forward to drape both arms around his neck. She finished off her little performance by planting a sickening kiss next to his lips. "Sure, honey, anything you say, only don't shout so loud. I'm right here."

Horn thoroughly enjoyed his situation. "Damned sure tootin' you're where you belong!" he bellowed even louder. "If I say squat, you squat! If I say jump, you damn better jump! And if I say lie down, you better pull up your dress and say how high, honey!"

Horn laughed hideously at his own dirty remarks, expecting everybody but Jessy Wiggins to laugh along with him.

Only three hard cases hooted and hollered.

Horn stood up; his chair went flying to one side. He grabbed his 30-30 rifle. Everybody in the room heard him work the rifle's lever. An angry snarl curled around his lips. "Now I said laugh! Everybody!"

Wally jabbed Beemis. "Laugh! All of us, laugh! No tellin' what he might do if he sees we're not!"

The room exploded with laughter. Some genuine, most not. Horn liked what he saw. He batted away some of the haze in front of his eyes. The glaze cleared for a second, long enough for him to recognize Wallihan. He started to sit down as he motioned for Wally to come forward. Delores saved Horn from an embarrassing disappearance behind his table by slipping his chair back under him in the nick of time. This time a genuine collective sigh of relief came from everyone in the room. Nobody wanted to be part of Horn's attitude adjustment if he had landed on his hinder!

"C'mere, Wallihan," Horn ordered. "Still got that big, ugly black box?"

Wally smiled. Horn was playing into his and Annie's scheme beautifully. "Why yes, Tom, it's outside! Want me to go get it?"

Horn smiled up at Delores. She moved in so he could put one arm around her waist. He drew her to him. "The only thing I haven't given you is my picture...How'd you like one of me? That way, after I leave this rat hole, you'll have somethun' to remember me by!"

Delores curled up on his lap while Horn laid his rifle back down on the table. She all but shoved one nipple into his mouth, blouse or no blouse! "But Tom, honey," she whined, "we were gonna leave together...remember? You promised me that when we went out back to count pelts the last time. Why do I need your picture?"

Everybody watched Jessy's face to get a read on him. He showed his true colors by lowering his head. He turned his back on Horn and his wife while he concentrated on re-wiping a tray of beer glasses that didn't need any attention.

Horn tossed his hat on the table. With Delores draped over and around him, he freed both hands long enough to plant a good-sized wad of spit in each. Then he plastered down his hair, daring anybody to snicker or laugh at his preparation for picture taking. None did.

Delores ran her fingers through his hair, messing up most of what he'd taken pains on getting to lay down. She gave him a big, sickening smooch. "You didn't need to do that, honey," she purred. "Your Deloresy would've found a comb. Alla ya gotta do is ask."

Horn rose, nearly dumping Delores on the floor. He pointed a finger at Wallihan. "Old man, you be ready to take my picture after I get back." Then he leaned on Delores and staggered for the door, one hand groping hard for her buttocks as they made their way outside.

"I've never seen anything so disgusting in all my life," Josie volunteered.

"Horn's been drinkin' hard for two days," said Wally. "Don't let that lean-on act to keep him walking fool you! He's sober enough whenever he needs to be! Saw that same thing pulled time and time again down in Arizona. The man is most dangerous when he's this way. Anything, anything at all, will set him off! So watch out!"

"I'm gonna change my plan! I'm gonna take Horn in and turn him over to that honest justice of the peace over at Hahn's Peak!"

This time Beemis had his say. "Annie, listen to me and listen good! Horn'll kill you at the drop of a hat! Haven't you been listening at all to Wally?"

Annie touched one of Beemis' hands. "Yes, Uncle, every word! I'm gonna have a little surprise waiting for Mister Horn when he comes back through that door!" She turned to Wally. "You go ahead and set up your camera; Horn's expecting that! That powder flash will blind him just long enough for me to rope him! Now, I'll need help when I drop my lariat down over him! He'll try to reach for his sidearms even when he's kicking and fighting my rope! Uncle Beemis! Josie! That's where you two come in! You'll have to hold him down until I hog-tie him for good! We'll load him into the two-seater and drive straight for Hahn's Peak! I'll get Justice Gooding to make him sign his name and when he does, I'll show him Isom's notice! And Wally will swear he saw Horn on the same day Matt was murdered! Yes, I know, it's all circumstantial, but it's the best chance we've got! The evidence will be too strong for Gooding to ignore or dismiss! He'll have to bind Horn over to the higher court for trial! This time there'll be no bill of sale to beat the odds!

We'll play Horn's game and beat him at it! Well, are you with me? Or do I have to do it as best I can alone?"

Beemis scratched his head, then his whiskers. "If you aren't the beatin'est! Even if Horn manages to beat the murder charges, we've bought ourselves a lot of time before Horn could possibly be released! That'll throw a pitchfork into Ora Haley's takeover plans! Alright, Annie, I'll go along!"

"Me too!" exclaimed Josie. "We're countin' on you, Sis! Don't you dare miss! You'll get only one throw!"

Annie, too, realized the terrible risk at stake! "I've got to get in some practice throws while Horn and Delores are busy out back. You get set up, Wally! That's the first thing he'll see when he steps back inside. You've got to make sure your powder flash will do the job!"

Wally hugged Annie. "Never seen a braver woman than you! I'm sure I saw several ropes on a couple of saddle horns outside. You do your thing while I do mine. Remember now, Horn's no fool! He'll shove Delores through the door first when they come back. Chances are he'll stick to her like glue, just in case Jessy or any of these jackals finds enough backbone for gunplay. Horn'll make sure they'll have to shoot through her first! They'll never get a clean shot at him! You can bet your life on that!"

"I just did!"

They played the deadly game of life or death inside and outside of Jessy Wiggins' cantina. Wally set up his tripod and camera near the entrance, then carefully paced the distance to make sure his powder would create a big enough and bright enough flash to insure blindness for a precious second or two.

Annie used Beemis and Josie as stand-ins for Horn and Delores. "Move closer to Josie this time, Uncle; I've got to make sure my loop is big enough to drop down over your head."

She reeled off four perfect throws, then one miss.

The enormity of what they'd taken on hit Josie. She rushed up to Annie and shook her. "Please, please, dear Sis, don't miss! This isn't back East or you practicing at the ranch. This is for all the marbles…and your life!"

Annie motioned for Josie to get back to her uncle. She then proceeded to toss twelve perfect throws without a miss.

None of Jessy's bar patrons gave a tinker's damn about Wallihan's photo preparation for Tom Horn's return. Several shrugged off the way Wally was going about getting set up as none of their business. So what if he was going to explode his flash powder when Horn returned with Jessy's wife through the open doorway? From where they stood, leaning against the bar, a new puff of powder smoke would be welcome change from the eye-watering and eye-smarting haze that hung over the entire room. Three others conversed among themselves, wondering if Jessy would even say one word when his wife returned with her skirt rumpled and her tight-fitting blouse mostly unbuttoned, mute evidence that she'd willingly submitted to Horn's flesh desires, lying on top of a stock of pelts in the back room. No, it was business as usual as far as they were concerned. Only one of Jessy's low-life customers had the gall to ask his partner if he thought Delores might take him on after Horn was through with her. He'd seen Horn operate this way before and knew Horn used his women for only one purpose and then discarded them like a used-up rag.

Beemis and Josie reappeared inside the cantina. "You stand back, a little, on this side of the doorway, and I'll do the same on the other side. Once Annie's rope drops, we've gotta be ready to jump him. Every second will count!"

Josie followed Beemis' instructions by moving a small table and chair to one side of the doorway. "We gotta look and act natural like we're customers sitting at tables on opposite sides of the door. Make sure your chair is turned enough so you can get out of it in a big hurry! Like you said, every second will count!"

Beemis found another small table and pushed it over toward the doorway. "Good idea, Josie!" He handed her an empty whiskey bottle. "Put that on the table in front of you…gotta make Horn think we're drinkin' customers, not mountain lions ready to pounce."

Annie came in. She looked at Beemis, then Josie and smiled. "Good idea, nothing looks out of place. I'll take a chair behind you, Sis. When I tap your shoulder, you duck down, so I can get my throw off quicker. I'll turn my head when Wally signals me, so my eyes won't have to stand the flash. Horn should be blinded long enough for me to nail him good!"

Long, exasperating minutes dragged on, like time's step-children who refused to budge for fear something terrible might happen should the hands of time be allowed to move forward. The four exchanged glances, each alone with his or her thoughts, each wondering if Horn's liquor-numbed reflexes would give them the edge they needed, the edge between life and death itself!

All four heard the shuffling of feet on the plank-board sidewalk. The hairs on the back of their necks stood erect. Four faces drew tense, eight sets of knuckles turned while, and four foreheads began to perspire.

Wally stood beside his camera, his hand raised high, his powder-laden flash ready for instant explosion.

Horn stopped just short of the doorway to dally with Delores once more. He pushed her up against the wall. She obliged by letting him raise her off her feet, so he could penetrate the folds of her skit as though nothing was there except soft, yielding flesh. She was more than willing to let him take a crack at anything and everything. She wrapped both arms around him and locked her legs behind his. "Gee, honey," she purred, "I feel something I like...thought we took care of that just a few minutes ago, countin' pelts! Never run into one like you. The more you drink, the more you're ready to go!"

Horn changed his mind when he let Delores' feet touch the planks. "My gut's growlin' again. See if you can't do something 'bout it this time by fixin' me some decent grub! We'll go back 'n count pelts some more after that!"

They entered the bar exactly the way Wally said they would. Horn made Delores enter first, with him all but living off her hips, that's how close he kept to her. One hand flexed above his sidearm, ready for any comers, while the other pushed her forward. When she moved, he moved. No one could've gotten a clean shot without going through Delores!

Horn and Delores walked straight toward Wally and his camera setup.

"Hey, Tom," Wally shouted out, "never got a shot of you like this. How about it?"

Horn's trained eyes covered the room in an instant. He saw nothing unusual or suspicious. "Alright, old man," he answered, "but make it quick! Got other things on my mind!" He shoved Delores aside. "Wallihan just wants my picture!"

Horn's own vanity played right into Annie's plan.

Poof! The extra powder turned Jessy's dim-lit bar into the blinding flash Wally had to have. Horn blinked while Delores tried to shield her eyes.

Annie's rope coiled and serpentined over Horn's head. By the time he glanced up, it was too late.

"I'VE GOT HIM! I'VE GOT HIM! QUICK! HELP ME!"

Beemis' cane flew in one direction while he and Josie tackled Horn together. With Beemis' considerable weight pinning him to the floor, Josie had time to help Annie put the finishing touches to her tie-down job. Satisfied Horn was helpless, Annie quickly removed his sidearm.

"Bring my chair over," said Beemis. "We'll set him up in it and tie him in it, just for good measure!"

Horn's profanities bounced off the walls and the ears of everyone there. When those finally died, he concentrated on Wally. "You dirty, double-dealing sonofabitch!" he screamed. "Wait'll I get free! I'll take care of you!"

Wally showed no fear whatsoever. "You mean like you took care of Matt Rash! Not this time, Horn! You're gonna be spendin' a lot of time trying to explain your whereabouts to the law. I saw you the day you murdered Rash! Got it written down in my journal! All we gotta do is match your handwriting!"

The profanities stopped. Horn turned silent. Did he have an ace up his sleeve? Or was his silence an indication he had nothing to trade for his freedom?

Beemis watched the half-dozen drifters at the bar, paying close attention to Jessy Wiggins. He didn't trust any of them. The last thing he wanted was a lynching. It was time to move before they put their whiskey-sponged brains together long enough to try to interfere with Annie's plans or his purpose.

The jackals turned their fear and cowardice into newfound aggression against the man who had bullied and cowered them into helpless, sniveling whelps for two long, drunken days. Now it was payback time!

Jessy finally showed he had a little backbone. Out from behind the bar, he charged, gun in hand, to kill Horn. He cocked the six-gun and pressed it against Horn's head. "Had your way with my wife," he screamed. "Two days! Two days! Think I was about to let that go?"

Horn never flinched a muscle. "She was willing...more than willing! Go ask her!"

Jessy felt something hard, round, and cold press hard into his ribs. "You blow Horn's head off, and I'll blow yours to kingdom come! Don't think Mister Wiggins wants that...Annie, go back our two-seater up to the door. Josie, go with her!"

Beemis waited until they left. At least now he felt they were safe for the present. Then he turned to face the half-dozen hard cases who hadn't made up their minds, one way or the other. "Jessy, better tell your friends that if one of them decides your hide isn't worth saving that you still get it first! Mister Horn is going to be escorted to Hahn's Peak for a hearing! A fair hearing! We've got evidence, plenty of evidence! So there's no need of any of you to get involved! Hear that? No need! Now either get the hell outta here or get back to your drinkin'!"

Beemis' words left a good impression, the lasting kind. Several grumbled and bitched to the others, but none appeared ready to back Jessy. The

Mexican stand-off between Beemis and Jessy over Horn's departure remained just that.

The sound of horses and riders approaching greeted everybody's ears. This was the one thing Beemis feared. "Wally," he barked, "go see who it is and tell the women to hurry up!"

Wally rushed out. A minute later, he poked his head back inside. "Four riders coming, all look like cowboys, not whiskey bums! The lead one looks all business! Annie and Josie are all backed up, ready for Horn!"

"Borrow Annie's gun and get back in here NOW!"

Beemis was worried, plenty worried. More arrivals could mean more trouble, the last thing he needed now.

Wally's news brought beads of perspiration out on Jessy's forehead. He feared Beemis could be getting help, the last thing he wanted to happen. He snarled at his wife, mad as hell at her behavior, especially around Horn. Horn had made his point. Delores had been willing, far too willing to accommodate him any time, any way he wanted her. He'd been humiliated to the point that he had to do something to protect what little integrity and respect he had left. He snarled at Delores, who'd left the Mexican stand-off to begin serving his old customers once more. "Damn you," he snarled. "You're the cause of this! You've been too damn loose about all of this! You been back at it agin, actin' up your old ways like a whore! Only this time, I ain't seen one gold coin outta Horn left on my counter. Ya been givin' it away for free!"

Delores, for all her faults, decided to add one more. She aired the family laundry and linen out for everyone to hear, whether they wanted to or not. She served one customer, then stood at the end of the bar and shouted to Beemis. "Go head, shoot the bastard! Can't count the number of times I've covered him when he always ran a little short! That's the story of your life, Jessy! Short of money and damn short where it counts with a woman!"

Beemis heaved a big sigh of relief when he recognized the four entering Jessy's cantina. Adam Hoy was the first to cross the planks, followed by Deke Landry and two other cowpokes from the Hoy ranch.

Hoy saw Beemis holding a gun on Jessy and Jessy, in turn, pressing his gun hard at Tom Horn's temple. What puzzled him most was the way Horn was tied up, defenseless to do anything about either. "Is this kinda private, or can anybody get in on this? What's goin' on, Beemis?"

"We got the goods on Horn for murderin' Matt Rash! Jessy here is tryin' to take exception 'cause his wife's been overly friendly with Horn! Wants to shoot Horn without givin' him a fair trial! Annie roped him, and we were about to run him over to Hahn's Peak for a hearing!"

Adam forged a smile despite the high drama he'd walked into. "Hell, Beemis, you oughta be thankin' Horn for doin' the law's job instead of tryin' to Shanghai him outta here!"

Horn sensed he might have found an ally, so he seized the chance. "Nobody saw anything! I'm innocent! And I can prove it!"

Adam motioned for Deke and the others to follow him. "When I say draw, all of you show Jessy that his minutes on earth are numbered unless he hands over his peacemaker! DRAW!"

Four guns put the business end of their barrels to good use—against Jessy's head. "Give it up, Jessy! Live to sell another shot of your rotgut! That's the only thing waitin' on you…unless you'd like to have your brains spattered all over the floor! Well, which is it?"

Jessy was glad, in a way, that Hoy gave him a way out. He meekly dropped his sidearm and handed it over to Adam. "Damned woman wasn't worth gettin' killed over anyhow…"

The four watched Jessy resort to his old self by working one end of the bar while Delores purposely stayed away from him at the other end. Satisfied Jessy was not about to interfere, Adam motioned for Beemis to put his rifle down. Beemis obliged. "Now then, let's see if anybody can get to the bottom of this! Where's your proof, Beemis?"

Beemis turned to Wally. "Get Annie in here and tell her to bring that note Horn tacked on Isom's door."

A minute later, the high stakes drama continued in earnest as Annie showed Hoy the note. "I also saw the same note with the same handwriting on Matt Rash's door before he was murdered!" She pointed to Wally. "And this man is willing to swear he saw Horn trying to slip outta the Park on the same day Matt was murdered."

"That right, Mister?"

Wally nodded. "Yes, it was Horn alright! I'll swear to it!"

"LIAR! LIAR!" screamed Horn.

"You're the liar," Annie shouted. "Wally had it written down long before he even knew about Rash's murder!"

Adam shook his head. "That right, Wally?"

"You bet, Mister Hoy! Annie's right as right can be! Horn's trying to pull a fast one to save his neck from rope burns when they hang him for murder!"

Adam approached Horn. "Well, Mister Horn, the goods are piling up pretty high on you! Annie doesn't seem like the lying type, neither does

Wally here! Unless you can come up with some pretty hard stuff, I'm gonna help Beemis load you up! And I'll send my man, Deke Landry, along to help drive the buggy! Got anything you'd care to say?"

Horn resorted to old habits. He squirmed and wiggled in his chair, but Annie's rope-tying job cut into his flesh, making him madder by the second. The Spanish flew from his lips, the guttural kind that curled your hair and turned your cheeks rosy red, even if you'd never heard it before! There was no mistaking the way Horn used it. Then came an incoherent mix of Spanish and barroom English, the kind that didn't need an interpreter at all! Then he stopped as suddenly as he'd started. He mumbled something in low tones.

Adam cocked his head. "That last part...say again..."

Horn's eyes went wild, his cheeks moved, and his muscles tensed. He screamed. "I can't be in two places at the same time! Now can I?"

Horn's outburst startled everybody. Nobody had a clue in the world as to what he was ranting about. Beemis spoke for everybody. "Mister Horn, you're right! You can't be two places at the same time. What in hell are you talking about?"

Tom Horn realized it was now or never to make his point if the seeds of doubt were ever to be planted. "What day was Matt Rash murdered?"

Horn's question drew an immediate response from Annie. "July eighth, as if you didn't know!"

"I was in Denver on July eighth! You'd better cough up somebody else, like Isom Dart! All of you know about the bad blood between them! Dart's the man you're looking for, not me! Now untie me!"

Horn had dropped a bomb! Annie and Wally exchanged disbelieving glances. Beemis and the others were dumbfounded. Finally, Beemis rallied his common sense. "Mister Horn, neither my niece nor my friend Wallihan are liars! So I guess we all know where that leaves you! Unless you have some proof, I'm gonna load you up for long haul to Hahn's Peak!"

"I do have proof! I mailed a letter to Matt from Denver! Look in his cabin if you don't believe me!"

Another bombshell! Horn knew he'd driven more than the proverbial wedge into the proceedings. Hoy took mental stock in the growing controversy. "Mister Horn, I'd still like to see your handwriting. Annie's got the note found on Dart's door! Well, how 'bout it?"

Horn weighed the request against the stockpile of mounting charges. "Alright, on one condition! Send one of your men to Matt's cabin! Make sure he covers every inch of that cabin! If he returns with the letter I wrote, the proof I told you about, then you have to let me go! Is it a deal?"

"I'll volunteer to go!"

Deke's pronouncement seemed to satisfy everybody, including Horn. Deke added his own thoughts. "Horn, you're a liar, and I'm going to prove it! Nothing in all this world would give me more pleasure than to escort you to Hahn's Peak. We all know you're stalling! There's no letter! You can't pull a rabbit out of somebody's hat like Matt Rash did to you with that bill of sale! That's why you murdered him! Rash outsmarted you, Mister Cattle Detective! Mister Braggart! Mister Nobody!"

"Get goin' Deke! The sooner you check out Horn's B.S., the sooner we do what we came for!"

Deke pumped Beemis' hand. "Not 'til Horn writes for us! Annie's got him nailed, but good! Those writin's will match closer than twin colts just born!"

"Untie Horn's hands! But only his hands!"

Hoy's orders were obeyed to the letter. Annie went to the bar and came back with a pad of paper and a lead pencil she personally sharpened. Even the bar customers crowded around now. None of them cared much for Horn after the way he'd bullied them, so they were eager to see Horn disposed of.

"Okay, Horn, put your John Henry down on that piece of paper!"

Horn never hesitated a moment, following Hoy's orders. He seemed glad to oblige, and that bothered Annie to no end. The signatures had to match! Nobody was more sure of that than she.

Horn handed the pad back to Annie. She pulled out Dart's note and laid it next to his handwriting. The circle of spectators closed in around her, crowding her to the point she barely had enough room to compare.

"It's a match! It's a match!" Annie shouted for all to hear. Then she forced her way between the bodies and shook her finger at Horn. "Never thought I'd say this, to you of all people, but thanks for helping us put a noose around your neck!"

"Free drinks for everybody! It's on the house! Horn's gonna get what's comin' to him!"

Jessy's invitation had plenty of takers—the same bunch whom Horn had run roughshod over for the past forty-eight hours. They shoved and jostled each other to get back to the bar to be served by Jessy. Delores refused to be part of the celebration.

Josie could only shake her head. "Look at them! Worse than hogs gettin' to the slop trough!"

"Yes, but didja notice Delores...the way she's acting. I think she really has some feelings for Horn. He's been a taker not a giver all his life."

Wally's candid observation about Horn was short-lived by Horn. He waited for most of the excitement to wear down at the bar. He turned his head in Beemis' direction. "Ain't you folks forgettin' part of our little deal? Like sending one of your idiots to Rash's cabin to check out my alibi?"

Beemis raised his rifle to remind Horn just who was very much in charge. "We'll go through the motions, Horn! Don't you worry your stretched neck about that!" He waved Deke over for some last-minute instructions. "Give Rash's cabin a good goin' over, then get back here as quick as you can. The way these hyenas are soppin' up the free whiskey, no tellin' what this could still turn into."

"You sound like Horn needs to be spirited out of here before Jessy and his pack of wolves might decide to take matters into their own hands."

"No matter what I think of Horn, he deserves the same fair-shake Rash got at Hahn's Peak!"

Deke stood between Horn and Beemis, so Horn couldn't hear. "Something about this whole business bothers me. Horn was too eager to sign his John Henry…can't figure why he volunteered to help stick his head in his own noose."

Beemis mused a moment. "You once told me Cassidy always had a backup plan, a way to get out of a jam if need be…now I figure Horn's every bit as smart as Butch…maybe he's no different."

"There ain't no letter, Beemis! Hell, how could there be!"

"Time to find out, Deke! Time to find out!"

Deke left the noisy cantina with Beemis' remarks still ringing in his ears. "Deke! Deke! Wait up!"

Deke had one foot in the stirrup, ready to swing his leg over the saddle. He felt Annie's hand touch his shoulder. Oh how he longed to feel both her arms around his waist, then let them slide up to his shoulders. "Lord-a-mighty, Annie, you sure make a fella plum forget what's he's supposed to be doin'! Man, would I ever like to kiss you again!"

"Well, why don'cha? Who's stopping you?"

Deke barely had time to plant both boots on the ground before Annie was in his arms. In two seconds flat, Annie removed all traces of every nighttime fantasy and daydream he'd ever had about her with the real thing—her lips and her body.

"Oh, Annie, oh, my Annie," he softly breathed. "Soon as I get back and this mess gets put to bed…there's so much that needs to be said between us…so much, Annie."

"Does that mean you're coming back? To the ranch? To me?"

He broke from their embrace. "See you later…gotta settle Horn's hash once and for always!"

Annie watched him put a real charge into his mount. Little puffs of dust followed an ever smaller speck of black until both became part of the horizon. She smiled to herself, glad, oh so glad for their chance encounter. She thanked God, in her silent way, for letting him come back into her life once more. Good things were about to happen between them—she could feel it! "Oh dear Lord," she spoke out, "let Deke be part of my life once more…let the past stay buried, where it belongs…let our future begin today. One small step at a time, if need be…but please, please, let it happen."

Adam and Beemis huddled. Delores was nowhere in sight while Jessy opened bottle after bottle of free booze. Beemis slid his specs down off the bridge of his nose; it was time to talk turkey. "Deke's gonna come back with nothin' but air between his fingers! Every one of these hyenas has a score or two to settle with Horn. We'd better relieve 'em of their hardware now before all this waitin' around gets to be too big a temptation for a hangin' party. You go over to the other end of the bar, and I'll take this end. I'll have Wally reach in to pluck their hardware, free and easy-like…"

Four loaded rifles were trained on the bar customers. "Gentlemen, may I have your attention! Raise your hands! BOTH OF THEM! NOW!"

Jessy looked up to see Beemis move his rifle in an upward motion. He raised both arms high to show the others he wasn't about to argue. "Do as the man says! Never argue with a loaded rifle unless you don't give a rat's ass about tomorrow!"

One by one, Wally moved among the hard cases, using his camera box to deposit their hardware. As he moved, one of Adam Hoy's cowboys moved with him, rifle poised. Two customers had other ideas, but felt several sharp jabs in their lower backs from the rifle barrel, a solid reminder that someone else was in charge. When Wally finished, he brought the wooden box back to Beemis.

"Thank you, gentlemen! Thank you for your cooperation! When we leave, you'll find your hardware down the main trail about a mile from here! Next to that lightning-struck tree stump!"

The hard cases found that being stripped of their hardware left them a whole new avenue to do what they collectively did best. None were a match for Horn on their own, but laced with too much liquor and too much time on their hands, they turned jackal and began yelping. Led by Jessy, they left their places at the bar and gathered as close to Horn as they dared, trying to provoke him into a running battle of words. Horn refused to play their game of taunts, so they did the next best thing, trying to outdo each other by bragging what they'd do to him if given the opportunity.

Jessy waved a whiskey bottle at Horn, then turned to his new-found drinking buddies. "Horn still looks like a Mex to me," he said. "And you know what we do to Mexicans around here!" That brought out a fresh round of belly-belching hollers from the five others who joined him. "We either string 'em up like sheepherders or else we drag 'em Apache-style, behind a pony over rocks and boulders, 'til the hide is stripped off and then cut the rope to watch him quiver and die!"

Another hard case wasn't about to be outdone. He used an ugly set of snaggle-rotted teeth to pull the cork out of his whiskey bottle. "Seen this done up on the Snake River! It's just right for a man like Horn! You let him dangle with a rope round his neck, but don't let nothun' but the toe of his boot touch the wagon seat under him. Then you watch him squirm and kick and yell fer mercy! When his juices run dry, that's when the fun begins 'cause there ain't no more fight left in 'em! Then the rope burns takes over and his eyes bug out and 'bout a pocketful of puke slithers out the corner of his mouth 'cause his own weight does him in! Now that's somethun to see alright! Sure like'ta see Horn's eyes bug out!"

A third hard case got caught up in the wishful thinking. He left his bar buddies and approached Beemis. "Any of them ideas catch your fancy? Turn Horn over to us…we'll take good care of him…like he done us!"

That brought out a fresh round of hoots, hollers, and whiskey cackles from the assembled pack of hyenas. Beemis pointed his rifle at the man. "Better get back or else we'll put you in a chair and set you next to Horn to keep him company! How'd you like that?"

Beemis was not about to be persuaded to do anything with Horn until Deke got back. The third hard case saw Beemis set his jaw. His cold stare told the man to move back or suffer the consequences. The man rejoined his newfound friends.

Annie shielded her face to keep from being overheard. "Sure wish Deke would hurry up. He's so damned honest, he'll tear Matt's cabin apart just so he can truthfully say he looked everywhere, even though we all know there's nothing to find. These lowlifes give me the willies. Drunk or sober or somewhere in between, I sure wouldn't want them to ever call me their friend."

Josie finished Annie's thoughts. "Yeah, I see what you mean. The only thing I'd care to do with them is set a Saturday-night bathtub in front of them, throw a bar of soap in their direction, and run like heck."

The fourth hard case came forward on wobbly pins. He swayed and staggered, holding his whiskey bottle in front of his face, trying his darnedest to line up the top of the bottle with his bleary eyes on either Annie or Josie's face. He missed badly on both accounts! Realizing the futility of such action, he tried to concentrate on Annie. He let his eyes do the feeling, trying to stare holes through her men's work shirt, so he wouldn't have go guess what a firm, trim figure she had under the shirt.

Annie sensed what was on his pickled mind, so she turned her back to him, cheating him out of his numbed, flesh-sorting pleasure.

Josie was next. He ambled over as far as he dared go without provoking a hostile rifle barrel being jabbed in his belly. He took considerable time to focus on her figure, especially her ample breasts as she sat facing him. She was truly in her prime, there was no hiding her obvious charms, no matter how drunk he appeared. If anything, her modest dress only enhanced his hungry stares and wanton desires.

He pointed to his whiskey bottle with a wavering hand and directed his question at her. "See this here bottle?"

Josie said nothing.

"I know ya see'd it." He wobbled some more, trying to steady himself. "Been suckin' on this...but it ain't worth suckin' on no more...not when there's somethun' a whole lot better in this here room to suck on..."

Beemis shifted positions. Every single soul followed him, knowing full well he was more than annoyed at the direction the hard case had chosen to take. "That'll be enough outta you, Mister! Take your bottle back where you belong and stay there!"

The hard case seemed to understand Beemis' order. He slowly turned; then to everybody's surprise, he let his bottle slip out of his grasp. He turned to Josie, grabbed his crotch with both hands and shouted, "After the suckin', there's something even better! This!"

Those who saw what happened next would be willing to swear Beemis sat in a spring-loaded chair. He was in front of the hard case before his whiskey bottle stopped rolling. He rammed his rifle barrel into the soft belly of the hard case again and again and again. The man winced with pain, so Beemis poked harder than ever until the man went down into a crumpled heap.

Beemis planted his boot across his throat to keep the man's head pinned. Then he forced the barrel's end into his mouth. "Go ahead, Mister! One more dirty thought, and it'll be your last!"

Adam Hoy stood beside Beemis. "Let him up, Beemis, we got bigger fish that needs fryin' tied up in a chair!"

Beemis finally pulled the rifle end out of the man's mouth. The man was so terrified that he never tried to get up. Everybody watched him crawl back to the bar, without daring to retrieve his whiskey bottle.

Wally had never seen such an obscene gesture in all his well-traveled days. He took the initiative, more for the women's sake than anyone else's. He stood between Josie and Annie, purposely blocking their view. "Deke should be getting back soon…How about you two being his welcoming committee outside?"

Annie took the hint. "C'mon, Sis! We belong outside, not in here!"

They passed in front of Tom Horn on their way outside.

"Dunno what in hell your beef is with me, but you sure can throw one helluva rope. Best I've seen ever!"

Annie halted a second, tempted to really let Horn get a full plate of what she really thought of him. Two hard stares from Beemis told her to leave well enough alone.

Josie caught up with Annie outside. "That was Horn's way of complimenting you. Never thought I'd live to see that day."

"Or what that drunk wanted to do to you, Sis! Will I ever be glad to see Deke come back so we can get this over with! Deke wants to come back…to the ranch…and I hope to me."

Josie hugged her sister. "Oh, I'm so happy for you. What did he say before he left?"

Annie kept the hug intact. "It's not so much what he said, it's the way he said it. I can tell. Always could read him like a book…"

They parted. Annie let her thoughts fly right along with her heart. The tears welled up, but she never even asked Josie for a hankie. "When I saw Deke today…I knew right then and there, there's no man who can take his place. Matt Rash wouldn't even be a bad second—you were right…all along…I just hated to admit it. I've asked God to forgive me a thousand times for my big mistake…only hope He's been puttin' the same thoughts into Deke's head."

Josie touched Annie's hand. "You're really a one-man woman, but you do have a way of rushing into things and men…without taking the time to sort them out with your mind as well as your heart. That's where you get into trouble."

Annie blinked to clear the mist from her eyes. "Thanks, Sis, for sticking by my side."

"That was the mother in me talking…now, as your sister, let's make sure Deke knows he's being appreciated when he rides back."

Inside the cantina, time not only stood still for Beemis and company, it appeared more like it was on a long vacation. Beemis drummed his fingers incessantly on the table, trying to make it march forward so the business with Horn could be settled and they could be on their way to the Hahn's Peak jail.

"Wouldja mind not doing that, Beemis! It's getting to me!"

The old scout lowered his head just enough to squint over his specs at Hoy. "Sorry, Adam," he mumbled. "What in hell's taking Deke so long?"

Hoy rocked back on his chair. He was glad the subject of Deke had come up. "Deke's no cowboy…never was…never will be. Took him in so he could get time to sort things out. Always kept closemouthed whenever your Annie's name came up. Just the same, I could see he was hurtin' plenty, inside. Heard some old hen's cacklin' that she got mixed up with that handsome devil, Lay, and then Matt Rash, too! Anything to it?"

Beemis thought long and hard about Hoy's question. He hated dredging up the past, especially his family's soiled laundry. However, here was a golden opportunity to cement their relationship with the truth. "Yes, on the first, and hell no about Rash. That's all I'm gonna say on the matter."

Hoy seemed satisfied with both answers. "I take it then Annie made a big mistake and that's what drove Deke over to my spread. Deke's ready to come back. Never would come right out to tell me he wants to…but I watched your Annie and him today. Their minds are in the same corral; now…hope it works out for 'em."

"Me too! Annie's paid and paid, and paid some more for that big mistake. Hope Deke can still find room for my Annie in his life…soon." Beemis leaned forward. It was past time to change subjects. "With what you just said about Deke, I've got me an idea. Let me run this by you. There's only three trails to guard…what say we share our hired hands and post guards up on top of those trails? Keep track of who's comin' and goin'. I'd be willin' to bet my best Arabian we can stop those night riders colder'n hell! Give Ora a little more to think about, along with putting his hired killer in jail."

Adam liked what he heard. "There'd be no more gobblin' up our ranchers' homesteads…Haley would have to settle for what he's grabbed so far…and he can't move his herds in 'til next season with no grass to feed 'em." He offered his hand. "Let's shake on it! What'a we got to lose?"

Beemis chuckled; his spirits rose sky-high. "Like it or lump it, in a way we could thank Horn for being holed up in this rat's nest. Brought Deke back and gave us a plan to beat Haley at his own game!"

Hoy's dead-serious expression softened a mite. "One other thing…hope it's not out of line, but the Widow Benson speaks very highly of you…any chance you might think that way about her?"

Beemis shifted in his chair, then seemed distant for a moment. He scratched his beard, his symbolic way of revisiting the past. He returned to the present with his answer. "When a man's been blessed with the best mate he could possibly have for more years than I'd care to count, it makes taking on another awfully hard to do…"

"Deke's coming! Deke's coming!"

None of Beemis and company cared if it was Annie or Josie who shouted out the good news. The room sprang alive with anticipation and final resolution. Horn's freedom had dwindled down to its last few minutes, on that there could be no doubt.

Hoy left one last order, before joining Beemis and Wally outside. He pointed to Luke, one of his cowpokes. "Keep your rifle trained on Horn! If he so much as wiggles, shoot him! If any of those whiskey hounds strays from the bar, shoot them!"

Deke's reception committee gathered long before either the horse or its rider could be separated as distinct objects. Deke hit the ground a running while his horse slid on its haunches on all fours.

Annie rushed up. "No letter! No letter! Right?"

Deke wrapped one arm around Annie's shoulder. Inside his shirt, he produced the evidence. Horn's letter. "I still can hardly believe it! I've read this three times! It's dated July eighth!" He turned it over. "See! It's even postmarked, Denver, July eighth!"

Jaws dropped, mouths opened, eyes nearly popped out of their sockets, and deep furrows formed across a lot of virgin forehead territory. Those who saw and those who saw and heard still couldn't believe their senses. All turned to Beemis for an answer.

"My hide's burnin' like hell, but we gotta let Horn go!"

They all heard, yet most had to have another minute for Beemis' pronouncement to fully sink in. Hoy was visibly upset. Wally kept repeating, over and over, mostly to himself, "I know who I saw. I know who I saw…on

July eighth. It was Horn…Tom Horn…I know who I saw…"

Annie looked up at Deke. "You didn't have to find it! Could've burned it or lost it on the way back. I know he's Matt's hired killer, I know…and so do you…all of us know."

Deke squeezed Annie, his way of agreeing. "I know we gotta let him go…don't like it! Still don't like it, but Beemis is right; somehow Horn pulled a rabbit out of the weeds…guess he was smarter than we all figured."

Beemis went back inside. He motioned for Hoy's two guards to leave; then he put his sizeable bulk between Horn and the hard cases. He spoke in low tones. "Guess you must've heard, your letter was found. Your sidearm and rifle are waitin' for you outside. When you ride outta here, I'd strongly suggest you make it a point to never come back. We gave you the benefit of the doubt…gave you time to make your point…that's why I'm gonna cut you loose! Next time you decide to hole-up, I'd pick better people to drink with or else you may not be so lucky next time. You heard 'em! Everyone behind me wants you more dead than alive!"

The minute Beemis' knife cut through the last rope, Horn's smugness and arrogance took over. He rubbed both wrists, stretched the kinks out of his legs and took his sweet time getting out of the chair. He took mental note of every face at the bar who watched Beemis set him free, logging each in his mind for future paybacks. It was Horn's way of doing business. Beemis figured Jessy would be losing everyone who drank at the bar with him. No doubt, he figured, they'd move on, probably as far away from Horn as they could possibly get if they wanted to draw breath on a regular basis.

Horn glared at Beemis, his dark eyes penetrating the stocky man's face. "Don't expect any thanks from me, and tell Wallihan the next time we meet, I'm gonna put on my own little surprise party for him."

Tom Horn walked out like he owned the place instead of being held prisoner inside. He turned at the doorway to give Beemis his parting shot. "Don't know who you are, Mister, but tell that ropin' gal who was with you to watch her step, too! She's liable to rope the wrong person next time and Wallihan won't be around to blind him while I make her dead meat!"

Horn mounted his horse and glared at his send-off committee, leaving no doubt that he'd just as soon kill them as look at them; all he needed was one more excuse.

Delores rushed out, carrying a satchel. No doubt it contained all she owned in the way of clothes and what money she could lay her hands on. She didn't wait for Horn to help her up. Instead, she raised her dress way too high, trying to get her foot in Horn's stirrup so she could swing her body up and leg over behind him.

Horn jabbed his horse hard. His mount bolted, knocking Delores down into the dirt. She lay in the dust, her modesty, if any, compromised beyond repair. She neither cared who did or didn't look. All she wanted to do was leave with Horn.

Horn was angry. He charged at Delores, determined to ride over her and knock her down once more.

"LOOK OUT!"

Horn heard Josie's warning. At the last instant, he apparently changed his mind. He leaned down and helped her up.

"Tom, honey! I knew you weren't going to leave me! Make your horse hold still! I've been good to you for two days! Treat me right, and I'll never look at another man! I promise! Just take me with you!"

Horn's belated gesture and gravity helped pull Delores' dress down once more. He jerked his hand away from hers. "You're gettin' too old! You're about all used up!"

Delores picked up her satchel then brushed some of the dust from her dress. "I'm not too old for you! Take me anywhere, and I'll prove it! You promised me, Tom, honey! Now you keep your promise!"

"Better see Jessy! Maybe he'll take you back! I got no use for you anymore! I like my women younger, better looking, smaller boned, and a whole lot tighter! That leaves you out, all around!"

Josie played the good Samaritan by helping Delores finish brushing the dust off her dress. Together, they watched Horn use that peculiar toe job. He rode away the way he'd come—full of conceit and contempt for those who crossed his path.

Delores tried not to show how deeply she'd been hurt. She turned away from Josie, tears streaking down her pasty makeup. She covered the hurt with a guttural offering. "Men! Ha, they're all the same! They promise and then they poke! Then they promise some more and poke even longer! Ain't a good one in the whole damn lot! Only difference, I like the way Horn done his promisin.' He looked me in the eye and lied like hell, and I took it!"

Beemis, Josie, Annie, and Wally got ready to leave. Adam Hoy and Deke walked to the buggy. Adam pumped Beemis' hand. "I'm gonna have Deke move over to your ranch tomorrow morning to help guard Irish Trail. The other two are closer to my end of the Hole. If this idea catches on, maybe some of the other ranchers will pitch in to spell us off so we can keep up with our own ranch work."

"Thanks, Adam. Let me know if we can lend a hand over your way. We'll post three guards startin' tomorrow morning, figure you'll do the same. Once a week, we need to get together…go over things we might have to come up against. Next Saturday, you and any you'd care to have come with you are welcome to supper. See you then!"

Hoy tipped his hat. "I'll be there! Heard about Josie's cookin' from Deke! That's something I aim to see for myself!"

Deke approached the buggy on Beemis' side. "I'd like to stay…well, what I mean is after we get this guard thing going okay…do you suppose you might consider taking me on again? I'd be willin' to start all over…"

The old boy's eyes told it all before the words came tumbling out. "You're coming back on one condition, Deke Landry! You're either my foreman or you might just as well take the same trail Horn did. Well, which is it?"

Deke was all smiles. He knew he'd be welcome—more than welcome. Yet, it had to be done his way.

"Deke?"

"Yes, Annie!"

"Do you still have that heavy, old cardboard suitcase? The one that needs a rope tied around it to keep everything from falling out?"

He scratched his head with the brim of his Stetson. "Yeah…needs two ropes now, instead of one…why?"

"When you come back to me…I mean when you come back to stay, I'd like to buy you a real suitcase…but like Uncle Beemis said, it's got one condition tied around it."

Everyone there saw what true love could do between two people. It could transcend all else, even those who want something good to happen again. "Shucks, Annie, I liked the way you put it first…but yes, if that'll make you happy, then go ahead, buy it! What's the condition?"

"I'm hoping things will work out between us…If it's alright with you, I'd like to keep the suitcase in my room…until it's needed for our honeymoon! It's never to be used if you plan on leaving again. Deal?"

Deke wanted to kiss her, to hug her so hard she'd squeal with delight. He wanted to hold her so tight, Beemis would've had to get a crowbar to pry them apart. He wanted to do other things too, provided she gave him the right encouragement, the kind only lovers sense and understand. Yet for all those feelings, he was obliged to keep those thoughts and feelings bottled up. He offered her his second best, his hand.

The electricity between them sizzled the second he felt hers slip into his. He tried to come up with some well-chosen words to tell her he shared her love, now more than ever. Instead, he blurted out the obvious. "It's a deal!"

It was simplicity itself, yet to Annie, no poet could've fashioned a better response regardless of the words chosen. "See you tomorrow, bright and early!"

The ride back to the Markham ranch started in silence, except for the occasional clucks Beemis gave to his team. Everyone was alone with his or her thoughts. It was time to reflect on the day and to draw from it, what each had contributed and received. Beemis stopped to let Wally drop off the guns they'd collected from Jessy's customers.

Wally dumped the hardware next to the lightning-hit stump, then just stood there.

Beemis waited a tolerable length of time and then said, "Wally, it's over! Horn's gone, and we're all alive and kicking! Try to look at it that way! Get in!"

Wally's anger erupted. "By lettin' him go, it makes me out a liar! I'm not a liar, Beemis! Don't care if Horn wrote two-dozen letters, I know who I saw on July eighth! It was Tom Horn! Nobody better say different!"

Beemis turned to get a read on Josie and Annie in the backseat. Neither gave him any support. "You're not a liar, Wally, Horn played it out his way! The smart ones always do! That's why they stay alive and people like Rash and all the other cutthroats and outlaws end up gettin' hung or shot! Horn's just like Cassidy, always figurin' a way out, always having a backup plan."

Josie broke her silence. "Maybe they're alike that way, but don't you dare compare Butch Cassidy to that animal we had tied up! I know what Delores is, but he had no call to treat her that way! She liked him! Maybe even loved him!"

Beemis let Josie's words settle the dust, so to speak. He turned to have his say, looking directly at her. "Cassidy and Horn are closer to bein' alike than you realize, Sugarplum. When Cassidy needs a woman, don't worry, he uses them the same way Horn does...You were his only exception...leave it at that. With Horn, there are no exceptions, just more like Delores!"

Annie decided neither her uncle nor her sister were ever going to change their minds about Cassidy or Horn. "Get in, Wally! Let's see if we can put our heads together to figure out how Horn pulled this off."

Wally took his seat next to Beemis, and they were off. Nobody ventured another word or a thought until they passed under the main gate leading to the ranch. "Stop the team! Stop the team! I know how Horn did it!"

"Whoa! Whoa, there!" Beemis brought his team to a complete stop. "Alright, Annie, how'd he do it? How'd he manage to be in two places at the same time?"

Annie had everybody's attention. "Wally, you were right! You did see Horn on July eighth, the same day he murdered Matt Rash! Horn wrote the letter from Denver alright, but he dated it, allowing enough time so that he could ride here to do his dirty work, and then have somebody back in Denver mail it for him. That way he could prove he had been in Denver if things didn't pan out the way he expected. We were the fly in his ointment! We almost had him! He had to use the letter as his way out! That's why he sat there so smug and arrogant! He knew Deke would find that letter! And, of course, we let him go!"

Everybody felt drained from the struggle Tom Horn had put them through. When Beemis suggested that everybody hit the hay, no one objected. There was now an overwhelming consensus that no matter what showed up next, for the most part, they'd seen it all! Though not spoken in just so many words, each in his own way felt that they had somehow turned the corner on stopping Ora Haley's complete takeover. True, no guards had been posted yet to stop Haley's night riders, but they had a plan—a workable plan. And for the first time, tomorrow offered them something besides more murders, hangings, lies, and deceit. Tomorrow offered them hope and a reasonable chance of security.

Josie wrestled with her pillow and bed sheets. Her covers had been kicked to the floor long ago. Butch Cassidy's name had stirred old feelings in her, feelings that would not go away. There was a restlessness within her heart and her body that must be answered in the only way she knew how to control them: It was time to share those feelings with Annie.

Down the hall she went, clad in her thin, cotton nightgown. It was too warm to slip on a robe for just twenty feet to Annie's bedroom. She grasped the doorknob and pushed in. Beams of moonlight flooded the room, turning it into half daylight. Annie had opened her curtains and sat on the window ledge; she, too, was not ready for sleep.

"Thought I'd catch you up...care for some company?"

"Sure, pull up your nightgown and join me."

They looked out the window, their faces and upper bodies bathed in ribbons of moonlight. "Butch is on your mind again...saw it the minute you tried to defend him against what Uncle Beemis said. Wasn't going to mention this, but since Butch has center stage again, Wally ran into Sheriff Neiman while in Denver. Neiman says the law's more than certain Butch has skipped the country. Best guess, according to Neiman, is South America."

Annie saw the look of relief cross Josie's face long before the words came. "Thank God! Maybe in a new country, he can make a fresh start...turn his life around."

"You mean like he tried to do here? That pardon business that failed when he wanted to marry you?"

Josie's handsome face came into play. "No...not the same as here...In a new country, they won't know him; he won't need that pardon."

"Depends on what he does for a living, Sugarplum. If he's not well heeled wherever he's at, it'll be business as usual, and we both know what that means, don't we?"

Josie refused comment. "What about you, Sis? What kind of a day did you have?"

"I've never been so happy and angry at the same time! Horn got away with one, and we both know it! He's worse than a wolf in sheep's clothing! He's a killer first and a cattle detective second! Not the other way around!"

"What about all that happiness? I hope Deke's coming back had something to do with it?"

Annie hugged her sister. "Everything! I never truly realized until today how much he means to me...Boy, do I ever love that mop of red hair that calls himself Deke Landry!"

Josie released their embrace. "Any other thoughts?"

"I know what you're leading up to! No, Sis, ten Elza Lays could never get to me...not anymore! There's only one man I love! I've been handed a second chance, and believe you me, I won't muff it this time!"

"Good! I'm so happy for you! Wish I felt as happy as you do tonight..."

"You will! You will! Just give yourself time; it'll happen!"

Josie laughed. "We sure do know each other. No wonder we get along so well!"

This time Annie had the last laugh. "That wasn't always so, was it? One other thing, Sis, how did Deke and Adam Hoy happen by Jessy's dive at the right time?"

"This time I've got the answer. Deke and Hoy rode here to see Beemis. Shorty told them we were at Jessy's. Deke had talked Hoy into coming here...seems he had about the same idea about guarding the trails that Uncle

Beemis came up with."

"Anything else?"

Annie had opened her heart up to her sister, so it was time for some good advice. "It took an awful lot for Deke to swallow his pride and hurt feelings to want to come back. When that mop of red hair shows up tomorrow morning, make sure you give him plenty of reason to stick around."

"Is that Sugarplum talking or just another motherly lecture?"

"Both!"

CHAPTER EIGHT

Old Henry said, "I seen this certain look on the old cowpoke's face—like he'd just been told all the Confederate money he'd hid for years in his mattress wasn't worth dry spit."

Annie slipped into the bunkhouse in time to catch Deke washing up. She pressed a finger to her lips, letting Shorty McCallum know that she wanted to pull off a big surprise.

Deke was hunched over the washbasin, his eyes closed, trying to locate the towel on a peg above him. Once, twice, he reached up with no success. "Dang it, Shorty! I'm too damned tired for games! Now gimmee the towel!"

Annie slipped the towel into Deke's open hand and stood directly behind him.

"That's better!" He raised up to wipe his face. "Since when have you taken to wearin' perfume? Lord a'mighty, you smell good 'nough to kiss."

Tex and Slim let out a roar. Deke turned to see what was so funny.

Annie stepped out behind him. "Will I do? I don't look much like Shorty, but maybe you can make allowances."

Deke grabbed Annie before she could finish her sentence. While in their embrace, he motioned for the other three wranglers to skedaddle. Finally, his lips left hers. "Annie, Annie, oh, my Annie," he breathed. "Haven't had much chance to be around you since I got back…Beemis is determined that we hold up our end of the guard duty. We keep three men up on top at all times…doesn't give us much time to catch any sleep."

"Who's up on top of Irish Trail spelling you off?"

"Got Cleve and Clyde Dreschler to give me some time off. Angus McLaren is the third man." He hugged her hard. "Oh Lord, you feel so good when we're like this…'course I probably smell pretty strong. You probably think a billy goat smells better'n me. Just let get the Saturday-night washtub down, and some clean duds, then I'll be presentable."

Annie stayed right in their embrace. "You smell like a man to me! All man! My man! Say, couldn't I pitch in? I'm as good with a rifle as most men!"

Deke threw up the caution flag—his forefinger. "Now, now, Annie, it's no dice and you know it! Beemis made sure you're not to stand guard! That's his strict order to me! We don't know if Horn is in the park or out of it! In any case, you are the one person Horn might try to take a potshot at!"

Annie appreciated the deep concern Deke and Beemis had for her safety. "Let's not be forgetting Isom Dart, either! He's under the same orders."

They walked to the door, hand in hand, their eyes, their body movements using a whole new language—the kind only lovers use and understand. Deke broke the spell. "It's working, Annie! It's working! Four weeks gone by and not one single soul has been rousted outta bed in the middle of the night!"

"How much longer? I mean we hardly spend any time together. At first, I was just plain happy to see you again…know that you're near. But now that I can see you again…that's not enough…I want more. Don't you?"

He squeezed her hand. "Since I've come back, all I think, talk, and sleep about is you. Beemis said these are going to be the hardest times for both of us…so close again and yet so far from what we both want. I'm gonna pass up the bath until I get some work done around here! We're way behind! Beemis will come down to the stables wavin' another buy order, and we won't be near ready! I'll work this morning and grab some shuteye this afternoon."

"Okay, but let me fix breakfast first! I'll fix your favorites, buck wheats and sausage. That way, I'll get to see you a bit longer…even if you've got a fork and knife in your hands instead of me!"

Deke was right. Gradually, most of the ranchers rallied around Beemis' plan to post guards at the three trails' entrances. Some called it vigilante business, others simply said it was association work that needed doing. Whatever the handle, it made sleeping at night a whole lot easier for all of the

Park's residents. As more and more volunteers showed up, a roster was developed so that Deke and the Hoy brothers could devote more time to getting their own ranch work back to their normal routines.

Those who worked around Beemis and those who loved him saw a remarkable change in the man. Gone was the "hanger-on" look of a man waiting for something to happen—either bad or good! Instead, he was his old, take-charge self once more. He was up at the crack of dawn, expecting breakfast to be waiting for him as he rounded the hallway corner into the kitchen. If it wasn't, a kindly rap on Josie's bedroom door meant the old boy was hungry as a mountain lion.

He'd pause after the first rap, and if he heard Josie stirring, he'd say, "You'll find me down at the stables; call me when breakfast is ready!"

Isom Dart was an entirely different situation. It made no difference if Beemis had given the order or he imposed the sentence on himself. Either way, he refused to go anywhere without at least one of the Markham wranglers accompanying him. Father Time, too, had exacted his own sentence on Isom. The years suddenly caught up with him. His hair went from coal black to snow white in only a matter of a few months. Those who worked around and with him couldn't help but note the change in his muscular build. They noticed the first signs of sagging flesh taking hold in a man whose body had been the envy of every man he met. Deke said he had the look of death about him; the only thing missing was the time and place. For all the changes that had claimed the man, nobody ever accused Dart of shirking any job given him, provided somebody was nearby. The fear of death stalked him. It showed in his eyes, his face, and even in the words he used.

One Sunday afternoon, the usual poker game was in progress. Shorty McCallum had lady luck perched on his shoulder; he'd licked the pot clean five straight times. Isom stood behind Shorty, watching his run of good cards, hand after hand after hand. Shorty turned to the Negro. "C'mon Isom, sit in on a hand or two! Make you forgit 'bout other things…"

Isom shifted stances. "Shorty, now, don't take this wrong…ah means don't git all mad…but ah hopes yo lose a hand or two…'cause ah gots to go see Pa Jones real bad! Ah needs yo to go wit me!"

Shorty looked across the table at Deke. His boss gave him the nod. "Sure, Isom, I'll go! Just let me play out this hand!"

They left and the card game continued. Tex tossed in his hand. "Still can't believe a man as big and strong as Isom is needs somebody to stand outside the can while he's inside doin' his business!"

Slim folded his hand too, leaving Deke and the cook to settle the round. "Yeah, one look at Dart and you'd have to say he'd never need a rifle to take on a grizzly bear; either his bare hands or a buggy whip would do just fine!"

Deke slept in late after finishing his three-day guard duty at the top of Irish Trail. Josie's breakfast had been history now, as they say, a good four hours ago. Annie brought down coffee, toast, bacon, and scrambled eggs on a tray to his bunkhouse. She passed the steaming cup of java under his nose, hoping to tease or tantalize him into kissing her good morning, or at the very least, getting him to sit up. On the second pass, she felt two very hot, passionate lips, surrounded by three-days' worth of stubble, doing their best to let her know he was wide awake.

"Love, the lips can stay, but that beard has got to go!"

Annie rested the tray on his lap and waited for him to dive in. He didn't disappoint. Between bites of toast and bacon, he managed to say something that pleased her. "You're gettin' pretty darned good at this breakfast thing. Sure beats the heck outta tough, old beef jerky, cold beans, and coffee that shoulda been thrown out two days ago!"

"It's payday! Or haven't you noticed? I need another good-morning kiss before I leave you alone to finish your breakfast and get cleaned up."

He put down his coffee cup long enough to grant her request. After, he said, "I'd like to improve on that last kiss; maybe we can get in some practice later on..."

She liked where his thoughts were headed. "Deke, we haven't taken one ride together since you came back. I know Beemis would insist that we take our rifles with us...just in case...but that shouldn't stop us from being together whenever we can, now should it?"

She made a good point. He no longer could hedge his answer. "I've been puttin' off our rides; if we ride, it might mean stopping somewhere...where we might be tempted to use our saddle blankets for something besides what they were intended for. Old memories might come back...lots of hurt could creep in again, and I don't think either one of us could handle that again. I know I couldn't."

He, too, had made a good point. Annie decided not to push it for now. "At least come on up to the main house to get paid. Beemis would like to see you...Josie, too! And having you around me would really be great...even if going for a ride is the farthest thing on your mind...for now."

Annie left Deke to finish breakfast and get cleaned up. She walked the well-worn path back to the main house, her mind on just one thing: getting Deke in her arms long enough to make his passion come alive. She knew she could make that happen. All she needed was the right opportunity. Ever since his return, she'd felt his eyes upon her many times, trying to undress her over and over in his mind, trying his best to remember how much of her body he'd touched and enjoyed. She wondered how he could stand being so close to her again and not take the chance to try again. She was also convinced that if she let him explore her charms again, the old hurt would go away because she would make sure he wouldn't have time to think about it; he'd be too busy trying to knock on the gates to paradise.

Beemis sat on the porch in his rocker with his three favorite people gathered around him. Supper was over, the dishes were done, everybody had put in a good work day, and it was time to enjoy each other's company amidst the gathering shadows of dusk. He rocked back and forth a dozen times and then stopped. "Never seen it so quiet and peaceful-like…'Tain't natural considering how things have gone so far…"

Josie leaned against one of the thick timbers, which supported the roof over the porch. She continued Beemis' thought. "You're saying this might be the lull before the storm. Mister Two-Bar has been too quiet…far too quiet."

"Yeah, here it is late September, and everything's goin' our way. Not one night rider and nobody's seen hide nor hair of Horn. I tell ya, it ain't natural! Two-Bar's too big an outfit to run and hide like a whipped dog! My Army days taught me one thing. When things are going too good to be true, that's when you'd better expect trouble."

Annie and Deke sat together on the top plank step. She had absorbed her uncle's and sister's thoughts about Ora Haley's sudden no-show. She turned to Deke with her own question in mind. "When you're up on top, do you see anything of Haley's cattle herds or the man himself?"

Deke rose to stretch the kinks out. "Never see nothin' of Haley, but you can sure hear his herds milling around. Boy, are those cattle ever noisy! They start to stray our way and then either some of Ora's point riders or swing rides come turn 'em back."

Beemis smiled. "Swing riders? Point riders? Guess those cowboying days over at Hoy's ranch taught you their language."

Deke laughed. "Yeah, I used those words 'cause I didn't want you folks to think my days over there was a total waste! Which they were!"

Everybody gave out a hearty round of laughter. Even Deke joined in.

Annie was the first to stop laughing. "Any other thoughts, dear?"

He helped her up. "Yeah, just one! I'm ready for a little race to the horse stables! How about you?"

Annie couldn't believe her good fortune. At long last she knew Deke had come back to her—all the way back. Every bone in her body, every nerve in her stomach told her that he wanted her as much as she needed him. Her question was a check on reality. "Does that include a little ride, too? After the race?"

"You bet!"

Annie was the first down the plank steps. Already her heart was on fire just thinking about what she knew was going to happen. She used the toe of her boot to draw a line in the soft dirt beside the steps. "Sis, you say go when we're ready!"

Beemis and Josie stood behind the two as they inched up to the line, ready for their mad dash to the horse stables. Annie turned to her sister. Josie read the soft smile spread across Annie's face, and the love fairly dancing in her eyes. It was sister-to-sister talk, the kind that spelled victory for one, deep satisfaction for the other.

"Ready! Set...GO!"

They were off! Deke took an early lead, then slowed down to let Annie draw alongside. When they were even, the elbowing and pushing reduced the race down to little more than a snail's pace.

"Look at them, Uncle! Didja ever see the beat of it? They're still a good hundred yards from the stable door and neither gives a darn who gets there first! Betch'a I know what'll happen when they get to the door!"

"Yeah, Sugarplum? What?"

"They'll close that door and boy will the kissin' ever begin!"

"Good! That'll give us time to fetch their rifles on their way out for that so-called ride! They're both so ready for each other, neither's thinkin' about takin' some real, long-range protection with 'em!"

Josie hugged her uncle. "You know those two pretty well, don't you?"

"Yup! One's the same as my daughter, and the other is going to be the son I never had! Deke's got two things on his mind...just hope Annie can separate the wish from the want and turn it all into a downright need for both of 'em to see their way toward a preacher!"

Josie and Beemis tactfully waited for the stable door to finally open. When it finally did, each handed up a rifle to the surprised riders. Off they went, down the trail, toward the main gate. When they reached it, both stopped to wave back at Josie and Beemis.

"You said Deke had two things on his mind. That's why he told Annie, in a couple of ways, he was ready. Care to tell me what they might be?"

Beemis put his arm around Josie. They started back to the main house. "Deke's bustin' at the seams with a man's love for our Annie. Now, now, he wants to do the right thing by our Annie…trouble is, his manhood could keep him from doin' what's right. Annie's got to help him see it so both of 'em get what they want…"

Josie kept her uncle's thoughts to herself until they reached the porch again. "Are all men like that? I mean that terrible man at Jessy Wiggins' place only had one thing on his mind…"

"You're right, Sugarplum! That's the difference between a real man and an animal. A four-legged animal only sees it one way! Nature made him that way! With a man, he's given the choice…it's up to him! Either stand up on two legs and be a man about it or else get back down on all fours and act like he just left the monkeys and the lions behind."

Deke picked the pace as they rode side by side along the trail toward the clump of cottonwoods next to Vermillion Creek. Annie watched his every move, hoping to get a better read on him. She felt sure they would not be stopping at their old spot; yet she couldn't help wondering just where they were headed and exactly what he had in mind on such a lovely evening. Just the mere anticipation of him in her arms, letting her take him as far as she wanted him to, made her heart do flip-flops. She was prepared to give him anything he wanted, if only she heard the right words without having to coax them out of him. That was her one condition: He had to profess his love for her of his own free will.

They approached the trail leading directly to the cottonwoods. Annie slowed down a bit, waiting for Deke to take the led, giving her a true indication of just what he had in mind.

Her heart skipped several beats as Deke never even looked toward the old, inviting cottonwoods. Instead, he opened his horse up, ready to really give his mount a good blow. "Follow me," he shouted back.

Annie opened Glory up as the horse responded to her master's commands. "C'mon, Glory! C'mon! Don't let Deke say you're getting fat and sassy when we stop! Go, girl! Go!"

Deke veered sharply to the left. He headed toward a grotesque-looking promontory of sandstone mounds and buttes that jutted out in this section of the Park. Up, up, he went, picking a little-used and little-known path between the lower reaches. Suddenly, he headed toward a small box canyon wedged between two huge mounds. It gave him what he wanted: complete privacy.

By the time Annie caught up, Deke was waiting for her with open arms. She leaped into his arms and their passion was on.

He tore two buttons off her work shirt in his haste to get at her breasts.

"Deke, Deke, my love, slow down. I'll let you have them…just take it easy…"

She quickly unbuttoned the other three buttons, not wanting to return with all her buttons missing. Josie might be waiting up, and she never missed anything!

He peeled her shirt back. "Oh, Lord, Annie, they're better, much better than I remembered…stickin' out so…oh, Lord, Annie!"

He went at them like a famished child who'd been denied his nipple and milk for two days.

Annie could only hold on and smile, letting him suck to his heart's content. She watched the immense satisfaction spread across his face. Even the smacking sounds he made seemed extra special, it was that good between them. She waited for him to change nipples; then she stroked his hair. "I love you, I love you, I love you," she kept saying over and over, urging him on.

Suddenly, he left her breasts and stood up. He went for her lips. Everything about him was on fire. Even in their most passionate moments before, she'd never seen him like this. He kissed her hard, then harder, trying in some way to make up for all the lost time he'd missed not savoring her buds, her soft, cherry lips.

"Deke, Deke," she managed to murmur, "please slow down…so we can both enjoy—slow down…"

Some of her words finally sank in. "I'm sorry, I'm sorry," he blurted out. "It's that I love you so much, want you bad. I can't stop."

He had opened the key to her heart with the right words without so much as one subtle little hint or bit of coaching. Now Annie was on fire. Down came her jeans, then her pantaloons. She wanted him to see, then take.

Deke didn't disappoint. Not this time. He dropped to his knees and kissed her navel and then went lower into her thatch.

Annie held on, sighing over and over, holding his head, urging him on with her body movements. Lord, what pleasure! What exquisite pleasure each was giving the other.

Suddenly, Deke raised up. He wanted in. How could she refuse him? He slipped one of her boots off, so she wouldn't be hobbled for what he wanted to do to her.

"Shouldn't we use one of our saddle blankets? It'll be much better that way, love."

She didn't hear him answer one way or the other. Instead he tried to lift her up so she'd be in a position for his shaft. "Can't wait," he replied. "I'm too hot! Too ready! I want you so bad! Put your arms around me and open up!"

Annie tried to hook her legs behind his to help him hold her up. She now realized he was more than on fire, he was ready to explode. "Here, love, let me take hold..."

The second she took hold, it was all over—her.

"On, my Lord, oh, my Lord!" he said, so embarrassed, so angry with himself.

She kissed him. "It's alright, love, it's alright, I understand. Let's finish it off. Just give it to me...I'll do the rest..."

She let Deke stroke into her thatch, draining him dry. When it was over, she kissed him again and again, trying to reassure him that it was alright, that he'd gotten in too big of a hurry, that's all!

Deke let her slide back down. Yet they stayed locked into their embrace.

"Deke?"

"Yeah?"

"I liked what you did to me. I know you love me more than ever...I've never seen you like this...so full of love...so ready to give me what I need."

"Yeah, and so out of control. Promise you won't laugh or bring this up...I'm so sorry...all this way out here and look what a mess I made...all over you."

She kissed him again. "Deke, most of your love went where it was supposed to go...Next time we'll both do better and we'll both slow down."

"Annie?"

"Yes, love."

"I think we'd better set a date to get hitched. A bed will sure beat the heck outta this. Didn't want to bring this up, but my back was killin' me. Only when you said go ahead...well, I kinda liked it too."

They kissed again. This time both savored the moment and each other's kiss.

"When do you want to get married? We'd better make it soon. After what happened between us, the sooner, the better!"

"How about next payday? We only work half a day; it'll give everybody an excuse to celebrate."

"And Josie will bake our wedding cake. I'll let you get the preacher."

"Annie."

"Yes, my love, my darling husband."

"There's an awful lot of work to do back at the ranch. How 'bout hangin' a sign on your bedroom door sayin' don't bother us for two days? Maybe just slip into the kitchen for a little grub and then back into your bedroom for more honeymoonin'."

"Fine by me! We'll keep that new suitcase I bought for our first wedding anniversary. Then we'll really take a trip...go somewhere..."

Deke turned his back on Annie while he tried to put everything back where it belonged.

Annie smiled at Deke's return to modesty. "Hey, hey, Mister Landry! When we're married, there'll be no turning our backs on each other, either when we're dressing or undressing! Agreed?"

"Well...okay, it's a deal!"

"Oh, Deke?"

"Yeah, Annie, now what?"

"As long as your back is still turned to me, how about pulling that farmer-sized hanky outta your pocket and loaning it to me? Got some wiping up to do!"

Deke's near-miss and his display of raw passion bonded him to Annie like never before. The two were inseparable! The minute they were around one another, whether at the stables or up to the main house, their obvious love for each other smoldered near the spillover point. Beemis took note of the situation and remarked, "Thank God, they're gettin' hitched! I've never seen two people more ready to jump into bed with each other than those two!"

Josie smiled at her uncle's candid assessment of the two lovebirds. She, too, added her own thoughts to the upcoming nuptials. "Annie says she's gonna hang a sign outside her bedroom door. 'On our honeymoon, do not disturb for two days.' I might just as well hang my sign under it. It'll say, 'Leave two pieces of wedding cake by the door and knock!' That's about as far away from the bedroom as they're going to get for two days!"

Beemis and Josie had more than a good chuckle over each other's thoughts.

"Did Deke get ahold of a preacher?"

"Yes, dear Uncle, he's coming all the way from Vernal. The Reverend

Enoch Schaffer will be here by this weekend. Annie's even thinking about having him stay over to hold regular Sunday service, once a month, from now on."

"Let me guess! Charley Crouse's schoolhouse will be put to use! Too bad old Charley's building never got used for what it was built for."

"Well, Deke and Annie's wedding will be held there! That's a start!"

"Guess those two years at the academy did Annie more good than we first thought. Besides coming down with sore knees and learning to play the organ, our Annie's got religion!"

Angus McLaren motioned for Deke to come running. "Hurry, Deke! Over this way! What should we do?"

Deke chambered a cartridge into his rifle. It could be the first sign of trouble—Two-Bar trouble! He ran up to the crest of a small hill to join Angus. "Where? I don't see any Two-Bar riders...just a small herd of Two-Bar cattle comin' this way. They've been branding for two weeks that we know of."

Angus pointed to the two dozen or so cattle headed their way. His Scotch background did most of the talking. "Maybe they're Two-Bar and maybe they ain't! Can't spot a brand on 'em, anywhere! What say we make a little money for a change? Let Ora Haley foot the bill!"

Deke licked his chops at the prospect. "These were missed during the branding. I count them as mavericks; they're fair game for whoever brands 'em first! That's range law! Learned that from the Hoys!"

Ben Ulrich, the third guard, joined them. "Damned good idea! Let's let 'em pass! Then get somebody to brand 'em, and we're in business!"

Angus was already counting his share in his head. "I ain't got any branding irons..." He looked at Deke. "Your uncle's got the best damn brand-man in the business working for him! We'll cut him in for a share! All ya gotta do, man, is ask him!"

Deke's enthusiasm dimmed considerably. "Isom won't budge from the ranch for love nor money...He thinks Horn is still around, ready to kill him if he ever goes anywhere alone."

Ulrich, like Angus, liked their chances. "Now, Deke, we all know what's on your mind these days, what with your wedding less than a week away. How about doin' Angus and me a favor by askin' Dart if he'd care to make some extra money? There's an old line shack up near Summit Springs. That'd be just right for our little branding operation. Make sure you tell Dart he won't be alone! Betch'a he'll go for it if you tell him that!"

335

Angus backed Ulrich. "Deke, it's in the man's blood! Once a brand-change man, always a brand-change man! Man, don't let this pass us by! Ask him!"

Annie and Josie watched from the kitchen doorway while Deke, Angus, and Ben gave Beemis their best reasons for picking up considerable spare cash by branding twenty-eight mavericks from the Two-Bar herd. Beef prices were high, which meant even if they had to split another share with Isom Dart doing the branding, the take for each man's share would be considerable.

"Oh, oh! There goes Beemis' specs down off the bridge of his nose. He's heard enough! I don't think they're going to like what he's about to lay on them!"

Beemis rose from his chair, cane in hand. "Got two things to say, and I'll expect all three of you to abide by what I'm going to tell you! First off, you shoulda run those cattle right back up the trail toward the main herd! But since your pocketbooks got in the way of your brains, and those cattle are in the Park, you can go ask Isom if he wants in. If he says yes, then let him do it, but all three of you will have no truck with such dealings. You're out! All of you! I'm responsible for guarding Irish Trail, and so help me, Hannah, so long as you're takin' orders from me, none of my guards are gonna get mixed up in this! That's my final say on the matter! Any questions?"

"What if Isom doesn't want to do the branding?"

"Well, Deke, since you three saw fit to let 'em walk right by all of you, it'll be up to you three to drive 'em right back up Irish Trail and hand 'em over to the nearest Two-Bar cowpoke you can find!"

Beemis opened the front-room door and pointed outside with his cane. "Good day, gentlemen! Deke, you can speak to Dart about this, but before you go, I need to have a word with you."

Josie turned to her sister. "Boy, you sure called that one right. Wonder what Beemis is holding back for Deke's ears alone?"

Annie smiled. "He's going to remind Deke about some things…like responsibility and such. He'll close the door, so we can't hear what's really on his mind."

Beemis winked at the two sisters as if to tell them he wouldn't be too hard on Deke, then closed the door to keep his conversation private. He waited a full three minutes, watching Deke stew in his own uncertainty. Next, he put his arm around Deke's shoulder. "Son, I know and understand about your life. You come from hard times, and this was your chance to come by some easy money." He crooked one finger in front of Deke and said, "Let's take a little walk."

Down the front-porch plank steps the two went. Beemis and Deke exchanging small talk, the typical kind a father and son would indulge each other in. When they stood on a small rise near the clothesline, Beemis lifted his cane and with one sweeping motion covered the immediate horizon. "See it, Deke? The land, the buildings, the big herd of horses, plenty of pasture! Looks pretty good, doesn't it?"

Deke nodded.

Beemis laid his other hand across Deke's shoulder. "Four days from now, son, it's all yours! All yours for you and Annie to run and operate as you see fit. Son, I know your life's not been an easy one! You know the feelin' of hunger gnawing at your stomach 'cause you've missed more than a few meals. I know you've had to take any kind of work just so you'd have something to eat and a place to stay. I also know you've missed a good many regular paydays and that you've never had much money left after those paydays finally came. That's all in the past, Deke, where it belongs! If you and Annie play your cards right, you'll never have to worry about work or money for the rest of your lives…"

Deke interrupted. "I still want to line up for my payday just like the rest of the crew."

"Fine, son, fine by me! Just remember, any time you need something, from now on you won't have to wait for next payday to get it. All you gotta do is tell Annie how much you need and it's yours! She'll pay the bills, and she'll show you our book. I think you'll be more than a bit surprised at how healthy the Markham ranch really is!" He pulled Deke in a little closer. "Son, there'll never be a need to look at easy money comin' down the trail again for the takin'! Are you catchin' my drift?"

Deke gulped. "I see what you're drivin' at…There was no need to even be thinkin' about the quick cash those unbranded cattle would bring!"

Beemis was all smiles. "Exactly, son, exactly! We're not in the cattle business and certainly will have no need to meddle in it! When I retire, four days from now, my job will be to make sure all of our back-East customers know that we will continue to breed the finest Arabians this side of the Atlantic! I'm going to write to every one and tell them that I'm not dead or dying and that the Markham ranch is a family business and will continue on that way. I'll also introduce you and Annie in my letters so that later on, when you folks do go back East, they'll know who you are and what you're up to!"

"You've got it all worked out, haven't you?"

Beemis toyed with his cane. He liked the compliment. "Yes, Deke, I have! All that's left is for you and Annie to say 'I do.'"

"What about Josie? I'm sure you haven't forgotten her, have you?"

Beemis was delighted by Deke's question. "No, son, I sure haven't! After you're married, ask Annie to let you peek at Josie's account book. There's enough money in it for her to be independent for a good many years if she chooses to follow that trail. Josie's a ranch-type woman, so I expect she'll get married and start her own family before too long…she's really waitin' on you two! You do know that, don'tcha?"

Deke pumped Beemis' hand. "Well, in four more days, she can stop worryin'! We'll be hitched and then she can get married to Cleve Dreschler."

"Son, marriage proposals just don't drop outta the sky like rain drops! Josie will stick around to see how you and Annie are handling the ranch! Then she'll drop a hint or two in Cleve's direction that she's thinking 'bout settling down. If he's half the man I think he is, he'll be over here every evenin,' courting the heck outta her until she finally says yes. Josie's not the type to be pushed or rushed into anything. That's what that Mormon-nice outlaw, Cassidy, never learned when he showed up here! Thank the good Lord for that!"

They continued their little stroll. Beemis would stop every few yards or so to point out and make suggestions about things around the ranch that needed doing in the near future. Then he'd always end up with his patented one-liner. "Of course, Deke, these are only suggestions; you and Annie do as you see fit…"

Deke finally told the old boy to stop. "You know, Beemis, my folks dumped me out to take on the cold world at the age of twelve. Never had much of a father…but if I had, I'd sure want him to be an awful lot like you!"

A coughing jag overtook the old boy. The specs came off his ears, and he blew his nose and wiped his eyes, and coughed some more, trying to clear his throat from some imaginary obstacles lodged in it. Having succeeded, the specs went back of, only this time they stayed down on the nose, so he could peer over them at the young man he thought the world of. "Bless you, my son! Bless you! You're as close to being my own son as I'd ever want!"

Isom Dart handled Deke's news about the maverick herd with a relish Deke had thought was long gone. His eyes bugged out, he licked his chops, figuratively and literally, and finally said, "Is you sayin' they's mine? All I haft'a do is brand 'em, then sell 'em! Man, oh man! Isom, hear dat cash money jinglin' in yo' pocket once more! Is'e gonna sprout wings n' fly dis here jail Horn done put me into! Californeee, here Is'e come!"

Deke stood before the mighty hulk of a man. "Before you get to celebratin' too much, Beemis is waiting up for you. You'll find him in his favorite rocker on the front porch. See that he's not kept waitin' too long!"

Isom's long strides took the Negro up to see Beemis in record time. Beemis kept moving his rocker back and forth, trying to tone down Dart's obvious excitement. "I take it, by the way you practically flew up here, you've decided to brand those mavericks!"

"Yes, Sir, Mistah Beemis! I done give some idee on it…an' Is'e willin' to do it! All I gotta do is stop by my place to git my brandin' irons n' such!'"

"Did Deke tell you that if you go ahead, you do it without any help from us! We want no part of this! Is that understood?"

Isom rolled his eyes from side to side. "Oh, yes, Sir, Mistah Beemis! Is'e knows jus' who to git…won't be no trouble, no how!"

Beemis rocked some more. "Yes…I was sure you'd probably come up with somebody. One last thing…if you leave here, you can't come back! I won't have a job waitin' on you or a bunk! Is that clear?"

Dart seemed in a big hurry to get the conversation over with. His ham-sized paw swallowed Beemis' hand like it was missing. "An Is'e thank yo, Mistah Beemis, fer what you done fer me. Sho' won't fo'git dat! Yo'all has a good day now an' a good weddin' too with Miss Annie and Deke!"

Beemis rose from his rocker. "Horn could be around! Aren't you afraid anymore?"

Dart puffed up his chest like a barnyard rooster ready to crow. "No, Sir, Mistah Beemis. Figure if'n Horn was here, ah'd know'd 'bout it by now!" He held out both hands to Beemis. "See! Dem shakes is all gone! No mo' shakes! No mo' Horn!"

Beemis watched the big Black walk away. He'd been a model wrangler, always taken on any job given him without some of the usual bitches and gripes that usually accompanied one or two of the not-so-pleasant tasks associated with horse breeding and raising. It wouldn't be the first or last time a man, any man, would succumb to the lure of easy money. He hoped Dart's latest go for freedom and independence would pan out.

Isom Dart was his old self again, master of what he did best: branding cattle. Even the remoteness of the old line-shack blended in beautifully with his little branding operation. There'd be no prying eyes or embarrassing questions about how this many cattle had managed to fall into his hands. Dart had no trouble finding three willing partners to help him do the branding. George Canty, Longhorn Thompson, and Joe Davenport were the perfect type of people he needed. Each had bent the law, considerably, outside of their safe refuge in the Park, and two of them had been whispered about as being the holdup men who worked with Jessy Wiggins. Rumor had it, whenever a stranger frequented his establishment, if Jessy thought he had money, he'd arrange for an "accidental meeting" away from his dive. The customer's money would then be lifted in exchange for his life and the proceeds split with Jessy.

Dart got a late start on his first day of branding, so the four rolled out their bedrolls and slept in the shack. Longhorn Thompson looked up at stars through the numerous holes in the old roof. He wisecracked, "Don't know why in hell we bothered coming in here, I count damn near as many stars inside as outside!"

The second day dawned in brilliant sunshine. The cold, crisp October air made the four glad that they had warm blankets wrapped around them. Isom was the first to leave his bedroll. His breath hung heavy as he urged the others to do the same. "Hey, dere's cash money comin' from those moo's you done heard. Only twelve more to go and we'se headed for Jessy's joint. He done promised sixty dolla' a head! Let's git to it!"

"Hell, Isom, we can get a hundred dollars a head, anywhere on top! Jessy's stickin' it to us!"

Isom eyed Joe Davenport. "Ah ain't 'bout to drive these here cattle past Beemis' post men. Ah'm gonna takes what ah kin git, and fly dis here jail! Californeee, here ah comes!"

"Didn'tcha at least bring a coffee pot? Christ, my gut's growlin' somethun' fierce! A cup'a java sure would help quiet the noise!"

"Quit'cher bitchin,' Longhorn! You can fill your gut later at Jessy's. Maybe give Delores a goin' over too, if she's willin' to go out back."

George Canty's remark to Longhorn took care of the complaints. It was time to get outside, start the pit fire to warm up Isom's branding irons, and make some pretty fair change, as they say.

Dart left the shanty first, followed closely by George Canty and Joe Davenport. Longhorn Thompson was still inside, huddled under his blankets, waiting for the fire to get started so he could warm the chill out of his bones.

He lumbered along; he could feel the weight of the gold coins rubbing a sore spot in his front pants pocket, there'd be so many to count. He looked up just as the early morning shadow from a big ponderosa pine crossed his face.

Kerwhang! Kerwhang! Two rifle shots rang out in rapid succession. Dart never knew who or what hit him. His knees buckled, and the big Negro hit the ground with a mighty thud, killed instantly by two bullets through the head.

"GET BACK! GET BACK!" screamed Canty, who turned on a dime in his mad scramble to be first back inside the shack.

Davenport turned white as a sheet, then sprang into action, knocking Canty down in his haste to get back. They crawled over each other, neither giving an inch. Finally, Canty leaped over Davenport, landing just inside the open doorway.

"BAR THE DOOR! BAR THE DOOR!" yelled out Davenport.

Longhorn Thompson shot out from under his blankets like he'd met up with a rattler. "Hey, man," he shouted back to Joe, "you do it! It's your idea!"

All three cowered in the farthest corner from the doorway they could find, each expecting Horn to step inside and empty his rifle on them, making sure he'd left no witnesses.

One, two, three agonizing hours passed, and no Horn. Joe Davenport finally mustered up enough courage to slither toward the door on his belly. He raised one boot to the bottom door frame, and kicked at it. The door creaked and groaned, its rusty hinges allowing it to travel far enough to close with a faint click.

Longhorn peered out through a shattered piece of window pane.

"See anything? What's Horn up to?"

Longhorn answered Canty. "Damned if I know! Why don't you walk outside n' find out? If he doesn't nail you, we'll know it's okay to get the hell outta here!"

They passed the daylight hours, each daring the other to be first to open the door and step outside. There were no takers!

The fading lines of dusk filtered through the lone window before Joe Davenport came up with a solid suggestion. He'd found an old handsaw under a pile of broken-down bedsprings and bunk boards. He waved it at Canty and Thompson. "There's brush and trees right behind us. Look for a weak spot in the back wall and we'll saw our way out. After it turns dark, we can slip away."

"What about those mavericks outside? We just gonna walk away from all that money? With Isom gone, there's only three ways to split instead of four!"

George Canty answered Longhorn. "You dumb jackass! Isom ain't gone!

He's still out there! Shot through the head! Tell you what! Soon as I get the hell outta here, you can have my share, too! How's that suitcha?"

The three forgot about making any money; just staying alive suddenly took center stage in their minds. They took turns, hacking, gnawing, and cutting their way through a section of half-rotted boards. Into the black of a moonless night, the three slipped away.

George Canty took time out from his run for freedom to knock repeatedly on the solid oak door at the main house of the Markham ranch. Beemis appeared in his nightgown, holding a kerosene lamp. The minute he recognized whom his unwelcome guest was, he made sure there was no chance for Canty to step inside.

"Isom's been killed! Happened this morning! Horn did it!"

"Didja see Horn do it?"

"Did I?" Canty held up both hands in front of Beemis' face. He held his two forefingers a quarter inch apart. "I was damn near this close when Horn dropped him in his tracks!"

"But didja see Horn do it?"

"No...not exactly...but it was Horn alright!"

Beemis was beginning to do a slow boil. The wee hour in the morning didn't do much for his disposition either. "'Not exactly' doesn't cut it, Canty! Not with me! Let me show you where to put Dart's body. Got a visitin' preacher here, so we'll take care of the burying after breakfast."

The old sage had inadvertently put Canty in a real pickle. Canty tried to cover his cowardice. "Dart ain't here...left him up by that shack near Summit Springs."

Beemis exploded. "You mean you took all day to finally get around to tell me Dart's been shot this morning?"

Canty defended himself as best he could. "Ya gotta understand, Horn was ready to murder us if we dared make a move. Had to saw our way out the back of the shack...only way we could escape!"

"Yes, I can see your predicament alright. Must've taken a lot of brave blood to saw your way out, especially if no one was there watching you do it! Who was with you?"

"Longhorn Thompson and Joe Davenport."

Beemis held the lamp close enough to singe the beard on Canty's face. "Tell you what, I'm gonna give you three brave souls another chance to show me what kinda stuff you're made of. You go back up there and bring Dart's body down here! Like I said, we do have a preacher to conduct the service.

Now, do you think you're up to doin' that?"

Canty showed his true colors. "Let the buzzards have him! Damned if I'm gonna risk my neck to help plant a dead nigger!"

Beemis was outraged. "My advice to you is to get the hell outta my sight! And be quick about it or else I'm gonna pretend I'm Tom Horn and blast you to kingdom come!"

Beemis took charge early that morning like a true general. He had everybody up and ready to roll at the crack of dawn. He even managed to put the Reverend Schaffer aboard the gentlest Arabian he had as the trail up to Summit Springs was too steep for a horse-drawn buggy.

They found Isom Dart lying in a pool of dried blood. Beemis immediately had Deke, Shorty, Tex, and Slim take turns manning the pick and shovel, digging into the hard ground until they had a hole deep enough to his satisfaction. Then he told the reverend to bring the blanket. Beemis laid the blanket next to Dart's body, rolled him over onto it, and wrapped it around him. Both ends of the blanket were tied with short pieces of rope cut from the makeshift rope corral Dart had fashioned.

Beemis approached the reverend. "We're ready for your words, Sir."

Everybody removed their hats out of respect while the reverend put forth a good effort. He let his blue-grey eyes survey the Markham Ranch crew gathered around Dart's blanketed body. Once he had their proper attention, he raised both arms in an upward, outstretched gesture toward the heavens, as far as his six-foot, slim frame would allow. "Good Lord," he began, "in all my fifty years here on earth, I've never buried a black man. I've buried Indians and Chinese, but never a Negro. Yet we all will meet our Maker, no matter what the color, when our time has come." He then spoke of man's purpose on earth and hope that somewhere along Isom Dart's troubled path through life, he had done some good things, things that would make him proud of the time he had spent with his fellow man. He then closed with two short prayers.

Deke and Shorty lowered Isom's body into the grave, using more rope from the corral. Annie left the burial scene to scout around. She went to the back of the shanty, saw where Canty and company had hacked a rough hole to make good their so-called escape. Next, she walked the same path Dart had used, continuing on past the big ponderosa, then circled back to watch Deke and Shorty finish scraping the last few shovels of dirt into the grave.

"Find or see anything?" Beemis asked.

Annie opened the palm of her right hand. "Two 30-30 shell casings," she said. "Found them behind that big pine! They're from the same kind of rifle Horn always carried."

Deke stood up to wipe his forehead. "Don't prove a thing, Annie. Since I've come into this park, I've seen at least two dozen other men, besides Horn, with 30-30s."

Shorty broke up the conversation. He pointed toward the corral. "What'll we do with those critters?"

Beemis supplied the answer. "You and Deke drive 'em down to the widow Benson's place. I heard she's hurting for payment money on her place…maybe these cattle will help do some good after all."

Annie stayed to have a word with Deke. "I don't feel much in the mood for our wedding, dear. Tomorrow's payday…Josie's probably baking our wedding cake right now."

"Me neither, now that this has happened. When we get to the ranch, I'll talk to the reverend…see if he'd be willin' to wait another week before going back…"

"Thanks, love, I'm glad you see it the same as me. After all, we've got our whole lives ahead of us…In another week, I'll be ready by then. There is one little problem, though…"

"What's that?"

"Uncle Beemis! You know what a sweet tooth he's always had. Josie will be faced with two choices: either stand guard over our wedding cake and shoo him off or else let him sample it and fix it up an hour before our wedding, so no one will know he's had more than his thumb into the frosting."

"Speakin' of Beemis, did you see the way he still sets his horse? Man, oh man, he must've been some kind of scout in his younger days."

"Wallihan told me before he left, he saw Beemis ride back East, when he was young. Said I reminded him of the way Beemis used to ride…none better was the way he put it."

Annie gave Deke a good-bye peck. "Don't forget how much I love you…see you tonight for supper. We'll both feel better when we're back at the ranch where we belong…on safe ground…away from Horn."

Beemis, Tex, Slim, and the reverend mounted up, ready for the ride back to the ranch. Shorty came running up to Beemis. "There's no marker on Isom's grave! Shouldn't we put something on it? There's already too many unmarked graves scattered all over heck in this here park! Shows nobody cares!"

"You're right, Shorty! Let's see if there's anything around we can use…"

He spotted Isom's branding iron poking out of its bed of cold coals in the fire pit. "That branding iron will be a most fitting headstone! It will call to mind that Isom was a branded man the minute he was born a slave down South! It will also call to mind that he had a choice to make when he reached free territory and that the choice he made was the wrong one! I believe Horn when he said nobody was any better at using that branding iron than Isom Dart. He was so good at it that it cost him his life!"

Tom Horn's here! Tom Horn's there! Tom Horn's everywhere! Or so it seemed! Every time one false lead or sighting popped up, ten more took its place.

The murder of Isom Dart served notice to all the small-time cattle rustlers in the park that none could guarantee they'd live to see another sunrise. Even if Horn hadn't murdered Dart, his system that never failed did a thorough housecleaning—something no law man had done or dared to do.

The exodus of the park's cattle-rustling element reached epidemic proportions. They fled their one-time sanctuary like rats leaving a sinking ship. Everyone wanted to get out and go as far away and as fast as time, money, or horseback allowed. Joe Davenport complained that the Park's winters had always been too harsh—Missouri had a much better climate. Longhorn Thompson jumped into the ice-caked Snake River to avoid a showdown with a rifle-toting stranger he swore was Tom Horn. George Canty said he had a peculiar ailment that could only be cured if he lived in Mexico. And so on and so on, the list of small-timers with built-in excuses grew like some gigantic tumbleweed that had been ripped from its roots and allowed to blow over an endless prairie. But the biggest surprise of all was the sudden departure of Jessy and Delores Wiggins. They loaded up two freight wagons one night and headed out for parts unknown and were never heard from again.

The week's delay of Annie and Deke's wedding solidified the Reverend Enoch Schaffer's standing in the Park. The good reverend and Annie prevailed upon Charley Crouse to let them hold once-a-month church services in his schoolhouse. The organ that had once been a permanent fixture in Beemis' parlor now would be moved to the schoolhouse where Annie would provide the music as the church organist. For five days, Annie and the preacher collaborated on the appropriate music so that come next Sunday's first ever preacher-held service, both would be ready. And then at two o'clock that same day, Deke and Annie would be united in holy wedlock as the nondenominational church's first married couple.

Even Beemis smiled and chuckled over the latest developments. He popped into the kitchen to make sure Josie's wedding cake was still in good shape. Josie caught him in the pantry, giving it "the finger test," as he called it. She scolded him. "Shame on you, Uncle! How in the world can you stand there and tell me a little sugar frosting just happened to catch on your finger when I see enough cake crumbs and frosting trapped in your beard to make you look like Santa Claus dived in head first?"

Beemis came up with a dandy. "Now, now, Sugarplum, let me make you a deal! I'll stand behind it tomorrow afternoon while you're doin' the serving. That way no one will ever see that big hole I accidently put in it, and it'll save you all that fuss, tryin' to patch it up!"

Josie's hands went to her hips. Even her little foot stomp and pretended look of exasperation were filled with such love for the man. "What in the world am I going to do with you?"

Again, Beemis had another gem. "Well, for starters, you might fetch me a towel and tell me where to wipe and then give me your best hug and tell me I'm still your favorite uncle!"

Josie laughed. "That's easy, you're my only uncle!"

Sunday morning finally arrived. Annie was so excited about her big day, she beat Josie to the kitchen. When Josie showed up, Annie poured her a cup of coffee. "Mrs. Deke Landry! Or should I say Mrs. Ann Landry! Sure like the sound of both!"

Josie, still half asleep, mumbled her approval.

"When are you gonna make it Mrs. Cleve Dreschler or Josephine Dreschler?"

Now Josie was wide awake. "That's none of your business, Ann Barnett! I'll get around to that when I'm darned good and ready!"

Annie laughed. "I'm in too good'a mood to worry one way or the other! But you're running out of time calling me Ann Barnett, so you better say it as many times as you want to…between now and two o'clock, that is."

Josie put her cup down and rose. "We're having flapjacks, sausage, and eggs. While you're down the hall, better rap on the reverend's door. You know how Beemis hates to be kept waiting at the breakfast table, even if a man of God is staying under his roof!"

Annie flounced around the kitchen, doing an impromptu dance step. "I'm happy…Deke's happy…you're happy, too. The preacher's here and Uncle

Beemis, and oh, Sis, I've never seen him any happier."

"Fine, Sis! Now get a move on! Time to wake up all our happy folks!"

Josie started on the flapjack batter. Thirty seconds later, she heard Annie scream. She rushed down the hall and found Annie hugging Beemis. Somehow she had found the strength to raise him up off his pillow. Back and forth she rocked him. "Oh my God! Oh my God! Make him wake up! Please, please, dear Lord! For me! I can't get him to wake up!"

Consumed by grief, Josie closed the door and joined her sister. She let out a horrible scream and threw herself on the bed, on the opposite side of Beemis. Sobbing hysterically, she hugged and kissed him between Annie's rocking motion.

"Annie! Annie! Listen to me! It's Deke! Now open the door! Got the reverend here!"

The Reverend Schaffer rapped politely. "Miss Barnett, please listen to me. We need to get your uncle ready...need to dress him...clean him up...comb his hair...maybe shave him. Your sister's in her room...It's been two days. She's worried about you. Please come out...unlock the door!"

Deke rapped harder. "The reverend's right! Now unlock this door!"

"Leave me alone...go away."

Deke and the reverend exchanged glances. "I'd better get Josie! They're pretty close! Maybe she can talk some sense into Annie."

They returned with Josie, who looked terrible, but seemed to have recollected most of her good sense. She rapped on the door. "Annie, it's me, Josie! Come to the door...we need to talk."

No answer.

"Annie, unlock the door. I'm the only one who will come in."

Finally, a feeble voice came through. "I...I...can't..."

"Annie, why not?"

"If I leave him...there's nobody...He'll be alone...I'll be alone."

"Listen to me, Annie! You're not alone! Deke's here! I'm here! And we both love you very much! Now come to the door!"

The untimely death of Beemis Jay Markham shook Brown's Park to its deepest roots. Without question, he had been the Park's champion, the steadying influence in the Park's recent rash of turbulence and violence. He had been the rallying point for the small cattle ranchers even though he had never owned a cow. In short, Beemis had been a man's man in as desperate a time as history ever recorded in the place where the old West refused to die.

They filled Charley Crouse's schoolhouse to overflowing for the funeral. Those who came late stood outside and waited their turn to file by his coffin to pay their respects to a man who'd earned it and more.

Inside, the Reverend Enoch Schaffer looked down on the sea of faces gathered before him. He ran a boney finger or two through his thick shock of grey hair and looked down at the coffin before him. "Folks," he began, "I had a speech all prepared for you. I was going to tell you about all the things Beemis Markham had done or accomplished during his lifetime. Then I looked down at him and realized that this would never do. I dare say, there isn't a man or woman here today who hasn't personally known Beemis longer or better than I. Yet for all of that, I knew him every day that we were together as a good and true friend. No man could wish or want more than that said about him when his life is over and he is remembered. I came to this park to celebrate a joyous union of two people. Instead, I must conduct a service of remembrance, one of sadness and sorrow."

Those who came were in general agreement, that the short service the good reverend gave would've been the kind Beemis undoubtedly would've ordered had he been given that option. Josie and Annie had to be restrained from one last view, their grief was so overwhelming. Deke had Shorty drive them back to the ranch to give them time to apply cold washcloths to their tear-stained faces and red eyes before serving the cake Beemis had sampled as Annie and Deke's wedding cake.

Considering how devastating Beemis' death had been, Josie and Annie showed remarkable poise when it came time to play host for the serving of cake and coffee. Deke left instructions that in no way were the two sisters to be allowed out in the private graveyard for a final good-bye while he handled the burial.

Deke, Shorty, Tex, and Slim lowered Beemis' coffin down into the ground next to his beloved Maybelle. Shorty could see how choked up Deke was when the coffin rested at the bottom of the Hole. "Me n' Tex and Slim can finish this up…maybe you'd better go on inside."

Deke wiped his eyes, then blew his nose. "It was hard enough when we buried Isom ten days ago…but this…No, I'm going to stay. I'm going to see this through. I have to…for Dad's—I mean Beemis' sake."

Deke packed the last few shovels of earth down hard on the fresh dirt, his way of saying good-bye to the man who'd meant the most in his life. He closed the gate and never looked back. To do so, he would've been sorely tempted to start digging Beemis up.

The minute Deke reached the main house, he headed straight for the kitchen. He used the dipper in the water bucket to splash cold water on his face. One of Josie's dishtowels served nicely as a washcloth. He saw his own reflection in the bucket. Satisfied that he didn't look as bad as Annie or Josie, he kept himself busy by busing the empty coffee cups and plates back into the kitchen. This way, he avoided much of the aimless condolence conversation, yet Annie could see he was nearby if she suddenly lost her composure and needed his shoulder to cry on.

Gradually, the crowd thinned down to what he considered manageable. He recognized the widow Benson, who had Josie's attention.

"Your uncle, bless him, Josie! Those cattle he had Deke and Shorty drive down to my place were a Godsend! Just wish he were here to thank personally..."

Josie blinked, and bravely replied, "So do I...so do I."

Sheriff Charley Neiman handed Annie his plate and cup. "Beemis would've been tickled to hear this. Routt County is gonna get split in two— west half will be named Moffat County. I'm gonna take the west half. There's talk that we might even keep a deputy sheriff here in Brown's Park with a jail to boot! That depends on what money we get."

Annie smiled, then wiped away a tear. "You know what Beemis would've said to that, don't you?"

"Yeah...it'd go pretty much like this: 'So far it's all talk...Show me that deputy restin' his boots up on his desk in the Park's jail, then I'll believe it!'"

Annie forced her own laugh. "Boy, you sure do remember how he'd put it! Even the words you used were pretty darned close."

"You take good care of this ranch, Annie...and hurry up and marry that Deke fella, who keeps runnin' in and out of the kitchen. I hear he's a lot better around horses than he is with your cups and plates."

They both laughed. "I will, I will, sheriff! Just as soon as I get to feeling up to it."

Thirty more minutes of sympathy handshakes and hugs, and promises of "if you need something, just let me know," dwindled the funeral reception crowd down to a few hangers-on. The ordeal was starting to wear on both sisters, who exchanged glances that said it all to those who dawdled: *I don't mean to be unkind, but please leave. I don't think I can take much more of this.*

Three gossip hens surrounded Josie while Annie was left standing alone with her thoughts and her pain. She turned away, and through swollen cheeks and bleary eyes, she started to pick up some of the silverware to give Deke a hand.

A voice behind her said, "I'm so sorry for your loss; please accept my apology for showin' up late."

Hi Bernard stood before her, dressed up in a dark-colored business suit complete with new, black boots.

Her first reaction was he looked good in it, like he belonged wearing it. She put her handful of silverware down. "Let me get you some cake, and I believe there is a little coffee left."

"No thanks, Annie, just wanted to stop by. Your uncle was a remarkable man in many ways. Didn't always see eye to eye with him, but he's the only man in this hole I'd care to take the time for or travel this far."

Annie fought hard. Her lips quivered, and a fresh run of tears took over. She broke down sobbing her poor heart out. Hi tried to comfort her the best he could by letting her cry it out as he held her close.

Between sobs, she looked up. "Oh, I miss him so...so very much...so very much."

Hi bent down to console her by planting a paternal kiss on her forehead. Suddenly, his lips pressed her wet cheeks, and he moved on until he found her lips. "Annie, Annie, I know how you feel...I've missed you so very much too."

Annie didn't have a second to respond. Two strong arms tore them apart.

"Get the hell away from her! And get the hell out of this house! Now!"

She turned to Deke. "Stop it! Stop it!" she screamed. "What's the matter with you? I just buried the man who was more a father to me than an uncle! And here you are, having a jealous fit! This man is a dear, dear friend! I demand you apologize! Go ahead! Apologize!"

Deke was hurt and embarrassed by Annie's remarks. He saw a lot more than red. He pointed his finger at Hi. "I'm not blind," he shouted. "This man, this...this dear, dear friend of yours meant much more by his kiss...a whole lot more! You're the one who's blind, Annie, if you can't see what he's up to!"

"You're making something outta nothing, Deke...so leave it at that!"

Deke would not back down. "I know you've put in a tough day! We all have, Annie, so I'm going to make an allowance for just this one time! Now walk your dear, dear friend to the door and tell him good-bye and not to come calling again. Say good-bye to him, and I'll leave it at that! Tell him, Annie! Tell him that or else I'll be the one going to the door, and I'll be the one sayin' good-bye!"

Deke had forced the issue. The three gossip hens fled out the front door, fearing a good, old-fashioned knock-down brawl was just one swing away. Josie rushed over to Annie with a look a blind man couldn't mistake. She expected Annie to do as Deke demanded.

"You're forcing me to choose...and I won't be forced! No man is ever going to force me! Not even you, Deke! I won't choose! I won't!"

Deke remained strangely calm for being in the middle of such a volatile situation. The red left his face and normal color returned. "Then I will! Good-bye, Annie!"

Three people watched Deke Landry walk out the front parlor door and out of their lives. Two were in shock; the third gloated a bit to himself.

Annie still felt she stood on solid ground. To her, Deke had pushed too hard, too fast. She patted Hi's hand. "That red hair gets Deke into trouble once in a while, goes with his temper...He'll cool off once he gets to the bunkhouse."

Hi excused himself, too, after taking careful stock of the situation he'd provoked. "My first intention was one of sympathy, Annie...until I held you...until I kissed you...Then it all changed. I'll come callin'...after the proper time of respect for your uncle passing."

Hi's black boots hardly had time to find the last step before Josie had her say. "Haven't smartened up a damn bit, have you, Dear Sister? Deke's worth ten of him! You'd better get your fanny over to the bunkhouse pronto—like before you see the south end of him and his horse headed north."

"I will not! He owes me an apology, and by heaven I'm gonna wait right here 'til I get it, even if I have to stay up half the night!"

"Better take Beemis' rockin' chair and sit a spell and wait for your hair to turn grey 'cause you've seen the last of him, my dear!"

"If he loves me as much as he says he does, he'll be back! He wouldn't dare lave me...not now...not after today."

Josie shook her head and gave Ann an exasperated look. "Some people just can't stand happiness...guess you must be one'a 'em! It's been a long, long day. Think I'll hit the hay! Leave those cups and plates; I'll tend to 'em first thing in the morning!"

Twice Ann started for the front door and twice she retreated, positive all she had to do was tough it out and Deke would come up the front steps, his old, sweat-hardened cowboy hat in hand, swallowing a water-dipper full of hurt pride and say, "I got a little carried away," Deke's way of saying, "I'm sorry" for acting like a damned fool.

Ann tossed and turned that night until fitful sleep finally claimed her. At the first hint of grey in her room, she was up bustling about in the kitchen. Josie wandered in, blinking her eyes, sure that she must be dreaming. Annie put on her best cheery smile and said, "Good morning, dear Sister! Breakfast is ready and waiting! Even made Deke's favorite, buckwheat flapjacks and sausage. How 'bout doin' me a favor?"

Josie finished rubbing her eyes. "Like what?"

"Knock on the bunkhouse door and tell Deke breakfast is ready! Soon as he sees the food, he'll forget about our little tiff...you'll see."

Josie poured herself some coffee. After several sips, she left the cup on the breakfast table.

"Good! Now that you've had your eye opener, tap on the reverend's door on your way out to the bunkhouse."

"I'll tap on the reverend's door alright, and I'll tell him to forget about your weddin' 'cause Deke's long gone! And you'd better forget about the bunkhouse unless you're invitin' Shorty up here!"

Ann had had enough. "Alright, I'll go myself! I know Deke better'n you'll ever know him. He's there, I tell you! He's there!"

"Well, then this is as good'a time as any to find out for sure! Let's see you bring him up here for breakfast!"

Annie marched straight for the bunkhouse and rapped soundly. "Deke! Deke!" she called out. "Time for breakfast! Made it myself! Your favorites!" She put her ear to the door and listened intently. She recognized several sounds midst the usual grumblings and scuffling around. She stepped back with as pretty a victory smile as ever seen in the Park.

"Okay, okay, I'm comin'," called out a voice on the other side of the door. "Just hold your horses!"

Inwardly, her heart rejoiced; it sure sounded like Deke, it had to be him! It just had to! And that was one of Deke's favorite expressions, too! She was tempted to jerk the door open and fling herself into his waiting arms, that's how much she wanted the voice to come from that mop of unruly red hair.

The door opened and there stood Shorty McCallum, in his bare feet, one red suspender trying to do the work of two, keeping his half-buttoned pants up, covering nothing but wrinkled skin and aging bones. He gave Ann his best toothless grin. "Oh, Miss Annie, Deke ain't here...left in a big tizzy last night. Never seen a'body so shook up! Kicked the hell outta that old battered box he calls a suitcase. He ripped the top blanket off'n his bunk and tied his junk in that! Oh, was he ever pissed! Oops! Didn't mean that, Miss Annie...meant to say madder'n hell...yeah, that's what I had in mind all 'long."

Ann felt somebody had pulled the plug to her life. "Did...did he say anything, anything about where he was headed out to?"

Shorty gummed his lips a mite, then wet them with his tongue. "Miss Annie, as mad as he was, none of us was crazy enough to ask any questions. He looked mean alright...mean enough to kick the hell outta all of us at once't. Ain't that right, boys?" Shorty got several nods from three others before he rattled on. "Last thing he said to me was to pick up his money next payday and go out and get drunk on him, that's how p-p-p—angry he was...'cause you know, Miss Annie, Deke don't drink anymore...not since he come back." Shorty saw that Annie couldn't check the tears that rolled down both cheeks. "Are you alright, Miss Annie? Kin ah do somethun' fer ya?"

It took two wipes with her hands to quell the tears, leaving only a broken heart to contend with. "Do you like buckwheats and sausage for breakfast?"

"Do I! Are...are you askin' me up to the main house, Miss Annie?"

"Sure, why not?"

"Gimme five minutes, Miss Annie, I'll be right up!" He turned to the others. "Okay, where'd you hide 'em this time! Dang you, Slim, you gimme my clackers back! Ain't gonna gum no buckwheats, I dang sure guar...ran...tee ya! No, sireee! Not this time!"

"Annie! Annie! Wake up!"

Josie shook Annie hard this time. Annie raised up, tried to rub some hard-won sleep out of her eyes and glared at her sister. "First decent sleep I've had in a week! Can't this wait 'til morning?"

"Shorty's in the kitchen! The stallion's gone crazy! Kicked the boards down in his stall! Now he's raising cane with the young mares who aren't ready for breeding! Won't let anybody near! Do something!"

"Why come to me? Tell Deke to—Oh my Lord!"

The realization hit home like never before. Beemis was buried and Deke was gone. Annie threw back the covers. "Tell Shorty I'll be out in a minute or two..."

Josie couldn't help but comment how much Annie had changed. "If Deke was to see you now, he'd barely know who you are! There's nothing to ya, 'ceptin' a hank or two of blonde hair and some bones and skin that lost their softness and most of their prettiness."

"I don't care how I look...I just want him back."

Somehow a year slipped by, though Annie could not account for this passage of time. She was kept too busy trying to fill the boots of the best two men in the horse business who she'd had the good fortune to know and work beside. She continued to make inquiries as to Deke's whereabouts, hoping against hope that somebody somewhere had either seen him or heard of him. And as always, she was met with either no news or a blank stare. As far as she was concerned, Deke Landry had simply vanished from the face of the earth without so much as a well-deserved go-to-hell from him. Even that, she would've welcomed at this point in her life!

Deke's absence gave Hi Bernard all the more reason to come calling on Annie. He now pursued her on two fronts, both socially and economically, as Two-Bar had gained sizeable holdings in the bottomland in the Park. He became a persistent caller and escorted her to every social event on the calendar. Annie treated Hi with kindness and a measure of respect, but nothing more, even though on several occasions, he pressed her for at least an understanding. Once he got that understanding, he felt sure marriage would then be just a preacher away.

The second year dragged by and signs of the inevitable began to take hold. Both Hi and Josie realized the Markham ranch was slowly, but surely, going under. On one particular morning, Josie brought fresh-baked pastry, two coffee cups and the coffee pot on a serving tray to Annie. She sat behind Beemis' old desk, a look of hopelessness etched clearly across her face. Annie pushed aside a stack of bills and letters to make room for the tray.

Josie poured two cups. "That bad, huh, Sis?"

"Got two buyers coming up from Craig today. Had to sell half our breeding stock…"

"That's good, isn't it? Even Beemis' best order from back East never amounted to that many."

"I had to settle for less than one-third of the back-East prices we used to get, so I could pay up our past-due bills." She pointed to another stack of bills. "Those are new bills, and there's no money to pay them. Good thing we're still getting by on the reputation Beemis built up over the years. Most of the people we owe still think we're good for it because Beemis always met his bills!" She turned to Josie. "Sis, we're strapped for cash! Don't know what to do…"

Josie put down her cup and walked behind Annie. She opened the bottom desk drawer and withdrew a bookkeeping ledger with her name on it. She handed it to Annie. "Here, use this if you have to! There should be enough to keep us afloat for a while!"

Annie picked up the fresh Bismark Josie had baked. She studied her sister, then heaved a big sigh of relief. "This is your money you're handing over to me. Are…are you sure you want to do this? If Deke were here, I'd use part of your money to make that trip back East! Deke and I would meet every old customer Beemis had! Then the orders would start coming in again! I've written to every customer Beemis ever had! I can read between the lines, Sis! You know what the problem is? Really is?"

Josie picked up her Bismark. "No, not really…"

"None of them want to do business with a woman! That's the real problem!" She picked up one open letter. "See this? It says, 'We have found a reliable Arabian breeder and supplier near Boston! Thank you for your inquiry.' My foot they have! They all but said they don't know who Ann Barnett is and since I'm a woman, they don't want to do business with me! I even explained in all my letters that I'm Beemis' niece and that I'm carrying on the Markham Ranch name."

Josie took another bite out of her Bismark. She cleared her throat after two swallows. "Now I'm beginning to see why Beemis was so bent upon you and Deke going back East on that honeymoon that almost was…Maybe it's not too late yet! Why don't you make that trip? There's still enough money!"

Annie gave Josie's suggestion some careful thought. "Without Deke…without him with me…no, Sis, it'd be a waste of your good money. I've got at least half a dozen other places crying for some of that money. Thanks anyway for the suggestion."

"I take it after half our stock leaves, there'll be some more changes around here."

Annie stood up. "You've got that right. I'm going to close one of the bunkhouses. No more Chinese cook, and no more crew from one of them! We can't afford their wages! With only half our stock left, Shorty, Tex, and Slim will have to do more…put in longer hours and do their own cooking if they want to stay on. That's the choice I'm going to give them today! Just hope they'll appreciate getting first chance!"

Josie picked up the tray, but left Annie's cup. "Speaking of giving them a choice, how'd you like to have the choice you made between Deke and Hi all over again? Wouldja do anything different?"

Annie never hesitated. "Sis, I'd make that choice so quick, Deke'd never have time to blink! Sure wish I could take it all back…"

Josie started for the kitchen and then stopped. "Seems to me, you've already had a second chance when Deke came back. Most women would dearly love to have that chance, and as usual, you blew it!"

"You sure don't mince your words or where you stand, do you, Sugarplum!"

"Not when it comes to Deke. You really passed up the best for…oh yes, for your dear, dear friend! Well, was Hi worth it?"

Annie refused to comment, figuring Josie already knew the answer. She had a wistful look about her. "Wonder where Deke is? What's he doing? Does he ever think of me or even care for that matter? Heck, he may even be married for all I know…"

Josie laughed.

"Hey, what's so funny! I was just wonderin' about Deke…"

"If you two aren't the beatin'est I've ever seen! Never seen two people so in love and so happy when you're together…and I've never seen two more miserable people when you're not! No, Deke's not married! He's too miserable to even think about marrying somebody else! Same as you!"

"Ann, I've known you more than a good, long while. Neither of us are gettin' any younger as they say. Let's grab some of that happiness other folks have been tellin' us to do! Let's get married! Got a new house, just built in Laramie, waitin' on your touch to turn it into a home! Whataya say?"

Hi's marriage proposal was exactly what Annie had been expecting for at least six months. It didn't come from out of the blue. There was no passion in his voice on bended knees, and no flurry of excitement when he popped the question—just a meat-and-potatoes type of proposition, stripped of the gravy of romance, hot kisses, and bodily embraces that telegraphed a common need to be one in the eyes of God.

Annie was flustered. A red-haired ghost still haunted her daydreams and captured all her nights. She went to the window, trying diplomatically to find a way to say no and still keep his friendship. She finally faced him. "We both know this ranch is going under, but no matter what does or does not happen, this ranch is mine…I have no intention of leaving it! It's my life! Does that answer your question?"

"Okay, then I'll stay here with you on the ranch!"

He could've knocked her over with a feather. This was hardly the answer she'd expected or wanted from him. Somehow, some way, Annie felt her polite no had been turned into a conditional yes. "I don't think you've thought this through…I mean really through! I'm not leaving!"

"Neither am I, if you'll marry me!"

Annie's mouth dropped open, but nothing came out. Finally, her shock turned to words. "Are you saying that you'd leave Mister Two-Bar himself, Mister High and Mighty, just to marry me? Hi, are you sure you really want to do this?"

"Give me your promise; I'll do the rest!"

What to do? What to do? Annie went to the window once more. A dozen thoughts, all about Deke, circled in and out. Was it truly time to get on with her life since Deke had made no attempt to contact her anymore? Could she learn to love Hi the way she'd always loved Deke? Could she? Could it be done? This time she faced him less than one foot away. "Let's clear the air about this so there can be no misunderstanding. If I marry you, you agree to leave Ora Haley for good! Is that correct? You're out of anything connected with the Two-Bar Cattle Company?"

He patted her hand. "Yes! Yes, Annie! Just say you'll marry me!"

"I promise…"

Hi finally got around to giving Annie a fatherly-type kiss and hug. "Are you gonna tell Josie tonight about our good news?"

"Yes, soon as you leave. Good-night, dear! We'll work out the details tomorrow night over dinner."

For the first time since Beemis' death, Ann smelled victory within her grasp, albeit a small one at best. She could readily imagine the indignation and anger Ora Haley would feel when Hi Bernard confronted the mighty cattle baron with the news that he was no longer his Colorado range boss. Oh, just to be privy to that conversation would be consolation enough. She kicked Beemis' old rocking chair with a gusto and glee she hadn't felt in months. "We did it! We did it!" she exclaimed out loud for the four walls to hear. "Your guard patrol was a great idea! And now this! Oh Lord, if you were only here to see this!"

Down the hall she raced, full of a new vitality she thought had died. She never bothered to knock, just bolted on in to find her sister, clad in her nightgown, brushing her shoulder-length hair. "Get up and dance with me, Sugarplum! At last, I have good news! The best yet!"

Around and around Josie's bedroom they danced 'til their legs gave out. Out of breath and exhausted, they fell on Josie's bed, still hugging each other for dear life. Josie finally spoke. "Tell Deke to wait up! I want to kiss him and hug him, too! Oh, Annie, your prayers have been answered!"

Annie sat up. "Deke? Who said anything about Deke being here? It's about Hi! He proposed to me, and I said yes! Oh, Josie, he's gonna quit Ora Haley and settle down right here with me! I mean us!"

Josie rose from her bed; an anger Annie had never seen before flashed from her eyes. "Haven't learned a damned thing about men, have you? You're so smart in many ways, and so stupid when it comes to men! You marry Hi Bernard, and I'll be the next one leaving!" Josie started to shake; her disgust boiled over. "If I thought it'd do any good, I'd slap you until I knocked some sense into that pretty, thick head of yours! But all I'd get for my trouble is sore hands! There's no hope for you! You'll never learn! Stay miserable the rest of your life! See if I care!"

"Fine! So go! Who needs you?"

Early next morning, Annie stood by the window in the front parlor, coffee cup in hand. She watched Shorty lug two of Beemis' old trunks down the front steps to be loaded into the buggy for Josie. Josie came out of her bedroom, clutching her porcelain doll and an old picture of Beemis and Maybelle, taken in New Orleans shortly after they had been married. She paused a second in the parlor, started to say something, then changed her mind.

Annie watched with total indifference while Shorty and Josie conversed alongside the buggy. Shorty helped seat Josie, then returned to Annie.

"What is it, Shorty?"

"Josie told me to tell you not to worry about the money she loaned the ranch 'cause pretty soon there won't be nothin' left to worry over."

"Was that it? Everything?"

Shorty fidgeted, first on one leg, then the other. "Miss Annie...there's a bit more...not very ladylike..."

"Go ahead, Shorty, let's get it said and be done with it!"

"Aw, Miss Annie, please!"

"I said go ahead!"

"Miss Josie said just in case there is somethun' left someday..."

"Yes, Shorty."

Shorty chomped down hard on his mail-order teeth 'til he was sure the upper plate was secure enough to relay Josie's words. "Don't 'member 'zactly her words, but aw'l do my best...Seems like she said if'n there was somethun' left, when you was out seein' Ma Jones...you was to stick it where the sun don't ever shine."

The little man's eyeballs looked large enough to pass for pullet eggs. He shoved his dilapidated slouch of a cowboy hat back 'til it rested against two big, elf-like ears. He was more than a bit puzzled by what he had just repeated. "Miss Annie, where in tarnation might that be?"

Annie soon learned that silence could be deafening. Alone in the main house, she was certain that the hallway sprouted new creaks and squeaks. Funny, she thought to herself, she'd walked those plank boards a thousand times before and never noticed a single peep. She rattled around the kitchen, making as much noise as possible when she fixed her own meals. Anything, anything at all, to break the thunderous silence that nearly consumed her waking thoughts. Once or twice, she thought she heard Beemis' heavy footsteps and the swish of Josie's petticoat after it had been starched. She rose from the kitchen table on several occasions, positive that she felt the vibrations of someone coming down the hall toward her. In panic, she shouted out, "Who's there? C'mon, show yourself! I know you're there!"

Then her sanity and logic took over. "C'mon Annie," she scolded herself out loud. "Your mind's playing tricks on you. You're just wishing too hard for too much!"

Annie stalled off her wedding with Hi in one last desperate effort to reach out to Deke. She made sure her name appeared in the society columns of the weekly newspapers in Rock Springs, Wyoming; Craig, Colorado; and Vernal, Utah. In that way, she hoped Deke would know that she was still single and available, despite her promise to Hi.

News that a new couple had taken over Jessy Wiggins' establishment prompted Annie to drive over to meet them. She was pleasantly surprised to see fresh-stocked shelves, bolts of cloth, two glass-lined counters, and barrels filled with apples, flour, cookies, and hard candy. She picked up what few items she needed, then gave the new owners, Aaron and Constance McLarty, a thumbnail description of Deke. "Sorry, Miss Barnett," said Aaron. "Haven't seen a red-haired man stop by since we opened three weeks ago. If we do, what should we say?"

"Tell him he's needed, more than ever, at the Markham ranch."

"And be careful on your way back, Miss Barnett," cautioned Constance. "There's been two holdups of our customers after they leave the store. Looking for money, mostly!"

Annie did not relish the idea of being out alone in her buggy after dark during the long ride back across the Park's floor to her ranch. She urged her team to pick up the pace, and they responded to her clucking. She thought about the storekeeper's wife and what she'd said. Butch Cassidy came to mind. There'd be no such highwayman's dealings while he was king of the outlaws in the Hole. No indeed! Butch's brand of law could be counted on to protect all who called this hole their home. How strange, she mused to herself, that she now thought of him in this manner. A kind of lawman, no less, enforcing his own no-touch, do-not-harm code of conduct.

The long tentacles of darkness closed in on Annie, leaving her still five miles from the main gate. A late April chill filled the air, making her thankful she'd remembered to bring along a heavy jacket. She stopped the team long enough to reach back behind her seat to retrieve it. The moon eased out from behind a bank of clouds, bathing the valley floor in semi-light. There would be no need to use the kerosene lantern to pick her way home at a much slower pace.

She heard a rider approaching fast, judging by the rapid staccato the horse's hooves made. There was no time to try to make a run for it. She reached under her seat to grab her equalizer, her rifle. She chambered a shell and levered it, ready to drop the rider at the first sign of danger.

"Stop! Stop!" she shouted her warning out. "Stop or I'll shoot!"

The rider heard her threat. In an instant, he raised up in his stirrups and pulled back on his reins. "Whoa! Whoa, there! Whoa, Thunder!"

"Thunder? Thunder! Deke! Is that you?"

Annie never waited for an answer. She threw her rifle in the buggy and came running. Deke's hat flew skyward as he hit the ground a running. They collided halfway between Thunder and Annie's buggy. They kissed and hugged, and kissed some more, each unwilling to part long enough to get a word in edgewise.

There was no need for words, both knew it. Each knew what the other wanted, and each was bound and determined nothing was going to keep them from it. Deke carried Annie to her buggy, deposited her on the seat and climbed in. The race was on, each stripping down to get ready—to make love.

Annie accommodated him in every possible way, even helped him to enter her. She gasped and held on; tears of sheer ecstacy and joy rolled down her cheeks. She whispered their first words. "Please, love, please! Don't get in too big a hurry…like last time."

Silhouetted against a full moon, the lovers rocked the buggy to and fro. It was clearly the kind of romantic setting fit for a poet's best efforts to match those going on in the limited space the buggy seat provided. They took and gave until their cup of love runneth over.

"Deke, Deke, hurry, hurry, I can't hold back any longer!"

Deke sensed they were on the verge of something extra special. He wasn't about to disappoint her or himself. He met Annie with everything he had until they experienced the ultimate—the climax lovers dream and fantasize about. When it was over, they lay locked in their union, each satisfied beyond all expectations, so taken with their experience. Neither wanted to be the first to break apart.

Deke finally broke their union. He raised up and looked about; a puzzled expression played across his face.

Annie looked into his eyes and pulled his head down to meet her lips. "Oh, my love…it was beyond words. What a feeling! What are you looking around for?"

He kept their kiss intact while he managed to move some of their clothes behind him. "My other boot…I knew it was next to the other I just found…"

Annie giggled, then broke out into laughter. "Guess we made the buggy bounce a little too much. Look underneath it!"

He gingerly stepped off the foot step, down onto the cold ground. "Yup, you're right, here it is! Hand my clothes down, will ya?"

Deke dressed while leaning against the buggy. The last thing he did was toss his Stetson into the buggy. Annie stayed in it to finish her dressing. "Come back up, dear, we have a lot to catch up on."

He climbed back up and sat beside her. Annie began to cry. Deke tried his best to comfort her. She shed tears of joy, so he let her have a good cry. When the sniffles were under control, she kissed him again and again. "Oh, my love, I thought I'd never see you again…Oh thank God, you're back and in my arms to stay!"

"Not to stay, Annie, just passing through…"

She put down her handkerchief. "I…I don't understand. What we did a few minutes ago…doesn't that show how much you mean to me? How much I love you? You came back…that's all that matters."

He let Annie rest her head against his chest. "It's plain luck I ran across you. New folks at Jarvey's old store put me onto you…rode like the dickens to catch up. Was really on my way to see Josie and Cleve Dreschler."

She raised up and looked him square in the face. "Deke, I've got a confession to make to you! Josie and I got into it! I mean really got into it! She left in a big huff and married Cleve. I wasn't even invited to her wedding! Can you believe it? Me, her sister! You'd'a thought she would've overlooked our past differences long enough to at least invite me!"

Deke nodded his head. "Okay, that explains a lot! Let me back up a second! When I left here, I headed west. Wound up near Vernal…found work at a small horse ranch near there. The man I worked for has a brother around Lander, Wyoming. He's in pretty bad shape, I understand…looking for somebody to take over his horse ranch up there and gradually buy him out. Couldn't be a better situation for me, so I'm on my way! Figured only on seeing Josie and Cleve, then on up to Lander."

"But love, you won't have to do that now! Deke, I've got another little confession to make. I'm broke! The ranch hasn't sold any horses back East in almost two years! I'm down to just Shorty, Tex, and Slim! Josie loaned me some of her money to keep the ranch afloat! As soon as we get married, there's still time to save the ranch! Beemis' old customers don't want to do business with a woman! But we can turn it all around! We'll go back East and meet them personally, just like Beemis wanted us to do in the first place! Surely, you can see, having you back with me will make all the difference in the world!"

"Sounds good, Annie, but what about your dear, dear friend?"

"I don't understand…what does Hi have to do with us and the Markham ranch?"

"That's a darned good question! Guess I'd better back up some more. Here goes! Lately, I was in Vernal, visited the barbershop…got me the twenty-five cent special, a shave and a haircut! I had plenty of time, so I went through a lot of the old newspapers the barber hadn't gotten around to throwing out. I read about Josie and Cleve gettin' hitched and wondered why your name wasn't mentioned…now I know. I went through most of the old society news, and darned near every one had your name in it, and right next to your name, about as close as them printed words could get, there was your dear, dear friend's name, too!"

Annie laughed. "It worked! Oh Deke, it worked!"

Deke scratched his head. "Guess I must be missing something…know my readin' ain't the best. What worked, Annie?"

"Don't you see it? I did that on purpose! Made sure my name was mentioned as much as possible! That way, if you ever picked up one of those papers…*and you did*…that way you'd know for sure that I was still single and waiting for you to come back to me…*and you did!*"

Deke mulled over Annie's explanation in his head. "Alright, so far, so good!"

Annie snuggled up to him. "Hand me my jacket, love...don't want to catch a chill."

Deke obliged; then a big grin spread across his face. "Little while ago, the only thing that jacket would've been good for was a cushion beneath us. Sure wasn't worried about gettin' a chill then..."

Both laughed. Annie finished buttoning up her jacket. "Love, I've covered all the questions that might've bothered you pretty well, haven't I?"

Deke kissed her tenderly. "Yup, you've changed, Annie...and I like the new you even better! No more holding back...waiting for me to shake all the truth outta you or push you into a corner until I wormed it outta you."

Annie liked what he said about her. "Tell you what, dear, ask me anything, anything at all, and I'll give you the straightest answer you've ever heard. Go ahead, Deke, try me!"

He picked up his battered Stetson off the floorboards of the buggy. He used it to scratch his mop of hair. "There is this one thing...still pesters me some..."

"C'mon, Deke, what is it? Ask me!"

"You and Josie...always lookin' out for each other...backin' each other all the way...must've been something mighty big for her to leave in such'a big huff...What was it, Annie? Give it to me straight like you said."

"Deke, first thing I'm going to do after we're married is drive over to see Josie and Cleve! She walked out on me, but it really doesn't matter anymore because I'm going to do the apologizing first, regardless of who's at fault."

"Alright, Annie, I'll even go with you if you want me to...but what was the big blow-up all about?"

She turned every bit of her charm on. The moonlight put a sparkle into her eyes and played across the prettiest face he'd ever seen. It even touched her moist lips so he could see them glisten, waiting for him to gather the nectar from them again and again. "It's really not important anymore...I covered that before, remember?"

"Annie, you're holdin' out on me again. Are you gonna tell me or do I have to get it straight from Josie when I see her?"

She erupted worse than a volcano. She kicked at the front boards of the buggy until Deke clamped both hands over her legs to keep from scaring the team. "Just couldn't leave well enough alone, could you!" she screamed. "Why, Deke? Why now? After the way we made love! Why?"

"Still waitin' on that straight answer...Annie...still waitin'."

She jerked her body out of his grasp and stood up. "Alright, here goes,

Deke, like it or lump it! After Josie walked out—I never knew how lonesome a person could get until then…There's nothing worse than being left all alone! Can…can you try to understand that? Even a little?"

"Sure I can, Annie…happened every time you broke your promise to me and I had to leave."

"Alright, we're getting somewhere! Hi kept after me…wanted to marry me…I held him off…had my name put in those newspapers like I said…like you read…"

"But did you promise to marry him, Annie? C'mon, the truth!"

She dropped to her knees before him, begging forgiveness in her way. Fresh tears formed and rolled down her cheeks; their moistness added to her own facial beauty. "I…I did promise…but…but that was before tonight…before you came back, before we made love." She looked up toward the stars and the heavens. "As God is my witness, I never wanted to marry Hi…only you, Deke! Only you!"

Annie's words moved him. He was almost swayed—almost. He stepped out of the buggy, planted both boots solidly on the ground—where he belonged. "You're awful good at making promises you never keep! You'll never change, Annie! Never!"

He started to walk away.

"Come back, Deke! Don't walk out on me! Please, Deke! Please!"

He put his foot into the stirrup and swung his leg over.

Annie stepped out of the buggy and rushed over to him. "Don't leave me," she begged. "Where are you going? What are you going to do?"

He looked down at her. "Help you keep your first promise…I was just passing through…remember? Good-bye, Annie!"

She broke down sobbing her poor heart out. Then she raised her fist in his direction as he turned his back on her to ride away. She called him everything but what he was: a simple man. The more distance he put between them, the worse the insults. He reached the point where she'd have to shout or scream at him. Suddenly, he stopped, turned Thunder around and faced her.

"Annie! Annie!" he called out, just loud enough to keep from shouting.

"Damn you, Deke Landry! Now what?"

"Maybe this will help. Got this here rule that follows me around most everywhere I go. Didn't pick it outta no book neither…just come natural for me. Always tried to live by the word I give…If I can't do that…then I don't give it."

One week to the day, Hi and Annie drove to the bustling town of Craig, Colorado. They looked up a local justice of the peace to perform their wedding ceremony. Afterwards, Hi rented the nicest room on the second floor of the Peabody Hotel for their honeymoon suite. He passed through the hotel lobby with Annie's suitcase under his arm and happened to meet several business acquaintances. He handed back her suitcase along with the room key. "You go on ahead…it's number fourteen. I'll be up shortly…got some business to take care of."

Annie climbed the stairs and inserted the key. The room looked spacious and well furnished as she laid her suitcase down on the big double bed. A huge mirror over the vanity table caught her eye, so she sat down on the padded vanity bench. Her reflection in the mirror pleased her. A new, short-cropped hairdo under a fashionable hat complimented her face. Even her dark-blue dress helped accent her petite figure in all the right places. A short strand of pearls around her neck completed the picture. Everything, including the new hairstyle, came as a result of her shopping spree before she had said her vows. Hi had been most generous.

"Alright, Annie," she said aloud. "Time for a little pep talk! Time to put the past behind you. Deke's outta your life for good. You're a married woman now…and starting today, you'd better smarten up and act like one. Hi will be up here any minute now, so pull the covers back, get undressed, and make darned sure you don't disappoint him. Got it, lady? Don't disappoint, no matter how much you have to fake it!"

One hour passed, then two, and still no new hubby with his Texas nasal twang. Annie banked a pillow behind her and sat up, ready to do whatever Hi's passion demanded. She wondered just how passionate he would actually be when he wanted her. She hoped deep down that he'd be at least half as passionate as Deke had been; it'd make her job, fulfilling his needs, just that much easier.

Annie awoke from her troubled sleep, hugging the other pillow. It was a poor substitute for a mop of red hair with more than enough passion spread around to meet or beat every possible women's need she'd ever experienced. The hour had to be late, she told herself. Where in the world was Hi? Had something happened downstairs?

She climbed out of bed to open her suitcase. Her first impulse was to put on a robe over her revealing nightgown and go downstairs. Her second impulse was to turn out the two kerosene lamps and wait for him in the dark. Much more romantic, she allowed. Hi would certainly appreciate a little wifely planning when he made his grand entry to claim his bride.

The faint smell of two kerosene lamps just extinguished filled the room when Hi threw the door wide open and staggered in. He stumbled over an upholstered chair and went down in a heap.

Annie's eyes were already accustomed to the dark. She rushed to his side. "Hi! Hi, honey! Are you alright? What took you so long?"

He used Annie and the tipped-over chair to get up. "Damnit!" he growled, "leave the lights on! Can't see a damn thing in the dark! And don't you ever call me honey, you hear me? Honey is what the whores call all their customers! Soon as we got some light, I got some talkin' to do! Now find those lights!"

Annie relit the lamps. Hi stumbled over to the bed and sat down.

"Can't it wait 'til morning, dear?"

"No!" Hi waited for Annie to sit down by him. "Got rid of the Arabians! Made a pretty good deal...those three you got workin' for you go with the horses as part of the deal! Took me too damn many drinks and too damned much time, but I finally swung it!"

Annie was alarmed and upset. "You shoulda talked to me first, Hi...Don't exactly cotton to the idea of you going over my head."

"Had to," he answered. "You're ranch ain't made a dollar in a 'coon's age! That's all gonna change mighty soon! We're about to start making money, Annie! Ya hear me? I said money!"

Annie tried her best to keep calm. "Doing what, Hi? Exactly what?"

"Raising cattle, Annie! That's where the money is!"

Annie got up, mad as all get out. "You mean the Markham ranch is going to be turned into a cattle ranch? I don't know a thing about cattle!"

"But I do, Annie! Just leave it to me! We'll have our own herd in a few days and things will start to turn around! Here, help me off with my boots..."

It took twenty minutes to get Hi ready for bed. By the time Annie draped his good clothes over the chair, she was totally out of any romantic mood whatsoever. Yet she saw the way Hi looked at her as she pulled his boots off and then proceeded to help him out of his dress shirt and pants. She started to unbutton his underwear when Hi raised his hand.

"Leave 'em on...I ain't hankerin' to be naked as a jaybird."

Annie left him alone and climbed into bed. She stayed on her side of the bed, determined that if he needed her, he'd have to make the first move and then some. To her surprise, he started to snore. Annie pulled her pillow over her head and tried to get some sleep, hoping the pillow would cushion some of his loud snoring.

"Annie! Annie! Wake up! I need you…"

She had no idea what hour it could possibly be, only that Hi was jabbing her in the ribs. She rubbed her eyes and tried to accommodate him. He lay on top of her and tried to kiss her. His breath reeked of whiskey, so she kept turning her head to avoid any contact. He gave up and concentrated on getting into her. She couldn't bring herself to help him. Finally, he made it in. Annie felt violated as she lay there through his limber pokes. He moved a little back and forth until she felt his pokes produce a little drizzle. She wanted to push him off of her and roll over to get away. He finally withdrew and turned his back to her.

Minutes later, Hi felt Annie's body quiver as she tried to muffle her crying. "Annie, Annie," he called out in the darkness. "We'll do better next time…got our whole lifetime ahead. No more whiskey when I need you next time…that's what slowed you down…right?"

The muffled sobs continued. Between a series of sniffles, Annie tried to answer as best she could. "Guess we both fell a little short of our expectations…let's leave it at that."

Their third day back at the ranch was another episode of how a marriage could be strained without either deliberately going out of their way. Annie was rudely awakened by the incessant bawling of cattle. She slipped on a robe, grabbed a cup of the thick varnish Hi called coffee and proceeded to find out what the commotion was all about. She opened the front door of the parlor and discovered she was in a whole new world—a world ruled by critters who wore cowhide clothes, bawled all the time, and stunk even worse. Hi had put her out of the Arabian horse business faster than he could move his mustache to accommodate his slow Texas twang.

Annie had never realized, 'til now, how irritating and slow his speech could be. She wondered how she had once thought there was anything romantic or wonderful connected to it. She watched Hi move the five hundred head of cattle while she stayed glued to the porch. She was glad of one thing. Thank God Beemis wasn't around to see what she was going through. He'd have thrown up his hands, cussed a blue streak, and then washed his hands of anybody and anything connected with it. She thought about asking Hi how in the world he had managed to start with such a large herd. Hi supplied the answer when he hailed her as he rode by.

"Made a lot of money for Ora…an awful lot…figured he owed me this much at least. They're mavericks I cut outta his herd; all they need is a brand and they're legally ours. Hired three cowpokes away from Ora. They'll be takin' over the bunkhouse. We'll do the brandin' next week…"

Annie's next surprise came without warning. Hi came up to her in an extremely agitated state—even for Hi. "Get your ridin' duds on," he ordered. "No time for talk. I need you to help me move the herd west! Now!"

Four hours of backbreaking hustle and determination paid off for Hi and his cowpokes. With Ann's help, they had managed to move five hundred head of cattle to the far western reaches of the Park. No sooner had they stopped moving the herd than Hi began branding. Ann rode over to him, looking for some sort of reasonable, rational explanation. "How come we're way over here in Utah? Why aren't we doing the branding back home?"

Instead of answering his wife's pointed questions, Hi cupped his hands and shouted toward his three hired hands. "Finish that one! Leave the irons in the fire! Grab your rifles outta the wagon and follow me! Ann, there's a sign in the wagon! Bring it and come on high with your rifle!"

Five minutes passed and the mystery clearly considerably when Ora Haley rode up with five of his men, accompanied by a large man with a handlebar mustache, sporting a sheriff's badge.

"Arrest them! Arrest them!" Haley charged. "Those are my cattle!"

Hi took one long look at his ex-boss. "The sign! The sign! Show the sign, Annie!"

Ann did as she was told. She held up the sign for all to see. It said, "Branding in Utah." Those three words did more than a fifty-man armed posse to diffuse Hi's close call. "We're in Utah! Got no business here! Now get along or else I'm gonna put you to work helpin' with my branding!"

Ora whipped his horse with a quirt, riding back and forth in front of his men, trying to figure a way to arrest Hi. Finally, the sheriff settled the issue the only way he could. Hi had pulled a rabbit out of the bag; he'd beaten Ora on a technicality. "Stay here, Ora, and don't you make a move across that line! We got no jurisdiction in Utah!" The sheriff shoved his rifle back in its scabbard, then rode the final fifty feet separating the two sides. "Order your men to lower the rifles!"

Hi's men did and the sheriff stopped in front of him. "The law says you got the right to move mavericks and strays off your property, but that don't mean you got the right to run 'em all the way into Utah!"

Hi turned to his men, then back to the sheriff. "What strays? What mavericks? Next time you see my cattle, they'll all be branded legal-like!" He tipped his hat first at the sheriff, then toward his fuming ex-boss. "Charley must be gettin' awful lazy these days...won't even take the time to ride out this way anymore."

The sheriff said, "I'm the new sheriff, name's Joe Jones! Guess you folks don't get outta this hole much. Had us an election up on top...Charley lost out bad, I mean real bad! And who might she be?"

"She's my wife, Sheriff Jones. Name's Ann, Ann Bernard."

A twinkle came into the sheriff's eyes. "Well now, Queen Ann, how does it feel to be associated with such high falootin' company as what your husband's into these days?"

Ann didn't care for either her new name or the insinuation it carried. "Whataya mean, Queen Ann?"

"Charley Neiman told me some about you. He said we got ridda the two kings of cattle rustling, Matt Rash and Isom Dart! But I guess he fergot to tell me 'bout the queen of rustling. That's gotta be you, Queen Ann!"

Ora Haley could only watch while Hi Bernard continued branding his mavericks and strays. He shook his fist and shouted several obscenities mixed in with some pretty stout Irish. Then he rode up close to the imaginary border to get in a final parting shot. "You were a damn-good ramrod, Hi Bernard, best I ever had...but you lost your brains and all your common sense around that fool woman you married. Thought we got rid of all the big-time cattle rustlers, now I find you've become one, too, along with that damned, no-good woman! You haven't heard the last of this yet!"

Ann had all she could do to stomach this latest round of accusations, which branded her as a cattle rustler right alongside her husband. She could still pick out Ora's derby hat as the sheriff's posse grew smaller and smaller in the distance. Then she let Hi have it. "Damn you," she charged. "I'm not a rustler! Never have been, never will be! Next time you need help to make a drive across the border, forget about taking me!"

Hi did not cotton to airing the family's dirty linen in front of others. To him what he'd done was perfectly legal, although it certainly didn't justify the wild drive to escape legal jurisdiction.

"Let's talk about it back home...You got a lot to learn 'bout range law, my dear."

Ann jerked Glory's reins and rode off in no mood to hear another word. Hi called out in vain after her. "Hell, we lost more'n this in the first month down on the Yampa and Ora never even picked his nose over it!"

Still seething with outrage and indignation as being branded queen of the Park's latest cattle-rustling operation, Annie came upon a small buggy heading east. What really caught her eye and held her attention was the fresh canvas sign tacked on the back of the buggy: "U.S. MAIL."

She passed the old gent handling the team and waved to him. "Wait up! Wait up!" he said.

Ann stopped to let him catch up. "Hello there! Since when are we getting regular delivery from Vernal?"

The old boy got out of the buggy and stretched before answering. "Since today, miss...startin' once-a-week mail service to the mercantile in the Park. Been long overdue." He took off his hat and scratched what little was left of a once glorious head of silver-tinged hair. "Danged Park's still better'n forty years behind, from what I see...been a safe place far too long for the scum of the earth." He had a pleasant smile to match his receding hairline, the kind a doting daughter would love to kiss. "About the Park, miss...I didn't mean nothin' personal." Then he pointed back to Hi's branding operation. "Can't figure that mess out! The sheriff and his men ride like billy blazes to get there, then they come back by me, all quiet-like, except one of 'em. He's a wild man, I tell ya...still cussin' and swearin' somethun' awful...even heard some Irish cuss words I ain't been around in fifty years, I reckon...Don't make no sense, no how!"

Ann decided to fill him in. "The sheriff got there too late to stop the branding because it's across on the Utah side, and he's our Colorado county sheriff."

The old man cackled and cackled and cackled some more. "Utah, huh? C'mere, let me show ya where Utah really is." Ann followed his arm and one long bony finger as he pointed to a small butte a good mile behind Hi's operation. "Look up there...up on that little butte...the one below that great big one...see it?"

"Yes, I see it...so what?"

"Look real hard—my eyes ain't what they used to be—can you see that pile'a rocks with one stickin' up on top?"

Ann strained and strained. "Yes, I think I see it...just barely..."

"Well, that's where Utah begins...not down there where them cowboys is at!"

"Are you sure? I mean really sure?"

"Lady, I should be 'cause I was part of the official United States government survey team what divided Utah from Colorado! Matter of fact, I held the rod up there on that pile'a rocks I was pointin' to, and down underneath that pile is the metal stake I drove into the ground myself to mark the boundary!"

Deserved or not, Ann Bernard was stuck with the reputation of being involved with cattle rustling, and of course, the name "Queen Ann," which Sheriff Joe Jones so readily bestowed upon her. At first, she paid little or no attention to it, but as time wore on, people would stare at her and point and then shield their faces and lips. Often the braver ones would confront her with a snide remark such as, "And how are you today, your highness?" Before Ann could counter the charge, another would step forward to chastise with a cruel verbal shot: "Say, I hear there's Two-Bar cattle on the loose again. Try the Wyoming line this time, it's a bit closer!"

Hi Bernard was totally indifferent to the sarcastic gossip spread about his wife. When Ann finally confronted him about the jokes and name calling, he merely shrugged his aging shoulders. "Got better things to do with my days than argue and defend what was legally mine to take and brand in the first place. If you want to give 'em some more ammunition…that's your business."

Life at the Bernard Ranch continued to be anything but tranquil for Ann or Hi. Fortunately for Ann, the years her husband spent as the range ramrod for Ora Haley had made him a man of simple tastes. She never claimed to be in the same class as Josie when it came to a wife's domestic chores. She kept a decent house and put out good but plain food when the spirit moved her. They would go for hours on end without so much as a kind word or otherwise passing between them. Occasionally, Hi would take her to task over her obvious lack of interest in the day-to-day operations of their cattle ranch. To those charges, she fired back, "Well, Hi, as far as I can tell, your cattle and our marriage are both a matter of convenience! Let's leave it that way!"

The one thing that did bother Ann to no end was the countless swarms of flies that made life miserable and nearly intolerable for her. Time and time again, she would beg Hi to do something about them; they were everywhere. "Do something about them!" she would scream at her husband. "They came with your cattle! You brought them!"

Old Hi would wait for Ann's temper to cool down a bit; then he'd nail her with the same patented slow response he always gave back. "Notice them cattle is always mine when you get to talkin' 'bout all them flies they bring in…but when you got new duds on your mind and you want to go to town to buy, how come you always ask me how much will our cattle bring?"

The one thing that Hi and Ann enjoyed together was the occasional dining out. As Hi's herd built up and became more profitable, Ann saw to it that they did dine out more often. This not only gave her an excuse to dress, fit to kill, but it allowed her to spend a precious few days or so away from those smelly four-legged critters back home who were the feeding troughs for all the pesky swarms of flies that clustered around every door and window in their ranch house, just waiting to get in.

This crisp, late November day found the two engaging in another shopping spree for Annie. Several new shops had opened in Craig, Colorado, and Annie made the most of it. Hi was loaded down with packages as he followed her from store to store. That night, they dined in near-royal splendor at the Peabody Hotel.

Across the aisle, in the fine dining room sat a well-dressed young man, who looked to be in his early thirties. He sat alone while he finished a most delicious meal. He was about to order dessert, then changed his mind. He couldn't take his eyes off the young, richly dressed woman, who sat opposite him, a scant ten feet away. She was the epitome of everything that attracted her to him in the first place. Besides her obvious good looks, he'd overheard enough of the lady's conversation to know that she was well educated. He was amused by the fact that the woman's conversation took a decided one-way tilt as the older gent she was with seemed ill at ease in keeping his end of the conversation up. He concentrated only on getting the few remaining drops of soup from the bottom of his bowl and in keeping his napkin tucked in under his chin.

The young man was totally taken in by Ann and longed to engage her in polite conversation. Proper etiquette dictated that he speak to the old gent first. He looked about him and his table to come up with a subject that would give him the opener he needed. He picked up his newspaper and pointed to it. Twice, he cleared his throat, hoping Hi would look up. "Excuse me, Sir," he began, "but did you happen to read this Denver paper?"

The slurping sounds of Hi spooning his soup was the only thing that greeted the man for his effort. "Sir, Sir, do you do much reading?"

Annie used a not-so-polite kick to Hi's kneecap under the table. "Hi, the man is talking to you! Answer him!"

Hi raised his head. "What was the question?"

Again the young man pointed to this newspaper. "I'd say it's about time!

They finally hung that no-good killer, Tom Horn, up in Wyoming on the twentieth for murdering a fourteen-year-old boy! Too bad Butch Cassidy skipped the country two years ago! Shoulda had a double hanging is the way I see it! Both were the worst kind! Horn bent the law every chance he'd get! Cassidy lived outside of the law, all the time! Hightailed it out just in the nick of time! The law was hot on his trail, I'll tell you!"

"Sounds like you knew both…purty well…did you?"

The young man pointed to himself. "Me? Never met either! But if I had, I'll tell you things would've been different! A lot different!"

Now Hi was amused—slightly. "Oh? How?"

The young man jumped at the chance. "I'da hired the best! Hunted both, day and night, 'til they'da dropped in their tracks with no sleep or food!"

Hi picked up his soup spoon and pointed it at the young man. "Seems to me, they did hire the best to try to nail Cassidy. Far as Horn goes, he was the best! Done the law's job in more places than you ever heard of, son!"

The young man was surprised by Hi's answer. "Sounds like you know a bit more about them than I do! Where'd you run across them?"

Hi put his spoon down. He seemed to enjoy the shift of attention. "Never crossed Cassidy's trail…but yup, I know'd Horn…he was a stock detective lots'a places. First run into him near Laramie. Big cow man…name of John Coble hired Horn up there. Done a first-rate job of cleanin' out the big-time cattle rustlers…done the same thing down in the Hole, too—that's Brown's Park to you, son."

Now Annie's interest perked up, too. This was the first time she ever heard Hi admit he had known Horn before Brown's Hole. She wondered what other connections Hi had had with Horn after Matt Rash's narrow escape at Hahn's Peak. Before she had a chance to ask Hi a very pointed question, the young man came over to their table. He shook hands with Hi.

"Glad to make your acquaintance, Sir. Have never met anybody who knew either, personally! My name is Douglas McKee."

"The name is Hi Bernard." He nodded in Annie's direction. "The lady here knew both of 'em…"

McKee couldn't believe his good fortune. "Really! Say, I've got a great idea! A great idea! What's your room number, Mister Bernard?"

Hi was a bit taken aback by the personal question. He hesitated, then answered. "Number fourteen…why?"

"I was about to order dessert, but am I ever glad I waited! How about me ordering my dessert now, and have your lady here join me at my table? I'd like to hear all about Cassidy and Horn! If that's alright with you, Sir?"

Hi and Annie exchanged glances. "Guess that'll be alright…" He turned to Annie. "Don't be too long in comin' up to our room, Annie…gonna get an early start at first light."

McKee pumped Hi's hand. "Don't you worry about a thing, Sir! When Annie's through telling me about Cassidy and Horn and we've had dessert, I will personally escort your daughter up to room fourteen!"

Hi Bernard did a slow boil. He rose from the table, his linen napkin still tucked between the top two buttons of his dress shirt. He jerked the napkin out, then let go. "Young man, this lady is my wife, not my daughter!"

Annie's suspicions loomed large in her heart and in her mind. She now suspected Hi had a hand in bringing Horn into the park to murder Rash and Dart. She intended to more than confront him once he set foot inside their hotel suite. The longer she waited for Hi to show up, the more her suspicions gnawed at her.

A half-hour later, he made his appearance. Annie jumped all over him. "How much, Hi? How much did you pay Horn to kill Matt or Isom? I demand an answer!"

Hi was in no mood to talk about Rash or Dart. He grabbed Annie's left hand. "Where's your weddin' band?" he snarled at her. "Coulda saved a lot of worthless time with that young buck in the dining room! Next time we come to town to buy and eat out, you have it on! You hear me?"

Annie jerked her hand away. "I left my band at the ranch. My ring finger's broke out! See! And for your information, we didn't come here to buy and eat out! It's called shopping and dining out! And that worthless time is called engaging in polite conversation! Something you know nothing about!"

Hi was far from finished. "He wasn't interested in small talk, he was interested in only you!"

Annie, too, wasn't through. "That's called attention, Hi! Something I haven't gotten from you since the day we married! Shoulda married one of your smelly cows! She'd get more attention than I ever got!"

Hi dropped the verbal confrontation; he knew better than to rile Annie up further. He turned abruptly and headed for the big vanity mirror. Annie was right behind. She waited with folded arms while he peered close into the glass.

"Now that you've had a good look at yourself, how much did Ora Haley give you to pay for Horn's services? I'm waiting, Hi!"

He ignored Annie and her question. Then he turned around to face his wife. "Tell me…do I look that much older? Enough to be your father?"

This time Annie ignored Hi's questions. "You stopped off at the bar again; I can smell hard liquor on you from here! Tell you how it's going to go 'til I get some straight answers from you! There'll be no more trying to kiss me in the middle of the night! And you can forget about rolling me over!"

Eight years somehow slipped by, though Annie seemed lost in every one as it passed. Hi kept to himself as much as possible, and so did Annie. Whenever they spent any time together, neither had a kind or considerate word for the other. Their marriage was strained to the breaking point, yet neither seemed on the verge of "splitting the blanket" as it was called, the Hole's way of saying, "I want a divorce!"

Annie had heard through the Park's grapevine that Josie had two children, a girl and a boy. She wondered if she'd ever get the chance to meet her niece or nephew. Several times, when Hi was away, she was sorely tempted to drive over to see Josie, hoping each would let bygones be bygones. She missed her sister's once close friendship, more and more with each passing month. Yet pride stood in the way, a mountain of it!

With so much time to herself, her thoughts always drifted back to a mop of red hair, and the passion and romance that always came with it. She found herself wanting to feel truly loved again, the way Deke had fulfilled her every need on that fateful night in her buggy. Many a night and day since he'd touched her was spent trying to regain and keep that ultimate feeling he'd left her with. Often she'd find herself either moist or wet from such thoughts, a poor substitute for the real experience, at best, she privately conceded to herself.

Hi took to spending more time away as the ranch prospered. Ann never bothered to question where he went or why he needed to be gone so much. Even after he came home, their life fell into the same old pattern for her. If anything was to be said, she'd have to initiate the conversation and force-feed it, or else it would surely die, along with the day that only promised more of the same. Everything about the man exasperated and exhausted her.

Hi returned from another trip—this time to Denver in the spring of 1911. And wonder of wonders, he stepped into the parlor, ready to talk. "I heard you playing on the organ as I drove in…That always means you've spent some time out at your family's plots…left flowers, too, I suppose."

"Yes, I cut some wild daisies; they're so beautiful this time of year." She put down her book and cocked an attentive ear in his direction. "Alright, you go first!"

"Ran into Ora Haley…we drank some…buried the hatchet. His and my past is where it oughta be…"

"Finish the sentence! Finish the sentence!"

He blinked both eyes, then mumbled, "Where was I?"

Ann threw up her hands; the book on her lap tumbled to the floor. "Who knows? Anything else, Hi?"

He sauntered over and took her by the hand. Ann hadn't the faintest idea what he wanted or had in mind. To her surprise, he stooped down to plant a fatherly kiss on her cheek. His dull eyes cleared up a bit. He seemed ready to divulge some dark, hidden secret. Ann tried to help him out. "Is there something you've been wanting to tell me? After all this time?"

Hi looked at her with the saddest expression she'd ever seen. "Can't remember if I told you this or not…long time ago…that young man in the hotel in Craig—guess, I already told you…didn't I?"

She wanted to scream, she wanted to tear her hair out, but she remained calm.

"It's about Ora Haley and you hiring Tom Horn, wasn't it? Never could get you to own up to it! Well, go ahead! Better late, I guess, than never!"

"See…must've told you…you already know about it…"

"Not all of it, Hi! Not all of it! Tell me the rest!"

He thought a spell and then the words tumbled out. "Paid Tom Horn five hundred dollars to kill Matt Rash…five hundred for Dart, too. It was Ora's money. He…he was afraid Horn would blackmail him…That's why I did it, Ann…that's why. Now you know."

Hi Bernard had finally let the cat out of the bag, eleven years too late. What Ann had long suspected had, indeed, come true. "Alright, now you've finally told me! Now tell me how come you waited so long!"

He took her in his arms and tried to will the answer out with a feeble hug and a squeeze. His soft, easy words in her ear were pathetic. "Made you wait all these years 'cause I know'd you still cared for that drifter…that red-haired lad your Uncle Beemis hired. Figured by now it's way too late…You won't leave me now…not now, Ann? My Annie?"

She broke away from his grasp, eyes spitting hate and disgust. "Should've stayed with what you do best, raising cattle and flies! You're no mind reader, Hi, and after today I'm no longer your wife!"

Ann wasted no time packing and leaving. The very first thing on her mind was some fence mending, the kind that needed an overdue trip to the Dreschler ranch to see Josie and apologize. She was determined to do or say whatever it took to be friends with her sister once again. She was surprised to see several bands of sheep nibbling on the short grass in front of the old Dreschler homestead. A thin, scraggily toothed man met her at the door. Two young boys clung to his wife's patched dress and peered out whenever their shyness deserted them. "Where's Josie Dreschler?" Ann asked, "Isn't this the Dreschler ranch?"

The man pulled out his Bull Durham sack and neatly rolled his cigarette. Flame spewed from his farmer match as his thumbnail engaged the match's head. He sucked in 'til the end of the cigarette glowed bright red. "Twas 'til a year ago; I moved 'em up to Rock Springs." He nodded toward his wife. "Me and the missus bought out Mrs. Dreschler and them two younguns a'hers."

"You said Mrs. Dreschler; what happened to her husband, Cleve?"

He left Ann's question up in midair, along with the smoke from another suck on the cigarette. "Guess you're not from 'round these parts or else you'da heard. Cleve Dreschler broke his neck...horse stumbled into a badger hole." He snapped two grimy fingers. "Made her a widow just like that!"

Ann was in shock. She needed two full minutes to regain some semblance of composure. "You did say Mrs. Dreschler is in Rock Springs?"

"Yup, last we heard she was." He turned to his wife. "Did the widow say anything to you 'bout what she was gonna do up there?" The wife shook her head. "That's all we know, lady..."

"Thank you." Ann started to turn away, then stayed a bit longer. "Thought this was cattle country, but you're running sheep! How come?"

The man shook his head and smiled. "Damned Two-Bar outfit ran so many head, the grass ain't got a chance to grow high 'nough round here anymore. Had'a sell off my herd'n buy them woollies you see out yonder. Even they had a tough go...it's slim pickins at best!"

The man's wife whispered into her husband's ear, then stepped back, a dirty smirk written from ear to ear across her face. "Okay, let's have it!"

"My wife figured out who you must be. Judgin' by them spiffy clothes you're wearin,' cattle rustlin' must still pay pretty good over your way, Queenie Ann!"

No matter what the cost in pride, Annie was determined to locate her sister. Five days later, she turned off of Main Street in Rock Springs. The dusty side street was much quieter than the main business district; however, nothing greeted her except a string of one-story buildings that had seen better days. Several storefronts were boarded up, and old posters from last year's carnival were still tacked up, leaving the swirling gusts of wind to scatter any good memories.

At the far end of the second block, she got out of her rented buggy and tied the team to a broken-down hitching rail. She walked up the boardwalk to the front door of the weather-beaten old building. In the corner of one window, a small sign told her she had the right place. It read: "Room and Board." She hesitated a second, then looked around as if to reassure herself. Fresh-starched curtains hung from two large front windows. Her hand gripped the cleanest brass-plated doorknocker she'd ever felt or seen. Her knees knocked, she was so excited. Yes, she had the right place; everything was clean and spotless—Josie clean and spotless!

Rap! Rap! Rap! She waited, too excited, too breathless to put off this meeting one second longer.

"Yes, who is it?"

The door opened. Eleven years of time froze while the two sisters fought to control their emotions.

"Oh, Josie! Josie! Forgive me!"

The two rushed into each other's arms. They hugged, they kissed, and they cried. It was the reunion of reunions. Josie stepped back to get a second look. "Haven't changed a bit—same hourglass figure, clothes right out of the best store window. Oh, Annie, Annie, I've missed you so!"

"And look at you! You're a mother! And I'm an aunt!"

They hugged again. Josie stepped back. "Yes, and look at me, twenty pounds heavier and three inches wider…oh, I must look a sight!"

"Best sight I ever saw! Where's my nephew and my niece?"

"In school! That's why I bought this boarding house. They're putting up a high school and so help me Hannah, my two are gonna go through it and get the education I never had! All the way through twelve grades! Maybe college later!"

They sat down and talked of their missed years, including all the trivial things that somehow seemed larger than life. Josie looked up at the clock on her kitchen shelf. "Still got two hours before you get to meet Ethan and Ann Marie. Ethan's nine and Ann Marie's eight! She was named after you! Care to tell me what happened between you and Hi?"

"Like you said, I was a fool to marry him…should've listened to you all along…Now it's too late. God only knows where Deke is by now…or if he's still alive. Anyway, he's probably married. Hope his marriage turned out a lot better than mine. I split the blanket with Hi…we're divorced now…got a pretty decent settlement, considering everything. Never learned a darned thing about the cattle business, Josie, not even after eleven years! The truth of it is, I never cared to! Isn't that awful?"

Josie squeezed her sister's hand then let go with a rip-snorter of a deep-belly laugh. "Not true, not true, dear sister! You learned how to be Queen Ann, queen of the cattle rustlers!"

"You heard it, too? Oh Josie, I've been branded for life! Still don't think I deserved it!"

Their conversation returned to a more serious note. "What are your plans, now that you're free as a bird to light where you please?"

"Last time I saw Deke, he had a job promised him up around Lander. I'm gonna go up there to look for him. If he's happy with his job and married, I'll leave him be…"

"C'mon, Annie, deep down you're hoping he's as miserable as you, so you'll still have a chance to lasso him. Hey, I'm your older sister, and I know you better than you know yourself!"

Ann went to get her purse. "Since you think you still know me, here's a little surprise for you." She handed Josie an envelope. "Go ahead and open it! Count it out if you want to! It's half of my share from the ranch. Beemis would've wanted you to have this; so do I!"

Josie never touched the envelope. "Sis, you have changed. No, I don't need it now. Keep it for yourself! Could come in handy in your future plans. Next week, the carpenters and lumber will arrive. Going to add four more rooms, and then I'll be able to make a good living for my family. It's all paid for."

Annie was startled by Josie's refusal to accept the money. She looked around at the plain, drab furnishings. "Sis, how can I put it without hurting your feelings or your pride? Looks like you could still use this money…please take it."

Josie turned deadly serious. "Can you keep a secret? I mean a secret you can't tell anybody? Not now, not never? Think about that before you try to answer."

"Alright, I promise. Shoot!"

"Six months ago, Butch Cassidy looked me up and left me some money to help out."

Annie's jaw dropped. "It can't be him! He's dead! Been dead for years...that... that big shootout down in Bolivia! It was in all the papers! I read about it!"

"Well then, guess that must've been a pretty lively ghost that kissed me and handed me an envelope just like yours!"

"I...I can hardly believe it! Anybody but you, and I wouldn't! How'd he look?"

"Changed quite a bit—put on some weight...face looks different, too...can't use that cowlick anymore to hide that scar. Hair's too thin...but believe me, it was Butch alright. He still kissed me like he used to...out of this world..."

The two sisters sat in silence, Ann too stunned to know what to say next, and Josie getting more than full satisfaction just watching her astonished sister. "Ready for another big surprise? Another real corker?"

All Ann could do was nod yes. "Elza Lay is out of prison! Butch looked him up and brought him here."

Again, Ann's jaw dropped in total disbelief. "He...he was sentenced to life down in New Mexico...How can this be?"

"Worked the same old charm he used on you! After Elza left here, Butch told me Elza had the warden down there eating out of his hand. Used to ride in a buggy around the streets of Santa Fe with the warden! Can you beat that! That warden even helped to get his sentence changed to he could be released! Now if that don't take the cake! Goes by the name Ellsworth Lay now. Butch says Lay dug up some money he'd stashed away, came up here, bought a ranch near Baggs, Wyoming, got married and settled down. He's into oil prospecting too, around the Powder Wash country. How's that for a new batch of fresh-baked cookies?"

Ann could only shake her head. "Butch isn't dead...he's back here...Elza isn't in prison for life...he's out and going straight...Josie, are you sure about this—all of this?"

Josie pointed to Ann's chair. "Butch sat in the very chair you're holdin' down and Elza—I mean Ellsworth, used that one over there by the back door. Remember now, don't ever ask me to swear on a stack of Bibles 'cause I won't dare go near 'em."

To Ann's surprise, Josie put on a light sweater and headed for the back door.

"Going somewhere, Sis? Okay if I tag along?"

Josie motioned with her finger to follow.

Ann shrugged. "Alright! Why not?"

They walked back to Main Street and the business section. Josie pointed to a large, three-story building. "It's called the Claremont; it's the best Rock Springs has to offer."

After they were seated in the dining room, Josie went over to the waiter to have a private word. He then disappeared. She returned to their table, pleased as punch.

"Tell me about Ethan and Ann Maire. What do they look like?"

Josie reached across to touch Annie's hand. "Ethan is looking more like Cleve all the time. Ann Marie takes after you...blonde hair...same blue eyes..."

"I hope she's not as impulsive as I used to be."

Josie laughed. "Not to worry, Sis, she acts like me, but looks quite a bit like you. Won't let me call her Annie for short, either! It's Ann Marie or else!"

Josie saw the waiter approach. When he set the teapot down along with the pastry, Annie hugged Josie. "This, this is too much, Sugarplum! Real Boston tea cakes! Oh, if only Beemis could be here now! You know what he'd say, don't you?"

"Yeah, Sis, that's all he talked about when he came back with you." Josie dropped her voice. "I tell ya, Josie, those were the best tea cakes I ever ate! Trouble was, I had to eat a plateful to find out how good they was."

Annie laughed and laughed and laughed. "Boy, you've got Uncle Beemis down to a tee! Even sounded like him, too! Thanks, Sugarplum, for giving me back the most incredible day of my life! I shall never forget this day, as long as I live...Thanks again."

A tiny tear used Josie as its temporary home. "Gosh, Sis, I haven't heard anybody call me Sugarplum in years. Only three people ever called me that after dad was buried: Uncle Beemis and you, when you wanted to be my special friend...and..."

"Deke, after he got to know you better. I wish...never mind, Sugarplum, that's wishing for the impossible. I have no right to ever expect that wish anymore."

"Don't give up hope, Sis...look what this day has brought both of us already..."

"Well, I suppose we'd better be getting back...Gosh, what a day! What a day!"

"Let's stick around a few minutes longer. Ann Marie and Ethan won't be home for a bit…I could go for another round of tea cakes, how about you?"

They had their teapot reheated and were served more tea cakes. "Go ahead, Sis, nobody's lookin'; lick the icing off your fingers…just like you used to do back at the ranch."

Annie did. Then a wistful look appeared. "Seeing you today couldn't make me any happier…or sadder, in a way…Wish we were back at the ranch with Uncle Beemis, Aunt Maybelle, too, as long as I'm wishing…"

The hotel manager interrupted their fond memories. He chased down the man who was clearing several tables behind Josie and Annie. "Look, I'm not going to tell you again! Put more dishes on your tray! It'll save your leg from making so many trips!" He looked over in Josie's direction. "Look, Mrs. Dreschler, it's not working out! He does alright in the kitchen, but he can't handle the job out here! Shoulda never hired your cripple in the first place!"

"I'm not your busboy, I'm the dishwasher! You promised me you'd have one here today!"

"Can I help it if he didn't show up? I'll contact the school tomorrow, see if I can get another boy. Darned kids…nobody wants to work these days."

"Yeah, I know all about promises and people who make 'em and break 'em all the time. Had me a gal once…loved her more than anything else in all the world. She always tried to play that promise game with me…"

The voice sounded somewhat familiar, even the bit about the gal breaking her promises. Annie shot out of her chair. "Deke! Deke Landry! Is that you?"

The man didn't answer. He kept his back to Annie and started straight for the kitchen door. He hit the swinging door with a full load of dirty dishes, dragging his left leg.

Annie was hot on his heels. "Oh no, you don't, Deke Landry! Look at me! Have I changed that much? Look again?"

He sat his tray down on the counter. Two week's worth of unshaven stubble, steeped in kitchen sweat, gave up the ghost. "Changed, Annie? Lord a'mighty! You're better lookin' than the Annie in my dreams!"

"Then why didn't you answer me? Why, Deke?"

"Look at me! I'm a cripple! Nobody's got the time a'day for a cripple! Yesterday, I got a new name when I was out front. A little girl pointed at me and said, 'Look, Mommy, see the gimp!' Well, Annie, take your pick: cripple or gimp!"

Tears welled up in Annie's eyes, but that didn't keep her from slapping his face. "Stop it! Stop it! I don't want to hear one more word about you feeling sorry for yourself! Deke Landry, do I make myself clear?"

"Sure, you're whole! Not like me!" He took one step away. "Look at the way I have to drag my leg! Piece of dried-up beef jerky looks better! Got Josie to thank for getting this job or else I'd really be out of luck! Nobody wants to hire a broken-down old horse wrangler like me! Nobody!"

"I do...if you'll take me back."

"You're just feelin' sorry for me. I wouldn't take that...not from you of all people, Annie...ah got nuthin' left to throw in with ya. Got so bad, after my accident, I had to sell my horse, saddle, bridle, and gun. When a wrangler's down to that, there ain't nuthin' left, Annie! Nuthin'! It's worse than bein' stripped down naked and run through town with a cattle prod goosin' you!"

"Still haven't told me you still love me..."

"Then you ain't been listening to me! All I ever cared about, ever dreamed about is you...said it ag'in and ag'in in them words I told you about my string of bad luck..." He motioned with one arm. "Look 'round ya, Annie, this is it! This is my range! Can't sit a horse no more, so I sits down on the stool to save my back so ah kin scrape and scrub down pots n' pans. Can't lead a horse or gentle one down, so I goes pearl diving in them tubs of dishwater, wishing it was Vermillion Creek with us on your Indian blanket gettin' ready to make love...Don't that kinda' tell ya how I feel 'bout you or love you?"

The swinging door opened and in walked one steamed-up manager. He turned on Deke. "You're falling behind again! Get out front! One more warning, and you're fired!"

Annie stood up to the manager. "Mister Landry doesn't work here anymore! He's with me!"

The manager threw up his hands. "Fine by me, lady! Hope you know what you're letting yourself in for! Nobody will take him! He's a charity case!"

"You're wrong! I will! He's going to be my husband, if he'll have me! Not the other way around!"

As soon as the manager left, Annie pulled up a chair. "Okay, let's hear it, accident and all! Last time I saw you, you were headed for Lander, Wyoming. Said you had a job on a horse ranch with the chance to buy out the owner. I think you said he was ailing..."

Deke sat on his stool. "First off, I ain't no charity case! Two years ago, I had it made...had saved enough to buy out my boss. It wasn't no big-time ranch like Beemis had, but it was worth puttin' my money into. I was gonna buy him out, then come lookin' for you...see if you still felt about me like you used to..."

"Oh, Deke, if you'da come back, I'da said yes, much more than just yes."

"Okay, here comes about my accident. Had this rodeo one Sunday. A neighbor brought in this here jughead. Danged horse couldn't make up his mind whether he was part mule, part jackass, or part Brahma bull! Anyhow, nobody could ride him, much less break him. One hundred dollars went to the first man who could stay on him 'til the count of thirty! Annie, I had that hundred in my pocket already...at least in my mind. Now, ah ain't never been throw'd from a plug that I couldn't dust off the seat of my pants and git back on. Oh, this jughead twisted n' turned like he was part snake, too, but he couldn't throw me..."

"So, what happened?"

"He headed straight for the chutes, twistin' more ways than I could count, but I was still on board. Then he crowded the hell outta me against those chute boards, but he couldn't shuck me. All a' sudden, my chaps got snagged on a nail stickin' out...next thing I knew, I was under him and he stomped me all to hell. I got peeled off faster than a 'tator gets skinned for the boilin' pot! So help me, Annie, that's what happened! That's all I remember 'cept it took every dollar I saved to pay up my hospital and doctor bill. Sold my horse n' such down here in Rock Springs and run into Josie."

Annie pecked him on the cheek. "Do you suppose that horse ranch still might be for sale?"

"Reckon so...but Annie, like I said, I can't sit a horse longer than ten minutes. My back and leg go numb; then the pain comes shootin' in..."

This time Annie really gave him a kiss, the kind both remembered. "Deke, you've forgotten more about horses than most men will ever learn in a lifetime. Why, I'll just bet you could sit in a chair out by the corral and tell our new hired hand just what to do and how to do it!"

His eyes lit up like Roman candles. "Yeah...yeah, Annie...see what you're drivin' at...sure I could!" Then his disposition changed. "But that takes money...I'm flat cleaned out. Sure like your idea, though..."

Annie, too, was excited. "I have some money...probably enough to buy that ranch, including the horse stock, hire a good wrangler, and still leave enough for us to get by on until we sold our first shipment."

"Guess your dear, dear friend left you better fixed than I figured. What happened?"

"You made me keep that promise when you rode out of my life. Believe it or not, Deke, that's the one promise I should've never kept or made...You were right about not giving your word unless you can keep it. My marriage was one miserable, big mistake...Josie was right about that, too." She looked at him. She saw neither the cripple that he was nor the man that he used to have been. She saw only the right man for her. "There is one little string attached to that money I brought with me…"

"What's that, Annie?"

"Marry me!"

It was a good day to do a lot of things, such as get married and start a new life. With congratulations and good-bye hugs from Josie and her brood, Annie and Deke rode out of Rock Springs. They came to a fork in the road and Deke stopped the buggy team. He pointed. "That arrow points to Cheyenne and the other points toward Lander. Got any suggestions?"

Annie snuggled up. "You know how Beemis would handle this, don't you?"

Deke laughed. "Yeah, I can see him now. Down that nose, his specs would slide—"

"They call them glasses, nowadays…but go on…"

"He'd blink at least five or six times over them. He'd get red in the face— wanna finish it off, Annie?"

"Yes, love. Beemis would say, 'What in Sam Hell took you two so long to get back together? Sure hope you weren't waitin' 'round for a personal invite from the Man Upstairs!'"

Also available from PublishAmerica

THE DEBACLE
by Jeff Prebis

Buxxum, North Dakota. The town was named after its lone resource, Buxxum. The lives of the people depend on this resource. Without it, there would be no jobs for the people, no food on their tables, and no hope for survival. But what happens when the resource attacks? When every man, woman, and child becomes part of a diabolical role reversal that leaves no one safe?

Man has dominated the world for a long time. But now a new predator is on the loose that wants a piece of the pie. The adults are dead by daybreak. The children are missing, under the control of deadly beings. A few scattered survivors are left to sort through the corpses for fragments of the lives they once knew.

Paperback, 215 pages
6" x 9"
ISBN 1-4241-6583-0

Danny thought he had the world at his fingertips. He is a provocative painter who seduces the ladies of Buxxum and leaves them longing while he chases his next conquest. He is forced to do the unthinkable: to help someone else for the first time in his life. June has loved Danny since they went to high school. She finally has her turn with him and the world falls apart. Can she find him before she is killed? Can they escape the madness?

Martha is a simple schoolteacher who loves her son and longs to move from Buxxum to find a better life. They are separated at the outbreak of the debacle, and she has to fight against the gathering storm of evil to save her boy. Can she find him before it is too late?

Willy is a dirty little boy. Frequently he is picked on by his school chums. Will he take a shower? Will he put on a pair of trousers? Or will he become a beast that rivals the Buxxum?

Available to all bookstores nationwide.
www.publishamerica.com

CHRISTMAS SONG
by Suzanne Trammell

Pauley Sutton is an aspiring singer, but she needs a job. When she finds an advertisement for an opening at the prestigious Benson Group, she jumps at the interview, believing this may just be the break she's looking for. However, she finds out the job is more then she bargained for. The arrogant Eric Benson has other plans for his employee. Will she be able to survive this deceit?

Paperback, 73 pages
6" x 9"
ISBN 1-60610-829-8

About the author:
Suzanne Trammell was raised in the Washington, D.C., area but has traveled and lived in many different areas within the United States and overseas. Trammell now resides in a community in central Florida.

Also available from PublishAmerica

DEAR CHURCH

by Kathryn Cooper

Dear Church is the author's belief that Proverb 31:10-31, The Excellent Wife or Virtuous Woman, is in fact the Bride of Christ, His church. It is His call to excellence and was meant for such a time as now, to ready her for His coming. It is her belief that the proverb was not just a wise saying but a prophecy for today.

The author has taken the verses of the proverb as a guide to what the Bride of our Lord should be, especially for this generation. It is a message to the Body of Christ to come together under His headship as one body, one spirit, and one mind—His.

Paperback, 87 pages
6" x 9"
ISBN 1-4241-7310-8

About the author:

Kathryn Cooper was born in San Diego, California, and lived there until age fifteen when her family moved to Salem, Oregon. She attended South Salem High. She has three children and five grandchildren, and currently works as a revenue agent for the state. She enjoys playing games with family, fishing, and going on trips to the coast.

Available to all bookstores nationwide.
www.publishamerica.com